The Burden of Faith

a novel by

DAMON J COURTNEY

Novels by Damon J Courtney

THE DRAGON BOND TRILOGY

Baptism of Blood and Fire
The Burden of Faith
The Fate of Champions

damon@damonjcourtney.com
www.DamonJCourtney.com

For Julian and Norah.
Without you, this book would have taken less time to write.
But with you, my life has so much more.

THE

PRELUDE

THE OGRE CHIEFTAIN'S greatsword looked six feet long as it swung down to cleave Gortogh's head in two. Though, it was hard to tell from his current position on the ground. Things always appear larger looking up. Probably why the ogre looked ten feet tall himself.

Gortogh spread his legs and leaned back. The blade passed right before his eyes to slam into the ground. Even one as strong as the ogre chief moved slowly wielding a blade of that size, it seemed. Goblins were much quicker than their ogre cousins.

And Gortogh was quicker than most goblins.

As the ogre drew back to strike again, Gortogh flipped his legs over to roll back and to his knees. Pushing up, he bounced to his feet. It should have been an impressive display of balance and grace, but he had to stumble back another step to avoid losing his head. The greatsword passed just in front of his face for the second time. He steadied his feet and sized up his opponent.

He's bigger than ten feet.

The biggest Gortogh had ever seen. The ogre grinned a big, yellow-toothed grin as Gortogh tried to get his balance. He's just toying with me. Backing up another step, Gortogh felt a shove as one of the goblins ringing

1

them in a circle pushed him back in. He readied himself for another swing, but the ogre wasn't even paying attention. He was too busy walking around the circle with his arms wide and his sword held high.

The crowd of goblins booed and snarled while a small group of ogres on one side of the circle cheered and laughed. The ogre chieftain bathed in it all, the cheers and the jeers, and roared all the louder. This ogre would no doubt kill him in a fair fight. And so far, this had been a fair fight.

No more.

Gortogh squeezed the hilt of his sword and felt the magical power of the blade flow through him. His arms bulged, and he felt a sharp pain as his muscles grew and tightened against his stretched skin. In spite of himself, a little smile crept onto his lips as the ogre turned back to face him. Gortogh hated the fighting, but he found that he actually liked the idea of putting this ogre in his place.

Gortogh walked slowly and confidently across the circle, sword at the ready. The ogre obliged and came to meet him. They swung, their swords clanging loudly as they met. Unlike before, Gortogh's sword held strong, unyielding. The ogre's eyebrows flew up, but Gortogh revealed no emotion. As if nothing had changed. Their swords pushed against each other. The ogre's greatsword pushed against his magical blade, and Gortogh couldn't hide a little smile. With a shove of his other hand, he sent the ogre sprawling backward, arms flailing for balance. The brute managed to keep from falling as he stumbled back, but his attitude had vanished. Gortogh pointed his sword.

"Swear loyalty to Ogrosh champion!" Gortogh yelled. "Join us now. No more fighting."

The goblins cheered at the mention of their god and began chanting his name.

"Ogrosh! Ogrosh! Ogrosh!"

The ogres did not join the celebration. The chieftain's eyes narrowed. His massive hand tightened around the hilt of his greatsword. Gortogh saw the fury in his eyes and shook his head slowly from side to side.

Why must it always be this way?

"No make me kill you, Malakar," Gortogh said.

Gortogh truly did not want to kill the mighty ogre. He had killed far too many of Ogrosh's children in the last six months. Good warriors, all. Many of them the chiefs and champions of their own tribes. Some of the best goblin warriors he'd ever seen. They had all come to challenge him, to be Ogrosh's Champion.

And they had all died.

Such is the way of the children of Ogrosh.

Gortogh had offered each one a chance to swear loyalty, knowing that none would take it. Loyalty is earned through blood. When he killed Malakar, and he had no doubt that he would, the ogres of his tribe would swear their loyalty to him. Never had an ogre knelt before a goblin that Gortogh knew. They had always seen themselves above *puny* goblins.

But these ogres would kneel before him.

Malakar yelled and charged. Gortogh stood, unmoving, unblinking. The ogre swung his greatsword for his head. Still, Gortogh didn't move. Calmly raising his arm, the greatsword clanged off of his blade in a crash of metal. Gortogh's sword hummed and vibrated, his fingers going numb around the hilt, but the mighty swing had not even moved his hand.

Malakar rained blows down in rapid bursts, trying to

drive Gortogh to his knees. Gortogh didn't move an inch. He was done dancing and dodging. Instead, he brought his sword to meet every blow, turning the greatsword aside with the flat of his blade. The sharp sound of metal on metal rang out through the trees and echoed off the mountains so loudly that some of the goblins covered their ears. But Gortogh did not flinch. He made no move to attack, only stood there and let the ogre see how easily he could turn aside every strike.

A cheer rolled through the goblin ranks.

It was a familiar sight for them. Gortogh heard their cheers, and it should have bolstered him, but it only deepened his sadness. Always more blood. The ogre stopped swinging, and Gortogh could see his chest heaving with each breath. Malakar was growing tired from his assault and could not keep it up. He stepped back and eyed the little goblin with renewed anger, and some suspicion.

"Me no want kill you, Malakar," Gortogh said calmly.

The ogre charged again and tried to shove him back from his stance. Gortogh set his foot and met the charge head on. The brute smashed into him with a force Gortogh had not felt in all his fights with other goblins. The ogre was more than twice his size, and he had clearly underestimated his strength. Gortogh flew through the air and landed near the edge of the circle with a great crash, barely keeping hold of his sword.

A cheer went up from the ogres this time, and Malakar held his arms wide and turned in a circle. He roared at the prone goblin and laughed.

"You are not champion of Ogrosh! You are weak and puny goblin! Champion of Ogrosh should be him chosen people! Ogres bear name of Ogrosh!"

The ogres cheered again, louder this time. Gortogh was still trying to recover from the jarring hit. His head was muddled, and he felt a sharp pain in his chest that made it hard to breathe. With the strength of magic flowing through his veins, he managed to put his hands down and push to a kneeling position.

"Yes! Kneel before mighty Malakar!"

Gortogh grimaced and felt for the hilt of his sword. His hand closed around it, and he waited, his breaths shallow and stinging. Time to end this.

Malakar did a few more turns for the crowd and then charged with a great yell. His sword was high, ready to deliver a killing blow. Gortogh remained on his knees until the ogre was almost to him. Tensing every muscle in his body, Gortogh leapt to his feet. As the greatsword swung down for his head, he stepped under it and raised his own blade. The magical longsword hummed with power, almost hungry.

It sliced cleanly through the brute's arm just above the elbow.

The arm went tumbling through the air with the greatsword still in its grip and landed at the feet of the crowd who stumbled back in stunned silence. Malakar looked at his arm lying on the ground. Confusion flooded his face. Then his eyes went to the other half of it that still hung from his shoulder, spurting blood.

The ogre bellowed and screamed and stumbled around the circle in pain. Gortogh stood calmly, waiting for rage to replace the panic and pain. It always does. Malakar howled some more and staggered a few more steps before falling to his knees and holding the stump of his arm. A growl formed deep in his chest. His head shot up and his eyes burned into Gortogh, his whole body trembling.

There's the rage.

With a roar, he stood as one of the ogres behind him helped him to his feet and tied a leather cord around the remainder of his arm. Blood poured from the stump, but Malakar didn't seem to care. With his remaining hand, he grabbed the other ogre's sword and charged. Gortogh went forward to meet him. As their swords clashed again, he could feel the depleted strength behind the blows. The loss of blood and his sword arm left Malakar with very little ability to continue this fight. But he would continue, Gortogh knew.

He will fight with every last breath.

Gortogh dodged under a wild swing and kicked out with his foot, catching the ogre in the gut. Malakar stumbled back, his sword tip dipping into the dirt. He no longer had the strength to keep it up. He tried to steady himself, but Gortogh kicked him again, knocking him to the ground.

Ten feet of ogre hitting the ground makes an awfully big thud. The circle shook, and the gathered goblins cheered and jeered. The ogre tribe tightened ranks and drew their swords. The goblins all cheered and cried out in unison.

"Fry! Fry! Fry! Fry!"

This is what they came to see.

It's what they always want.

They wanted Gortogh to release the lightning magic stored in his wicked sword and destroy the ogre chieftain. Gortogh wanted this to end *now*. No more blood. No more magic. He hated using magic to best his opponents. Except for the magic he used to make himself stronger and more agile, of course. Without that, the fight would have been over in seconds and with a *very* different outcome.

The first chiefs of the goblin tribes that joined him all had fought him in that same ring. They had come seeking glory at besting the champion of Ogrosh. In those battles, Gortogh would fight with *all* of his might and magic. He stoked the crowd with laughs and hand waving just as Malakar had done. He enjoyed it. Reveled in it. When his opponents were all but dead, he would offer them one last chance to join him. When they refused, and they all refused, he would unleash the lightning in his sword and fry them.

"Fry! Fry! Fry! Fry!"

They wanted Malakar to fry.

The bloodthirsty goblins always wanted to see the most spectacular end. Gortogh had lost his taste for it. Too many strong warriors had died at his hand. For no reason other than to show his superiority. He wished, just once, they would join him without a fight.

But that was not the way of the children of Ogrosh.

The ogre chief pushed himself to stand and faced Gortogh with a grimace. He had one good arm and a strong sword. In a fight with any ordinary goblin, that would have been more than enough. But Gortogh was no ordinary goblin. If what the goblins believed was true, he was imbued with the power of his god. If Malakar had believed it, he might have accepted the offer to join without a fight.

If only he'd believed the lie.

Both combatants stood steadfast and waited for the other. The goblins surrounding the circle continued their chant. The ogres on the far end had formed a tight cluster around themselves with their weapons drawn.

Gortogh looked around the crowd and then back to the ogre chieftain. They stared long and hard at each other as the chants grew louder and more insistent. Paying no attention to them, Gortogh lowered his sword and motioned Malakar over with a wave of his hand.

Malakar's brow creased. He brought his sword up with his remaining hand, the blood dripping steadily from the stump of his other arm. Gortogh made no move toward him but simply waved his hand again. When the brute refused to move, Gortogh reached his hand back and slid his sword into the leather scabbard that hung from a belt over his shoulder. The ogre's brow scrunched up even more, and Gortogh waved again.

The crowd grew silent.

The cheering stopped, and the goblins stared in confusion. This was not how the fight was supposed to go. Malakar took a few cautious steps toward him, and Gortogh waved once more, never inching toward his weapon. The big ogre let his sword slip to his side as he took a few more steps toward the center of the ring.

He looked back at the ogre tribe, but they all just watched in silence. A few more steps brought him within striking distance, but Gortogh made no move for his sword. He waited patiently for the ogre to draw nearer. Once he was close enough, Gortogh leaned forward and spoke.

"Join us. I will not make you kneel. You can lead your ogres as your own tribe under my command."

The ogre's eyes narrowed.

"I don't want to kill you," Gortogh said.

Malakar continued to stare but said nothing. Gortogh could see the thoughts playing out on his face. He had to know that he would lose this fight and most likely his life. He was being offered a chance to live, but it went against the ways of the tribes.

"We *all* fight for Ogrosh," Gortogh said. "You will still be chief of the ogres. You will lead the tribes as my commander."

Malakar straightened and looked around at the goblins watching silently with great interest. He looked at the ogres of his tribe, but they looked just as confused as the goblins. He looked back at Gortogh and stared long and hard. Seconds passed in total silence with the whole crowd watching. Slowly, the ogre nodded his head as the tip of his sword dipped to the ground. He turned to address the circle.

"We will join champion of Ogrosh!" he shouted. "I will lead ogre tribe in Ogrosh name!"

Gortogh breathed a little sigh of relief and watched as confusion registered on all the goblins gathered. No one cheered as he had hoped. It was the opposite, in fact. Once the realization dawned that there would be no spectacular bloodletting, many began to boo and growl. More howls quickly joined them. Weapons were drawn.

They called out for blood.

They called out for him to fry.

Gortogh snatched his sword out in a quick motion. Malakar jumped and brought his own blade back up, but Gortogh was already turning away. With a single thought, the energy stored in his sword coursed down the blade and then leapt from the tip in an arc of blue lightning.

It shot through the air with a loud thunderclap and struck a tree high above the crowd. The trunk of the tree splintered and cracked in a great explosion, sending shards of wood flying. Gortogh held the sword high and turned in a circle to meet their eyes, challenging any to disagree.

"I am the will of Ogrosh!" he shouted.

The goblins fell silent. No one dared speak or jeer. Gortogh turned back to Malakar who was staring in amazement at the blackened tree that was now missing a huge chunk on one side. The ogre looked down at him with his eyes wide, staring, unmoving. His face cracked into a toothy smile. Then the smile turned to laughter.

"Boom!" he shouted and laughed louder.

The goblins began laughing with him, and Gortogh sighed with relief.

"We fight for Ogrosh!" Malakar shouted. "For Ogrosh! For Ogrosh!"

The crowd took up his chant and shouted to the heavens. Malakar stood beside Gortogh and shouted for Ogrosh. Even Gortogh got caught up in the fervor and shouted to the blood god. He watched the ogres who were still looking on with confusion, but they began to chant as well.

For Ogrosh.

All for Ogrosh.

With a slap on Gortogh's back, Malakar went to stand with his ogres, still chanting. Gortogh turned and walked to the other side where the goblins were cheering and chanting as one.

"For Ogrosh! For Ogrosh!"

Over his shoulder, Gortogh heard a great yell, followed by the unmistakable sound of a sword cleaving through flesh and bone. He spun back in time to see Malakar's head roll from his shoulders and fall unceremoniously to the dirt. It rolled several turns before coming to rest in the middle of the ring. His mouth still turned up in a smile as the lifeless eyes stared at Gortogh.

The headless body tumble backward with a thud that shook the circle. The cheering stopped in the moment it took them all to realize something had happened. Goblins in the back were pushing and scrambling forward to try and see what was going on.

Gortogh stared into the eyes of the ogre holding a bloody greatsword in his hand. Malakar's greatsword. Matching his stare, without looking away, he raised the sword high above his head. Blood dripped from the blade to land on his shoulders and head, but he held Gortogh's gaze and paid it no attention.

"I am Brog!" he yelled. "*I* am ogre chieftain!"

Everyone stood in stunned silence. Some of the ogres behind Brog looked confused. Many more were smiling or nodding. Some even laughed. Brog's gaze drifted around the circle, meeting the eyes of the goblins.

"We fight for Ogrosh!" he shouted.

Without missing a beat, the goblins took up their chant again, louder this time. Brog met Gortogh's stare as his eyes came back around. Gortogh turned and strode from the circle without another word. The crowd parted at his approach, some falling to kneel before him. A great cheer went up from the goblins as some jumped into the circle to tear the body apart and play sport with the severed head.

Such is the way of the children of Ogrosh.

CHAPTER ONE

A Walk in the Woods

ERYNINN'S ALMOND EYES watched the battle between Gortogh and the ogre chieftain with disbelief. He had never seen a goblin with such strength or power. The goblins worried him even more now.

He had been watching them for months, ever since the attack on the village of Jornath. Ever since he found the hole they were hiding in. Though, in truth, he could hardly call it a hole. There was no hole in all the Twin Crest Mountains that could hold a goblin army of this size.

And now ogres had joined them.

Not many, thankfully, but if the massing goblin tribes were any indication, more would come. Eryninn had never known an ogre personally, but in his years of fighting them, he had never seen one cooperate willingly with a goblin. Much less be subjugated by one.

But this goblin chief, Gortogh, was unlike any goblin he'd ever seen. And he had seen a lot of goblins. His power was not his own, Eryninn could see that plainly enough, but it mattered little where it came from. All that mattered is what he planned to do with it. After witnessing the attack on Jornath and seeing the growing size of his forces, he had no doubt that whatever he was planning would not be good.

Eryninn heard a shout from the camp and saw the fun break up instantly as goblins scrambled to grab their weapons. He was on his feet in a second and scurrying down the tree he'd been hiding in. He thought about moving closer again to see what was going on but decided against it when a small group of goblins left camp and headed his direction.

More patrols.

He relaxed a little and hid behind the tree as he waited for them to pass. The patrols were getting more frequent. Probably because Eryninn made sure that none of them returned. Or, if any did return, it was with a horrible tale of slaughter by the one they called the Wood Elf.

Wood Elf.

Father would have laughed. Eryninn couldn't help a little smile too. Pulling his cloak tighter around him, he pressed himself against the tree and watched as they passed. He could watch from afar with his elven eyes, a gift from his father, without ever needing to get close. His enchanted cloak, his father's cloak, allowed him to hide in the forest where not even the most sensitive animal could detect his presence. He watched and waited.

Was this what it was like for you?

His father once protected the people and these forests. Long ago, this was the home of the ancient elves, now home to animals and goblins. His father was gone now, dead for more than a decade. For so long, Eryninn had refused the mantle of the Wood Elf. He would not die for others as his father and mother both had. He watched with indifference as the goblin tribes gathered. When they entered his forest, he tracked them and fought when attacked, but as long as they let him be, he let them be.

Until they massacred the nearby village of Jornath.

Without knowing it, he began to walk the steps he imagined his father once took long before he was born. Is this how it started for you? Is this how you became the Wood Elf? By helping people when you could not ignore their cries?

Was it truly his father's doing, or was it his human mother's gentle soul that set him on the path? These thoughts rolled around Eryninn's mind as he watched and waited. It seemed he had nothing *but* time to think now.

The goblins argued with each other as they walked, each one fighting for leadership of their little band. Always fighting to lead. They passed Eryninn just a few trees away, none of them even looking to where he hid. In his father's cloak, he could hide from the goblins and track them through the forest without them ever knowing he was there.

In his father's cloak, he *was* the Wood Elf.

He stalked the goblins from the trees, following along beside their route but never close enough for them to hear. Not that they would. Goblins were not the most sensitive when it came to listening for trouble. He kept pace with them from afar. When they stopped, he stopped. When they moved, he moved. He was their unseen shadow. He followed and waited for them to get far enough from their camp.

Far enough away from the safety of numbers.

When they stopped at a cross in the game trails and started arguing, he saw his chance. The two biggest goblins were shouting and shoving one another, each pointing in a different direction. Pulling the bow off his shoulder, he took aim. The two kept yelling even as another let out a strangled cry. It wasn't until they saw the arrow protruding from its chest that they even knew something was wrong.

The five remaining goblins yelled and scrambled, bumping into each other and falling down. Eryninn drew and shot again, killing a second one before they had extracted themselves enough to take cover. He stood patiently and waited as they all ran to hide wherever they could find.

He slipped between the trees, the power of the cloak concealing his movements, and made his way around behind them. He could see the goblins hiding and searching for the location of their attacker, but they would not see him no matter how hard they looked. A few more steps, and he was at their backs.

He loosed, catching one through the back and pinning it against his tree. The three remaining all scrambled around to put some cover between them and this new attack. They ran into each other as much as the trees themselves.

Eryninn could only smile at the absurdity of it all.

One of the goblins shouted to the other two, and they shouted something back. Eryninn didn't understand the goblin tongue, but he had little doubt what they were planning. They all turned and ran. Eryninn shot again, striking one in the back and dropping it. The other two ran faster, and he was all too happy to take up the chase.

Eryninn tore out from behind his tree and ran after

them. Now that they were running scared, he no longer made any attempt to hide himself. The goblins were quick, quicker than even him perhaps, but they were barreling through the forest at too fast a pace to pay much attention to where they were going. The one in the lead went down first, tripping over a tree root. The one behind it went down next, tripping over the first goblin.

Eryninn stopped short and drew another arrow. As the two goblins fought with each other to stand, he pulled back and loosed. The one on top fell forward, its dead weight pinning the last one to the ground. It struggled to push its fallen comrade off, but its arms were pinned, and it couldn't lift the body.

Eryninn slung his bow over his shoulder and walked slowly toward the trapped creature. The goblin squealed and fought even harder to get out from under its burden, but it was no use. Eryninn folded his arms and waited.

"No kill! Please no kill!" the goblin cried out and closed its eyes.

It kept repeating over and over. Eryninn waited for it to finish. When the goblin finally quieted down to a whimper, he bent toward it.

"You run, I shoot."

The goblin's eyes went wide and stared at him. He pulled the bow off his back and shook it in the air for emphasis.

"No running."

The goblin looked from the bow and back to his eyes and nodded. Eryninn bent down and pulled the dead goblin up. He tossed the body to the side and then held his hand down. The goblin threw its arms in front of its face and squealed. Eryninn shook his head and held his hand down again.

The goblin peeked out from behind its arms and looked into his eyes. It seemed to understand as it reached out and grabbed the proffered hand. Eryninn pulled the creature to its feet and then reached out and dusted some of the dirt off. The goblin eyed him warily but made no move to run.

Eryninn pulled the hood back from his cloak, letting the goblin see him fully. Its eyes darted over the features he could now see. Pointed ears. Blond hair. Stubbled chin.

"Wood Elf!"

Eryninn shook his bow again, reminding it of the consequences of running. The goblin quieted down and stood there shaking.

"Yes, I am the Wood Elf."

"Please no kill! Please!"

"Stop, stop. Be calm."

The goblin stopped screaming and stood trembling. Eryninn saw a stream run down its leg and puddle at its feet. He shook his head and rolled his eyes.

"What's your name?"

"Orp."

"Orp, I need you to do something for me."

The goblin nodded enthusiastically.

"I need you to take a message to Gortogh. Can you do that?"

It nodded again.

"Tell him if he doesn't stay out of my forest, his blood will be the next I spill. Got it?"

The goblin nodded, its eyes wide.

"Good."

Eryninn spun its shoulders around and planted his boot in its backside.

"Hurry now!"

Eryninn watched as the goblin ran off through the forest with all speed, crashing into low branches as it kept looking back over its shoulder.

"Watch where you're—"

The goblin smacked headlong into a tree. Eryninn groaned.

"Goblins."

CHAPTER TWO

TRAINING

RINN DUCKED UNDER the sword that was aimed for his head while driving his shortsword in from below at the same time. The blunted tip of his sword bounced harmlessly off the mail armor of his opponent, but he smiled just the same.

"Good!" Berym shouted. "Your reflexes are much faster this morning."

"Either I'm faster or you're slower," Rinn said.

"Maybe a little of both," the knight said with a grin.

The two of them stepped back and stood ready. Berym launched the attack this time, coming in with a vicious, overhand chop that would have been a stinging hit if Rinn were still standing there. He had stepped forward into the attack and then spun to Berym's left where he stabbed twice with his dagger.

"A good hit, but I've warned you about that dancing. I know it's fun in single combat, but on a battlefield, moves like that will get you killed. Look at where you are now."

"I'm behind you."

"Aye, and my men are behind you. Keep your enemy

in front of you and your friends at your back, you'll live longer for it."

They each returned to their side of the little circle and brought their weapons to the ready. Rinn launched the same overhand chop Berym had just used, but the knight brought his shield up to the side. Rinn's blade struck hard and lodged into the edge of the wooden shield where it stuck fast. He yanked it free a second later, but he knew it was already too late. Berym's blade came down and chopped his sword arm, dropping his weapon.

"Ow!" Rinn said.

"You don't have the reach for chopping. Don't try it unless you know you have the kill."

"I thought I did."

"Do you think this shield is here just to make me look pretty?" Berym asked with a laugh.

"One more," Rinn said.

Berym backed up and stood ready. They charged, Rinn chopping again from up high. Berym raised his shield, but Rinn reversed his swing and went low. Berym dropped his shield and swung down with his longsword, but Rinn had already moved to his right and stabbed with the dagger in his left hand.

"Excellent! You're getting faster. I think this combination works well for you. Just remember that even though you can block with the dagger, you should always be looking for an opening to attack. The more you can practice your attacks with both hands, the better off you'll be. We might be able to find a dagger with a longer cross though. It would make it easier to catch a sword when you have to."

"It feels right. I'm still not used to the sword though. It feels better than the longsword, but it's heavier than my dagger."

"Switching between weapons can be difficult, but knowing how to use whatever you can get your hands on is a useful skill. Your dagger will not always be at the ready. And to some creatures, a dagger is nothing more than a nuisance."

Rinn nodded. He swung the shortsword a few times to feel it in his hand and then jabbed with the dagger in his left hand. They both still felt a little awkward. The sword was heavy and much longer than the dagger he was used to, and he wasn't accustomed to using his left hand.

When he had begun training with Berym a few months ago, he had started with the classic longsword and shield combination favored by the knights. He practiced for several weeks, but while the sword and shield worked well for someone fighting straight on in heavy armor, they had quickly decided that it didn't suit his more *subtle* talents. Berym switched him to a shortsword after that and then quickly traded his shield for a dagger in his left hand. He was starting to get the hang of it now.

"Care to try again?" Berym asked.

Rinn looked to the sky and felt the sweat dripping from his brow. It was already nearing midday, and they had been out in the sun since early morning.

"Can we rest a minute?"

"Of course."

Rinn walked over and sat down on the long wooden bench at the edge of the practice circle. He grabbed the water skin hanging from the weapon rack beside him and took a long swig. He wiped his mouth and looked around the circle where others were practicing.

The town of Havnor acted as one of the main homes of the Knights of Gondril. The practice field they were in was one used by knights to instruct and train new squires and to keep their skills sharp. There were only a few knights training today, and no squires. Rinn was glad of that.

When he began training with Berym, they all assumed he was just an older squire and treated him as one of them. Once they learned he was not, they shunned him and kept to their own. He was glad they were gone. He took another drink from the water skin and hung it back on the hook as he stood. Berym waited for him to return to the circle.

"Are you ready?" the knight asked.

Rinn nodded.

"Care to try again with the longsword and shield?" Berym asked.

Rinn looked back at the weapons rack and scratched his head.

"I think I want to stick with these," he said, holding up the dagger and shortsword.

"Very well then."

Berym walked over and set his longsword and shield down against the rack. He looked the training weapons over briefly before selecting a shortsword and dagger for himself. He turned and marched back into the circle.

"Let's try this then," he said with a smile. "Try to block with the flat of your shortsword and then use the dagger for a quick strike."

Rinn lunged for him.

**

Elody took a deep breath and reached her thoughts out across the field. She could feel the magic tickling the ends of her fingertips. It was so faint it was almost imperceptible, but she'd become more sensitive to it even in small amounts. It was there, just out of her reach, and she ached to take it. She scrunched her eyes and pushed hard, trying to touch it.

Nothing.

She opened her eyes and huffed. Jalthrax stared at her, unblinking.

"I can't reach it," she shouted. "It's too far!"

The dragon cocked his head to the side but made no move toward her. She threw her hands up and stepped another ten feet closer. Flinging her hands out, she closed her eyes and concentrated.

She could sense the magic stronger now, and she reached out and felt her fingers touch it. It was cold. Like she had put her hands into an icy river. It didn't rush into her like it did when Jalthrax was right beside her, but she could pull enough to cast a small spell. The little dragon's magic was just waiting there for her to take.

She drew the magic to her and felt her hands tingle with raw energy. With practiced ease, she flicked her hands and fingers in intricate patterns in the air, weaving the magic. Thin, blue strands hovered between her palms as she pulled them like threads. She finished with a flourish and cupped her hands to her mouth.

"I did it," she whispered into her hands.

Jalthrax looked up as the spell carried her low whisper on the wind to his ears. He snorted, blowing a puff of frozen air that clung to the grass in front of him. He stared down at it a moment and then drew in a long breath. Stretching out his neck, he pushed his breath out hard, and a cone of ice and snow flew across the field.

The blast only extended a few feet in front of his nose, but every bit of grass it touched froze in place and wilted. With another huff and a shake of his head, he looked back to Elody. She crossed her arms and tapped her foot.

"Are you done?"

Jalthrax returned her stare but eventually nodded.

"Good, because we need to keep practicing."

She walked the length of the field to where he stood, taking care to go around the frozen patch. When at last she stopped in front of him, she knelt down and reached her hands up to touch his face. He leaned in and let her hands slide down his neck. Elody smiled as she felt a little rumble of pleasure.

How did he get so big already?

She couldn't believe how much he'd grown in only six months. Though his body was no longer than a horse and much lower to the ground, his wingspan had already grown to more than twelve feet across. He was so much bigger now than when he hatched the previous fall. It seemed like so much longer than only six months ago. As she rubbed her hands up and down his neck, Elody admired his scales. They were still duller than most adult silver dragons, but the muted gray color had started to give way to shiny metal beneath.

"You wanna try something new?" she asked.

Jalthrax opened his eyes and stared at her.

"I promise, *nothing* dangerous."

The dragon continued to eye her with suspicion.

"Oh, be quiet."

She rose from her knees, straightening her robes out of habit. She walked away a few paces and then turned back to face him.

"Ready?"

A puff of cold air was her only response. Elody rolled her eyes and then closed them tightly in concentration. Her first time with a new spell always made her anxious. And a little nervous if she was honest with herself.

Relax. You can do this.

Taking a deep breath, she reached out to pull the magic from Jalthrax. At this distance, it practically leapt into her hands, and she immediately felt them tingle with energy. They started to burn as more magic flowed in, but she held on longer and kept pulling. The spell she was attempting was one she had never cast before, and it required more magic than most of the spells she was familiar with.

When she finally had enough, her hands started moving quickly. She had to force herself to slow down. The raw magic burned to get out, but she had to take her time. All the new spells she had attempted had not turned out right. So far she had not failed to complete a spell, but she had yet to achieve the intended effect either.

Elody slowed her movements and went through the motions of the spell. They were burned into her mind after weeks and weeks of studying them. She followed them now, tracing each one from her memory. In the periphery of her senses, she could feel Jalthrax edging away from her, but she ignored it.

Focus. Concentrate.

When at last the spell was complete, she threw her hands out in front of her and opened her eyes. It was as black as night. Darker even. She couldn't see a thing. Not even a speck of light. Through the darkness she heard a snort and felt the cold blast of air a moment later.

"Well, the darkness was right! Just not in the right

place. It was supposed to be across the field."

No response.

"Oh, be quiet."

Another huff, and cold air hit her face. Elody walked in the direction of the cold, feeling her way through the darkness. Thankfully, the field was pretty flat, and she knew it well enough to know there were no major pitfalls between them. She could feel Jalthrax near her before she could touch him.

"Not a word," she said, passing him.

Sometimes it was actually better that Jalthrax hadn't learned to speak yet. Elody slowed her steps and kept walking until she emerged from the ring of magical darkness. The bright sunlight made her eyes snap shut, and her hand shot up to shield them. It took another minute for them to adjust, and in that time she felt Jalthrax move up beside her.

"I don't know what to do. These spells are all wrong. I need someone to train me, but every dragonmage I've met is too damn busy!"

Jalthrax stared at her and then looked up to the sky.

"Thrax! Are you listening?"

She blinked her eyes rapidly and shielded them to look down at him. He snapped back to her and then looked back up.

"Again? You just ate this morning!"

He nodded.

"Fine, but stay close. I want to try again as soon as my eyes stop watering."

With two beats of his wings, Jalthrax flew into the air. Elody turned back to look at the cloud of impenetrable darkness sitting in the middle of the field.

"Not too bad."

She shrugged her shoulders and then folded her arms with a smile.

***

Rinn cursed as the blade struck his ribs. The practice blades were blunted, but they were still made of solid steel like a real weapon. They were just as heavy and hurt just as much to be bludgeoned with. He skittered back just out of range of another hit and nearly tumbled out of the circle.

Despite his heavy armor, Berym moved impossibly fast. Rinn was wearing nothing but a shirt and breeches, a combination he regretted each time he got hit, but he still found it hard to keep away from the encumbered knight.

"Not as old as you thought, eh?" Berym said as they returned to their sides. "You can be much faster with a dagger than someone blocking with a heavy shield, but you have less reach. You're more agile, but you have to get in closer."

Berym charged.

He stabbed over the top with his shortsword while coming in low with his dagger. Rinn stabbed at the knight's legs with his dagger, but Berym caught it with his own and pulled his arm up. He twisted, jerking Rinn's arm, and Rinn couldn't stop the sword coming for his chest.

"Ow!"

Berym pulled back and lowered his weapons. Rinn stood panting for a few moments before the knight spoke.

"You should have let go of your dagger."

"I didn't want to lose it."

"You'd rather lose your life? You still had one good

weapon, and you could have used it if you hadn't been so desperate to hang onto the other."

Rinn tried to catch his breath. He stumbled over and collapsed onto the bench. Berym remained in the circle swinging his weapons slowly, testing their weight. He finally gave up and plopped down beside Rinn. They sat quietly for another minute, staring out across the circle as Rinn's breathing slowed.

"I'm glad you're back," Rinn said.

"As am I. I look forward to resting a while if the knighthood will let me."

"You've been gone a lot lately."

"Aye. Things are happening. The knights received a request for help from the dragonmage conclave, but so far we've been unable to offer anything."

"Did you ask them about Elody?"

"I did. Their answer is the same as you've heard from others. Every dragonmage who can wield magic is off protecting a dragon mother. There is no one they can spare to train a new mage."

"I guess there is never enough help to go around. I see far fewer knights training in the yard these days."

"Called away to guard other towns, no doubt. The knighthood has been shrinking for years. Though I have heard rumors of new recruits of late."

Rinn nodded as he grabbed the water skin and took a long drink.

"Have you thought more about my offer?" Berym asked. "The knighthood would welcome a man of your character."

Rinn looked down at the sword leaning against the bench beside him.

"I've thought about it," he said, "but I don't think I'm

cut out to be a knight."

"There is no doubt of your bravery, Rinn, I have seen it for myself. You are older than most squires, but you are skilled enough with a blade. You would not be starting from the same place."

"It's not that, it's just… I don't know what I want to do with my life yet, but I know I don't want someone always telling me what to do."

"Well, that you can't escape. You still have to work and eat, and there will always be someone there to tell you how you have to do it."

"It's just not the life I would choose," Rinn said.

"It's not so hard."

"It just seems lonely."

"It can be," Berym said.

"Some part of me still wants to go back to the farm and start a family," Rinn said. "Didn't you ever want a family?"

Berym stared off, watching two other knights sparring in their shining armor.

"Family means different things to different people. My family was not like yours. It was not something I ever aspired to have."

"Yes, but all the moving around. Don't you ever want to just stop? Call someplace home?"

Rinn thought he saw him wince a little, but he said nothing. They sat in silence.

"When my time as a knight is through, I'll find a little village to settle down in."

"What do you mean when your time is through?"

"When I become too old to be a proper knight. Too old to fight."

"That's when you want to settle down? When you're

too old to enjoy life?"

"There's a lot of life left in a man long after his fighting days are done."

Rinn took a swig from the water skin and stared at the ground.

"I don't want to wait my whole life to start it," Rinn said.

"Well, you keep staying out all night, I'm sure you'll find the right girl soon enough."

Rinn snapped his head around and looked at him, but Berym just smiled and crossed his arms.

"You don't think I know why you come to practice so tired all the time? I may be a knight now, but I wasn't always you know."

"I thought I hid it well."

Berym burst out laughing, and Rinn had to laugh with him.

"You don't hide it well at all," Berym said. "Don't worry, I won't tell your aunt. Just make sure you don't get into too much trouble."

Rinn sprang up.

"Damn! I forgot to get the herbs for Aunt Jelena."

"Well, don't sit around having fun with me all day then. Go on."

Rinn hurried over to put his weapons back in the rack. He grabbed his own dagger and stuck it into his belt before running off.

"See you tomorrow," he called back.

"Bright and early!" Berym said. "And not pickled like a herring!"

Rinn chuckled as Berym laughed out loud at himself.

***

Rinn jogged through town and out into the woods. Once

there, he slowed his pace and fished around in his pocket for the list his aunt had given him. With his frequent trips to the forest, he had gotten quite good at locating and identifying the various plants and herbs his aunt used regularly. His first few weeks were spent mostly groveling around in the dirt and returning only to find he had grabbed the wrong thing. On one occasion this turned out to be a plant poisonous to the touch that had earned him a few days in bed.

Glancing down the list, it was nothing but the usual today. He memorized the list and then tucked it back into his pocket. Looking back up, the trees parted and opened onto the field the dragonmages used for training. He slowed his steps when he heard something. The grass was higher than his knees, making it hard to see anything, but he definitely heard something. A light rustle. A small movement.

His thoughts turned to rabbit stew as he drew his dagger and crouched low. Stalking through the field with only his eyes above the grass, he slid as much as walked on bent knees. He heard the grass shift again, louder this time. Taking care not to make a sound of his own, he crawled closer. A sudden shift ahead made him draw his dagger back, but when he saw a head pop up over the top of the grass, he dropped back down.

Elody.

She was dusting bits of grass from her robes and staring at the sky. He smiled to himself and came up with a new plan. Tucking his dagger back into his belt, he continued sneaking. With her back to him, she never had a chance of seeing or hearing him coming. She held both hands to her brow and continued searching the sky, oblivious to his presence.

When at last he had gotten close enough to her, he leapt forward and wrapped his arms around her waist in a great squeeze. She screamed and tried to scramble away, beating at him with her fists. One good punch connected with his nose and dazed him enough that his grip slackened. He fell back, and she spun around and punched him again before he could say anything. He tumbled back into the grass and hit the ground with a thud.

"Rinn!"

Elody ran over to him and pulled him up. He was still reeling from the hit, but he managed to get his feet under him. He put his hand to his nose and felt the blood running down.

"You punched me in the nose!"

"Well, I thought you were attacking me! You shouldn't sneak up on people!"

"Ow!"

Rinn rubbed at his nose some more and pinched it together to staunch the bleeding.

"That really hurt," he said, his voice sounding funny. "You hit pretty hard for a girl."

She raised her fist as if to hit him again, and he flinched back a step.

"You flinch like a girl," she said, and they both laughed. "What are you doing out here?"

He let go of his nose and rubbed it a bit.

"Looking for herbs. Aunt Jelena says she has a birth tomorrow."

Elody nodded. Their aunt had an uncanny way of knowing when one of her mothers was going to give birth. They used to question and tease her, but she had proven right every time. She was a witch after all.

"Want some help? Jalthrax has been gone for half an hour, and I'm bored."

"Sure. You take half, and I'll take the other half."

He tore the list in half and handed her the harder ones. She scrutinized it and frowned.

"You gave me the hard ones."

"Oh, fine."

He grabbed the paper from her and dropped the other one in her outstretched hand.

"Big baby," he said.

"Thanks!"

She skipped off ahead of him toward the trees, and he could only shake his head and chuckle as he trailed after her. They walked together through the woods, one of them dipping off the path every few minutes to grab at something next to a tree or in some underbrush and tuck them into the pouch on their belt.

"Getting any better with Jalthrax?" he asked.

"A little. I can get a little farther away now and still keep the link, but it's harder than I thought. Master Cythyil said that other dragonmages would train me, that the conclave would arrange it, but every one I've met since we've been here was only passing through. I didn't think I would have a hard time in a big town like Havnor."

"Berym said that most of the dragonmages had been assigned. They're all worried about the wizard who's killing the dragon mothers, and no one knows what happened to the goblins after Jornath."

They both fell into silence at the mention of their home. Rinn bent down to move some underbrush aside and pluck a few flowers beneath it before standing to catch up to Elody. When he caught up to her, she was staring at the ground.

"I miss Dad," she said.

"I do too."

He put his arm around her, and she leaned her head against his shoulder.

"Is it wrong that I don't miss mom?"

She could feel Rinn tense against her, but he rubbed her shoulder.

"No," he said after a pause. "You were so little when she died."

"I think I've forgotten her," Elody said, and he could hear the sadness in her voice.

"Aunt Jelena looks a lot like her. Just older. And meaner."

Elody chuckled, and he pulled her closer. They walked a while more before stopping in front of a large oak tree. Rinn pulled his arm back and stared down at the piece of paper with a sigh.

"Why does she always need fresh acorns?"

"They can't touch the ground, Rinn," Elody said in her best impression of their aunt. "They have to be from the top of the tree, Rinn."

Rinn laughed and stared at the tree. Tucking the paper into his pocket, he grabbed the lowest branch and hoisted himself up. Pulling from branch to branch with ease, he climbed to the top of the great tree. Leaning his back against a bough, he reached out and plucked some acorns and put them into his pouch. Once he had enough, he turned and scanned the sky. He was high enough in the great oak to be over most of the treetops.

"Hey, I think I see Jalthrax," he called down.

"Really? Tell him to get his scaly arse back here!"

Rinn laughed and squinted at the flying spec in the

distance.

"Can't you just send him a message or something?"

"He can't hear me this far away. We're still working on the communication thing. I might be better at it by now if I had a *damn* dragonmage to teach me."

"Such language, little sister!"

He grabbed a few more acorns and tossed them at her head, each one bouncing off of her skull and shoulders in rapid succession.

"Hey!" she shouted up, but he was already climbing back down.

"That's everything on my list," he said as he reached the ground.

Elody looked in her pouch and then consulted the torn piece of paper in her hand.

"That's all of mine."

"Let's head back to the clearing."

They fell into step beside each other and strolled back to the field. When they were close, they heard a screech up ahead, and they both started to jog.

"Thrax!" Elody called out.

"He sounds different," Rinn said from behind her.

The trees opened onto the clearing, and they were met with an unexpected sight. A large dragon with dark red scales swiveled its long neck around as they came out of the woods.

The air around them grew suddenly hot as the beast drew in a great breath.

CHAPTER THREE

RESTLESS

GORTOGH STOMPED INTO the cave, nearly kicking the sniveling goblin at his feet as he passed.

"Move!"

"Forgive me, Mighty One! Kurgh is always in the way!"

The goblin bowed repeatedly and planted his nose firmly in the dirt. Gortogh walked past him without a second glance and stood with his back to the little shaman. He stared into the low fire surrounded by mounds of fur for seating and took a deep breath. The smoke clung to the air, and he wrinkled his nose at the smell of cooked fur and old meat.

The cave was musty and hot, which suited Gortogh just fine. Goblins were not keen on cold weather, and Gortogh less than most. He could hear the shaman shuffling up in the sand behind him.

"Your tribe becomes stronger with the ogres, Mighty One."

Gortogh turned with an annoyed glance, but Kurgh was facedown, not even looking at him. He turned back to the fire.

"Yes, the ogres are strong."

"And tough. The chief took much punishment from our mighty champion before he fell. He should have surrendered sooner. He could not match the champion of Ogrosh."

"He would only have lost his head sooner. The ogres tolerate no sign of weakness in their leaders. He was dead before he entered the circle no matter the outcome."

Gortogh made no attempt to hide his intelligence and speak as other goblins in the presence of the shaman. Kurgh truly believed him to be the champion of Ogrosh, and thus, perfect.

"Who leads the ogres does not matter. The Mighty One will lead all the people of Ogrosh."

Gortogh snorted and then winced at a pain in his side.

"Are you hurt, Mighty One?"

Gortogh was angry at the way the fight had ended, but the anger drained away with a sudden, sharp pain in his chest. He reached his hand up to grab at his armor. His body was not bleeding that he could see, but he was having trouble breathing. Probably a cracked rib from the solid hit he took. He pushed on his chest and sucked in his breath sharply.

"Rest, Mighty One. Let Kurgh heal you!"

The goblin had inched across the cavern floor until his fingers were lightly touching Gortogh's feet. He kicked them away in disgust and felt another sting in his side. He thought for a moment of throwing the little toad out and just pushing through the pain, but in truth, it was becoming quite uncomfortable. With as deep a breath and a sigh as he could muster, he laid back on the pile of furs nearest the fire and waited.

Kurgh scurried closer again, the bones he wore around his neck and waist clattering against each other with every movement. He moved like a crab, crawling along on his hands and feet. He always stayed low to the ground in Gortogh's presence, but he always stood tall among the other goblins. Long black feathers he wore from his belt tickled Gortogh's legs as he climbed up the furs to rest beside him. Gortogh looked at him and saw a giant smile on his face. It sickened him.

"Get this over with."

"Of course, of course, Mighty One."

His hands slid across Gortogh's body and a shiver went up his spine. The tiny shaman closed his eyes and breathed deeply as his fingers tittered lightly across his skin. Gortogh turned his head and closed his eyes to hide his revulsion.

"Ooh. So mighty is the champion of Ogrosh. Only a single broken bone. It would heal on its own with your godly strength, but Kurgh can help it. It will heal much faster with Kurgh."

"Just do it."

The shaman closed his eyes and threw his head back to the sky. A gleaming knife of white bone appeared in his hand, and as he chanted softly to the heavens, he dragged it across his arm. His chanting never broke, as if the cut gave him no pain. Blood poured from the wound and flowed to Kurgh's hands, answering his call to Ogrosh.

"The blood is strong. Blood will heal you."

The shaman laid his hands on Gortogh's chest and continued chanting. The name of Ogrosh was invoked repeatedly as he asked the blood god to heal his champion. Gortogh wondered, as he had so many times before, if this would be the time he was denied as a fake. How could he receive the blessings of a god he did not worship?

Gortogh was no champion of Ogrosh.

A few breathless moments passed, and Gortogh felt the warmth spread through his body. In an instant, his breathing eased and the pain lessened. It seemed Ogrosh would help him a while longer.

"His champion is healed! Praise Ogrosh!"

Kurgh leapt from the furs and danced around, singing his praises to Ogrosh as blood from his arm splashed the cave walls. Gortogh rolled his eyes and poked gingerly at his ribs. The pain was gone, completely healed. He sat up and watched the shaman skip around the cave in a circle.

Kurgh held his arms to the sky, and they both watched as the deep cut on his arm slowly began to close. In moments, the blood was gone and not even a scar remained. The shaman began to dance again, shouting the name of Ogrosh. Gortogh would have laughed if he didn't despise the pathetic creature. He heard a high whistle from the darkness of the cave and swiveled his head.

Kurgh immediately stopped dancing and glared into the dark.

"Leave me," Gortogh said.

"I should stay with you, Mighty One."

Gortogh turned his glare on the shaman, and he immediately shrunk to the floor and scuttled away. When he was out of sight, Gortogh stood and walked alone into the darkness.

"It is unwise to keep that sniveling toad in your confidence," he heard a voice say.

"He is just another worm who serves me," Gortogh said.

"He worships you because he believes you are the embodiment of his god."

"Then I should not have to fear his dagger at my back."

Velanon stepped out from behind an outcrop and stood with his arms folded. They stared in silence for several breaths. Gortogh looked him up and down and felt a twitch in his sword arm. The elf was no taller than a goblin and half as big around. He wore no armor, no obvious weapon. It should be such an easy thing to draw his sword and chop the weakling in two.

But Gortogh knew better.

"It's about time, wizard," Gortogh said. "It has been over a month."

"I have been busy and have had no need of you."

"You have had no need of me for months now. My warriors grow restless with nothing to kill. I don't know how much longer I can keep them here with nothing to fight but each other."

"A while longer, perhaps."

"You come every month and tell me the same thing. Gather the tribes. Gather more warriors. I am growing as impatient as my people, wizard."

"If you are not happy with our arrangement, feel free to leave at any time."

Gortogh stared hard at him, then finally looked down.

"That sword you carry, the amulet you wear, every bit of strength you possess is mine to give and take. When I pulled you from the mud, you were as weak and sniveling as that bootlick you call a shaman. I gave you the power.

I helped you kill the chief of your tribe. You are alive only as long as I allow you to be, never forget that."

Gortogh nodded, his eyes never leaving the dirt.

"Then we understand each other," Velanon said.

"This cannot continue as it has. The tribes follow me, but my hold over them is weak at best. I can command them easily enough in their presence, but I cannot be with them every minute of every day. Old wounds run deep, and only more blood will fill them."

"Can I not trust you to handle this one task? I do not have the time to babysit you and your kin."

"You order me to gather the tribes, and I have done so! You order me to wait, and I have waited! But you *cannot* have both! You cannot order goblin tribes to live beside one another and offer them nothing on which to bloody their blades. Even Ogrosh himself could not achieve what you ask."

Velanon glared long at him, but he would not turn. He held the wizard's gaze until at last he shook his head and spoke.

"Perhaps you are right. One cannot keep a bow drawn taut for too long. His hold on the string weakens with each passing moment. Very well. As it is, I do have need of you."

Gortogh eyed him.

"Why now?" he asked.

"The why is my concern. In a little less than a fortnight, you will have your fight. And, oh what a fight it will be."

"Two weeks? I cannot keep them together for even a week! Fights have already broken out among the larger tribes, and the tension mounts with each day."

"The town of Molner is ten days hard march from

here. That should take some of the piss out of them. Between here and there is the village of Derne. Take your army and destroy the village on your way if you wish. But be in Molner in ten days."

"And what then?"

"Await my instructions. I have other business to take care of until then."

"And what if you don't come?"

"Well, wouldn't that be nice for you?"

With that, the elf turned and walked deeper into the darkness until Gortogh could no longer see him.

Wait. Always wait.

Gortogh walked back to the fire where he plopped down on his throne of furs. Only a few moments passed before he heard Kurgh slithering back in on his hands and knees.

"May I enter, Mighty One?"

Gortogh grunted, which was all the invitation the shaman needed. He crawled up until he was across the fire and stayed low to the ground.

"You should not be speaking to that pointy-eared demon," he said in a low voice.

"You should not be spying on my affairs!" Gortogh said, his head snapping around to glare.

Kurgh whined and prostrated himself in front of him. He pushed himself as deep into the dirt as he could. Gortogh had no doubt that if he could dig a pit to climb in, he would.

"I meant no disrespect! I was not spying, Mighty One! I only saw him through the darkness. I heard nothing!"

He glared at the blubbering fool and shook his head.

"Stand and look at me!"

His head snapped up, his face covered in dirt, and stared across the fire. He reluctantly stood and faced Gortogh on wobbly knees.

"I'm sorry, Mighty One. I'm sorry."

"What did you see?"

He whined and looked down again. Gortogh could see his knees shaking, no doubt wanting to collapse and bring him to the position he was most comfortable in.

"What did you see?"

"I saw you talking with that pale, pointy-eared demon. You should not deal with such devils, Mighty One. He is not of our blood."

"He serves his purpose."

"He is not of Ogrosh, Mighty One. His blood is poison."

"The elf is not your concern. I have him under control."

"Of course, Mighty One, of course. You are using him for the glory of Ogrosh."

"Exactly, yes."

There was a commotion outside. Gortogh could hear a lot of curses flying and a lot of shouts for blood. He leapt to his feet and strode for the cavern entrance.

"More fighting between the tribes?"

"Another lost patrol, Mighty One. A survivor stumbled into camp with a great gash on his head given to him by the Wood Elf. I have healed him, but he said all the others were killed. He told me to tell you that you are to leave the forest if you want to keep your life."

Gortogh growled and drew his sword.

"This damn Wood Elf! He mocks me and strikes at me while hiding in the forest like a coward! For months he has played this game with me, and I grow tired of it!"

"Send another hunting party to find and kill the devil. String his guts from the trees for the birds!"

"Another hunting party?" he shouted. "How many must we lose?"

Gortogh squeezed the hilt of his sword and felt its power flow through his muscles. He swung it to the side where it clanged loudly into rock and bit deeply, tearing off a chunk. Bits of stone and dust flew behind him and scattered across the ground. Gortogh closed his eyes and took a deep breath. When he had calmed, he sheathed his sword and turned back to find Kurgh in his usual position on the floor.

"He hides and fights like a coward. I will give him no more of my men."

Kurgh looked up and nodded. Gortogh returned to his fire. The silence dragged on uncomfortably.

"I am going to tell the men the tale of the great city of Ogrilon tonight," Kurgh said sheepishly. "The shamans of the other tribes are going to come together to pray to Ogrosh as one. Will you join us around the fire?"

"No."

Kurgh looked back down.

"Find the new ogre chieftain and send him to me," Gortogh said. "Then go and tell the tribes to make ready to march tomorrow."

"We march, Mighty One?"

Gortogh stared long into the fire.

"We march."

CHAPTER FOUR

A DARK MAGE

"ELODY, RUN!" RINN yelled as he grabbed her arm and slid in the grass.

Elody was sliding too as they both tried to turn and run. The red dragon had raised its massive wings and head, which sent her heart into a thunderous rush that seemed to drown all the sound in her ears. She heard Rinn say something else behind her and felt a tug on the back of her robe, but as she spun to flee, she slipped and hit the ground. Rolling to her back, she threw her arms up over her face.

"Tark, stop!"

She heard the shout over her pounding heart but didn't recognize the voice. She peeked between her arms and saw a man running from where the dragon had already drawn its wings back in and settled to the ground.

"I'm so sorry," he said as he neared. "He wasn't really going to hurt you, he's just been on edge lately."

Elody opened her mouth, but she was breathing so hard nothing would come out. Rinn had no such trouble.

"What in the nine hells is wrong with you?" Rinn

shouted.

The man was reaching down for Elody, but he quickly stepped back as Rinn got between them and slapped his hand away.

"I told you, he wasn't going to hurt you. He was just scared."

"*He* was scared?" Rinn yelled.

A screech cut the air, and they all looked up to see Jalthrax glide down and land just behind Elody where he quickly ran up beside her. With a hiss, he spread his wings. A cloud of frost drifted from his open mouth as his neck swayed back and forth.

Rinn reached down without turning his back on the man and grabbed Elody by the arm. He tugged her to her feet and pushed her back.

"You'd best get that animal under control," Rinn said. "Lot of people won't care whether he was going to hurt them or not."

"I'm sorry. We've been in some really hostile places lately, and he overreacted. I'm Eliath, and this is Tark."

He smiled and extended his hand, but neither of them reached to take it. Elody touched Jalthrax's neck and rubbed him until he calmed and pulled his wings back. Eliath's hand hung in the air for a few seconds before he pulled it back to scratch at his neck.

"Who is this little guy?" he asked looking at Jalthrax.

Elody wrapped her arm around the dragon's neck and pulled him to her.

"His name is Jalthrax."

"He's beautiful. And what was your name?"

"I'm Rinn, and this is my sister Elody."

"Glad to meet you both. I only just arrived in town a moment ago, and I came here when I saw no dragons at the Roost. This used to be where dragonmages met and practiced the last time I was here."

"The only dragonmages we've seen stayed a day at most," Elody said, standing up.

"Of course," Eliath said.

He scratched at a thick growth of beard on his chin as he stared off at the ground. He looked younger than Elody had first thought on seeing him. He was only a few years older than Rinn maybe. A dirty blonde tangle of hair covered his head, but his scraggily beard was more brown. His clothes were worn and far too heavy for the summer sun, but he didn't seem to notice as he stood awkwardly shifting his feet. She looked up and met his eyes as he caught her staring, and she snapped her gaze down.

"Well," he said. "I guess I'll be going then. Should be plenty of room at the Roost by the looks of it."

"They'll let you in the Roost with *that*?" Rinn said with a nod at Tark.

A low growl rolled out from the red dragon's lips as Eliath's eyes narrowed.

"Nice to meet you, Elody," Eliath said in a low voice.

He looked Rinn up and down one last time before snorting and turning back to Tark. Without another word, he slid expertly into the saddle on the dragon's back. Before he could even tug the reins, Tark beat his wings and thrust into the air, blowing the leaves and grass up around them.

Rinn and Elody watched in silence as they disappeared into the sky toward town.

"Come on," Rinn said at last. "We have to get home."

***

Rinn and Elody stumbled into the house just after

sunset. Aunt Jelena was waiting.

"When I ask you to bring me herbs in the morning," she said, "I don't mean whenever you damn well feel like it."

They both looked to the floor, but then Elody brought her head up and scrunched her eyes. With a quick step to the side, she skirted around her aunt and went up the stairs to her room, giving Rinn a little wave and a smile over her shoulder as she did.

"Thanks," Rinn called after her and then turned back to his aunt. "I'm sorry, Aunt Jelena. I was busy with Berym, and I lost track of time."

"Do you know how long it takes to prepare what I need? Mrs. Gelin will go into labor tomorrow morning, and I need to be ready."

Rinn looked down.

"I'm sorry," he said as he held out the pouch of gathered herbs. "Is there anything I can help with?"

"You can stay out of trouble," she said as she grabbed the pouch and pushed past him.

Rinn jogged up the stairs and knocked on the closed door at the top.

"Thanks for leaving me down there. That was really great."

Elody opened the door a crack after a moment.

"It wasn't my job to gather the herbs, I was just helping. I wasn't going to stand there and take a tongue lashing for it when it wasn't my job."

"Real brave, El."

Elody started to close the door, but Rinn stuck his hand out and held it open. She stared at him and cocked her head.

"What?" she said.

48

"I don't want you talking to that red mage," he said.

"Why would I talk to him?"

"Elody."

"*Rinn.*"

"I mean it. I know you."

"I have no desire to speak to some oaf with a red dragon," she said.

"I know you've been wanting someone to train you."

"He *has* no training and nothing to teach me."

Rinn stared her down a moment longer before pulling his hand away. She immediately closed the door. Rinn shook his head and went to his room. Pulling his own door closed behind him, he kicked his boots off and flopped down on his bed. Lacing his hands behind his head, he laid back with a little sigh, rolled over, and closed his eyes.

*****

Elody went back to her bed and sat down. She heard Rinn's door close and listened for any further movement in the hallway before pulling a book out from under her pillow. It was a small book, bound in leather with old, yellowed parchment inside. She cracked it gingerly and turned to the page she was reading before her brother had knocked.

The pages had small notes and pictures scrawled in the margins, but they were mostly filled with tiny drawings of hands. Each picture showed a hand position with some small arrows or a wisp of a pencil mark showing a direction of motion.

Elody stared intently at the drawings. Taking great care with the brittle pages, she bent the book back a bit so that it would stay open without her having to hold it. Satisfied it would not close, she laid it down on her pillow and scooted to the middle of the bed so that she could see it all at once. Moving her hands through the air, she attempted to follow the illustrations.

When she was sure she had it right, she turned the page with a little smile.

CHAPTER FIVE

AFTER MIDNIGHT

RINN'S EYES OPENED slowly and saw the moonlight pouring through his window. It was the only light in his room. He rolled over and saw the nub of wax that was the candle he left burning when he fell asleep. Taking care to sit up without making the bed creak, he paused and listened.

Silence.

He rose from the bed and crept soundlessly to the door. Opening it just a crack, he put his ear to it and listened for any sound. He heard nothing. The house was silent. He saw light pouring from beneath Elody's door but figured she had probably left her candle burning too. He smiled to himself and closed the door.

He grabbed the leather jerkin that was laid over the edge of the bed and quickly pulled it on. Reaching under the little mattress, he pulled out a pouch and jingled it in his hand with a grin. He tucked it into his tunic and laced up the front.

With the practiced ease of a hundred times before, he pushed the window open and slid one leg, then the other, out. His hands closed over the windowsill as he pushed the rest of his body out. He dangled in midair for a second as his feet searched around for a purchase. Once they found what they were looking for, he let go of the window and slowly lowered himself down.

Rinn climbed down the side of the house without stopping and dropped silently to the yard below. He heard a sound behind him and every muscle tensed for an attack. A blow to the back flung him to the ground, and he rolled over quickly and threw his hands in front of his face.

Too slow.

Jalthrax snorted, and a blast of freezing cold air hit his face.

"Aagh! Every damn night?"

Jalthrax huffed again, and Rinn felt his skin go cold. He wiped his face and pulled back to see actual frost on his hand.

"Enough!"

He jumped up and grabbed the little dragon by the face. With rapid motions, he started scratching down his neck.

"Enough, Thrax. Time to go. Now be quiet. I mean it this time."

He gave him one last scratch and then turned toward the gate. He made it a few steps before Jalthrax squawked at him, and he scrunched up his shoulders in response.

"Every damn night."

He shook his head and went out the gate and into the night beyond. With a skip in his step, Rinn turned up the street and moved to the other side where he could duck into the shadows between two houses. Havnor seemed perfectly still. Watching and waiting for a moment, he finally slipped out into the street.

Picking his way across the city, Rinn couldn't help thinking how different his life had become. Sneaking out at night was nothing new, he'd been doing that in his village for years. It was everything. If he were still in Jornath, he might have married and had his own farm now. He and his father would have built it together, maybe just down the road from the one he'd spent his life on. His father had pushed him to find a nice girl for years, but he could never seem to choose just one.

A sigh escaped as he thought of his father. Life with his aunt was so different. No chores, no rules, no work to be done. Not that he missed any of that, but it sometimes felt like he was letting his father down. He knew his aunt was only giving him time because of what had happened back home, but he had begun to think that maybe it was time to find what he would do with his life.

Rinn picked his head up when he heard the shouts up the street and saw his final destination ahead. The Chicken Coop tavern. He smiled at the little joke in the name he had only learned a few nights before. It was a jab at the Dragon's Roost a few streets over, and it was every bit the opposite of that fine establishment.

The raucous sounds of merriment and drunkenness floated out of the open door and into the streets. As he watched from across the street, a man stumbled out the door, laughing to himself. He made it a few steps before he turned to the alley and retched. Wiping his mouth with his sleeve, he just laughed some more and kept walking.

This was definitely not the Dragon's Roost.

A high-class establishment for all the dragonmages of

Gondril, the Roost was far too fancy a place for the likes of him. Fresh, roast meat every night. Elven wines imported from Nirorn itself. All the great dragonmages stayed in the Roost. The Chicken Coop, on the other hand, was a place where you might end up if you were a failed dragonmage.

Which he was.

Scanning up the street and seeing no one, Rinn finally stepped from the shadows and walked across to the door. Brushing the dirt off his jerkin, he patted the pouch tucked safely inside to make sure it was still there. One never knows what could be stolen traveling the streets of Havnor. Even if you're regularly on the side of those doing the stealing.

He launched into the tavern with a flair and dashed up to the bar, slapping his hand down repeatedly until he got the old man's attention.

"All right, all right," the old man said.

Rinn said nothing as he turned back to the crowd. The place was loud, but he saw that it actually wasn't that packed tonight. He heard a mug thud down on the bar behind him and spun back to smile.

"Thanks, Orus."

"Just keep it down in here tonight, all right? I've about had it with you and your friends there."

Rinn reached into his pocket and fished out a silver coin. He tossed it onto the bar and turned his back.

"We can always take our coin elsewhere if it's not good enough for you."

Old Orus snatched it as quickly as his big, meaty hands could take it and tucked it deep into his trousers.

"Ahh, Rinn. You know I'm just joking ya'!"

Rinn raised his mug in response. His eyes darted

quickly over the crowd, taking in every face in seconds. The Coop catered to a certain kind of patron. One that would sooner steal your coin purse as help you off the floor. It was a place for lowlifes. But Rinn liked lowlifes. They felt like his people.

And one was headed his way.

He saw her coming before she even got close, but he made no move to stop her or even acknowledge her. The girl slid up beside him as smoothly as she could manage in her overflowing dress and too-tall boots. She rested her hand firmly on his leg, slipping it higher and higher up his thigh. Rinn just sipped his mug without looking at her.

"Oh, Rinn. Aren't you tired of playing these games?"

"Oh, there's no game," he said. "I don't play games."

"Wonderful! No need to play a game anyway, you've already won. You just need to claim your prize."

She pushed her chest up, her breasts spilling out with so little to hold them in, and rubbed them against him. Just in case it wasn't clear the prize she was offering. Rinn smiled and shook his head.

"It's not the prize I mind, it's the price."

"I already said I'd do it half price for you. Five coppers, and I'll even let you stay a while after if you want."

"For five coppers, I'd better get to leave as soon as I'm done."

"You can do that too!" she said eagerly.

"I don't pay," he said. "Why pay for something I can easily get for free whenever I wish?"

"Not in this dump you don't. Only girl not working this place is the deaf one Orus has cleaning out the dung in back."

Rinn looked up when the door banged open and motioned to the group walking in. He emptied his mug and then slammed it on the bar before pushing the girl's hand away and walking over. He could hear her saying something behind him, probably an insult, but the bar was too loud and he didn't care.

"Be careful in here, Ariss," Rinn said as he approached with his hand extended. "Orus says he don't want no trouble from us tonight."

"We'll try and watch our manners," the man in front replied as he took Rinn's hand and pulled him close for a slap on the back.

The three boys behind him all chuckled. Rinn fell into step as they pushed their way through the crowd to a table in the back. It was already occupied by a couple of old farmers, but they quickly got up at the approach of the young men. Ariss took the far chair, and Rinn took the one beside him as the others jockeyed for the remaining chairs that didn't put their backs to the door.

Rinn recognized two of them as Balk and Ferix, two guys he'd gotten to know over the last few months, but the third he had never met.

"Kinda dead in here," Balk said.

"Where are all the girls?" Ferix asked.

"First of the month," Ariss said. "Merchants all got a little extra cash, so they go out for a good time. Girls are probably up the street at the Flagon. Better work than the lot that come in here. Nothin' but farmers and thieves in here."

"And here I forgot my plow," Rinn said.

They all started laughing a bit too loud as a girl appeared beside the table with a tray of mugs. Moving swiftly and ably between them, she set a mug down in front of each of them. Passing around the back, Rinn gave her a little smile and a wink as he slid in his chair to let her pass. She set the last mug down in front of the guy Rinn didn't recognize, and he reached his hand up to grab her bottom.

"Hey!" she said, smacking his hand away.

Rinn was on his feet in a flash, but Ariss beat him to it. Before Rinn's legs had left his chair, Ariss had his dagger drawn and pointing at the man's throat. The man's eyes went wide, and his hands shot into the air.

"I'm sorry, Yara," Ariss said. "I'm afraid my new friend doesn't know his manners."

Without a word, she picked up her tray and turned back to the bar. The man's hands stayed in the air as Ariss's dagger hovered above the table, and he let it hang there a few seconds longer. With a quick motion, he snapped it back into his belt and sat down. Ferix and Balk laughed and raised their mugs, but the others all sat in silence. After a few moments, the mood lightened, and the man found the courage to speak.

"What the hell was that, Ariss?"

"You don't piss where you sleep," Rinn said. "You go upsetting the girls, and the best you'll get is some spit in your beer. The worst is you'll get us thrown out of here. And we like it here."

"Who asked you, friend? I was talkin' to Ariss."

"He ain't your friend, Delek," Ariss said. "He's *my* friend. Me and Rinn go way back, and you'd best remember it. 'Cuz while he's an old friend to me, you I'll cut from ear to ear and throw down a hole."

Delek grinned and leaned back in his chair, eyeing Ariss as though he were waiting for a smile or a laugh. None was forthcoming. He finally held his hands up and shook his head.

"Hey, I was just havin' a little fun is all. Nice to meet you, Rinn. Ariss speaks highly of you."

Rinn nodded as he took a pull from his mug. The tension at the table hung in the air for several more minutes as the laughter and fun raged around them. Each man sat quietly sipping his beer and staring down at the table except for Rinn and Ariss. Finally, one of the others looked up and spoke.

"Well, this is fun and all," Balk said, "but if we're just gonna sit like a couple old fishermen with nothin' to say, we might as well get out of here and get to it. This beer tastes like piss anyway."

More silence.

Balk's eyes went around the table once or twice before he stared back down into his beer. Ariss drained the rest of his mug and raised it high, shaking it to no one in particular before he set it back down and leaned into the table. Everyone else leaned in with him.

"Big job tonight," Ariss said. "Can't say much about it here, but we're all gonna be busy. Things go well, all our friends could make out very well."

"I heard everyone is robbing the merchant district," Delek said.

Ariss sat back and narrowed his eyes.

"That what you heard is it?"

"Uh… that's just what I heard."

"Well, maybe you oughta shut your damn mouth about what you did or didn't hear, you know?"

"Sure thing, Ariss."

"Is he right though?" Ferix asked.

"Maybe so," Ariss said. "Maybe it's time for a bigger score."

"We can't go down into the merchant quarter tonight," Balk said. "They beef up the guard down there this time of the month to keep guys like us out."

"Guard won't be a problem," Ariss said.

They looked at him and then back and forth at each other.

"What about the knights?" Rinn asked.

"Can't do nothin' about the knights," Ariss said, "but there aren't enough in town to make much a difference. Everyone's real busy these days."

"We can't just go walkin' into the merchant quarter and take whatever we want," Ferix said. "If it were that easy, we'd have done it by now."

"We couldn't," Delek said. "There were too many dragonmages protecting the city. You seen any dragonmages around here lately?"

They looked around the table, and a smile crept onto their lips.

"I've seen a dragonmage," Rinn said.

Ariss cocked an eyebrow and turned his head to look at him.

"Saw one this morning," Rinn said.

"Just one?" Ariss asked.

"Just one. A dark one, with a red dragon."

Ariss waved his hand dismissively.

"Nothing to worry about with just one," he said. "He expectin' any friends?"

"I don't think so. Mages are all pretty busy protecting dragon mothers these days."

"What, dragons can't take care of themselves now?"

"Not from this they can't."

"So," Balk cut in, "you're sayin' we got a merchant quarter full of gold and valuables and no guard?"

"Well, no guard that'll do nothin'," Ariss said.

"Well, nine hells, boys," Ferix said. "What are we sittin' around here for?"

They all stood as one and shoved their way back through the crowd to the door. One by one they stepped out into the warm, humid night. Ariss moved to the middle of the street and sauntered off toward the town center. Rinn wasn't sure what he was doing, but he moved alongside him. They both got a chuckle watching the other three flitting through the shadows from building to building trying not to step on each other.

Rinn knew where the merchant quarter was, but since he had no idea what their final destination was, he just walked beside Ariss. They passed by the closed shops in the lower quarter and turned onto a street a few blocks up, heading again toward the town center. Ariss slowed his steps as they passed the front of the Dragon's Roost. They both looked beyond the inn itself to the dragon stables beside it and saw the red dragon, Tark, sleeping soundly.

Ariss chuckled and shook his head as he picked up the pace and walked on. Rinn stared a moment longer and then jogged to catch up. He occasionally looked back to see the other three creeping along about a block behind them.

"Come on, you slowpokes!" Rinn shouted.

They all froze in place as Rinn and Ariss roared with laughter. Fumbling to get around one another, the other three finally walked up alongside them down the middle of the street. In another few blocks they reached the merchant bazaar in the center of town.

Rinn had never really seen the place at night. At dusk, most of the merchants closed up shop and took their wares home for safekeeping, so there wasn't much to see or steal at night. Everything on the other side of the bazaar was the merchant quarter, and that wasn't a place they usually went. Much easier pickings in the lower quarter.

The bazaar looked abandoned. Through the darkness, Rinn could see a few torches and lanterns between the tents and shacks. He heard laughter coming from somewhere. Ariss paid no attention to any of it. He just kept walking.

Rinn started to get that nervous, excited feeling he got every night on a job with Ariss. He felt confident that if things went bad, he could hide somewhere and sneak off into the night without getting caught, but he wasn't as sure about Ariss. He had fallen in with a local thieves guild long before Rinn and Elody arrived in town, and he acted a little too invincible for Rinn's taste. Ariss was always taking chances they didn't need to take.

But Rinn trusted Ariss to see them all through. He always had. They had known each other for years, ever since Rinn's days training as a dragonmage in Baglund. Ariss had gotten him out of trouble a number of times through the years. Though he was also usually the one getting him into trouble.

Rinn looked to the side where Ariss walked with a calm look on his face. He didn't seem nervous at all about their adventure that night. Not the way Rinn always did. Ariss could always keep calm and get done what needed doing. When Rinn's bond failed, and he returned to Baglund without a dragon, Ariss was there. He walked Rinn the three days home and didn't say a word the whole way.

Rinn owed him so much for that.

They passed the old fountain at the heart of the bazaar, still bubbling in the night. Rinn saw some light up ahead. When they reached the lit tent, a few men sitting around a box being used as a card table looked up at their passing. Two shabbily-dressed men in robes, one with several missing teeth, smiled and waved at Ariss who smiled back. The other two players were members of the town guard from the looks of them.

"Care to join our friendly game?" the gap-toothed man asked.

"Not tonight," Ariss said. "Work to do."

The guards eyed the five of them as they passed, but neither made a move to stand. Ariss touched his hand to his brow as he strolled past. The rows and rows of tents finally parted as they neared the eastern edge, and they suddenly found themselves bathed in the light of dozens of lanterns and torches. The lavish homes of the city's merchant quarter lay open in front of them. Lights had been lit all along the street, almost giving the appearance of day. But just like the bazaar, the street was completely empty.

No guards. No knights. No dragonmages.

The merchant quarter stared back at them like a bright, open doorway inviting them in. And who were they to refuse such an invitation?

"This place is dead," Rinn said with a bit of reverence in his voice.

"Not dead," Ariss said. "Just sleeping. But it's just as good to us, ain't it boys?"

The other three could only nod. They stared ahead as though they were looking at a giant mound of gold. With no more fanfare, Ariss turned onto Aspen Lane and walked down the middle of the street, right out in the open.

Three guards rounded a corner up the street and marched in their direction. Everyone tensed, but Ariss only put his hand down to steady them. Rinn could feel his heart trying to climb his throat. Every instinct in him screamed to run, but he followed Ariss right toward the oncoming guards. Ariss only nodded as they passed, and the three of them just looked right past them and kept their eyes forward.

"They didn't see nothin'," Ariss said.

The others stared after the guards in stunned silence for a moment.

"Shouldn't we be at least a little cautious?" Delek asked. "Aren't there still a few knights?"

"Some," Ariss said, "but we'll keep an eye out for 'em."

Ariss led them to the first cross street and turned left. Rinn was on his guard and looking for any other sign of movement, but he saw nothing. The merchant quarter was truly empty. Somewhere on the periphery of his hearing, he heard a familiar sound.

The sound of jingling metal.

"Someone in armor's coming," Rinn said.

Ariss ducked into an alley between the two nearest homes, and the others followed. They waited silently as the sound got closer and closer. They could hear the loud clomping of metal boots striking the cobblestone streets, and they all shrunk deeper into the shadows. Rinn looked to the left and right and saw walls. The houses on this street backed up to the wall that cut off the merchant quarter from other parts of the city, leaving nothing behind them.

Nowhere to run if it came to that.

A figure appeared at the entry to the alleyway and paused for a moment to look down. The light behind him was bright and shadowed his face, but Rinn recognized the face immediately.

Berym.

Rinn looked down suddenly as though he was trying to hide his face and slinked back into the darkness. He bumped into Ariss who grabbed his arm tightly but had the good sense to not make a sound. They hid and waited.

Berym took a few steps into the alley, and Rinn saw Ariss slowly pull the dagger from his belt. Rinn's whole body tensed and he suddenly didn't know what to do. Unconsciously, he found himself drawing his own dagger. But he didn't know whose flesh it would find if a fight broke out. He held his breath for what seemed like minutes.

In another part of the city, the clang of a bell rang out. In seconds it was joined by more. Berym looked back at the noise and then turned back down the alley at a jog. Rinn let out his breath a little louder than he expected and received a thwack on the head from Ariss.

"You wanna get us killed?" he asked.

Ariss gave him another smack for good measure before pushing past the others and peering out of the alley. He held his hand back for another moment before waving them all forward. They filed out and turned left back toward their original destination. Wherever that was.

A few houses down, they found out.

Ariss stopped in front of a large house on the street and scanned it top to bottom. He looked down at his hand for a second and nodded to himself. Without a word, he disappeared along the side of the house and went around to the back door. The rest of them followed.

"You all know how we do this," Ariss said. "Delek's new here, but he ain't new to this. I go in first and subdue the help. Hopefully there won't be any more trouble than that."

"You expecting trouble?" Rinn asked.

"Maybe. Some of the merchants have been hiring mercenary help the last few months. I haven't heard about any at this house, but you never know."

Ariss reached out and tried the door but found it locked. He waved a hand, and Ferix stepped forward and knelt down. Fishing a small strip of leather from beneath his belt, he pulled tiny, metal tools and picks out and set to work on the lock. In only a few seconds, a loud click broke the silence, and Ferix turned the knob and pushed the door open with a smile.

Ariss crept past him and into the house, pulling the door closed behind him. Ferix stood back up beside the others, and they all waited. Rinn shifted from side to side on his feet when he could no longer contain his nervous energy. He hated the wait before the job. The more time he had to think about it, the more nervous he got.

Time crawled by without a sound.

Five minutes passed. Then ten minutes. They heard someone pass by on the street twice, but no one ever came around to the back of the house. Finally, the door opened a crack and then wider, and Ariss stepped out.

"Why aren't you guys ready? Masks."

Balk, Ferix and Delek all reached into their tunics and pulled out black masks that they used to cover the lower half of their faces. Rinn smiled and closed his eyes. Reaching inward for his inborn magic, he found his fingertips tingling in an instant. Years of practice and no dragon to rely on had made finding his own well of magic very easy for him.

Rinn heard Delek start to say something, then a smack, then he went silent. Rinn paid no attention. He was already focused on his spell. He moved his hands quickly and surely, as he had cast this spell many times before. It only took a few seconds to complete. Finishing with a wave in front of his face, the magic faded from his fingertips, and he felt it cover his body like a light snowfall.

Before their eyes, Rinn grew a whole foot in height and sprouted a great, black beard and mustache. His face became chubbier too, and his belly grew to match it. Delek stared at him with his mouth open, but the others just chuckled.

"A bit fatter this time, eh?" Balk asked.

"People are more comfortable around jovial-looking fellows," Rinn said.

His voice was just the same as it always was, but the rest of his body would be completely unrecognizable by even his own sister.

"How is it you cast without a dragon?" Delek asked. "You some kinda wizard? You didn't say he was a damn wizard, Ariss."

"Shut your mouth, Delek," Ariss said.

"No wizard," Rinn said quickly. "I just know how to draw the magic within me and weave it."

"No one I know's got magic except dragonmages and wizards," Delek said. "And I don't see a dragon."

"I trained for years as a mage," Rinn said. "It didn't work out, but the magic is my own. All of us have some magic inside though. Except maybe you lot."

Ferix and Balk snickered, but Delek still eyed him cautiously. Rinn waved his chubby arm at the door with a flourish.

"Are we going in or what?"

They filed in through the backdoor and into the kitchen beyond. Once inside, Rinn heard a muffled cry from the darkness and looked down to see two women and a man trussed up and lying on the floor. Their mouths had been gagged, and the man looked as though he'd been beaten a little. Rinn winced at the thought but kept walking behind the others who didn't even stop to look. Ariss turned back on them.

"You three down, me and Rinn up," Ariss said. "Silver, jewels, anything we can make out with without too much notice. Servants quarters are down that way, and ain't nothin' worth takin' down there, so stick to this side of the house."

His orders given, he walked past them with Rinn in tow and headed for the stairs. He crept slowly up, and Rinn followed behind. Neither made a sound. Not even so much as a creak. They reached the top and started down a long hallway of several doors. Just as they reached the first door, the next one down the hall opened in, and a man stepped out.

Wearing nothing but a robe and rubbing his eyes, he looked down the hall with a lazy look and saw them. His eyes went wide. He tried to turn, but Ariss got to him first. He grabbed the man from behind and quickly wrapped his thick arm around his head, covering his mouth.

The man tried to scream, but it came out as a muffled moan that no one would hear. Ariss spun him around to face Rinn whose hands were already moving through the motions of a spell. Ariss smiled and made sure his arm didn't cover the man's eyes as Rinn's hands flew through the movements. He spread his fingers out softly before the man's face.

He went slack in Ariss's arms, and Rinn nodded to his friend who then released the man. He was younger than Rinn would have expected, given the wealthy surroundings. He couldn't have been more than few years older than himself.

"Hi there," Rinn said, "I'm Ril. Don't you remember me? We met at spring fair last year, I think."

"Ril?"

The man blinked his eyes, and a sudden recognition washed over his face.

"Oh, yes, of course," he said with a smile. "Yes, I remember you, Ril. I wasn't aware we had friends over."

"We're very sorry to call on you so late, um... I'm sorry, what was your name?" Rinn asked.

"Terel," the man said.

"Of course, Terel. We're very sorry to call on you so late."

"That's quite all right. Friends are always welcome in my home. We just need to keep it down a bit. My wife is very tired these days, and she's just finally fallen asleep."

"We certainly don't want to disturb her," Rinn said. "We really hate to bother you. We were attacked on the road outside of town, and everything we own was stolen. I tell you, the world has gotten so rough these days. Everyone out to rob you blind and take what's yours."

Ariss chuckled behind Terel, and Rinn gave him a little wink.

"We got into town late with no horses and no food, and we just couldn't find a decent enough inn to stay in."

"They are all a bit shabby, aren't they?" Terel said. "Well, of course you're welcome to stay here. I would never turn a friend out into the night."

"Oh, Terel. I wouldn't dream of it, what with your wife being so tired. I would feel terrible if we woke her. No, we'll definitely go and find a nice inn to stay at. I hear the Dancing Unicorn is a very nice establishment. We were thinking we might stay there."

"Oh, yes. That is a fine place. I've stayed there a few times myself."

"Excellent. That's where we'll go then."

Rinn turned to leave, patting his vest melodramatically before spinning back with a chagrined expression.

"Oh, my. I forgot they stole our purses as well. We have no money to even find a place for the night. Would you have just a bit of coin we could borrow to get a room?"

"For you? Of course! Wait right here, and I'll get it for you."

Terel had skipped past them toward the stairs when Rinn stopped him.

"We'll come with you," he said. "I'd hate for us to stay up here and make so much noise that we wake your wife."

Terel paused at the stairs. He seemed to wrestle with himself.

"We're old friends, you and I, Terel. We'll just come along with you so we don't wake the wife."

Terel's eyes scrunched, and he unconsciously sucked on his lower lip. Rinn stepped forward and laid his hand on Terel's arm with a light pat. The conflict within him settled in an instant, and his eyes brightened as he smiled at Rinn.

"Yes, of course."

He started down the stairs, and Rinn and Ariss both couldn't suppress their grins as they followed behind him. They reached the bottom together and walked back through the house toward the kitchen. Rinn didn't see the other three, but he could hear slight sounds from other parts of the house. Turning down the short hallway to the servant quarters, Terel came to the door of a tiny room that probably belonged to one of the girls.

"The bugger hid it in the servant's room," Ariss said. "Smart."

Terel swung the door open and strode in and to the far wall. Pushing lightly on the wall three times, they heard a click as he slid a panel out of the way to reveal an iron box hidden in a cubby.

Taking a key from a thin chain around his neck, he quickly unlocked the chest and propped the lid open. Inside were dozens of small, leather pouches. Grabbing one, he turned back and held it out.

"Here you are. That should get you many nights stay, even in a finer place like the Dancing Unicorn."

"Wonderful, Terel. Thank you. You know, we really could use a bit more if you can spare it. We're in desperate need of some new clothes and maybe a fine meal."

"You know," Terel said, "I didn't want to say anything, but you do look a bit shabby. Those scoundrels must've taken everything."

He grabbed another pouch and handed it over to them. Rinn smiled and tucked it into his vest.

"Thank you so much, Terel. We really can't thank you enough. Though... we really could use a bit more. We need to buy a new wagon and horses. And maybe restock some of our supplies. Perhaps we could just take what you have."

Terel's eyes went wide.

"As a loan, you understand," Rinn added quickly. "We'd, of course, have it back to you in a week or so. Probably less. We just need to pick up some more supplies, and we don't know what everything will cost. But we do have some goods coming in just behind us, and we'd have all of this back to you in only a few days."

Terel's whole body trembled as he struggled with something inside himself. Rinn felt Ariss reach for his dagger beside him and gently motioned him back. With his other hand, Rinn reached forward and touched Terel's arm.

"It would mean so much to us, Terel. I promise we will have it back, in full, in no more than a few days. With interest, of course!"

Terel looked down at the hand touching him and then back up to Rinn's eyes and seemed to soften.

"Well, what kind of man would I be if I didn't help a friend who'd lost everything?"

He reached back into the chest and pulled out a larger bag tucked into the bottom and then started throwing the smaller pouches into it. When the chest was empty save for some papers and a few bits of leather, he closed it up.

"There you are. That should be more than enough to get you back on your feet. And you'll get it back to me in three days?"

"Two, more likely! Our shipment may come early. I'll be sure that you're paid back in full with some extra on the top. Maybe you and the wife could stay a few nights the Dancing Unicorn yourself."

"Well, she's not much in the mood for romance these days, but maybe I'll buy her some nice jewelry."

"I think that's a lovely idea," Rinn said.

He turned back to Ariss and his smiled widened.

"We really must be going, Terel. We'll head over to the Dancing Unicorn and get a room or two. We'll see you in just a few days."

"Excellent!" Terel said.

He followed behind them as they walked back down the servant's hall and into the kitchen. Rinn took the lead and went straight for the backdoor with Ariss behind him. Terel passed his prone servants without even noticing them as he walked them both out and stood in the doorway as they left.

Rinn and Ariss stepped out and found the other three already standing there waiting down the alley a bit.

"Goodbye!" Terel said as he waved.

"Goodbye, Terel," Rinn said. "And thank you again."

"For you, Ril? Anytime."

He continued waving as they all turned down the alley and headed back toward the street. Rinn carried the heavy bag over his shoulder, and he saw the others also carrying various loads. Ariss took the lead and moved to the head of the alley and peered out in both directions. With a wave of his hand, they stepped out into the street.

"For you, Ril," Ariss said with a grin, "anytime."

They all laughed hard as they hurried through the streets. The bag over Rinn's shoulder was heavy, and he kept having to switch sides to keep from getting too tired. His struggle wasn't nearly as hard as Balk's though. He was carrying a large painting almost as tall as a man and half as wide.

"What in the hells are you doing with that?" Ariss asked.

"I liked it," Balk said. "She's pretty."

"We get in a pinch, you ditch it quick."

One quick turn and two blocks, and they left the bright lights of the merchant quarter behind as they blended back into the darkness of the uninhabited bazaar. Rinn dropped his disguise as the others removed their masks. Walking as quickly as they could with their prizes in tow, they passed by a few town guards leaning against the side of a stall. Rinn saw Ariss extend his hand out and slide some coin into each of their hands as he passed, and they both pocketed them without a word. Once they were beyond the bazaar and safely back on their own side of town, everyone loosened up a little and walked with a little spring in their step.

"How the hell did you pay off the whole damn town guard?" Rinn asked.

"Wasn't just us," Ariss said. "Couple other guilds all pitched in to make it happen. The guard was easy. They're just as sick of all the gold going to the fat merchants as we are. We didn't even try to pay off the knights. We've tried before, and it never works."

Balk struggled with his painting. Rinn continually shifted his bag from shoulder to shoulder, refusing to let anyone else carry it. When they finally reached the Chicken Coop, they ducked into the alley behind it and crowded around each other. Ariss reached behind some crates stacked in the alley and pulled out a tarp that he laid in the middle of them. One by one they emptied their pockets and bags onto the tarp.

Balk tried to put his painting in the middle, but a

look from Ariss made him lean it against the wall instead. Once everything was in the circle, Ariss reached down and began divvying out. He started out taking a huge pile of the smaller pouches and shifting them over to his side and then split the rest evenly. The few bits of silver and jewelry the others found, he put into the pile in front of him.

"How come you get so much more than the rest of us?" Delek said a bit too loudly.

Ariss's fist shot out faster than Rinn could register, catching Delek in the jaw. He flew back and landed hard on his arse. Ariss had his dagger out in an instant, but Delek made no move to get up.

"The guild gets their cut first. Then I get my cut, then Rinn gets his cut, then Balk, then Ferix, then you. That's how the cut works. You don't like it, we can cut another way."

He twirled his dagger in the air in front of Delek's face. Then he pointed it down at the largest pile.

"That belongs to the guild. Got it?"

Delek nodded.

Ariss slid his dagger back into his belt and then threw the biggest pile along with his own into the sack. The rest quickly tucked their haul into their own vests and pockets. They all stood, and Ariss reached his hand down for Delek. With one tug, he pulled him to his feet.

"Now," Ariss said. "Who wants a drink?"

Nods all around.

"I can't be out too late," Rinn said.

"Oh, we'll get you home before your aunt wakes up," Ariss said, and the others laughed.

Rinn moved up beside Ariss as he lead the way, and he gave Rinn a slap on the shoulder.

"You did good tonight," Ariss said. "I love that friendly thing you do. Reminds me of the good times back in Baglund."

"To good times," Rinn said.

"Listen," Arris said, "after tonight, you should lay low for a couple days. Don't come out lookin' for us, 'cuz we won't be here. After a job like this one, lotsa people are gonna be staying gone for a bit. I'll send word when things are clear."

Rinn nodded.

"We should have time for a quick drink before everything turns lopsided though," Ariss said with a smile as he pushed open the door to the Coop.

CHAPTER SIX

THE FLESH OF DRAGONS

VELANON STOOD ON the side of the windy mountain and stared long at the path ahead of him. If that elven scout he'd beaten to death was telling truth, the dragon's cave was just up around the bend. He glanced over his shoulder down the trail but saw no one coming.

Velanon hated being back in elven lands.

He hadn't returned to them since leaving more than a year ago to begin his quest. Before that, he had spent more than a hundred years in the tower of his master, just inside the elven forest. Now he stood deep within their borders. It unsettled him. Though he was sure his recent actions were not known to his people, his beliefs and those of his master were.

He had no more friends in these lands.

From the side of the mountain, he could see all of the surrounding forest. Nothing looked dangerous or suspicious, but that gave him no comfort. He had wards cast on himself to detect trouble, but his eyes wouldn't see an elven scout near him until the blade was already at his neck. He cleared his throat and stared at the path in front of him. One foot in front of the other, he walked on.

A few short steps brought him around the last bend in the mountain trail where it disappeared into a deep cave. Reaching beneath his tunic, Velanon tugged at the simple, golden chain around his neck and pulled free its prisoner. A small, pink crystal dangled innocently in the air. Velanon closed his hand around it and felt the hum of power that radiated down his arm and through his whole body. He dropped it back out of sight and took a deep breath.

Moving his hands in swirling patterns, he began to speak in the ancient song of magic. The words flowed from his lips in perfect rhythm, each one building on the last. Strands of magic leapt between his hands, swirling and coalescing around them. He spread his arms apart as he finished, and the magic flowed around him, wrapping his body tightly. He shivered at the chill as the spell took effect.

Straightening his back, he strode into the cave.

It was deeper than it looked from the outside. He walked for several minutes with no sign of anything other than a few lizards. Gold dragons liked their caves deep and closer to the elements, he knew, but this was more than he expected. He finally reached a break where the cavern split into two and stopped.

An orange light and sweltering heat poured from one passage while the other remained cold and dark. The choice was easy. Gold dragons favored a lair built over molten rock. Taking the left passage, the heat immediately started rising. The wards he had cast protected him from any harm from the heat, but he felt his brow moisten the deeper he went.

There was a smell in the air just below the heat. He

couldn't discern it at first, but as he crept deeper into the mountain, it became clear.

Smoke. And cooking flesh.

A bright light up ahead spilled out from an open cavern, and he heard loud noises from that direction. Velanon took a deep breath and stood up straight. Taking extra care to make his heels click loudly on the stone to announce his presence, he sauntered into the cave.

It was even hotter in here. Almost unbearable.

A long, wide ledge ran the length of the place, but that was all. The edge of the rock to Velanon's left just fell away. That was where the heat was coming from. He could see the waves of heat and the orange glow from the lava below. It flowed through low canyons beneath the surface, peaking through the rocks in broken places.

Across from him, the gold dragon was crouched low to the ground, crunching loudly on the roasted bone and flesh of some recent kill. Its head came up as Velanon came into sight, but it made no move to rise. Loud breaths echoed through the chamber as it breathed in deeply, taking in his scent and his aura of power. The dragon went back to eating and tried to play uninterested, but Velanon could see how its body was now tense and ready to spring.

He smiled and began his speech.

"Greetings, Mighty Zarathalus'ul'Nutharr," Velanon said with a flourish of his hand.

The gold dragon chuckled in its deep, gravelly voice, shook its head, and went back to eating. Velanon narrowed his eyes.

"Do you know who I am?"

The dragon ignored him. It didn't even bother to look

up this time. Velanon clenched his hands and felt his fingernails dig into his skin. Oh, how he hated the arrogance of dragons. And this was the most arrogant he'd met.

"Whether you speak to me or not, I am here to kill you."

Now it looked up and gave him its attention. Velanon smiled smugly but quickly wiped it from his face.

The gold dragon started laughing. A loud, chilling laugh that shook the cave around him, causing rocks and dust to break away and rain down from the ceiling.

Velanon growled and began casting. He spoke the words of magic and whirled his hands to form a spell.

"If you keep this up, you will be the one dead, wizard."

The dragon spoke calmly and evenly. So much so that Velanon dropped his hands. His spell vanished from his lips and his eyes narrowed. This dragon was *definitely* the most arrogant he'd ever met. He cursed himself silently for losing the spell and started to chant again.

"I have killed dozens of wizards just like you, elf. Most not as powerful, perhaps, but I was much younger then."

Velanon stopped before the first words left his lips.

"Besides," the dragon said, "I'm not the dragon you're looking for."

"Oh? And what would you know of what I seek?"

"You came looking for a dragon mother. Males don't lay eggs as far as I know, though I confess I have never tried."

Velanon looked the dragon up and down.

"I was told this was a dragon mother's den."

"Oh, it *was*. Just not anymore."

"Where is she?"

The gold looked pointedly down at the large chunk of meat at his feet and took another great bite. Velanon couldn't hide the shock on his face.

"You killed and *ate* her?"

"Come in and sit down. If you'd like, I can cook you up some leg. Though I must admit roasting under intense heat chars the outside while leaving the inner flesh quite raw. Something we dragons like but your kind rarely does."

He bent back down and continued eating while Velanon stood still and watched. For once, he wasn't sure what to do.

"Sit," the dragon said more forcefully.

His voice held no authority for Velanon. He had no real fear. For all his bluster, the dragon could do nothing to harm him. But the dragon had intrigued him. None of the countless others he'd killed could make such a claim. Making up his mind, Velanon took a few steps closer and sat down.

The dragon kept eating, leaving the two of them in silence for several minutes. Velanon watched with disgust and did little to hide it from his face. Even the goblins were not so vile as to eat their own kind. Trying hard to ignore the sound of tearing flesh, he looked the beast up and down to get a measure of it.

The two horns on its head were thick and long. The frills on the side of its face were wide, and Velanon could see the long spikes going all the way down its back. All of its spikes and horns had grown in across the top of its head. Which made this dragon at least a hundred years old by his guess. Dragons lived so long, it was hard to tell sometimes.

His eating was distracting. And disgusting. Blood and juice from the dragon leg he was eating dripped down his chin and splattered to the ground. Velanon wrinkled his nose. Turning away in disgust, he looked off into the cave.

"You are the hunter, yes?" the dragon said at last.

Velanon swiveled back and found himself staring into the dragon's narrow, slanted eyes.

"You are the one that has been murdering the dragon mothers, yes?"

"Yes."

"Good."

The dragon lifted his horned head and sucked in a great breath. Velanon's body tensed to leap back, but he managed to control his fear and stay put. He cannot harm me. No matter how old he is.

The dragon blew a burst of fire from his mouth, charring more of the flesh and scorching the ground in front of him. As the fire flowed across the sandy cave floor, some of the flames neared Velanon, but he would not move. They licked at his body and then suddenly parted harmlessly to the side.

The dragon looked down with a wry smile as he leaned down and took another bite of the haunch of meat he had just heated back up. Throwing Velanon a wink, he chewed slowly and blew a small puff of fire straight at Velanon where it again flowed to the side, never nearing him.

"Neat trick. A field of anti-magic?"

Velanon folded his arms and said nothing.

"I can sense it from here. It's a good thing you stopped when you had the chance. Your skinny corpse would be something stuck between my teeth before you knew what happened."

Velanon snorted. A most unrefined sound coming from him, he noted.

"You dragons are all alike," he said. "Arrogant and superior."

"And you are not? Sometimes arrogance is earned, little wizard."

The dragon took another bite and smacked his lips.

"Is that Zarathalus you're eating?" Velanon asked.

"Was that her name? I suppose so. I can hardly keep up with all these young ones."

"And what shall I call you?"

"You may call me Kalus."

"Why did you kill her, Kalus? Surely there is other meat around here you could find if you are hungry."

The dragon glared and chewed, swallowing a hunk of meat before answering.

"She was a whore who gave away her children."

"So you would kill your own kind?"

"She was a traitor to her kind and no kin of mine."

Velanon arched an eye.

"Is that not why you came to kill her?" Kalus asked. "Yes, I know who you are and what you do. You don't just kill dragon mothers. You've killed dark dragons who sell their eggs as well. You've been quite the busy little wizard."

Velanon eyed him cautiously and tried to form a response. This was not going at all as he'd planned, and he couldn't know what this dragon was after. Is he after information? What if this is the one I cannot defeat. When he finally spoke, Velanon chose his words carefully.

"Yes, I came to kill her because she was a dragon

mother."

"Why should it matter to you what a dragon does with her eggs? Do you fancy yourself the last wizard on some great crusade against dragons?"

"She and her kind, your kind, destroyed my people. I am not the last of my kind, but I may be the last who cares about our destruction."

"She was not even alive when the wizards died out. I would venture to guess that you are older than she was."

"Then she has paid for the sins of her fathers."

The gold dragon chuckled.

"You elves have such long memories, but not nearly so long as dragons. You speak of a history you know nothing of and with such righteousness that it gives me pause to wonder which of us is truly the more arrogant."

"I have read the histories, wyrm."

The dragon shook his head and smiled.

"Elven history. I would sooner trust the scrawl of an ogre. You know nothing of history, little elf."

"And you do? Dragons being so adept at writing things down, you must have many books."

"We need nothing so fragile as paper and ink. Our history is passed from one generation to the next through magic and song."

"And you trust songs of glory over written documents? It is you who know nothing of history, wyrm."

"I know what it is you do not. I know that your books have lied to you. It was your kind, wizard, who started the war with dragons."

Velanon leapt to his feet.

"You lie!"

He immediately regretted the outburst and tried to

calm himself. He couldn't let this dragon see that he could get to him.

"Oh, no, it's quite true," the dragon said with a smile. "The elves were so good as to scrub the truth from the pages of their dusty books, but they cannot erase the memories of dragons."

Velanon laughed.

"Are you going to sing me a song, dragon? Tell me a tale of the old dragon ways? What makes your stories any more reliable than my dusty, old books?"

"I'm not going to tell you what I've heard, wizard. I'm going to tell you what I saw. I was there, you see."

Velanon chuckled and rolled his eyes.

"You cannot have been. The wizard wars were a thousand years ago."

"And I am over a thousand years old. I was still young during the war, but not so young."

"No dragon lives as long as that. You would be in twilight at least, old and weak."

The dragon raised himself from the floor and spread his wings, and a smile splayed across his scaly lips as he stared down at Velanon.

"Would you care to try?"

Velanon folded his arms and stared. Even if he thought he might stand a chance against a thousand-year-old dragon in a cave with no room to escape, he was too intrigued to try and kill him now. Kalus lowered himself down and folded his wings back behind him.

"It was called the War of Ways," Kalus began, "not the wizard wars or whatever you call it, and it lasted for over a hundred years. I tell you truthfully that it was the wizards that started it. You already know it was the dragons who finished it."

Velanon walked closer and folded his arms.

"What started the war? If it was the wizards as you say, why wage a war against dragons?"

"The first dragonmage was made but a decade or two before I was born. I know little of the history of that day, but it was a wizard who bonded the first dragon. And when he did, he learned of the immense power that he could draw from the dragon and channel into his own magic."

"Yes, I know this history. The bond wasn't strong enough, and the magic nearly destroyed him."

"The bond was weak because the dragon was too old. Its mind was already strong and set as stone. To form a stronger bond, he needed a younger dragon. His next attempt would bond a dragon at birth, when its mind is new and malleable. He became the first dragonmage."

"You are giving me a history lesson I already know."

"Then you know that it was a gold dragon who gave that first egg. And many more besides. Soon the world would be filled with dragonmages, as the dragons of light saw an opportunity to create a stronger, better world through the cooperation of man and dragon. Foolishness."

Velanon chortled.

"Yes, it seems quite funny today," Kalus said. "We should have known you would betray us."

Velanon stopped laughing and narrowed his eyes.

"Even though it was the wizards themselves who created dragonmages," Kalus continued, "some believed that the dragons allowed it and even strongly encouraged it as a way to control the magic of our world. Utter nonsense. Fools the lot of them. The wizards attacked as one, moving on us all across Gondril, thinking to snuff us out in one great blow we could not hope to recover from. They might have won too. Despite their hatred for our kind, they employed dark dragons to fight alongside them. But they underestimated our strength and numbers."

Velanon couldn't hide his interest now and edged forward. He had read all of the history books of the war, but he couldn't pass up the opportunity to hear about some of it firsthand. He would kill this dragon after.

"What happened?" he asked.

"The dragonmages rallied to our cause. Then the dragons of light convinced the dark dragons to turn on the wizards and fight alongside them to rid the world of them. Without wizards, we are practically invulnerable. The wizards thought we tried to enslave mankind by becoming the lone source of magic, but the dragons of light had no such ambitions. The dark dragons, though, liked the sound of it. You see, it was the wizards who gave them the idea and thus brought about their own demise. With their help, we turned the tide of the war."

"You said it lasted a hundred years."

"And so it did. But not all in great battles. Not like the ones fought in the beginning. Those were something to see. Wizards and dragons fought in numbers. Magic flowed like lava across the world and covered it in a blanket of fire and destruction. But it took nearly a hundred years for the wizards to be beaten into near extinction. And when there were too few left to hunt us, we stopped hunting them."

The dragon tilted his head down to look Velanon in the eyes.

"Perhaps we stopped too soon."

Velanon smoldered, and it made the dragon smile.

"There were still wizards alive," Kalus said, "mostly among the elves, but we no longer had quarrel with them. And they had no strength to keep up the fight."

"If what you say is true, and I don't believe it is, there is still something I don't understand. If you fought to destroy the wizards in order to save dragons and dragonmages, why are you here now, killing your own kind?"

Kalus looked down and spoke to the ground.

"Because I saw the truth of man in the war. The wizards showed me the heart of your kind. And you are not worthy of our children. I have tried for centuries to convince my brothers and sisters to stop giving our children to worthless, undeserving humans and elves, but they would not listen. They couldn't see that *we* were the ones who had become enslaved. A new age of peace would come from bonding, they said. They refused to listen, and I grew tired of asking. So I took it upon myself to stop them."

"But it's been centuries. Why now? I have heard nothing of you until today. Why have you waited so long and done nothing?"

"Because of you," the dragon said with a nod. "Hidden away in my mountain hole, asleep for most of the last century, I plotted and waited. When news reached me of someone slaying dragon mothers, I thought it was another dragon like me. Imagine my surprise when I learned it was a wizard murdering them. Some things never change."

"Sorry to disappoint."

"Oh, I am not disappointed. Wizards are no longer my enemy. If wizards were still here, there would be no need for mankind to bond with my kind. Our children would be free to be as they please. We were never meant to live together. Bonded mages and dragons are an abomination. No, wizard, I am not here to fight you. We are kindred spirits, you and I. We serve the same master."

Velanon stood and brushed the dirt from his breeches.

"I suppose we are in some ways. Since the dragon I came to kill is already gone, there's no reason to stay any longer. Thank you for the story."

Velanon turned and left without a look back and walked up the tunnel to where it sloped out into the sunlight. The cold mountain air felt exhilarating as it hit his face, and he took a deep breath of it and thanked the gods he was out of that heat. He was halfway down the mountain when he heard footsteps coming down the path behind him. A gold-skinned elf jogged up beside him and winked.

"I know who you are now," Kalus said.

"I am the one growing impatient."

"Your name is Velanon, yes?"

Velanon stopped and stared.

"You were Lorinan's charge. I can hear him in you."

Velanon stiffened and eyed him warily.

"How do you know my master?"

"He was my friend. We knew each other many centuries ago when I was... when I was among the elves. We became friends over the years."

"I doubt that very much. My master hated your kind."

"A fact he was all too happy to tell me each time I visited. He kept that anti-magic field you wear up for many years when I would come. Eventually he learned to trust me, that we shared a common goal."

"This is a trick. Just another lie."

"Yes, you sound just like him. You came to your master just over a century ago, yes? He mentioned your name the last few times I visited before I went into deep slumber. He was looking forward to having a student after having none for so long."

"You remember a name spoken in passing a few hundred years ago?"

"Dragon memories are not like your fragile minds, elf."

"And why have I never heard your name? Surely my master would have mentioned such a great friend."

Kalus chuckled.

"We were friendly, but old Lorin would not have called us *friends*, I think."

"Still. In a hundred years he never mentioned your name? You never came to visit?"

"I was in deep slumber, and Lorin was fading from this world. He would not have wanted me there in his twilight, and I honored that."

Velanon folded his arms and stared at the gold-skinned elf in front of him.

"Why would you befriend my master who hated your kind?"

"Because he hated me for the same reason that I hated him. I visited him every few years, and we would talk. We came to understand that we wanted the same thing, we just saw differently how to get it."

"What is it that you want?" Velanon asked.

"What do you want?"

"I want to free mankind from the slavery of dragons."

"What a startling coincidence, I want to free dragonkind from the slavery of men. You see? This is where old Lorin and I saw things differently but still sought the same result. But by the time we came to trust each other enough to do something about it, he was too old."

"And now you wish to enlist me?"

"I don't need to make you do anything. You are already following the last wishes of your master. I am offering to help you as I would have helped him."

"I don't need your help. My master left me all that I need to see this through."

Kalus chuckled.

"You would think that. Lorin was arrogant, just as you are. I know that you think yourself invincible, but you will need my help to see this to the end. I even managed to convince Lorin of that before he passed into twilight, but by then it was too late."

Velanon shook his head and looked out over the valley below.

"If you think to betray me, know that you will die."

"We are on the same side, wizard. We see our goal through different eyes, but the goal is the same nonetheless."

"You will not slow me in my task."

"Perhaps I can aid it. Let us do what your master could not. Together. Can you think of no use for an ancient gold dragon?"

Kalus winked, and Velanon rolled his eyes.

"Can you at least look less conspicuous?"

Kalus held up his arms and looked down, turning them over in the sunlight. It sparkled off the gold tone of his skin as tiny dots of light twinkled off of him.

"No."

They walked down the mountain together.

CHAPTER SEVEN

A New Day

"GET UP!"

RINN felt a slap on his arm, and his eyes shot open. The world was a blur. Light was pouring through the window, so he knew it was at least morning, but he couldn't focus enough to see anything else.

"Get out of that bed!"

A slap to his leg this time. He bolted upright and tried to blink the sleep from his eyes. His late nights did not agree with an early morning. When at last he looked up, his aunt was standing in front of him with a scowl and her arms folded.

"I need your help, and you're not going to stay in bed all day. I don't care how late you were out last night."

Rinn's eyes went wide, but his aunt had already turned her back and was out the door.

"Get dressed and downstairs," she called over her shoulder.

Rinn blinked and ran a hand through his hair. Standing slowly, he picked up his breeches from the floor. He was surprised to see he still wore his shirt from last night. He didn't remember much after getting home.

The magic must have taken more out of him than he'd realized. He briefly considered changing his shirt, but after smoothing it down, he decided it was good enough. He grabbed his boots and ran downstairs.

His aunt shoved a piece of buttered bread at him as he came into the kitchen, and he grabbed it between his teeth as he sat down and started pulling on his boots. He paused every few laces to take a bite and put the bread down on the table. Pulling the last lace tight, he saw his aunt walk back in and drop a bag down.

"You're going with me to a birth today," she said.

Rinn arched an eyebrow at her.

"I can't assist in a birth. I can't even be in the room."

"You're not going to assist in the *birth*, you're going to assist in getting there. I'm an old woman, and my bag and stool are heavy. You're going to carry them for me."

Rinn looked down at the bag and the odd-looking stool sitting across the kitchen. They looked just like the ones his mother had growing up. He walked over and picked up the leather bag. Big, but not too heavy. He looked at the stool and smiled.

It looked like a simple chair that someone had cut the bottom out of, creating a U-shaped ledge one could just perch on. He sat down and spread his legs to hold himself up.

"You know, we used to love to play on my mom's stool when we were kids. We'd see who could hold their legs open longest or who could close them the most without falling in. Mom didn't like us playing on it though."

"That's because it's a birthing stool, Rinn. That's where a woman sits and pushes out a baby."

Rinn jumped up from the chair and stared down at it in horror. His aunt burst out laughing, and he couldn't help his cheeks turning red. Through his embarrassment, he had the sudden realization that that may have been the first time he'd ever heard his aunt laugh.

"Why didn't you tell me before I sat in it?" he asked.

She just laughed harder.

Rinn shook his head remembering all the times he and Elody had played on their mom's stool. He wondered if Elody knew what it was and suddenly couldn't wait to be the one to tell her. When Aunt Jelena finally quit laughing, she rubbed a small tear from her eyes and brushed her dress down.

"Grab the bag and stool. We have to go."

Rinn picked up the bag in one hand and then very gingerly picked up the stool, making sure to grab it by the back and not by the seat. His aunt started to chuckle again and then just shook her head as she walked past him and headed for the door.

They made their way across town down a familiar path toward the lower quarter, the same path Rinn had traveled just the night before.

"How far are we going?" he asked.

"Merchant quarter. The mother is the wife of a merchant. It's her first."

Rinn shifted the things in his hands a little. His aunt walked purposefully in front of him and kept a brisk pace. Though he was quite a bit younger and stronger than she was, he was having to jog to keep up. The weight of her enormous birthing bag and stool didn't make his journey any easier.

Moving briskly through the lower quarter, they passed the Chicken Coop. Aunt Jelena looked at the place and waved a hand at it with disgust, and Rinn didn't miss the sneer on her face. The door was closed and windows buttoned up tight. Other than the weathered sign out front, it looked just like any other house on the street. They moved quickly through the quarter and out into the open bazaar in the city center.

The shouts of the merchants were deafening as soon as they were among the tents. Rinn lowered his eyes as he walked through the bazaar, just as his aunt had taught him and his sister to do. They can't sell you anything if they can't meet your eye, she'd tell them. He looked up only briefly to follow her and saw that she held her head high and stiff, almost daring someone to approach her.

She stopped at a stall ahead of him, and he caught up to her. Taking the opportunity to rest a second, he set the bag and stool down.

"A small pot of honey please, Banus," she said.

"Of course," the merchant said as he started fishing around in his wares. "Going to a birth or just stocking up?"

"A birth. How is your wife?"

"She's doing well."

"And your son? He should be walking now, yes?"

"Oh, yes. And quite the terror in my shop too. I have to move everything off the ground when he comes by!"

Jelena laughed as he handed her a clay jar. She pried the lid off and took a sniff. Holding the lid, she managed to free a finger to dip into the gooey pot. Popping her finger into her mouth, her eyes lit up, and she nodded with a smile. Rinn watched her and felt a sudden sadness. He had never noticed how much his aunt looked like his mother when she smiled. At that moment he couldn't recall seeing her do it. He wasn't sure which made him more sad.

Aunt Jelena quickly put the lid back on and handed

the jar to Rinn. He held his hands up and looked at her, but when she didn't look back, he just dropped it into her bag.

"Off to a new mother," she said. "Tell your wife I'll come by and see her next week. I'd love to get a look at that beautiful boy."

"I'll tell her!" the merchant shouted after her.

Rinn grabbed the bag and stool and hurried to catch up to his aunt who was already several tents away. He shifted the stool to his other hand, again taking care not to touch the seat. He skipped through the throng of people packing the bazaar and managed to catch his aunt when she stopped at a little jewelry tent.

Rinn moved up beside her and looked up to see what she was eyeing. He was sorry he did. He caught the eye of the merchant in the stall and instantly recognized the gap-toothed man he saw playing cards from the night before. His eyes went to the ground as quickly as they could but not quickly enough.

"Ahh, my friend! It is good to see you. Perhaps you will stop and buy something, yes? Something pretty for your mother here. Pretty mothers deserve pretty things."

"You are absolutely right about that," his aunt said, "but we aren't buying anything today. I know of a man who will be a new father soon, though. I shall tell him to come and visit you."

"I have very special things for new mothers! You tell him to find Worla. I will save something pretty for his wife!"

Jelena nodded and moved on, and Rinn was right behind her.

"Come and see me again, my friend! Any time, day or night!"

Rinn cast his eyes down and kept walking. Like the eye of a storm, they broke through the crowded tents and stalls into the city square. People were gathered there and moving through it, but it was practically empty compared to the narrow alleys of the bazaar. His aunt walked to the bubbling fountain in the center and turned to wait for him. Once he caught up, she grabbed her bag off of his shoulder and set it down.

She pulled two empty water skins tied with a cord from the bag and plunged them into the fountain. With each one full, she capped them and then draped them over Rinn's shoulder before turning and moving on.

The skins were heavy. Heavier than the bag they were carried in, which he *also* still had to carry. With a sigh, he shifted the stool to his other hand and grabbed up the bag as he walked after her.

Beyond the city square, they hurried through the other side of the bazaar and followed the crowd as it spilled out into the merchant quarter. Rinn could see from far back that the place was all abuzz. A large group of finely dressed men were all crowded around a figure standing tall in polished armor. Members of the town guard stood in a line in front of him and held back the posh merchant men as he shouted back at them.

"I told you all," the man shouted, "there was an emergency in another part of the city last night, and the watch was stretched thin!"

"What emergency?"

"What part of the city?"

They were all shouting such that Rinn could barely make out what they were saying, but he had a pretty good idea what the fuss was about. His aunt had slowed as they approached the crowd and listened as she walked past. Rinn almost bumped into her while watching it all.

"Lot of people are upset," she said. "Something *bad* must have happened last night."

Rinn pretended to pay attention to what the men were shouting so he didn't have to look at her, but he could feel her staring at him. She shook her head and sighed before moving on. She had to go around the gathering to get into the merchant quarter, and Rinn dutifully followed.

She walked up a few streets and turned onto Aspen Lane. Rinn got a sinking feeling in the pit of his stomach. Jelena looked back over her shoulder when Rinn slowed up and then stopped to wait for him.

"Something wrong, Rinn?"

"No," he said a little quickly. "This stuff is heavy."

"Why else do you think I had you carry it all the way down here for me?"

She turned another corner and continued down the street until she reached the door of a very familiar-looking house. Rinn stopped several feet back and watched as she knocked on the door. She looked over at him with a calm expression, even batting her eyes, and waved him forward.

She knows. She always knows.

Rinn was saved her stare when the door opened and a man stood in the doorway with an excited look on his friendly face. Rinn kept his face pointed down so he didn't have to look at the man.

"Good morning, Terel," Jelena said. "I trust I'm not too late."

"No, no, you're right on time! I had heard that about you, you know. You always show up at just the right time. And here you are!"

Jelena smiled and waved Rinn forward again after he'd taken a few more shuffling steps back. Terel stepped out of the doorway and waved his arm for them to enter. Jelena walked in with a smile while Rinn lowered his eyes as he stepped inside.

"You've gotten the straw like I asked?" Jelena said.

"Yes, it's already been put down."

"Wonderful. And the fire in the bedroom is lit? We have to keep that little baby warm once they're here."

"Fire has been lit!" he said smiling. "Anna's sisters are up there with her now. Her older sister has children already, and she came out and told me that we were getting close. I was just going to send for you when you arrived."

"It's a good thing I came then."

She turned to Rinn who was still standing awkwardly in the entry. The door was closed behind him, but he pressed himself as close to it as he could while still juggling his heavy load. Jelena frowned and shook her head. She motioned up the stairs.

"Terel, if you would be so kind."

"Yes, of course! Best get to it I should think."

With a skip in his step, he took the stairs two at a time. Jelena walked slowly and evenly behind him, and Rinn brought up the rear, dragging the stool and bag as he went. When they reached the top, Terel went to the second door down the hallway and stopped.

Rinn could already hear the sounds of labor from within. Jelena hurried to the door and motioned Rinn forward who was still lagging behind. She grabbed the stool, bag, and water from him and then shooed the two men away from the door before opening it a crack and peeking in. She looked over her shoulder at the men and then carefully slid inside, taking care not to open the door too wide.

Rinn peeked through the crack just enough to see that the room was completely dark save for some candles and a low fire in the fireplace. His aunt's head reappeared, her body blocking the door. She reached back and pulled the stool and then her bag in and then poked her head back out.

"Do not, under any circumstance, open this door. If I need the strength of a man, I will come and open it for you. Is that clear?"

"Yes, ma'am," they said in unison and then looked at each other.

Jelena nodded and then closed the door. A moment later, Rinn saw straw poke through the keyhole in the door. More and more filled the hole until it was completely plugged and nothing could be seen inside. Both men stood silently staring at the wooden door for several seconds before looking at each other.

"So, I guess we just wait here?" Terel asked.

"Looks so," Rinn said.

Terel stared at the door and then turned back to look at Rinn. Rinn looked down at his feet, watching from the corner of his eye for Terel to look away. A loud moan from inside the room finally drew his attention. When it died down, they both stared back at the door.

"My first child," Terel said.

Rinn nodded but didn't speak.

"I have several nieces. My wife's sisters have all had girls."

Rinn nodded again.

"I'm hoping for a boy, of course. Someone to take over my business when I'm gone."

Rinn looked up at him.

"Couldn't a daughter do that?"

"It's a very tough business. Not the kind women are used to doing."

"I don't know. My sister's used to some pretty tough business."

A loud moan that turned into a scream cut off Terel's response. They waited and watched the door again. A minute passed in silence with no further sound.

"Have we met before?" Terel asked.

Rinn shook his head.

"Your voice sounds very familiar to me."

Rinn shook his head again. Terel eyed him a moment longer before another scream. He started pacing up and down the hallway nervously.

"You been to a lot of these, have you?"

"A few," Rinn said.

"Does that sound normal to you?"

Rinn looked at the door.

"Mostly, yes."

"What do you mean mostly?"

"They're all different, but they all hurt if all I've heard is to be believed."

"Is there anything they can do for the pain?"

"Herbs, sometimes. Wine."

"Ooh, I left some wine in there like Jelena asked."

"That helps," Rinn said.

"What if there's a problem? What if something happens?"

"My aunt is very good at this. The best. She'll know what to do."

"Your voice really does sound familiar. Very soothing and friendly. I know I've heard it somewhere."

Rinn looked down and shook his head.

"We've never met," he said, pitching his voice a little lower.

Terel paced back up the hallway and stopped in front of the door as a long, loud moan filled the air.

"Should I have called a priest? Some of the other merchants said they paid for a priest to stand by in case something went wrong."

"If my aunt needs a priest, she'll call one."

Terel nodded absentmindedly and kept pacing. Rinn slid down the wall and sat on the floor where he put his head between his knees. He hoped that Terel would get the hint and stop questioning him. After another few laps, Terel walked over and sat down beside him. Rinn just kept his head down and waited.

Why was he here?

He'd learned enough about his aunt in the last six months to know that she was far craftier than she appeared or let on. It was no mistake that she made him attend this birth. He was starting to wonder if him robbing Terel had been no mere coincidence as well. Could she set something like that up? Rinn tried to keep his head down and talked to Terel as little as possible.

They sat, head down, for long stretches of silence. Terel would pick his head up every time there was a moan or a scream from the room and then settle back down a few moments later. All Rinn could do was sit and wait for it all to be over.

Time crawled by. Rinn counted the screams to pass the time and waited for the sound of the baby to know when it was over.

They heard one last long scream followed by silence. Then, finally, a baby's cry. Terel leapt to his feet and started pacing again. He went to the door, and Rinn almost said something, but Terel pulled his hand back after touching the knob. He stared another moment and then paced again. When at last the latch clicked, he ran back to the door.

Jelena came out holding the baby wrapped tightly in a blanket. Rinn instinctively stood and watched as she came out. Terel looked on silently and then slowly reached his hands out. He stopped a few inches away. Rinn could see his hands shaking. Jelena reached forward the rest of the distance and placed the babe in his arms.

"Meet your son, Terel."

Terel looked down in surprise and smiled so big that Rinn thought his ears would roll up into his head. Rinn watched as he cradled the baby in his arms and then held him close to his chest. Rinn felt awkward just standing there, but Jelena waited silently next to him. When Terel finally looked up, it was with a sudden thought.

"How's Anna?"

"She's doing just fine," Jelena said.

Almost as if on cue, the door cracked open, and a woman Rinn guessed was one of the sisters poked her head out and nodded.

"She's ready for you and the baby," Jelena said.

He nodded with the same stupid grin and then followed Jelena into the room, leaving Rinn alone in the hallway. He started to sit back down when he heard someone coming up the stairs. He recognized one of the servant girls from the night before, though she was tied up the last time he saw her. She slowed as she reached the door and stopped to listen.

"Is the baby born yet?"

"Yes," Rinn said. "A boy."

"Everyone is all right?"

"As far as I know."

She scurried off down the hall. Rinn watched her go, and she turned her head back to look at him again before disappearing through another door. He waited there until his aunt came out again. She handed her bag and stool unceremoniously to him and stood in the hallway waiting. Terel came out a moment later.

"Thank you so much, Jelena," he said. "It is true what they say of you. You are truly a miracle worker."

"Oh, just an old witch woman," she said.

Terel smiled and then looked down at the floor. He watched his feet for a few breaths and then looked back up with his eyes low.

"I'm afraid I can't pay you right this minute," he said. "I'm short on funds until later this week. Possibly longer."

He looked at her, waiting for a response. Rinn saw her glance sidelong at him before stepping up and wrapping her arms around Terel.

"You're a good man, Terel," she said. "You pay me when you have the money. I know that you will. You're a good man, and you'll be a good father to that little boy."

Terel put his arms around her in kind and held her a little longer before letting go and stepping back.

"Truly you are as good as they say," he said.

She patted his hand one last time and then let it go as she spun on Rinn.

"Let's go," she said.

She walked past him and down the stairs without another word or look back. Rinn trailed after her with his head hung low.

CHAPTER EIGHT

SPELL TRAINING

TOO MUCH. IT'S *too much*.

Elody could feel the immense power she was drawing from Jalthrax. Her hands were starting to shake but not from the power. Her fear at losing control was rising as she broke into a sweat, but she still didn't have quite enough to complete the spell. She needed just a little bit more. If she held it too long, it could harm her. She had to finish it. Pulling the magic as quickly as she dared, she finally had enough.

Her hands burned with the raw magic, and she immediately began swirling them. Around her, above her head, around her body. Twisting in a giant whirlwind. Throwing her hands out, she felt the magic fly from her in a burst and waited breathlessly. It took only a second for the spell's effects.

She heard a sound like a tiny rip in a piece of cloth, and then a creature stood before her. But it was not what she had wanted to summon. It was all wrong. The being was made of pure fire. Its body was a shifting shape made of flames that twisted and licked at the air and grass around it, setting the field on fire where it stood.

Elody gasped and stumbled back a step. Jalthrax flapped his wings and backpedaled away from the fiery thing as well.

"Go!" she shouted. "I release you!"

But the creature did not go.

Through the flames, Elody could make out what looked like a face, or at least eyes. They were watching her. Fire burst up from its body and formed into two long tendrils of solid flames that began waving around menacingly. It moved toward her, seemingly with great effort as it strained against some unseen bond. It managed only a step, but its intent was clear.

Elody tried to quell the panic rising in her throat. The tendrils of fire danced through the air, getting closer and closer to her face. She took a deep breath to steady herself and focused all of her thoughts on the being before her. *I* am in control. *I* summoned this creature, and I will send it back.

"Begone."

She spoke calmly and with power behind her word. The creature had no choice but to obey. In a blink it was gone, sent back to the plane from which it was summoned.

Elody blinked and then sagged down to the ground drawing breath after breath. The exhilaration had kept her fear in check, but now that it was gone, her body trembled. Jalthrax blew a long blast of freezing ice at the spot where the creature had stood, putting out the remaining flames that still burned in the grass.

She turned to say something to him, but a flap and a screech from above made her look up. Tark glided and touched down softly behind them. Eliath was sliding off of his back even before the dragon had landed.

"Mercy of the gods, what were you doing?" he shouted.

Elody's knees were weak, but she pulled herself up straight and faced him.

"I was summoning an elemental."

"Yes, I saw that, but what were you thinking summoning from the plane of fire? Do you know what that creature might have done had you lost control of it?"

"I *didn't* lose control of it."

"Really? It didn't look all that controlled from where I was sitting."

"I sent it home with a word. No one was ever in danger."

"I'll ask you again. *What* were you doing summoning a creature like that?"

"I don't answer to you," she said.

"No, it would seem you answer to no one here, and that is a very bad thing."

"I was in complete control."

"You were casting beyond your abilities, and you could have set this entire forest on fire for it!"

"You know nothing of my abilities. I was not casting beyond."

Eliath pointed a finger down at Jalthrax.

"He looks like he's about to fall over. Do you want to lie to me again?"

Elody looked down and saw Jalthrax sitting next to her. She realized he hadn't stood up since banishing the creature, and she saw now how he swayed from side to side as though he might topple over at any minute. She knelt down and put her hands to his neck.

"Are you hurt?"

Jalthrax squawked.

"You've drawn too much from him," Eliath said. "He needs to rest."

"He'll be fine," she said as she stood back up to face him.

The great red dragon behind Eliath let out a sound like a scoff and leaned closer to Eliath.

"They train them young in their hate," he said softly, but even the whisper of a dragon carries. "Leave this girl to her death and let us be gone from here."

Eliath watched her as the dragon spoke, but she was no longer paying attention to him. She couldn't take her eyes off of Tark. Whatever fear she had had on first seeing the giant red was gone now as she stared at him. His head was like a great bushel of spiked horns. Two large ones swept back from the top of his head toward his neck, and small, thorny bones jutted out from every corner of his face, even down from the chin. There was an odor of sulfur in the air as he neared her that grew stronger when he opened his mouth to speak.

"What are you staring at, little girl?" the dragon suddenly said.

"Nothing, just... I have never seen a red before. Only in books. I have only ever seen the dragons of light up close."

"Dragons of light," Tark said with a scoff, a puff of smoke floating up through his lips. "The only thing light about them is the way the sunlight shines off their metal arses."

"Don't let Tark frighten you," Eliath said. "Look all you like, he loves to be admired."

"I'm not frightened," Elody replied.

She took a step to the side to see more of Tark's long body. From head to tail, he must have been more than thirty feet long. She had seen many dragons in her time as a trainee, but none that looked as powerful as this. Red dragons were said to be the strongest and most terrible of all the dark dragons, and Elody felt a shiver rattle her shoulders in spite of herself.

"Come and look closer if you're not afraid," Tark said in his growling voice.

Elody *was* afraid suddenly, but she would not let them know it. Taking slow steps, she approached the mighty red with her hand out in front. As she neared, she reached to touch the side of his face. Tark's teeth extended out from the top and bottom of his lips, giving him a permanent grin that looked playful and wicked all at once. Her hand stopped just short of touching the hard, leathery skin.

"I can smell your fear," Tark said.

Elody jerked her hand away as his mouth opened and spoke, and she felt Eliath behind her suddenly with his hand resting on her back.

"Stop it, Tark, you're scaring the poor girl."

Elody held her hand close to her chest as though it'd been burned. She tried to pull away from Eliath's grasp, but he nudged her forward instead.

"You can touch him. He won't bite."

She would not let her fear beat her here in front of this man. Her hand shot out and touched the side of the dragon's face. She held it there, unmoving. It was harder than she had imagined. Like touching the jagged rock face of a mountain that could cut her with even the slightest move.

"It's so rough," she said, making no attempt to hide the wonder in her voice. "The dragons of light all feel like cold metal. Not at all like this."

Tark pulled his head up and away from her hand, and she pulled it back and stumbled into Eliath.

"I'm sorry," she said, pulling her hand back, "I didn't mean to offend—"

"You didn't," Eliath said.

She pulled away from him and walked back over to Jalthrax, who was still a little unstable.

"I need to continue my training," she said and turned her back on them both.

"Is that what you were doing?"

"Of course it was."

"Because it looked like you were about to burn yourself up. Why in the gods would you summon a creature from the plane of fire?"

Elody hunched her shoulders and folded her arms.

"I was trying to summon an air elemental so I could fly."

"Why not just cast a fly spell?"

"I don't know *how* to cast a fly spell."

"You don't know how to cast summoning spells either. I can show you how if you like."

"I don't need any help from an untrained savage."

"You need all the help you can get."

"You'll tell me when a trained dragonmage comes along then."

"You know, I've met many a dragonmage who hated me, but I always just thought it was something they learned over time. Tark was right. They train you to hate right from the start, don't they? I was only trying to help you. Did your master teach you nothing of casting beyond, or did your lessons focus mainly on contempt for those not like you?"

"He told us we should never cast beyond our abilities.

He said it was too dangerous."

"Your master was irresponsible in his duties," Eliath said. "Telling a child not to play with fire will not stop them from playing, it will only ensure they are burned when they do. Like all things, you must learn to do them safely. But you're right, *I* am the one who is an untrained savage."

She watched Eliath walk back toward Tark and pull on the handhold to vault himself up into the saddle high on the dragon's back.

"Wait," she called out.

She didn't know why she said it. Eliath stopped and looked at her.

"I... I haven't had any training since I got Jalthrax. None of the dragonmages I've met could stay long enough to help me."

"With how you treat new people you meet, it's a wonder why."

"I'm... sorry."

"That was almost sincere," he said, and Tark raised his wings.

"Wait! I'm *sorry*."

"Sorry for what exactly?"

Elody folded her arms and glared.

"Will you help me or not?"

Eliath leaned back in his saddle and stared for a moment before sliding down and striding over to stand before her.

"Where did you learn the summoning spell? Certainly not something your master taught you."

"From a book."

Eliath laughed.

"You learned that from a book and were able to cast it

successfully?"

"I wouldn't call it a success. I opened a door to the wrong plane."

"Yes, but you actually completed the casting from pictures in a book. That *is* impressive. Just don't tell any of your fancy dragonmage friends about it, or they'll kick you out of their club."

"I don't have any dragonmage friends."

"But you're so charming with new people."

Elody hung her head.

"I'm sorry," she said.

"You've said that already, no need to keep doing it. Now, would you like me to help you?"

"Yes."

"Excellent. Tark, can you take Jalthrax and find some food?"

"Of course," Tark replied.

"Wait," Elody said. "I... Don't we need him here?"

"Are you afraid to let him go with Tark or to be alone with me?"

"Both."

"That was not so difficult," Eliath said. "Honesty suits you."

Beside her, Jalthrax swayed slowly before settling his head down into the grass.

"I can help him if you'll permit me," Eliath said.

"What can you do?"

"Give him some strength. At least enough to get on his feet and find some food."

"What will you do?"

"Do you want my help or not?"

"Yes," Elody said. "I mean, yes, please."

"Manners become you, m'lady."

Eliath knelt down next to Jalthrax and laid his hands on the dragon's back. Closing his eyes and taking a deep breath, Eliath pushed his palms against Jalthrax's back and breathed out slowly. Elody could see the faintest hint of a magical glow beneath his fingers.

"What are you doing?"

"I'm giving him some of my magic," Eliath said as he continued breathing slowly.

"How... How can you do that?"

"Did your master teach you nothing?"

Elody bit her lip in silence. In another few breaths, Eliath was finished. He stood up and stepped back as Jalthrax climbed to his feet, steady as ever.

"He needs some food and to get some strength back," Eliath said. "Tark can take him if you'll permit."

Elody looked at the big red and nodded reluctantly. Tark spoke something to Jalthrax who then looked at Elody. She nodded again to him, and the two dragons leapt into the air. Elody watched them both go while Eliath stood quietly waiting.

"Tark will take care of him. He has taken care of me for a long time now, and despite his protests at having to do so, he's quite good at caring for those smaller than himself."

Elody continued to watch after them as they disappeared into the blue.

"Now, the first thing to learn is that you should never attempt to cast beyond with spells that harness the destructive elements. Fire, lightning, ice. Never attempt spells with that kind of power. Should you lose control, you could kill yourself, Jalthrax and anyone around you."

"I know that."

"Are you going to keep telling me what you already

know?"

"I wasn't trying to summon fire," she said, folding her arms.

"Which brings me to my next point. Summoning spells should never be cast beyond your skills. Drawing a being from another plane requires absolute power to control once they arrive. You can't rip someone from their home, even if they would serve you willingly, and keep them here to do your bidding without *total* authority."

Elody started to reply but closed her mouth and nodded.

"Good. Now that we have that out of the way, I should tell you that you really should avoid casting beyond completely. Even with simple spells, the results can be... unpredictable. Sometimes a harmless spell can go awry and do great damage."

"Do you ever do it?"

"I have before, yes. Once when I was in great danger. It saved my life, but I also fell unconscious when the spell was done. Had Tark blacked out from the exertion too, neither of us would be here today."

"How can I learn to control it then?"

"I can teach you, but your master would not approve of such training I fear."

"I have no master any longer. My brother says I shouldn't even talk to you."

"What does Elody say?"

She looked him up and down.

"Teach me," she said, a grin creeping across her lips.

"Very well. Let's start with that summoning spell you were trying. And if you can manage that, I have a few other simple spells I can teach you maybe."

"You just said I shouldn't cast summoning spells beyond my skills."

"And your brother said you shouldn't talk to me, yet here you are. I don't think you listen too well. Don't worry, we're not going to actually cast it. Now, show me your motions, and we'll see where you went wrong."

Elody shook her arms, letting the sleeves of her robe fall to her elbows as she began her spell.

***

Elody finished the motions of the spell and looked at Eliath with questioning eyes.

"Excellent!" he said. "When Jalthrax has his strength back, we'll try for real."

"What if I lose control?"

"You won't. But if something happens, Tark and I are here. Just remember to use Jalthrax's energy to summon the creature but then use your own store of magic to bind it. It will be a slow drain, but you should have enough to hold it here for as long as you need."

"I don't think my own magic is strong enough."

"You're stronger than you think," he said. "You just need more practice at it. Your well of magic is like a muscle. The more you use it, the bigger it gets."

Elody nodded.

"What should we do now?" she asked.

"We can work on a different spell while we wait for the boys to return."

They both turned to the sky for the tenth time in the last hour.

"They've been gone a long time," she said.

"Only a couple hours. Tark likes to hunt for bigger game sometimes. Or maybe he just wants more than one."

Elody cracked her fingers and rubbed each of her shoulders.

"Let's sit down," he said. "You're probably tired."

Elody didn't argue a bit as she plopped down into the soft grass. Eliath walked over and dropped down beside her, but not too close she noted.

"I'd offer you some water, but all of my provisions are with Tark."

"That's okay," she said. "There's a little spring not far from here if you want to walk with me."

"My lady, that would be lovely."

Eliath rose and offered his hand. Pulling her up in a quick motion made Elody groan from the soreness and aching in her shoulder.

"Oh, I'm sorry," he said. "I forgot. And here I was trying to be chivalrous."

Elody turned to hide the blush in her cheeks and walked toward the forest with Eliath a step behind her. They left the field and turned onto the road that led deeper into the woods.

"I probably haven't worked as hard as you have since I was in training myself. And that was a long time ago."

"Not so long, I think. You're how old?"

"Twenty two."

"That's not so old."

"Well, I feel much older. Years spent riding a dragon has given me the back of an old washer woman."

Elody laughed and then groaned and rubbed her shoulder.

"Sorry about that," he said. "We shouldn't have worked so hard. I forget what it's like to be in training and how sore you get."

Elody kicked the dirt along the road and closed her

eyes as a breeze blew by. Opening them, she found Eliath watching her and stared back for a moment before turning away.

"What was training like for you?" she asked.

"Oh, now you think I was trained? I thought I was a savage."

"I didn't... I mean... That's what we were told about dark mages."

"That we're not trained?"

"Not formally."

"I imagine your training was very formal."

"Master Cythyil... likes things a certain way. But he was a wonderful teacher."

"It would seem. You show many skills I never had at your age."

"So then what was yours like?"

"My training was... undisciplined. Joron was a drunk."

"Your master was drunk?"

"He was no master, and he was only drunk most of the time. He did manage to teach me a few things in his sober moments."

"Why would you choose someone like that as your master?"

"My father chose him, but when you're a dark mage, you take what you can get."

"Oh."

"Well, don't look so down. It worked out for me. I got Tark in the deal."

Eliath stopped along the road and picked a large, open flower standing alone in the grass. He handed it to her with a flourish, and they walked on. Elody put it to her nose to hide her smile.

"Why did you want to become a dragonmage?" she asked.

"Because my father wished it. My older brother was a copper mage, and my father wanted another in the family to protect his holdings. I was the youngest son and had nothing else of value to offer."

"If your brother was a copper, why did you choose a dark dragon?"

"I was never given the choice. When I was only ten my father tried to get me into a school. I was told I could start when I was twelve if there was an opening. My father was a local lord of considerable wealth and power and felt I should be given some privilege, but the master refused. So, he took it upon himself."

"When you were only ten?"

Eliath nodded.

"He bought Tark from an egg merchant who heard he was rich and looking for one. Paid a lot of gold for it. Red dragon eggs are not easy to come by."

"Are they as big as they look in pictures?"

"Bigger. The man drove it in on a wagon, and it took two servants to move it into the barn where it stayed until Tark hatched. We were told the egg would take almost two years to hatch. It hatched in one. Guess it had been laid earlier than the man thought."

"So you were eleven when you got your dragon?"

"*Almost* twelve, but yes. Thankfully, Joron had stayed awake long enough on a few occasions to teach me the bonding spells, though I don't even know if I cast them right. I think the spells had little to do with our bond. I slept in that barn for a year. Every night, on a blanket right next to Tark. I even tried sitting on his egg a few times like the chickens."

Elody laughed.

"You laugh, but I wanted that dragon so badly. I had seen my brother's dragon and the way my father looked at him with such pride. I wanted him to look at me that way. I was also just a boy, so I really just wanted a dragon to play with. There's not much more exciting to a young boy than the thought of his own dragon."

"I don't guess there was a ceremony when he was born?"

"No, no ceremony. Tark was born in the stables with no one but me and the horses. I woke in the middle of the night when a heard loud cracking noises. I was so scared. I wanted to run to the house and get my brother. But I needed my father to see that I could be brave and do it all by myself. I thought Tark would kill me when he came out, and they would find my mangled corpse the next morning. My family didn't even know until days later."

"That's awful," she said.

"It's how it was meant to be. We bonded instantly. I forgot all the spells and chants you're supposed to use. The minute our eyes met, it was like we knew that it would always be the two of us. Standing there alone in that barn, we both knew we were the only ones we could count on."

Elody ducked off of the road a few steps where a small brook flowed alongside it. Kneeling down next to it, she cupped her hand and drank handful after handful. She hadn't realized how thirsty she was. Standing back up, they both turned to walk back the way they'd come.

"And you just named him Tark?"

"I had a much more elegant name for him when he first hatched. Tarkanon'ul'Eliatharr. I spent weeks thinking on it, but when he came, he was just Tark to me."

"I like it. I call Jalthrax Thrax sometimes."

They walked in silence for a while, and Elody worked up the nerve to ask her next question.

"Are... Are dark dragons truly as they say?"

"Are you asking me if Tark is evil?"

"I suppose so," she said as she looked down.

"Don't look so embarrassed, you're not the first to ask. A dragon is no more evil than you or I. There is evil in all intelligent creatures, I think. There are tales of dragons of light laying waste to villages or demanding homage from good people. It is the actions you take that should decide how others paint you, not the manner or blood of your birth. Yet Tark and I are painted everywhere we go before we've even touched the ground. People cower in fear at our approach or look on us with disgust."

"I'm... sorry."

"Don't be. You did nothing a thousand others before you haven't done. You're here now at least, and that's a place to start."

"How can you bear it?"

"We try to make them see us for our deeds. If Tark's scales were gold, we would be welcomed in every part of Gondril as heroes. Instead they are afraid of us. It doesn't matter how many we've helped or how many battles we've won."

"Have you truly fought that much?"

"Too much."

"Was your training all in combat?"

"Sometimes I think that's all Joron knew. When he wasn't drunk, which was most of the time, he wasn't a bad teacher. He knew a lot. He's the one who taught me to cast beyond and how to control it. He just didn't stay sober for very long at a time. I hear that happens a lot to half-dead mages."

"What do you mean half-dead?"

"That's what they call them when a dragonmage loses their dragon. Half-dead. I've heard some call them neutered mages, but I think the loss of power is such a small part of it. More like losing half of yourself. Joron was a drunk, but the moment I sat in that barn looking into Tark's eyes, my feelings about him changed. I knew why he'd rather be drunk all the time."

"I think Master Cythyil is half-dead too."

"Many of the best teachers are," Eliath said. "What was he like?"

"A horse's arse."

Elody clapped her hand over her mouth, and they both burst out laughing.

"Sorry, that just came out. He was a great teacher, but he was very tough. A true master."

"Must be nice."

"Not really. He made us do chores all day. Clean up the house, clean out the stables, brush down the horses. When we weren't training, we were his own personal staff."

"Well, Joron definitely never made me clean anything. Unless you count the vomit I had to wash off of him most mornings."

"Well, I never had to do that, may Threyl keep me. Sometimes I think Cythyil was too strict. We weren't allowed to cast any destructive spells, only practice them without magic."

"Not a bad idea."

"Yes, but we never learned to truly cast the spells. He

would tell us when the movements were right, but we never felt the fire or the lightning in our fingertips. I wasn't ready for it when I cast it for the first time, and I didn't know what I was doing."

"Well, what's a little girl like you doing throwing fire anyway?"

Elody's smiled vanished in a blink.

"My village was destroyed by a goblin army on the day I took Jalthrax home. Rinn and I had to fight to save the women that the goblins had kept alive for fun, and I... I burned them alive."

"Oh."

"That's why I think we should have been taught to cast with real magic. I wasn't prepared to fight."

"You shouldn't have had to at your age."

"I am trained as a dragonmage. The minute Jalthrax was born, I was the protector of my village. That's what I was always told. It was my job to protect them."

"You say that like you blame yourself for what happened."

"I could have done something to stop it," she said.

"You did. You saved those women. You may be a protector, but you can't always save everyone. You can't think about the ones you didn't save, they will haunt you forever. Try and remember the ones you did save and how they are alive today because of you."

"That is why I want to train so badly. I want to see that what happened to my village never happens to another."

"A noble goal, but one you will not achieve I'm afraid. No one person can stop all the evil in this world, no matter the training they've had."

"Then I will train and be as powerful as I can be.

Maybe I can't help everyone, but it won't be because I didn't have the strength to try."

A shadow passed over them, and they both looked up to see the two dragons returning.

"We'd better get back," Elody said. "I'd hate for them to worry."

"Tark never worries," Eliath said. "Red dragons are like that. Too damn arrogant for their own good sometimes."

Elody chuckled as they headed back to the field together, side by side.

CHAPTER NINE

MARCH

ERYNINN WATCHED FROM a distance as the goblin tribes, now moving as one, packed up their camps and belongings and marched north. Even at a distance, his elven eyes showed him a very frightening picture. The goblin army was huge. They were thousands strong at least. More than he had thought possible.

Moving gracefully through the forest, Eryninn slipped behind the next tree over to get a little closer. There was some commotion down among the troops, and he wanted to get a better look. With all the noise of the troops packing up to march, he took a chance and snuck closer to hear what the fuss was over. Gortogh had emerged from his cave, and the goblins around him had all fallen to their knees.

Eryninn wondered, not for the first time, at the magic the goblin played with. He had seen his battles with the tribal chiefs and his most recent bout with the ogre chieftain. There was no doubt that his strength came from power that was not his own. But strength alone was not enough to create this level of subjugation in goblin warriors. They worshipped at his feet whenever he passed.

He watched as Gortogh walked silently through the throng of admirers, nodding at every one. As always, behind him was the disgusting little shaman, and the warriors were quick to fall to their knees as they passed. Gortogh stopped them and pulled them to their feet where he could grasp their arms firmly, but as soon as he passed, a glance from Kurgh brought them to their knees again. The shaman was revered almost as much as Gortogh. Even at this distance, Eryninn could see the disgust on the goblin champion's face when he looked over his shoulder.

With most of the goblin tribes already on the march, the rest made haste to catch up once Gortogh was past them. Eryninn was stunned to see the ogres bow, some even kneeling, at the goblin's approach. Even the new ogre chieftain bowed but did not kneel.

"I need you and your best warriors to lead the tribes," Gortogh said.

Eryninn was surprised to understand the conversation. Gortogh spoke more formally with the ogres it seemed and used the common speech of Gondril instead of goblin tongue.

"They will not take orders from me or my men," the ogre said. "They have their own chiefs."

"Do not question—" the shaman lifted his head and started to say, but a glance from Gortogh silenced him.

"*I* am their chief," Gortogh said. "They will do as I say. And I say they will follow you."

"And if they give me trouble?" the ogre said.

"They are of Ogrosh," Gortogh said. "They follow strength. You will show them the way."

Gortogh turned and started marching up the line of

goblins straggling behind his mighty army. Without a sound, Eryninn drew his bow and nocked an arrow. He had a clear shot straight into the goblin champion's back. A single shot through the heart, and even the shaman would not be able to save him before his lifeblood drained out.

"Where are we going?" the ogre shouted.

Gortogh turned back around.

"To make war on a village."

He spun back and continued up the line. Eryninn drew the string back and held his breath. But as he did a silent count in his head, the shaman bounded up behind Gortogh and began walking behind him, blocking his view. He breathed out slowly and dropped his bow.

There would be another shot.

Gortogh stopped suddenly, leaving the shaman to crash into his back, but he paid him no notice. He turned his head slightly and stopped. Then turned his body around to face the forest behind him. Eryninn could feel him looking at him, yet he knew he could not be seen. Still Gortogh watched, his eyes moving slowly from tree to tree. He stared for nearly half a minute before turning around sharply and marching on.

***

Gortogh felt the hairs on his neck stand up. And it wasn't because he had his back to the sniveling shaman. He stopped short, and Kurgh crashed into his shoulders, but he only rolled his eyes. He turned his head slightly and looked around. Something had made him stop.

Something he felt.

Turning his body, he scanned the trees. He could feel the ogres watching him with interest, but he kept his eyes on the forest. His head snapped right as a bird took flight and flew away, but he saw no other movement. He waited a few more seconds and then turned back around to join his troops on their march. He could feel Kurgh behind him in an instant.

"What did you see?" Kurgh asked.

"Nothing."

"But you felt something?"

Gortogh glanced at his shoulder and sneered.

"Maybe."

"You are blessed by Ogrosh. You can sense a presence when it is near, just as the shamans can."

Gortogh jogged to catch up to the front of his army but also to try and distance himself from the annoying shaman. He found, to his dismay, that Kurgh was right behind him as he jogged. He kept it up for a while, and found renewed energy when his men cheered him as he past. Still the shaman kept up.

"High shaman!" a goblin called out.

He came limping from up ahead. Kurgh stopped and pulled his shoulders back. It always made Gortogh uncomfortable to see Kurgh change so quickly. In private, Gortogh was the champion. Kurgh groveled at his feet. Out here, among the warriors, Kurgh was high shaman. One of only five in all the tribes. The highest position of power among goblins.

"What is it?" Kurgh asked.

The goblin whimpered and pointed at his leg. Gortogh could have used the distraction to slip away, but Kurgh would only catch up again. They both bent to look at the warrior's leg. There was a large gash down the side, and it was bleeding heavily. Gortogh could see white glimpses of bone beneath.

"You are a warrior," Kurgh said. "Can you not bind

your own wound and press on?"

"I can walk," the warrior quickly said. "But it hurt."

"We are not marching to the river for a swim!" Kurgh said. "Your blood is Ogrosh's blood. You bleed the blood of a *god*."

The way Kurgh spoke was not lost on Gortogh. In the months since the shaman had come to him and offered himself, Gortogh had seen many of Kurgh's faces. It was part of life as a goblin. Gortogh had many himself.

In private, Gortogh spoke as himself, and Kurgh spoke as a sniveling, stupid goblin. But out here, Kurgh spoke as himself and with authority. Gortogh still played the part of the common warrior to his men. Out here, *he* was the stupid goblin. He never let them know how smart he *really* was.

An old habit.

The warrior pulled himself up taller and nodded. He turned to limp away. Gortogh was about to say something, but Kurgh beat him to it.

"Stop," Kurgh said.

The warrior stopped and turned back.

Kurgh already had his knife in hand as he approached. He sliced into his arm, the blood flowing quickly to his waiting hand. Kurgh laid hands on the warrior's leg, their blood mingling together. As Kurgh prayed, the blood flow stopped, and the wound closed over.

"Go and rejoin your tribe," Kurgh said.

"Thank you, high shaman," the warrior said.

"Do not thank me," Kurgh said. "Thank Ogrosh. Praise his name and his blood."

"Praise Ogrosh!" the warrior said.

Kurgh smiled and nodded as the warrior ran off

ahead. Gortogh and Kurgh began walking again. They marched along beside the column of soldiers, and Gortogh took every opportunity to talk to a fellow warrior. It gave them pride and strength.

And he didn't have to talk to Kurgh.

"It was the Wood Elf," Kurgh said from beside him.

"What?" Gortogh asked, looking around suddenly.

"What you felt. It was the Wood Elf. Who else would be so close to our camp and we not know it?"

Gortogh stopped jogging and dawdled along as he thought on it. He could feel the shaman at his shoulder and jerked it involuntarily, sending him back a few paces.

"Maybe so," Gortogh said at last.

"He will be trouble."

"He *has* been trouble. Maybe he'll go away now that we're leaving his precious forest. That's what he wants."

"I have prayed to Ogrosh for guidance on this. He will be trouble."

Gortogh looked back over his shoulder and saw the long line of marching goblins now behind him. The paint and markings of each tribe stood out boldly with each goblin marching next to one of his own. They marched as one great army but with many collected groups within. Occasionally one would bump into, or maybe shove into, someone from another tribe and start an argument. A few times, a large fight broke out between two or more of the clans. Sometimes the other tribes surrounding them would break up the fight. Often they would just stand by and cheer them on.

Gortogh shook his head and sighed.

"We need no more trouble than we already have. Perhaps we should be the ones making trouble for him."

***

Eryninn followed the goblin army from the trees for as long as he could, but the forest was getting more and more sparse the deeper into the mountains they went. His cloak kept him hidden enough even as he moved between them, but if they caught sight of him, he would find himself in trouble very quickly.

He watched from below the last great oak growing nearest to the mountains as the tail end of the army disappeared around a rocky outcrop. Sitting down, he pulled some stale bread from his pack. It would be quite easy to follow an army this size, so he was in no hurry. Better to wait and then catch up under cover of night.

When at last night fell, he stood and tried to stretch the ache from his muscles. Pulling an apple from his pack, he polished it on his cloak before taking a bite and moving on through the darkness. His elven eyes adjusted to the darkness until he could see just as clearly as he did in the daylight.

He walked a while through the night until he saw the orange glow of campfires in the distance. The goblin army had camped in a large ravine and had filled it from end to end with barely room to spare. As Eryninn crept closer, he saw only a few tents sticking up through the throng of goblins. He didn't have to guess who slept in the pavilion tent in the center of the army.

The song and merriment from the goblins poured out of the narrow ravine. It seemed that Gortogh had been holding out. Eryninn didn't recall a night in the past six months when the goblins had had so much to drink. It looked like the goblin champion had been saving it for a special occasion.

Tracking back down the trail a ways, Eryninn found a rocky pocket to tuck into and scooted in. He pulled his cloak around him, covering himself completely, and laid his head down on his knees. The exhaustion of the day overwhelmed him, and he fell asleep without another thought.

***

Eryninn's eyes snapped open, and he had to force himself to remain still as he realized where he was. He didn't know how long he'd been asleep, but it was daylight out. Somewhere in the periphery of his mind he recalled something waking him. His pointed ears perked up to listen, but the rest of him stayed perfectly still beneath his cloak.

Goblins.

He heard them talking in their guttural tongue, and not far from his little hiding spot. He slowly lifted his head to look around. The rocky niche in which he currently found himself almost completely blocked him from sight on three sides, but that left the fourth side very vulnerable. If they found him there, he would have no choice but to fight his way out. There was no getting out the other directions.

He heard the goblins closer now. They made no attempt at silence. Not with an entire army behind them should trouble arise. Off to his right, he saw the arm of a goblin swing into view. It waved around in a circle while its owner talked loudly. Eryninn couldn't tell how many there were or what they were saying, but it was obvious they were arguing.

A heated discussion broke out between them. It went on for half a minute before Eryninn heard a much louder voice boom over them. An ogre probably. He still couldn't understand the language, but it was obvious that this new speaker was the voice of some authority. He sighed with relief when the arm disappeared and he heard footsteps receding into the distance. He waited several minutes after everything was silent before unfolding himself and peering out.

He stood up slowly until he could see over the rock and took a peek. Everyone was gone. There was no one in sight, and he no longer heard the raucous sounds of the goblin army up ahead in the pass. He took a few cautious steps and then stood up tall and stretched his sore muscles and aching bones. He definitely preferred life high in the trees to this crouching-under-rocks business.

Eryninn sat down and put his back to the mountain. Taking another apple and a hunk of cheese from his pack, he ate his breakfast and waited for the goblin army to be far enough ahead of him to continue following them. He ate for ten minutes before he was too anxious to wait any longer. He stood up from the rocks and brushed himself off. Coming around the bend, he saw the long, empty canyon ahead of him.

Eryninn walked a few steps and then stopped. The high, steep walls in the ravine gave him pause. Being at home among the trees, the high walls of rock gave him no cover and no place to quickly climb and escape. He rubbed at his arms and scanned the top for any sign of movement. The valley below was all but empty with only a giant mess left behind by the passing army. A few huge boulders dotted the landscape, making him even more uneasy.

They looked perfect for an ambush.

He stood perfectly still, watching and listening, waiting for any sign of trouble. Glancing up the sides of the ravine again, he shook his head slowly. Eryninn hated places he could not easily climb out of. Taking a deep breath, he took one step forward and then another. His steps were faster than he'd have liked, but he couldn't stop. When at last he let his breath out, he had almost made it to the first set of big boulders without so much as a whisper of the wind around him. Some part of him, his instincts, told him something was amiss. But another part, his head, said he was just being paranoid.

Should have followed my instincts.

He felt as much as heard the slight rush of wind from above. His instincts told him to leap to the side, and to his credit, he listened this time. He jumped sideways, turning slightly as he did to put his back to the mountain. Looking straight ahead, he saw a boulder nearly twice the size of his head crash into the ground where he had just been standing.

One hand reached for his bow while the other flashed to his sword. He followed his instinct again, or maybe the call of something else, and grabbed the sword, pulling it free of the scabbard just as an ogre came around the boulder in his path. With a great roar, the ogre raised his club and charged him. Eryninn kept his back to the mountain as he held his sword at the ready and felt a hum to the blade he had not known since his father was alive. It made him smile a little.

Hungry, are you?

His smile widened. Eryninn's sword was not his own. It was the sword of his father. Eryninn had become its owner when his father died, but for many years he would not carry it. Along with the cloak and the boots he now wore, it hung forlorn in his cabin waiting for the day it would draw blood again. The sword he now held was crafted by his father's people, the elves, and imbued with the magic to destroy their mortal enemy.

Ogres.

Surely the goblin champion thought it wise to leave some of his strongest warriors behind to kill the Wood Elf. He could not have known that there was no enemy his sword longed to drink from more. The blade quivered in his hand at the ogre's rush.

Then you shall drink.

The club came down in a heavy crash into the rock where Eryninn stood only a moment ago. The ogre's smile of victory turned to confusion when the dust cleared and there was not a crushed elf beneath its weapon. It didn't have long to ponder it though. A quick slash to the back of its knees brought the brute crashing forward into the rock. Its head smacked into the mountain with the full weight of its body. The howl of pain pierced the air and continued until a moment later when Eryninn's sword burst through its chest. The howl and the pain stopped abruptly as the ogre fell against the mountain and bled out.

Eryninn yanked his sword free and flicked his eyes to the rocky walls above and spotted two ogres at the top of the ravine hurling rocks down. Now that he was aware of them, it was a simple matter to watch their throws and keep out of their way. It was the five ogres coming from farther down the canyon that worried him most. The champion of Ogrosh was serious about killing him, it seemed.

Eryninn scanned up and down the ravine, but he already knew what he would find. No way out. Even with his father's blade, he could not kill so many. Another rock crashed down near him as he leapt out of the way. Eryninn's eyes flicked to every possible option around him, but none offered a way out.

He would have to fight.

And he would most likely die.

The ogres charged with a roar. Eryninn looked up the walls and briefly considered trying to scale them, but he would never make it before the ogres simply bashed him against the rocks or dragged him back down. Steadying his sword, he stood ready to fight and die.

The first ogre went down quickly. Eryninn stabbed out as it charged, and the hungry blade found its target with ease. The blade actually seemed to pull itself as Eryninn tried to direct it elsewhere, and he found it a bit unsettling. Almost as if the sword knew exactly what to do, and he was only there to hold it. The ogre stumbled back, its guts still in its body only by the hands holding them there.

Eryninn dodged a club meant for his head and then jumped to the side as another rock flew by. Four clubs were swinging at him relentlessly, offering him no hope of reprieve. He danced back to get some breathing room, but the ogres' long steps followed his every move. Ducking a swing, he came up and jabbed with his blade. It sang in his hands, and he could feel the hum as it cut through the ogre's stomach.

If I can dance long enough, perhaps the sword will take care of the rest.

Eryninn heard a loud battle cry behind him and thought for just a second that perhaps some reinforcements had come to save him. Daring a glance over his shoulder, he saw two dozen or more goblins charging up behind him. His silly hope vanished. It wasn't him they were there to reinforce. They were coming up from behind, cutting off any chance of escape. The champion of Ogrosh *really* wanted him dead, and he'd taken no chances this time.

Eryninn ducked a club and tried to think of a way out. Another ogre overextended his reach as Eryninn skipped back just as a small boulder flew down and crashed into its shoulder. The ogre shouted up to the top of the ravine and shook his club. The other yelled back down and threw a rock as his answer. Eryninn suddenly remembered who he was fighting. A plan formed in his mind.

The goblins were coming up fast behind him. Eryninn stabbed an ogre in the leg, bringing it to its knees where another slash across the neck ended it. Dodging another club, Eryninn tried hard to stay alive. He didn't even try to attack, only defend, but as an ogre got too close, the sword wouldn't let him hold back. A quick slash to the leg, and that ogre was limping back as fast as it could.

Wait… A moment longer.

Finally, the goblins were on him. They rushed in headlong, and Eryninn was glad to see these goblins were just as stupid as all the others he'd fought. A quick jab killed one before it could even swing its weapon. The fighting was too chaotic now for any of them to have a clean shot on him, but they kept trying. The others leapt in with no regard for their own safety, and Eryninn chanced a little smile. All the pieces were falling into place the way he'd hoped. He just had to stay alive long enough to see it through.

An ogre swung its club. As Eryninn ducked, it caught a goblin upside the head and crushed its skull in. A boulder from above crashed into another goblin, killing it. The goblins flailed about in confusion, some slamming into the ogres who were trying hard to reach Eryninn with their clubs. One of the remaining ogres picked up a goblin and, with a growl, threw it against the rocks.

That's it!

The fight changed so suddenly that Eryninn hardly had time to blink. With a howl, the goblins turned their blades on the ogres. The ogres smashed into the goblins with ruthless efficiency, killing several in seconds, but the goblins greatly outnumbered the remaining ogres. Eryninn danced out of the melee while they went at killing each other.

A boulder crashed into a goblin right beside him, and he barely had a chance to look up before another one struck him. The blow spun him half around, and he fell against the wall of the ravine as his left shoulder exploded with pain. Swallowing it down, he slipped along the wall, just out of reach of the fighting and tried to stay out of sight. He heard another boulder, but it was aimed at the goblins now.

All but forgotten in that moment, Eryninn turned and ran as fast as he could. He heard shouts from above as another boulder blasted the rock a few feet behind him, but all he could do was keep going. Pushing through the pain as best he could, Eryninn fled the ravine and into the waiting arms of the forest beyond.

CHAPTER TEN

FLY

ELODY ARRIVED THE next day eager to get some practice before Eliath showed up only to find him and Tark already there. Tark was lying lazily in the grass watching her while Eliath was standing against a tree on the far side of the field. Tark lifted his head with a little smile at her approach, and she heard a screech from overhead as Jalthrax glided down to land beside her.

"Hello, Tark," Elody said as she approached cautiously.

"Lady Elody. Nice to see you're not burning things up today."

Elody tittered nervously.

"No, I think I'll leave the burning things to the experts."

Tark gave a little chuckle that sent whiffs of smoke floating around his teeth and over his snout. Jalthrax snorted beside Elody and said something to Tark in the dragon tongue.

"I wish that I could speak dragon," Elody said. "I want to know what he's saying to you."

"He says he hates when you cast fire magic."

Elody looked down and wrinkled her brow.

"I know, I was stupid," she said to Jalthrax. "I won't cast beyond like that anymore."

"I do not think it is merely the way you cast them but all spells of fire. Fire is not kind to silvers, and they fear it instinctively from birth."

Elody knelt down and put her hands on either side of Jalthrax's head.

"I'm sorry, Thrax. I didn't know. I won't use them anymore if I can help it."

She stood back up and looked past Tark to where Eliath was still standing far away from them.

"Why is he all the way over there?"

Tark swiveled his neck around and looked on for a moment.

"He is speaking with the conclave."

"How is he doing that?"

"Through spells of sending. They pass words back and forth through magic, but it can be draining, and it is not convenient for longer messages. Most communication is done through wood dragons."

"Wood dragons?"

"Not really dragons, but they are distant cousins. Tiny things, but they're smart enough to understand simple commands, and they have an uncanny ability to find who they're looking for."

"The conclave sends tiny dragons to communicate with dragonmages?"

"They sent one this morning to tell us to keep waiting. He's trying to talk to them now and find us something useful to do, which will no doubt prove a waste of time."

"Why do you say that?"

Tark laid his head back down.

"Because that is all we have done for months," he said.

"Doing what exactly?"

"Waiting. Waiting for the conclave to let us help. They admit that they need our help, but they refuse it when it is offered."

"I don't understand."

"They don't trust us because I am a red dragon."

"Oh."

"They need our help, but they cannot lower themselves to take it. So we wait."

"They shouldn't treat you that way," she said

"Was it not *you* treating us the same just a few days ago?"

"Only because I didn't know you like I do now."

"And you believe that you do now? You have only known us both a few days."

"It doesn't take long to see the good in people."

"Dragons can be a little harder to read," Tark said.

"But Eliath loves you, so I know that you cannot be evil."

"The conclave does not agree with you."

"The conclave is making a mistake. And, as selfish as it is to say, I'm a little glad they are. It means you'll be here for a little while longer."

Tark chuckled.

"Were we to meet nicer people on our travels, I would suspect we would stay in more places longer. In truth, this has been a nice rest. Mostly because you are the only other dragonmage around. The less of them we see, the gladder I am for it."

"I'm sorry that I thought you were evil."

"You were trained to fear my kind. At least you stayed long enough to decide for yourself. Dark dragons are born no more evil than you or Jalthrax. Do not trust that every dragon of light you meet will be good either. I have known some in my life, bonded even, who were quite evil."

"Even bonded dragons?"

"They are often the victim. Dragons are not as emotional as you humans. Many is the good dragon who did evil in the name of a jealous or vengeful dragonmage."

"My master used to say the opposite. That dark mages often turn to evil, poisoned by the whisperings of a dark dragon."

"I suppose that could be said as well."

"But we each have a choice. The bond does not enslave the dragon or the mage."

"The bond is stronger than one forged of emotion or blood. A dragon or a mage will follow their brother into madness if that is to be the way of it. Would you not follow your own brother into trouble, even if it meant going against what you know to be right? Would you follow Jalthrax?"

"I don't know."

"Let us hope you never need ask yourself."

Just then Eliath yelled and cursed to the sky.

"Sounds like good news for you," Tark said with a huff of smoke. "We shall stay a while longer, I think."

Elody could only sigh. Eliath stormed over, crossing the field to stand beside Tark. He looked like he was going to say something to the red but then stopped.

"Good morning, Elody."

"Good morning. Tark tells me you'll be staying a few

more days."

Eliath slugged the dragon and then pulled his hand back in pain.

"Do that again and you might damage those precious fingers of yours," Tark said. "Then where would you be?"

"Right where I am," Eliath said. "Useless."

Tark stood and stretched, saying something to Jalthrax.

"If you are going to stand around and lavish pity on yourself, Jalthrax and I will hunt."

They both flapped into the air and were gone from sight a moment later. Eliath and Elody watched the sky for a while longer before turning back to each other.

"I'm sorry," she said.

"For what?"

"That… That they treat you the way they do."

"I don't need them. I only wanted to help, and at first they seemed eager to have it. Now I can do nothing because they won't let me."

"You're helping me."

Eliath smiled weakly.

"At least I can do that."

"Are you ready to start practice?"

"Can we sit for a minute? Speaking with the conclave has sapped my strength."

Elody moved nearer to him and sat down. She patted the grass beside her, and he joined her, close enough that their knees touched. They sat quietly for a while with nothing but the sound of the grass swishing around them in the wind. Eliath picked at the grass and sighed.

"Joron told my father this would happen. He told my father to sell the egg and not waste the money training me, but my father wouldn't listen. Joron may have been a drunk, but he was once a brilliant man I think."

"Why didn't your father listen?"

"He didn't care where the dragon came from so long as it was powerful. My only task was to protect him and his holdings, so it made little difference to him if I was an outcast."

"But Joron trained you anyway?"

"He just wanted more booze and a warm bed, but he *could* train me. He bartered with the only thing he had to offer."

Elody nodded.

"At first I just let him sleep and stole some of his books to read, but I didn't understand what they were saying or how to interpret the movements. So I started asking him for help when he was awake, which was rarely, and he would sometimes teach me how to read them. When I got as far as I could and realized I needed a real teacher, I begged my father to find me one. But Joron had convinced him that I was just a poor student."

"Your father didn't see him drunk all the time?"

"My father was rarely home, and when he was, Joron would manage to clean himself up for a few weeks and play the part. Then one day I started waking him every morning with a bucket of cold water from the lake. Threw it right in his face. He'd come up sputtering and cursing the gods, and I'd take off running."

Eliath laughed at the memory, and Elody laughed along.

"Then one day he caught me. Beat me good and told me to leave him alone and not make trouble for him or he'd make trouble for me."

"What did you do?"

"Next morning I hit him in the head with the handle

of a shovel instead of a bucket of water."

"Oh."

"Not so hard, but hard enough to give him a knot and put him out a few more hours. It was a stupid thing to do, but I was desperate. When he woke, I stood over him with that shovel in my hand and told him to remember that he was passed out a lot and when he was, I could and *would* do whatever I wanted. Surprisingly, after that, we got to be friends."

"Is that when he started training you?"

"Most days. I still had to wake him up with a bucket of cold water, but he didn't fight as much anymore. Oh, he'd curse my name, my family, my father, my mother, everyone I knew. But he never came after me again. After Tark was born, my father wanted to get rid of him."

"Why?"

"He had a dragon now, he didn't think he needed anyone to train me. My older brother insisted I continue training since I was so young, that I hadn't completed the required three years that he went through. Joron just didn't want to lose his free meal and booze. Between the two of them, they convinced my father to let him stay a while longer."

"Did you want him to stay?"

"Yes. We had become friends of sorts, but more than that, I wasn't ready. If my father thought my training was done, he'd send me out to protect his land. I just wanted to learn as much as I could and get out of there."

"Why didn't you just leave after Tark was born?"

"Ardina," he said with a sigh. "My little sister. I stayed for her."

Elody closed her eyes and nodded.

"Big brothers do that sometimes," she said.

"Well, don't look too highly on me. I ran away about a year later. Tark was old enough that I thought we could make it on our own."

"Where did you go?"

"We didn't make it far before they caught up to us. My father used my older brother and his dragon to track us down and bring us back. He threatened to take Tark away from me if I ever did it again. He said he owned Tark because he paid for him."

"Why would your brother do that?"

"I don't blame him. He was only doing what he was told. There was a war going on. Lords were losing their holdings by the acre as the kings took what they needed for the war, and my father had a red and a copper dragon standing watch over his."

"So you stayed?"

"Only until I knew I could get away. I'd had a little taste of freedom, and I wanted it more than anything. As soon as I could run again, I did. This time, Tark and I went as far and as fast as we could."

"Did they catch you?"

Eliath looked down at his hands nervously clenched in his lap.

"Two days after we left, King Hallex's men attacked my father's castle. I don't know everything, but I know they defended for several days before they were overrun."

"Gods. What about your brothers and sister?"

"I was told after it happened that they were all killed. Joron told me. After I left the second time, they threw him out on his arse. Turned out to be his good fortune when the place was burned to the ground days later."

"Eliath, I'm so sorry."

"There was nothing I could have done. My sister would still be dead, only I would have joined her. Tark too, probably."

They sat in silence for a long while. Elody started to say something a couple of times but had trouble finding words.

"I just want to help where I can," Eliath finally said. "But they don't want my help. Not really. Do you want to know where I was for the last three months? In the Frozenlands."

Elody jerked her head around, her eyes wide.

"You've been to the snowy north?"

"Many times. And this time, all the way to the White Vale. Trying to find a trace of the wizard doing all of this. The conclave told me I could be most helpful tracking down some killings up there, but really they were just tired of me asking and needed something to do with me."

"I can't believe you've been to the White Vale."

"And all across the King's Belt, from the west coast to the east. And south to the Seas of Sand as well."

"*Really?*" Elody said, a bit louder than she had meant to.

"Really. Tark much prefers the great desert to the north. He has no love for the cold places of the world. The heat of the desert is far more to his liking. Even met some dwarves down there."

"You've seen a dwarf?"

"Lots, actually. They still have strongholds in the mountains that border the desert."

"That's amazing. You've been everywhere!"

"Almost. As soon as Tark was big enough to carry me, we flew as far and wide as we could. Tark's a bit of an adventurer too. He really loves it most when it's just the two of us and the open sky. He really didn't want us to come back here."

"But you did?"

"I needed to. I've spent too many years running away."

"From what?"

"Nothing. Everything. I don't know."

"Then why stop now?"

"Because I want to be of help to someone. I may not have been strong enough to help when I was a boy, but I'm strong enough now."

"I understand. They won't let me help either, but I'm strong."

She understood all too well. Eliath smiled.

"You remind me of her, you know?"

"Who?"

"Ardina. Smart, beautiful… stubborn as a mule."

Did he just say I was beautiful?

Elody hit him as hard as she could, which only made him laugh, and she quickly turned away to hide the stupid grin on her face.

"And hits like a girl!" he said.

She swung again, but he leaned back suddenly, causing her to fall over. They both laughed until they couldn't breathe. When they finally stopped, Eliath stood and offered his hand down.

"Well," Eliath said, "are we going to practice some or just sit around all day telling sad stories?"

Elody smiled and took his hand. As he pulled her to her feet, she reached up slowly and put her arms around him. Eliath stood awkwardly at first but then wrapped his arms around her and squeezed tightly. They stayed locked in their embrace as time drifted by until Eliath let go and stood back. He turned and made a show of scanning the skies for the dragons, but Elody could see him wipe the corners of his eyes when he thought she wasn't looking.

"I wish I could see some of the places you've seen," she said as she looked off into the distance. "I always dreamt of traveling the world."

"Then travel the world! What's stopping you?"

"Nothing, I suppose. Jalthrax won't be big enough to ride for a long time though."

"I don't know. You're pretty small. Another five years or so, and you'll be flying everywhere."

"That seems like forever from now."

"Well, would you like to take a ride on Tark? He can hold—"

"Yes!" she shouted before he could even finish.

"All right then. When they get back. In the meantime, let's work on your spells."

"I practiced some last night."

"Well, let's see them then!"

**

The roar in Elody's ears was deafening. She heard Eliath say something from behind her, but she couldn't make it out.

"What?" she shouted above the wind.

He tapped her shoulder and pointed to his right. She looked out and saw Jalthrax pull his wings tight against his body and spin in a circle. She almost screamed, but he stopped just as suddenly and spread his wings to glide gracefully beside them. Looking back over her shoulder, Eliath was nodding with a great smile.

"No!" she said, but if he heard her at all, he didn't seem to care.

Eliath slapped Tark twice on the side, and the great dragon tucked his wings back and went into the same spin Jalthrax had just done. The whole world flipped around her. Land, sky, land, sky. Her body lifted slightly and pressed against the leather belt around her, the only thing holding her in. Her knuckles went white around the horn of the strange saddle as she held on for her life. Behind her, Eliath screamed and gripped her tighter around her waist, her body pressed closer to his.

Her heart beat even faster.

Tark finished his third spin and climbed back out of it with ease, his giant wings spreading out to either side to let him glide gracefully above the treetops.

"Pretty exciting, right?" Eliath yelled in her ears.

"Yes," she shouted over her shoulder. "Don't ever do that again!"

Tark's body shook beneath her as the big dragon laughed, his hearing obviously much better than hers up here. Jalthrax screeched, and she took a chance and removed one hand to wave at him. Tark flapped his wings lazily every few moments, keeping them aloft with so little effort that Elody could hardly believe it. As they slowed, the wind in her ears lessened, and she found she could hear herself a little easier.

"Well," Eliath said leaning forward, "where do you want to go?"

"Kingsport Bay!" she said "I've always wanted to see the twin fortresses."

Eliath laughed.

"I don't think we can make it there and back in a few hours. Or even a few days."

"What does that matter?"

"Well, I wouldn't want anyone thinking I had

snatched you away. Your brother would not like it so much, I think."

"How far can we go then?"

"We can fly for a few hours before heading back. I know it doesn't sound like much, but when you're not traveling by road, a few hours can take you a lot of places."

"Can we make it to Ilothen's Crown?"

"Of course!"

Eliath slapped Tark on the side, but the dragon had already begun to change direction without waiting for approval. Elody looked down at the ground flying by beneath her, felt Eliath's arms around her, and could barely keep herself calm. She knew he could feel her rapid breaths against his hands and could only hope he thought it was the exhilaration of flying.

They flew for hours.

The ride was smoother than Elody would have thought. She had watched Jalthrax fly many times, but Tark was so much bigger and his wings much wider. They mostly rode the currents with only the occasional flap of Tark's wings to adjust direction or move them back into the right wind.

When Ilothen's Crown finally came into view, Elody could hardly believe it. The part of her that always saw wonder in the great peak was breathless. The part of her that thought of her father wanted to weep. Until her village burned six months ago, her whole life had been lived under the watchful eye of the great mountain.

"Did you just want to see it," Eliath asked, "or do you want to land?"

"Can we land on the top?"

"Somehow I knew that's where you'd want to go. The

weather at the top is too cold, and we aren't really dressed for it. But we'll go as high as we can."

Eliath slapped Tark again, but the dragon paid him no attention. Turning slightly to the left, Tark climbed higher and made for the snow-capped peak. Jalthrax followed silently along beside them. Elody felt a rush of cold wind across her face and a rush of emotion through her heart. As a girl, she had dreamed of one day reaching the top of Ilothen's Crown. She wished she had dressed more warmly so that she might actually stand on it.

The air was getting colder, and Tark eventually stopped climbing and set down gracefully on a rocky ledge covered with a light snow. Elody tried to stand but couldn't get up with the leather belt around her.

"Slow down a minute," Eliath said.

His hands dropped down and deftly undid the metal buckle, releasing her from the saddle. She hadn't been aware of how tight it was, but her breathing became much easier as it released. Tark shook his body just as she started to stand, and she tumbled back into the seat.

"Hey!" Eliath yelled.

"Apologies," Tark said. "This damn cold makes me shiver. My kind is not made for it, though Jalthrax seems quite content."

Elody looked out and found Jalthrax rolling around in the snow on the ledge. She shook her head and stood back up. Eliath had already undone his belt and held out his hand to help her down. She climbed down the series of leather loops that hung from the saddle until the last when she leapt off and felt her boots crunch the snow beneath her. Eliath was down beside her a moment later.

"Why do they call it Ilothen's Crown?" she asked.

"The forest in the shadow of the Twin Crest

Mountains was the home of the first elven kingdom. When the elven god Ilothen made the elves, he made all of this for them and made the tallest peak so that whenever they wished, they could climb it and be nearest to him. That's the legend, at least."

"Is it truly the tallest mountain on Gondril?"

"I don't know. The Anvil is said to be its twin and almost as tall. I do think the Crown is taller though. The tops of both are always covered in snow, so I guess they're pretty high."

"I used to love the snow in Jornath as a girl," Elody said as she tromped around. "There's not much snow in Havnor in the winter. When it does snow, it melts away within a day or so. This was my first winter without real snow, I think."

"In the White Vale, the snow never stops. Well, it will stop snowing for days or weeks, but there is never a time when the ground is not covered."

Jalthrax squawked as he continued to roll around on his back in the snow. Elody watched with a sad smile as she thought of all the times she had done the same as a child.

"I love when it snows," she said. "It used to cover the village every winter and make everything look so clean. The world doesn't look so dirty in a blanket of snow."

"I'm sure the tribes of the Vale could do with less of it," Eliath said.

"I could do with none of it," Tark said.

"Tark did not enjoy our trip to the Vale."

"Every morning I woke to find my bones stiff and my muscles frozen. If ever you desired to quench the furnace of a dragon, that is the place to do it. Even as my inner fires burned, it felt as though I could never get warm."

"He's just mad because the tribes had no place for a dragon his size to sleep, so he had to stay outside. I found him still asleep most mornings covered in snow. You're right, though, he did look clean."

"I would love to see the Vale one day," Elody said. "When I was accepted for training, I made a list of all the places I would go in my life. The White Vale was one of them. I wanted to travel all of Gondril and see its wonders."

"What's stopping you?"

Elody turned and looked south to where the remains of her village would be. To Jornath. She couldn't see it from here, but she knew where it was. She could never forget.

"Tell me," Eliath said as he stepped closer. "What would you have done if your village were still down there? If none of that had ever happened?"

"I would be the village dragonmage, there to protect it."

"And now that it's gone?"

"One village is gone, but there will always be others."

"But you have the chance to be anything you *want* now. You don't owe anyone anything. You can travel the world like you dreamed, and no one can stop you."

"You just described yourself," she said. "You owe nothing to anyone, and you can go anywhere you like and do whatever you wish. Yet here you stand, wanting to help people with your magic."

Tark scoffed.

"She has you there," he said.

"I suppose she does," Eliath said.

Elody folded her arms across her chest and rubbed them. Her robes were not very thick and did little to repel the cold wind this high on the mountain.

"*I'll* show you the world," Eliath said at last. "You and Jalthrax can join Tark and I."

Elody spun and looked at him, her eyes twinkling with excitement.

"Where would we go?" she asked.

"I've already been to most places. I'll leave it to you. What are some of the places on your list?"

Elody smiled.

"Well, we're standing on one right now."

"Ha! See that? We're already off and on our way."

Tark's body spasmed, shaking loose some of the rock around them.

"Apologies," he growled. "It is this damn cold."

"I would say next time we dress for the journey though," Eliath said.

"Next time," Tark said, "pick somewhere warmer."

"We should probably get back," Eliath said. "Are you ready to go?"

Elody looked back to the south again. To Jornath. To her home.

No, no longer her home. Her home was the whole world now.

"I'm ready to go," she said.

***

Elody pulled the door closed behind her and listened to the darkness in the house. By the time they had returned from the mountain, it was quite late. Eliath had flown straight to the Dragon's Roost and then walked her and Jalthrax home from there. Her steps light, she crept up the stairs. As she reached for the knob to her room, Rinn's door opened, and he stepped out.

"Where have you been?" he said, his voice just above a

whisper.

"I was training."

"You can't train in the dark, El."

"I've been practicing light spells."

"I went to the field to find you a few hours ago," he said as he folded his arms.

Elody could feel the silence in the air as she tried to think of a lie. Thinking of nothing, she gave up and held her chin high.

"I was with Eliath," she said.

"I knew it. I told you to stay away from him."

"I don't care what you told me. I don't answer to you."

"No, but I'm the one looking out for you."

"I never asked you to."

"Dad asked me to."

"Dad's gone, Rinn, and you're not him."

"Eliath is nothing but trouble. You're going to get hurt."

"You don't even know him."

"I know enough about his kind."

"No, you don't."

She tried to push past him into her room, but he stepped in front to block the door.

"What do you want, Rinn?"

"I'll tell you what I don't want. I don't want you going out at night and getting in trouble or possibly getting hurt."

"Like you do every night?"

"What do you know about it?"

"Everyone knows, Rinn."

"Well, that's different."

"How is it different?"

"Because I'm a grown man, and you're still a girl.

Someone has to look out for you."

"I don't need your protection."

"I don't want you around him."

"Well, he told me he's leaving soon, so you won't have to worry about him and me anymore."

"Good."

Elody glared and tapped her foot.

"Can I go to bed now?"

Rinn stepped aside without a word as Elody shoved past him into her room. Pulling the door closed behind her, Elody leaned her back to it and listened. When she heard Rinn's door close, she stood and lit the candle on her tiny table.

Looking around her room, she started thinking of what to pack.

CHAPTER ELEVEN

GOODBYE

RINN WOKE TO a loud knock at his door. He bolted up in bed and had his clothes in hand before he had even gathered his wits.

"I'm up, I'm up!"

He snatched the door open and found himself staring at Berym's shiny, steel chainmail.

"I'm glad that I warrant such promptness, but you really could have pulled your breeches on first."

Rinn stared down where he was still holding his clothes in his hands and slowly closed the door. He had no trouble hearing Berym's roaring laugh from the other side. With his breeches firmly in place, he opened the door again where Berym laughed even harder.

"It's not as funny as all that."

Berym gasped and grabbed his sides. Rinn could see tears on his cheeks. The sight of the knight made him smile until he could no longer hold it in and was forced to laugh along with him. When they could both catch their breath, Berym lead them back downstairs to the kitchen. Rinn looked around and noted Aunt Jelena was gone. He thought maybe she'd gone to another birth, but he had a sneaking suspicion she wouldn't be attending another without her newfound helper carrying the bags.

"Sit," Berym said, pointing at a chair.

Rinn plopped down at the table and grabbed at the loaf of bread his aunt had left. Taking a piece in his mouth, he chewed silently and waited for the knight. Berym sat in the chair directly across from him.

"I'm sorry I missed our practice the last couple days," Rinn said between bites. "Aunt Jelena made me attend a birth with her. Which really just means I carried her stuff. She's been dragging me around since."

"That's all right. I thought you might have met a nice girl and decided to stay in bed a while longer."

"That would have been a much better time," Rinn said.

Berym chuckled half-heartedly but seemed to be struggling with something.

"I'm going away for a while," he said at last.

Rinn swallowed his mouthful of bread.

"Called away again?" he said. "Do they ever let you rest?"

"No, nothing like that," Berym said. "This is for me. It's actually something you said the other day while we were sparring."

"Me? What did I say? Don't listen to me."

"Well, this one time, it might have been something I needed to hear."

"Believe me, I'm not the one you want to be taking advice from."

"It wasn't advice so much. It just made me think a bit about my life and where I am. Do you remember when you talked about wanting a family?"

"Sure."

"I never met your mother, but if your father was any measure of your family, you have a lot to look forward to. I know you must think about him often."

Rinn swallowed hard.

"Every day," he said. "I know it's been six months, but I still can't believe he's just gone. I keep expecting to hear him stomp through the door yelling about me leaving the coop open again."

Berym's gaze went past Rinn to the window behind him where he stared in silence for several moments before speaking.

"I don't even know if my father is alive or dead. I haven't spoken to him in more than fifteen years."

"You don't even know if he's still alive? You haven't seen him?"

"He is not someone I care to see."

"But he's your father."

"I know that means something to you, and well it should. It should mean something to every man, but it's not always how it is."

"It can't be all that bad. I hated my dad sometimes too. He worked me like a mule. Made me get up every morning with him—"

"My father beat me until the age of twelve when he tried to sell me."

Rinn stared across the table.

"Sell you?"

"He was a drunk and a disgrace who had no money, but he had a title. He had lost every copper of the family's fortune, but he still held his *damn* title, by her grace. This was when titles meant something to people. He used it to barter for food sometimes, but mostly drink. I usually had to find my own food."

"Who did he try to sell you to?"

"He sold me as a squire to a knight. As a noble, I had the birth to become a knight, but with nothing else to our names, I was only worth the gold he could raise by selling me."

"That sounds awful."

"It wasn't. The knight who took me in was a better father than my own ever could have been. It is him I think of every day. But other than him and his sister, I have no one. So, when you talk about having a family, you can see where I might have a hard time imagining such a thing. It is not a dream everyone can have."

Rinn nodded and picked at the loaf of bread resting on the table.

"Why all this talk of family? Are you going to try and find them now?"

"In a manner of speaking, yes. I'm going to the village of Derne a few days ride from here. That is where my master, Pelen, was from. I spent some time there with him and his sister, Narissa. She still lives there. It's been almost a year since I've seen her, and I owe her a visit."

"His sister, huh? Is she the one you think about?"

"Think about what?"

"When you stare off for long minutes and get that dumb grin on your face."

Berym's grin spread wide, and Rinn could only point.

"That one," he said.

"I suppose she is," Berym said.

"And you love her?" Rinn asked.

"I do. I have for many, many years now. She is the light in my soul."

"Then why is this the first I've heard of you going to see her? Derne is only a two day ride from here."

"My duty is to those who *need* me first, and it leaves little room for visits. It never seems enough time, and I am always leaving too soon for the both of us. Saying goodbye just gets harder each time."

"So you would rather say nothing at all?"

"I plan on staying for a while this time, but I don't know how long," Berym said, clearing his throat. "I wanted to tell you so that you would know where I was going and that I might not be back for a bit. The knighthood knows where I am."

"And what if they send for you?"

Berym looked past Rinn to the window again.

"I will answer to my duties."

Rinn shook his head.

"Is it really worth it? Being a knight I mean."

Berym stared into his eyes.

"Someday you may be called to do something that takes from you what you truly want. Someone's life may depend on it. On that day, I hope you find the conviction to do what is needed over what you desire."

"I'll just sit back and hope that day never comes."

Berym shook his head, but a little smile crept onto his lips.

"Let us all hope," he said.

***

Elody's hands glided through the air in the motions of her spell while the blue threads of magic arced between her fingers. She opened her eyes for only a moment before holding her palms out and cupping them in front of her. The magic swirled and coalesced and then leapt up with a ripping sound. Perched upon her palms was an ugly, black crow.

"I did it!"

Jalthrax stared but said nothing.

"I think that's pretty good for only having studied for a few days."

The crow cawed, startling her, and she shook a finger at it. She used her own magic to bind the crow, just like Eliath had told her. Though she always thought of her magic well as being tiny, she knew it was enough to hold the little bird here. She could feel the tiniest tingle as it slowly dripped away.

Elody smiled to herself and sighed. Looking to the sky again for the tenth time in as many minutes, she started pacing. She was only practicing her spells to keep her hands busy as she waited, and she was already tiring from it.

How long have I been here? She had arrived just after sunrise, eager to see Eliath and talk more about their plans. She had briefly considered going straight to the Roost to meet him, but she didn't want to wake him too early. This was how they had met every day, right here in the training field, so she kept to that.

Jalthrax looked to the sky, and her eyes followed. She saw the unmistakable form of a dragon in flight off in the distance and instantly felt her stomach churn. Today was the day she would leave it all behind. Jornath. Her brother. Her whole life as she'd always known it. They would leave today.

Where would they go? She'd thought on it a hundred times just since last night. She watched as they approached, growing nearer and nearer, taking shape with each passing moment. Tark landed as gently as always, and Eliath slid gracefully from his back and to the ground. Jalthrax called out something in dragon, and Tark responded. Eliath looked at the red dragon with a raised eyebrow, but Tark paid him no attention.

"Are we needed?" Tark asked.

"Go," Eliath said with a wave. "But don't be gone long."

The two dragons leapt into the air, and with a few short wingbeats, they were high in the sky and quickly disappearing from sight. Elody turned to Eliath and let the crow jump up onto her shoulder.

"Did you summon that?" he asked.

"Yes!"

"Excellent! Better yet, not dangerous."

"Careful now. Crow-crow here could claw your eyes out."

"Crow-crow?"

"I gave him a name."

"Can you send Crow-crow back?"

Elody turned her head to eye the bird on her shoulder.

"Begone," she said calmly.

With a pop, the crow was gone.

"Ha ha," Eliath bellowed. "My best student!"

Elody laughed.

"That might mean something if you had more than one."

"Well, then you'll always be my best. And when you rule the conclave one day, I can say that I trained you. Have you practiced the other?"

"A little bit. It was actually pretty easy."

"Oh, ho? Well, let's see it then."

"I may not have enough in me to cast it."

"We'll never know unless you try, will we?"

Elody raised her arms to let the sleeves of her robe fall back to her elbows and closed her eyes.

"Uh, that way?" Eliath said.

Elody opened her eyes and saw him pointing away from him. She turned around with a smile and closed her eyes again. She had been with Jalthrax for so long now that she hadn't needed to use her own magic. In truth, she'd only used it a few times in her life, but she had practiced since then and had learned to reach it more quickly. In only a moment she could feel the magic tingle in her fingertips. It wasn't enough, she knew. Reaching deep inside her inner well of power, she pulled at it for more. When she finally thought she had enough, she started moving her hands.

The spell was fresh in her mind. She had practiced it many times in the last few days, even when she wasn't with Eliath. The movements traced in her thoughts like an ancient map of magic, and her hands and fingers followed every step. Completing the spell, she pushed her hands out in front of her as though she were throwing sand in someone's face and felt her hands grow wet and cold as a blast of ice leapt from her palms. When she opened her eyes, the field in front of her was covered in a light dusting of snow and ice.

"Amazing!" Eliath said. "You really are the quickest study I've ever seen."

"I learned from the best."

"You learned from what was nearest," he said with a laugh.

"Well, then I just got lucky that you were the best."

Elody turned and lifted her robes with a dainty pinch of her fingers in a little curtsy, and Eliath laughed out loud. She stood back up with the biggest grin and could hardly contain herself.

"I thought more about where we could go first," she

said. "I've already started packing."

Eliath stopped smiling and looked down.

"I, uh… I have to leave today. I'm sorry. That's what I came to tell you this morning. I received word from the conclave last night after we returned. It seems I must have convinced them of my sincerity yesterday. Or perhaps they just got too desperate."

Elody's smile lasted another second before her brain caught up.

"Go? Go where?"

"A gold dragon was murdered in the elven lands. The elves have kept their borders closed ever since this business started, and they must have thought they were safe."

"Then why are *you* going?"

"Until yesterday, the gold and silver dragons have remained untouched by this murderer."

"The queen was silver, and she's dead."

"Yes, but she lived outside of elven lands. And she was the only silver to do so. All of the golds and silvers live within the elven borders except for two. And one is now gone."

"So you're going to protect the silver and gold dragon mothers?"

"We have most of the rest protected here. The elves insisted they could protect their own, but now a gold has been murdered. They would never ask for help, it is not their way, but the conclave cannot ignore a threat against any of the dragon mothers."

Elody looked down and kicked a rock as her feet shifted beneath her robes.

"But I thought… I thought we…"

"I know. I promise, we will take that trip together. But

this is my chance, maybe my only chance to prove that I can be of help."

"I thought that didn't matter to you."

"That's what someone always says when they can't have something."

"I don't understand. We talked yesterday about going away."

"I know."

Elody looked down to hide the tears she could feel at the edges of her eyes.

"Will you be back?" she asked, afraid to look up.

"Yes! I *promise* you, we will take our trip. Together."

"When?"

"That I don't know. I leave here straight for Molner. I'll be there for a week or two to meet with members of the conclave, but then it's off to the elven lands for *who knows* how long. Maybe not until we stop this madman."

"But... What am I supposed to do until then?"

"Wait here for me. Continue your training. I would tell you to wait for another dragonmage, but I don't think you're likely to see one for quite a while. What few there are left unassigned are going to the elves now. You may not see another pass through until this is over."

"When do you leave?"

"As soon as Tark returns from his hunt."

Elody couldn't mask the quiver in her voice.

"That soon?"

"They said it was urgent. I wish that I could stay, but this is the first real chance they've offered me to help."

"I know why you have to leave," she said.

"I knew you would understand."

"I do."

"And you'll continue your training?"

"What little I can."

Eliath reached out and lifted her chin.

"You can do more than you think. Just keep at it, even if it feels like it's too hard."

"You too."

Eliath reached his arms out and wrapped her in a great hug. Elody took a deep breath and then hugged back, squeezing him tight. Tears welled up in her eyes, and she tried hard to blink them away. Eliath pulled back when they heard the flap of wings in the distance and getting closer.

"I'll send word when I get there," he said. "I can send messages to you, but you aren't yet strong enough to reply."

"Be careful," she said.

"Thank you, Elody."

"For what?"

"For being a friend. I really needed one. With you and Tark, I can now count two in this world."

Elody smiled and wiped the tears she couldn't manage to stop.

"I don't have a lot myself," she said.

"Keep close the ones you do."

Elody couldn't help it, she hugged him again, and he squeezed back even harder. They continued to hold each other until Tark and Jalthrax landed beside them. Eliath stepped back and reached his hand up slowly to her face. Using his thumb, he wiped the tears from her eyes and then turned away.

He moved alongside Tark and pulled himself up onto the red dragon's back and into the saddle. Tark said something to Jalthrax in the dragon tongue, and the little silver replied back with something Elody was left to wonder about.

"Goodbye, Elody," Eliath said. "I'll miss our talks together."

The lump in her throat choked her words. All she could do was wave, so that's what she did. With a flap of his great wings, Tark leapt into the air. In only a moment they were both gone from sight. Elody stared into the sky long after they could no longer be seen. She wiped her eyes, took a deep breath, and looked down at Jalthrax.

"I guess we're not going anywhere," she said as the tears rolled down once more.

***

Rinn was sitting quietly at the table, staring at a half-eaten loaf of bread when Elody returned home. She said something that broke his trance, and he blinked up at her.

"What are you doing?" she asked.

"What?"

"I asked where Aunt Jelena was, and you just sat there staring."

"Oh. Out, I guess," Rinn said. "I was asleep when she left this morning."

Elody opened the little closet under the stairs and peered inside.

"Her bag and stool are still here."

"I didn't see her leave."

Elody sat in the chair across from him and grabbed the remaining bread. Taking a bite, she chewed slowly as they both sat, each one staring past the other. Rinn finally looked up at her and saw the redness in her cheeks where she'd been crying.

"What happened?" he asked, his trance broken.

"Nothing," she said. "I hurt myself."

"Doing what?"

"Being foolish."

Rinn nodded and didn't press further. He still felt bad about how they had left things last night. Not so much that he regretted what he said, but maybe how he said it.

"What are you doing here?" she asked.

"Berym came by this morning," he said. "Said he was leaving for a few weeks."

"Oh, I'm sorry I missed him. That wasn't very long, was it?"

"A few days."

"And they sent him off again? I haven't even seen him in weeks."

"Well, it'll be a few more it looks like. He wasn't sent by the knighthood, but he said he may be gone for a while."

"For a while? Where's he going?"

"To visit family, he said."

"I didn't know he had any family."

"Neither did I."

"Eliath left today too," she said as she looked down at the table.

"Good riddance," Rinn said.

Elody's eyes shot up and glared, and he could see her lip quiver like she wanted to say something.

"What?" Rinn said. "I asked you not to talk to him, and you did anyway. You don't need to spend your time with someone like that."

"Someone like *what*, exactly?"

"You know what I mean."

"A dark mage?"

"Yes, a dark mage. You don't need to train with

someone like that. We'll find you a better teacher."

"Eliath taught me some important things."

"Like how to kill someone?"

"Isn't that what dragonmages are trained to do? What do you think they taught as at school all those years?"

"Yes, but it's *who* you kill that matters most."

"Eliath is a good man. If you had spent any time with him, you'd know that."

"I don't need to spend time with him. I know exactly who he is by the company he keeps."

"Tark is good too, you just didn't bother to find out."

"Did you listen at all when master Cythyil taught us about the dark dragons? They are born with evil in their hearts, El. Even if Eliath is a good man, that dragon will corrupt him and twist him until he is just as evil."

"You don't know Tark."

"I don't need to. There are creatures in this world that are born evil. They don't become it, they just are."

"I don't believe that."

"It doesn't matter if you believe it."

"People can change, dragons too. Haven't you ever done anything bad?"

"I wasn't born evil."

"If what you say is true, then humans are even worse. If a dragon is born to evil, they are simply as Anarr made them. A man who is evil does so because he chooses it."

She stood quickly and pushed away from the table.

"I have spent enough time with Tark to see the good in him. If he was born to evil, then he has fought against it and won. What excuse does a man have?"

Rinn had no answer as she stormed out the door. She had a point.

What was his excuse?

CHAPTER TWELVE

MISTAKES

THE MOON WAS full, casting a bright glow over the entire field. It was almost as bright as when Elody would practice early in the mornings, and she was glad for it. She had been waiting for weeks for the right night to try her new spell, and the time had finally come.

Eliath had only left that morning, but it seemed the perfect time to try something a bit reckless. She wasn't feeling in a particularly safe mood today. When he returned to take her away, she would be strong. She would be ready.

"Are you ready to try?" she asked.

Jalthrax shuffled his feet beside her and squawked.

"It's not a fire spell, I promise. I won't cast those anymore if you don't like them. I have other, more powerful spells I can cast now."

She rubbed her hands together and took a deep breath.

"This is a big one, but I've been practicing the movements."

Jalthrax squawked again.

"Oh, be quiet. Eliath taught me more about how to

cast beyond. I know how to be safe now. Don't worry so much."

Jalthrax huffed, but she had already turned her back to him. Taking a deep breath, she practiced the motions a few times without drawing any magic. She wanted to make sure she got the spell perfectly. She had considered asking Eliath for help with it, but it was *so far* beyond her skills that she knew he wouldn't approve. But Elody was confident.

I can do this. I don't need help.

Slinging her hands out and flexing her fingers, she brought them back to her chest and breathed out slowly. Reaching her mind out for Jalthrax, she could feel him there beside her, though a few steps back from where he was a moment ago. She took hold of the magic within him and started pulling. She pulled and pulled, taking more magic than she had ever drawn before. A spell of this much energy took more than any single spell she'd ever cast. It rushed into her fingers.

The magic in her hands burned to get out. She could feel it racing through her arms, and she wanted desperately to throw it out of her, to be rid of it. But she didn't have enough yet. She drew the last little bit that she needed for the spell and felt her arms spasm. They tightened up and ached, and she suddenly wondered if she'd even be able to complete the motions. She had never felt so much power within her, and she was beginning to doubt.

Curling her hands slowly at first, but picking up speed, she began to weave the magic. Blue strands burst from every fingertip, connecting to another on her other hand, and then flying back again to form another thread. It was as though she held a ball of yarn in her hand that got bigger with each arc of magic. She spread her arms wider to contain it all, but she never stopped moving her fingers. A scream built in her chest.

It's too much. I can't control it!

She opened her mouth and yelled, her body trying to expel the magic in any way that it could. Her voice grew louder and louder until she was shouting to the sky. With a final flick of her hands, all of the magic leapt to one hand in a great whoosh, and she pointed her finger to the heavens.

A boom echoed across the field as a great bolt of lightning flew from her fingertip and into the night sky. Elody watched in awe as it raced up, looking as though it might touch the moon itself. The clouds above lit up with a flash as it disappeared into them. When at last it was gone, she stared a moment longer before yelling and jumping up and down.

"Ha ha! I did it!"

She twirled in a circle and turned to Jalthrax.

"We did it, Thrax!"

But the dragon didn't move. When she stopped jumping long enough to look on him, he was lying flat out in the grass.

"Thrax?"

Elody ran to him and knelt down beside him.

"Thrax!"

She shoved on his body, trying to wake him, but the little dragon gave no response.

"Thrax, wake up! Wake up!"

She shoved him again, but he still didn't move. Elody's heart pounded in her chest. She dropped to her knees when they would no longer support her. She closed her eyes and reached out with her thoughts.

Please be okay. Please be okay. She could feel him. She felt his life connected to hers, but it was faint. His life force was distant. It felt as though he were all the way across the field even though he was right beside her.

"Help!" she cried. "Someone help!"

She looked up through the tears clouding her eyes and shouted for someone, anyone, to come and help her. But she knew no one would come. She had picked this night and this spot because no one ever came out here at night.

Elody leapt to her feet and started running. She had to find help. Rinn. Aunt Jelena, maybe. She would know what to do. But as she reached the edge of the field, she skidded to a stop and turned back to see Jalthrax lying still. He just laid there, unmoving.

I can't just *leave* him.

She ran back and grabbed his legs. Pulling as hard as she could, she started dragging the unconscious dragon through the grass. Even as a small dragon, he weighed a lot. The going was slow and the grass muddy. Her feet slipped from under her more than once, and she stumbled back and fell to the ground.

Crying and screaming, she tugged and pulled but knew it was no good. She couldn't drag the dragon all the way back to town. He was too heavy, and she was too weak.

"No!" she screamed to the night and grabbed him up again.

She pulled harder, slipping on the muddy ground with her feet. A roar of desperation formed in her chest, and she pulled with all of her strength.

The dragon's body wouldn't budge.

Sliding to the ground, she wrapped her arms around

his neck and screamed. Tears dripped down her cheeks and fell onto the silver scales, glistening in the full moon. The tears fell onto her hands and slid down off with little plops as they hit the grass.

Elody pushed her hands against Jalthrax's silver scales and hugged him with all her strength. Somewhere deep inside, she could still feel the tiniest spark of magic ready to leap to her hands. Even without thought, the bond between them was so strong that the dragon would give up his last drop of life for her.

Elody's eyes sprang open. She had taken too much, she knew. She had taken too much of his magic, and now he was dying. But she could give it back to him. Eliath had done it. He had taken from Tark's energy and given it to Jalthrax.

She could Jalthrax her own life.

Pushing herself to her knees, Elody leaned closer and put her palms flat on Jalthrax's back. She could still feel that tiny spark of magic. It was still in there, which meant Jalthrax was still there, somewhere. She closed her eyes and tried not to think about Jalthrax. She focused instead on herself.

Looking deep within her, she pushed her mind down for her own store of magic. The tiny well of her own power. It was nothing like the size of Jalthrax's, but she hoped and prayed that it would be enough. She found the magic easily enough and took it all up into her hands. Every last drop. If she failed, she would not need it anyway.

The magic flowed through her hands, and she pushed out with her thoughts, trying to somehow make it flow into Jalthrax somehow. She had watched Eliath do it, but she didn't know how it worked. No one had ever taught her. It was all instinct and fear alone. Her hands tingled with energy, and she pressed them against his body.

Slowly, she felt the energy begin to flow. She pushed harder, but it did not move any faster. But it did move. She could feel the energy leaving her hands and flowing through Jalthrax's body. Her hands jerked a little when the dragon's body heaved with a great breath, and she nearly cried out with joy. The last of the magic left her hands, and the blue glow faded beneath them. Elody leaned her head against Jalthrax to feel the deep, rhythmic rise and fall of his breathing.

Then she passed out and knew nothing else.

***

Alone.

That's all Rinn felt. Berym had left that morning. Elody wasn't speaking to him. He had no one. He thought he'd heard his aunt come in earlier, but she had not called out or made attempts at conversation. She probably didn't even know he was up in his room.

The candle on his desk sputtered a few times and then went out leaving long wisps of smoke. They floated up across the window where the full moon bathed his room in a soft glow. It was a foggy night, but Rinn could still see the position of the moon in the night sky. He closed his eyes with a deep sigh and looked down at the piece of paper in his hand.

Ariss's note had said he and the rest of the gang would be waiting for him. Rinn had been lying there thinking of what to do for hours. He had watched the candle growing smaller and smaller as the hours passed, a constant reminder that he needed to make a decision. Could he go now that he knew what he knew? It was so easy to steal from them when he knew nothing of their lives.

Damn you, Aunt Jelena.

Whether she meant to or not, she had thrown his head into confusion. Rinn suddenly found the idea of robbing someone a lot harder after seeing what it meant to the one who got robbed. The thought of doing a job wasn't as fun as it was a few nights ago.

But they would be waiting for him. Ariss had said it was a big job, and he knew they wouldn't go without him. If he didn't show up at the Coop, they would come looking for him.

Burying his face in his hands, he growled into them and then sprang up to sit on the side of the bed. He sat there a minute staring at the melted nub of wax that remained. Heaving another sigh, he got up and crept down the stairs. Reaching the bottom, a loud rumble startled him, and he almost leapt out of his boots. He muffled a quiet chuckle a moment later when he realized it was his aunt.

Her snoring continued softly as he stepped lightly across the entry to the study. Buried from sight behind the stacks of books, he found her sleeping in her reading chair. A giant tome lay open clutched against her chest, nearly dwarfing her entire torso in its pages. With a gentle hand, Rinn picked up one arm after the next and laid them to the side before lifting the book off of her and setting it on the stack beside the chair.

Jelena shifted slightly, but her breathing became much lighter without the weight on her chest, and her snoring grew softer. Rinn looked on and sighed deeply. When she was quiet, she reminded him so much of his mother. He ran his fingers lightly across her hair, careful not to touch her. With another sigh, he stepped away.

Taking care to stay silent, he vaulted back up the stairs with soft steps.

Twirling about his small room, he had his leather jerkin, belt, and dagger in place in quick order. He started to reach for the pouch of gold beneath his bed but then stopped. Nothing to celebrate tonight.

Is this really who I am now?

Whatever the job was, it was no doubt going to be robbing someone. Probably someone important judging by the weight Ariss had placed on his words. Was he going to just keep on stealing from people after what he'd seen? He couldn't do it, he decided. Stealing just wasn't fun anymore.

Resolved to go and tell Ariss and the gang he was out, Rinn turned to the window. A little smile crossed his lips when he realized there was no need to sneak out tonight. He skipped down the stairs and stopped at the bottom to wait for the telltale snoring from his aunt. A few deep breaths later, he quietly pulled the door open and stepped out into the night.

A thick fog immediately filled his vision. The lamps had all been lit going down the street, each one casting a glowing ring of light that marked his path. He wouldn't even need to take to the shadows tonight. The fog would be more than enough to hide his passage.

A shiver ran down Rinn's spine, and he felt his nerves falter. Telling his friends he was not coming along would not go over well, he knew. Despite their friendship, there was a very real chance they would beat him senseless. He silently hoped he knew them better than that, but something inside him harbored doubts.

Making his way through the fog, it took only a few minutes to make the trip. The front door to the Chicken

Coop stood open in front of him, as loud as ever. The fog tonight had done little to dampen the spirits of its patrons. The farmers were, no doubt, still celebrating their pay, and the rest were probably still reveling in the giant haul from a few nights before. Rinn wondered if the mood was as jovial in a place like the Dancing Unicorn across town. The merchants in that fine establishment were probably not celebrating as heartily.

Rinn put his head down and plunged into the steamy bar. The noise and laughter, usually enough to put him in the right mood, was overwhelming tonight. The oppressive heat of pressed bodies coupled with the fog pouring in through the open door had made the place nearly unbearable. Struggling to push past the throng of sweaty men and desperate women, he tried to make his way to the bar.

When he realized he didn't actually want a drink, he turned away from the bar and scanned the room. A quick glance around found no empty tables and no sign of his friends. The closeness of everything suddenly felt very uncomfortable. Any memories of fun in this place were washed away in a sea of sweat and raucous laughter.

A tap on his shoulder spun him around with his hand going instinctively for his dagger. He recognized Balk immediately, and his hand relaxed a little. But not completely.

"Outside in the alley," he said over the crowd and turned back out the door.

Rinn followed into the night, glad to at least be out in the open again. Balk disappeared around the corner into the alley behind the Coop, and Rinn dutifully followed. Hidden in the back by the thick fog, the rest of the gang was all there, including Delek from the other night.

"Finally," Ariss said. "Now we can move."

The others fell in behind him as he pushed past Rinn with a sour expression. Rinn started to say something, but the look on Ariss's face stopped him cold. There would be time to talk more when they stopped, he decided.

"Where are we headed?" Delek called out.

Ariss paid no attention and just kept walking without looking back, confident that everyone was following. Rinn fell into step beside Ferix and Balk with a questioning glance, but they both just shrugged and kept walking. Everyone picked up the pace to keep up with Ariss who was moving fast and with obvious purpose. If too much fog got between them all, they could lose sight of him.

"Not many guards out," Ferix said.

Rinn hadn't noticed it before, but he was right. A walk down a busy street like this one should have revealed at least one or two of the town guard on patrol. They always seemed to stay close to the Chicken Coop most nights, and with good reason. But tonight the streets were empty.

"Think the guild paid 'em off again?" Balk asked.

"Shut it, all of you," Ariss said from out in front.

The conversation ended quickly, everyone trudging along silently behind Ariss toward whatever their destination was. It wouldn't be long before they found out. Ariss suddenly stopped ahead of them and turned into an alley. With a shrug and a look back, Ferix followed in with Balk and Rinn behind him. Delek, acting as rear guard, pushed in after, forcing them all deeper into the shadows.

"That's where we're goin'," Ariss said looking out

across the street.

Rinn wasn't terribly familiar with this part of town, having had no real cause to ever go there. The thick fog made it hard to see, but he knew exactly where they were. He locked eyes with Ariss who only nodded behind him. Rinn turned around and let his gaze wander up the long spires of the building in front of them. It was just as he'd feared.

Havnor's temple of Threyl. One of the largest Threylian temples in all of Gondril.

Rinn shuddered. He could see some of the others shift uncomfortably, and more than a few nervous glances were tossed around. The whispers from the others told him they were all thinking the same thing.

"You wanna rob a church?" Delek asked.

"You see another place across the street?" Ariss shot back.

If Rinn hadn't already made up his mind this job wasn't for him, he needed no further convincing now. He spun around and walked straight up to Ariss, leaving little distance between their faces and spoke with his voice low.

"Can I talk to you?"

Ariss stared hard at him and looked past to where the others were watching the exchange. He nodded and motioned for Rinn to follow deeper into the alley. Once they were away from the others and separated by a layer of fog, Ariss turned back and stood with his arms crossed.

"I can't do this, Ariss."

"Never figured you for a holy man."

"I'm not, but that doesn't mean I can rob a church."

"What do you care who it is we rob? You didn't have

180

much problem robbing anyone else? Fact, as I recall, you're the one sweet talkin' 'em out of their life savings."

"That was before…"

"Before what?"

"Look, maybe Threyl called me to her breast, or whatever they say. Maybe I just don't think it's right, robbing a church. Anyway, I'm not doin' it."

His body tense, and with his hand straying to his dagger, Rinn turned to leave. He hoped in his heart that he and Ariss were as good of friends as he imagined. Otherwise one of them might not leave this alley. And he had a pretty good idea which.

"Nira's sick."

It wasn't the blow to the head he'd expected, but Rinn stopped dead just the same. He looked over his shoulder where Ariss was still standing, his shoulders slumped and his head down.

"Real sick," he said. "She's hangin' on, but they don't think she'll live another week."

Rinn turned around to face his friend.

"You never said."

"She's just a girl, Rinn."

Nira was Ariss's little girl. Six or seven? Rinn couldn't remember exactly. Her mother was a prostitute who'd died a few years ago. Of what, Rinn wasn't sure. Despite Ariss's rough exterior, his little girl meant everything to him. He'd often told Rinn, after far too many drinks, that he'd do anything for his little girl. Everything he did, the robbing, the beating, worse. He did it all to provide for her.

"I took her there," he pointed across the street. "And those sons of bitches wouldn't help her. They said we weren't *of* the church. That we didn't worship their *beloved goddess*, so they couldn't help her. She's just a girl. And they'll just let her die."

"Have you sent for someone else? Maybe my aunt can help her."

"I've sent for too many healers. Spent more money than I had for anyone who could help. Everything I took from the merchants the other night went for Nira. They all say the same thing. Can't be done without a priest."

Rinn could hear whispers down the alley and turned back to look. Unable to see anything but shapeless forms, his eyes trailed up the great spires of the temple once again. He stared at them for several seconds before turning back.

"I tried going to the temple of Ildun," Ariss said. "I've tithed there a few times over the years. Mostly before a big job, when I needed the luck, but they've seen me in there. They know I've given 'em money through the years. They wanted to help but didn't have a priest strong enough. Sons of bitches had the nerve to wish me luck as I carried my little girl out of there."

"What will robbing the temple of Threyl do to save her? You plan on stealing a cleric in there?"

They both forced a chuckle.

"When they wouldn't help her, I got desperate. I... I went to the temple of Vorrod."

Ariss cast his eyes down, and Rinn shuddered uncontrollably. The thought of even stepping in their temple told him how desperate his friend must have been to try.

"They said they could help her," Ariss said.

"I didn't think they did stuff like that. I thought they were happy to let people die so long as they were sent to Vorrod."

"They are, and I didn't figure on them helping me either. But they said because her death wouldn't be violent enough, she wouldn't go to Vorrod and that they could help her. But it would cost."

"How much?"

"I'd like to say too much."

"I have some money saved up. You can have it. You don't have to rob a church."

"They don't want money, Rinn."

Rinn shuddered again. He could only guess at what the Deathbringers might want in exchange for a life.

"They want some gem from inside *that* temple," Ariss said.

He pointed across the street, but Rinn just shook his head and muttered no.

"I bargained for her life, and that was the price."

"No, no, no."

"I don't have a choice, Rinn. If I don't do this, Nira'll die. Likely within days."

Rinn sighed and looked into the eyes of his friend. He tried to say no again, because that's what he really wanted to do, but he couldn't. The pain inside those eyes was too much to bear. His head dropped to his chest.

"I'll help," he said.

Ariss looked up with a little smile.

"But only to get this gem," Rinn said. "Nothing else comes out of that temple."

"What do I tell the others? They'll expect something for the job."

"Can you even trust them?"

"They're loyal to me. And if they cross me, they know I'll find them."

"Then you and I will pay them together out of our

own pockets. That should be enough to make them happy and keep their mouths shut."

Ariss walked forward and put his hand on Rinn's shoulder.

"You're a good friend, Rinn. I'm glad I saved you all those years ago."

He gave Rinn's shoulder a gentle squeeze and smiled before walking past him to the rest of the waiting men. With one last sigh, Rinn turned back to follow. They walked together into the midst of the others and all turned as one to stare at the great temple.

"We're looking for a gem," Ariss said. "A ruby. Big one. Nothing else comes out of there. We do this right, we'll all end up with some nice coin for our troubles."

"What're the guards like in there?" Ferix asked.

"Pretty light. They keep the damn front door open at night if you can believe that, but we'll never make it in that way without being spotted. Word is the ruby is on the main altar, but we may still have to look around for it."

They all nodded and looked back across the street.

"There," Rinn said, pointing. "Second story window with no light on the left side. We can go in through there."

Another round of agreement, and they each crept across the street one after another. One by one they boosted and pulled each other up through the window with Rinn following last. Peering over the window, he saw the room was a simple sleeping chamber. A single bed lay against one wall with a small writing desk next to it. The others were already pulling on their masks as he came up and over the windowsill. A quick spell, and he had his own disguise magically in place.

"How is that better than just putting on a mask?" Delek asked.

"Easier to look innocent without a black mask covering your face. Plus I can't breathe in those things."

Ariss shushed them and then went to the door. He gave them all another quick description of the ruby they were looking for, and they were off. Checking the hall each time, Ariss sent them out one by one. When it was just he and Rinn left, he smiled and gave a little wave as he went out the door, leaving Rinn alone in the dark room.

Last one. This is the last one. For Nira.

Rinn stepped up and peeked out into the hall. Seeing no one, not even his companions, he crept out and pulled the door closed behind him. If the size of the hallways in this place were any indication of the overall size of the church, it was huge. Three men could walk abreast and not touch elbows. With torches every twenty feet or so, Rinn found many shadows to stick to as he made his way around.

He knew he was on the far side of the church, and he wanted to get to the middle. Rinn turned a few corners and started to realize the temple might be bigger than he had imagined. He suddenly found he wasn't exactly sure how to get back to their empty little room.

Turning down another hall, he could see flickers of light spilling out from beneath a few of the doors, and he moved to the opposite side of the hall to avoid them. He gingerly opened a darkened door to find it empty and made note of it just in case he'd need a place to hide.

Rounding another corner, he faced another dark hall. He'd seen no one so far. No guards, no priests, not one of his companions. It was like the whole place was empty.

At least that was the thought that passed through his mind before he heard a shout. It cut through the stillness like a stone breaking the surface of a pond, and Rinn felt it ripple through him. A scream followed it. Then metal boots running.

Rinn's dagger was in his hand before he realized it. More shouting echoed around him, and the sound of the boots was getting louder and a lot closer. The whole temple was coming to life around him, and he was just standing there in the middle of a hall. He spun and darted back around the corner, running for the empty room he had just passed. Up ahead he felt as much as heard the sound of heavy running. He yanked the door handle and ducked inside.

The room was surprisingly bright for being empty. In the second it took Rinn to realize this wasn't an empty room, his eyes took everything in and fell to the woman sitting up on the bed. The grip on his dagger tightened, and he stood frozen in front of her. A low candle sat beside her on the small desk, and her hands were both holding a large book in her lap. She started to open her mouth, but Rinn cut her off.

"Don't scream," he said.

Her eyes flicked down, and he followed her gaze to the dagger in his hand. He tucked it behind his back and into his belt and held both of his hands up.

"Don't scream. I won't hurt you."

Outside the door he heard the thundering of metal boots run down the hall.

"Why shouldn't I scream?" she said at last.

She didn't sound frightened. More... curious.

"Because I'm not going to hurt you."

She closed the tome in her lap and pushed it off onto

the bed.

"Then what are you here for? And who are you?"

"I'm Ril. I came here to find something to save a little girl's life."

She folded her hands in her lap and looked him up and down.

"If you need healing, there are better ways to ask for it. Sneaking into our temple in the middle of the night is a sure way to *not* receive help."

"We already tried to get help for her. Your priests turned her away."

She eyed him warily and shook her head.

"You're lying. We turn no one away who needs our help. Threyl would not let us turn away those she has made."

"Well, someone did. She's dying, and I have to help save her."

"There is nothing here but the priests that can save her. You'll find no magic that can save your little girl. If you leave now and bring her to me tomorrow, I will help her. And if I cannot, I will find someone who can."

They both looked up as more boots came running down the hall outside.

"It's too late for that," Rinn said.

The boots stopped and a fist pounded on the door.

"Yes?" the woman said.

"Are you all right, Lady Oryna?"

She hopped up from the bed and pushed Rinn to the far side of the room as she passed him. Opening the door just a crack, she peeked out.

"Yes, of course. Is something the matter?"

"Thieves, m'lady. There are thieves running through the temple."

She made a dramatic gesture of turning her head and peering around her room. She locked eyes with Rinn for only a second before returning to the guard.

"Well, I see no thieves in my room."

"Of course, m'lady. I was just making sure you were safe. It might be best to lock your door until the temple is secure."

"Thank you," she said and then pushed the door closed. She turned back to face Rinn and put her back to the wall.

"Is that what you are? Thieves?"

Rinn looked long into her eyes and then dropped his chin to his chest.

"Yes," he said. "At least I was."

"It looks to me like you still are."

"Only for the little girl."

He looked up into her eyes, and she stared long and hard at him.

"Bring the girl to me, and I will help her."

"I can't. She's not mine. My friend has found someone who will heal her, but it will cost us."

The woman shook her head and huffed. Stepping across the room, she reached under her bed and pulled out a small, wooden chest. Popping the latch in one quick motion, she opened it and pulled out a leather pouch. Slapping the lid shut again, she turned and grabbed Rinn's hand and placed the pouch in it.

"If you will not let me help her, then take this and find someone else."

Rinn shook his head and pushed back at her.

"I can't. We'll find what we need to heal her. I can't take your money."

"So, you'll steal from my church but not from me? We

are one and the same. Take it. If you bring her to me tomorrow, you can bring it back to me as well."

Rinn pushed back again, so she grabbed it from his hand and slapped it against his chest. It stung, and he instinctively drew up his hand to grab it as she pulled her hand away.

"Go."

She shoved Rinn toward the door. He turned back to say something.

"Go," she said, cutting him off.

Rinn nodded and turned back to the door. Opening it just a crack to peer out, he checked the hall for guards. Seeing none, he gave her one last look before stepping out and pulling the door closed behind him. Moving quicker now, he dodged from shadow to shadow trying to stay hidden as he moved through the temple. Ahead and around the corner he could hear the sounds of a scuffle. He almost ran the other direction but then thought of his friends.

Glancing around the corner, he saw Delek fighting someone. Not a guard, by his clothes. He wore no armor, only a night shirt. But he carried a big metal shield and a long mace that he was currently trying to bash Delek's head in with. Delek dodged a swing and stabbed back with a short sword, but the man blocked with his shield.

Rinn stood frozen, not knowing what to do. The man's back was too him and completely undefended. A flick of his wrist could put a dagger into him. A short run and a stab, and the man would be dead. But still Rinn found himself frozen in indecision.

Before he could react, Delek made his decision easy. A stab of his sword broke through the man's defense and caught him in the gut. He screamed, and Rinn saw blood pour out and splash across the stone floor. Rinn fell back around the corner and closed his eyes as he looked to the sky. The blood in his ears was pounding, and he prayed silently for Threyl to save her faithful servant.

He heard Delek say something he couldn't hear, but the tone was clear. Rinn peeked around the corner again, and the man was huddled on the floor clutching his stomach and scooting along the floor. Rinn had no trouble deciding his action then. Taking two steps back down the hall, he ran around the corner as if he'd just burst onto the scene.

"Delek!"

Delek looked up from where he was about to stab the man again. Rinn leapt over the prone man and gently pushed Delek down the hall in the other direction.

"We have to go. There are guards everywhere. We have to get out of here."

Delek looked down at the wounded man again and then back up to Rinn and nodded. They ran beside each other down the hall and came around another corner. Rinn could feel that they were nearer to the center of the temple and wondered if anyone had yet found the ruby. He still had a job to do. They saw a big, bronze door up ahead of them on the right and went for it without discussion. As Rinn flung it open, they pushed their way into the main altar chamber of the church.

Rows and rows of carved wooden benches lay before them, and they were standing up on a raised platform looking down at them. Thankfully, the hall was empty. Rinn pushed the door quietly closed behind them, and they both stood for a moment catching their breath.

"Where to now?" Delek asked.

Rinn looked around, and his eyes settled on the set of

double doors at the far end.

"Those doors will lead right out to the front of the church."

"We run for it?"

"You wanna stay and fight?"

Delek seemed to ponder it for a second.

"No, I guess not."

They walked down the steps that separated the altar from the rest of the benches and stopped suddenly when they heard a scuffle outside the big doors. Rinn turned to look back at the door they'd come through when something caught his eye. Looking back up at the altar above him on the stage he saw a giant, red ruby encased in an elaborate gold setting at the front of the lectern. He spun back to say something to Delek, but he was already at the double doors listening intently.

Rinn leapt up the steps to the altar and drew out his dagger. He went to wedge it in but stopped just short of touching it. Reaching out slowly with the tip of his dagger, he tapped the gold setting and then jerked his arm back. When nothing happened, he reached out with his hand and repeated the process. Satisfied that Threyl wouldn't strike him dead just for touching it, he jammed the tip of his dagger beneath the ruby.

Closing his eyes and turning his head away, he applied a little pressure. The ruby didn't budge. Using the palm of his hand, he hammered the dagger a little deeper beneath the gem and then pried with all his might. A clink of metal and a sudden pop sent the ruby tumbling toward the ground where Rinn reached his hand out and caught it. He held it out at arms length and turned his head away again. When a few seconds had passed, and his hand hadn't erupted in holy flames, Rinn shrugged and tucked it into his belt pouch.

Skipping back down the steps, Delek turned back as Rinn bounded over to him. The sounds of battle outside the door had died down, and Delek finally mustered up the courage to open one door and peek out.

"Looks clear," he said over his shoulder.

Opening the door wider, he poked his head out.

"Do you think we can make it out the front?" Delek asked.

"Probably guarded. Better to find a side room and jump out a window."

Delek nodded and pulled the door open. Taking one cautious step after another, he crept out and then turned for a staircase leading back up. Rinn fell in behind him and was happy to let him lead the way if they got into any trouble. Rinn wasn't sure he could do more than run if it came to a fight.

They reached the top of the stairs and immediately heard more fighting around the next corner. Delek glanced down the hall.

"Ferix and Balk, fighting," he said.

Delek charged around the corner to help and Rinn silently cursed his luck. Drawing his dagger, he charged after Delek and toward the fight. Ferix and Balk were fighting two of the temple guards as far as Rinn could guess, and they didn't look to be doing too badly. As Delek joined the fight from behind, they quickly had it in hand. Rinn held back a little but not too much.

As the two guards fell bleeding to the ground, Ferix and Balk looked up and smiled. Then a crossbow bolt took Balk through the neck. Blood burst from the other side and splashed Ferix's face as the tip exited. A second bolt caught Ferix in the chest, nearly burying itself completely into his body as he turned to find the source of the attack. Rinn could hear shouts from around the corner, but he wasn't close enough to see. Delek stumbled back away from the dying thieves and bumped into Rinn who was turning to run.

Seeing darkness beneath the door to his side, Rinn tested the handle and pushed it open. Delek followed behind him, and they shoved the door shut. Rinn sighed with relief when he saw a window against the far wall. Three quick steps, and he threw his leg up over the ledge and jumped out. Swishing his hand in one quick motion, his descent slowed suddenly, allowing him to gently float to the ground.

Rinn looked back up to the window to see Delek staring is disbelief.

"You have to jump!" Rinn shouted up.

"Do that thing and make me float!" Delek called down.

"I can't cast it on you while you're *up there!*"

Rinn could hear more guards, some of them outside the temple now, but he stayed and waited for Delek.

"Jump, dammit!" Rinn yelled.

Delek cursed as he climbed out and hung himself down by his fingertips before letting go and falling to the cobblestone street below. He hit with a yelp. He rolled as he landed, absorbing some of the blow, but when Rinn tried to help him stand, his ankle wouldn't support much weight.

"Come on," Rinn said.

Helping him down the street toward the nearest alley, Rinn held Delek around the waist and let him lean on his shoulder. They limped along together down a few streets before they were a safe distance away. Once they reached the shadows, they both visibly relaxed. Making their way through the backstreets as quickly as they could with Delek's wounded ankle, they managed to reach the Chicken Coop without being spotted. They both collapsed in a heap when they finally wound their way into the back alley that was the meeting point.

As the magic of his spell faded, Rinn's disguise dissolved, but he barely noticed. He wasn't sure how long they lay there waiting. His panting had slowed to deep, heavy breaths when he finally sat up. Delek struggled to sit, and Rinn helped pull him up. They waited there for Ariss to return, both knowing the rest of their crew would not be meeting them. Rinn was beginning to wonder if Ariss had survived when he finally sauntered around the corner, the look on his face anything but pleased.

"Gods! Damn guards were everywhere all at once!"

He collapsed onto a box beside them and looked around the alley.

"No sign of Ferix or Balk?"

"Dead," Delek said.

"You sure?"

They both nodded, and Ariss sighed and shook his head.

"Once the alarm sounded, wasn't nothing we could do but run," Ariss said.

"I killed three before I ran," Delek said. "One of 'em a priest."

"I killed two guards and a priest I woke up when I tried to hide in his room. At least we gave better'n we got. Never did find the ruby we were looking for."

Rinn reached into his belt pouch and pulled the ruby out with a quick motion. He held it up in his hand so that the light from one of the windows in the Chicken Coop made it sparkle in the dark alley. Ariss's eyes went wide and then his lips smiled wider.

"You son of a bitch," he said.

"Where'd you get that?" Delek asked, staring as well.

"Pried it off the front of the altar when we were trapped."

"You son of a bitch!" Ariss yelled. "I knew you'd get it! Threyl be praised!"

They all laughed as Ariss snatched the ruby from Rinn's open hand and held it up in front of his eyes.

"Blessings of Threyl, boys!" Ariss said. "We're all gonna be stinkin' rich once the Deathbringers pay up for this beauty!"

Rinn cocked his head, but as the words hit him, his eyes turned cold. Ariss must have noticed because his smile suddenly disappeared.

"And I'll be able to get Nira healed," he quickly added.

He reached out and patted Rinn on the back.

"Thank you for saving my little girl, Rinn."

Rinn nodded and stood to leave.

"Where are you going?" Ariss asked. "We have to celebrate!"

"Two friends died tonight. I don't feel like celebrating. I'm just glad Nira will be all right."

"Oh, come on, Rinn. Have a drink with us. For Ferix and Balk."

Rinn looked down at Delek who was nodding and then back up to Ariss who was smiling and nodded his head.

"That's the spirit!" Ariss said. "Come on, I'm buyin'."

Rinn reached down to help Delek up and pulled his

arm around his shoulder to support him. They hobbled into the Chicken Coop behind Ariss who they could already hear triumphantly shouting that the next round was on him.

***

Rinn stumbled over the threshold of the Chicken Coop and staggered out into the night. He felt a shove from behind as Ariss fell into his back, and they both tumbled out into the street, Ariss landing on top of him. Their laughter filled the silent street.

"You guys drink like women," Delek said as he came out behind them. "You didn't even finish four pints. I drank five, and I'm not drunk at all."

Rinn rolled Ariss to the side where he lay catching his breath and then sat up in the street.

"I've really gotta get home," Rinn said. "My aunt will start wondering where I am."

"I'm glad I don't have a mom," Ariss said.

"I *don't* have a mom."

"I didn't mean like that. I meant like no one telling me what to do."

"She just worries," Rinn said.

"Nira worries about me too. She's tough though. Been takin' care of herself since she was four seems like."

"We're gonna get her healed up," Rinn said.

Ariss's brow creased, and he tried to blink his eyes open.

"Yes," he finally said. "I'll go see them priests tomorrow."

"I'm going," Delek said.

He turned down the street and tried to walk straight but didn't have much luck. With his ankle, he managed to look more hurt than completely drunk.

"He's drunk," Rinn said, eliciting another loud laugh from Ariss. "Come on. We'd better get home before someone robs us in the street."

"No one's gonna rob us! I'd bring down the whole weight of the guild on 'em if someone was stupid enough to try that!"

"Still… Still stupid to be out on the street like this."

Rinn put his arm around Ariss's waist and pulled him closer so they could use one another to steady themselves. Slowly, one step at a time, they walked up the street. There was a lot of swaying, but they kept moving forward and didn't fall at least.

"Are those priests really gonna heal Nira if we give them that thing?"

"Huh? Oh, right. They said they would. Damn Deathbringers may creep me out, but I think they're honorable. They'll give me what's owed."

"What was that you said about us being rich?"

"Did I say that? Well, I figure they want this thing so bad, they can heal Nira *and* throw in a little coin for the trouble. Ferix and Balk died in there. They owe us somethin' for that."

"You're gonna try and change the deal?"

"Hey, I never said that *I* was honorable!"

Ariss broke into laugher again, and Rinn chuckled beside him while trying to keep them both upright. With fingers too nimble to be drunk, Rinn reached into the small pouch on Ariss's belt and plucked out the ruby. With a quick hand, he dropped it into his own pouch and then staggered along after Ariss. They continued their slow walk through the empty streets until they reached an intersection in the lanes.

"This is where you get off," Rinn said as he pulled his

arm away.

Ariss looked around confused for a second and then nodded.

"Yup. Looks like it."

He turned left toward his own home while Rinn kept going straight. He kept his steps slow as he stumbled on, eventually stopping to lean against another house where he watched Ariss disappear from sight. When he could no longer see him, Rinn pulled himself up straight and brushed off his jerkin.

He jogged the rest of the way home.

When he reached the door, he made a few quick movements with his hands, summoning a ball of magical light to his palm, and pushed the door open. Cupping his hands together to cover the light, he waited for several seconds, listening. Satisfied that he heard nothing, he tiptoed through the stacks of books and found Aunt Jelena still snoring softly in her chair, right where he'd left her. Careful to keep the light from her, he pulled the blanket she had draped across the back of the chair out from behind her and laid it gently over her, tucking the edges in around her body.

Padding up the stairs, Rinn reached the top and ducked into his room. He set the ball of magical light in his hand down before stripping off his jerkin and laying it gently over the chair that was pushed under his little table. With a wave of his hand the light went out, leaving him bathed in the full moonlight pouring through his window.

Rinn sat on the edge of his bed and took the ruby from his pouch. Holding it up to sparkle in the moonlight, he admired it for a second before shoving it under his pillow and falling into bed.

Despite fear and a sense of dread, the part of him that felt at peace found sleep quickly.

CHAPTER THIRTEEN

CHANGE

ELODY STARTLED AWAKE when Jalthrax shifted beneath her. Her whole body ached, and her eyes stung from the morning sun when she tried to open them.

"Thrax?" she said hesitantly.

The little dragon opened his eyes and stared at her.

"Are you okay?"

Jalthrax stared back at her, unblinking.

"I'm so sorry," she said, her voice barely a whisper.

Elody closed her eyes. Her body started to shudder with silent sobs as she leaned against him. *I almost lost him. And it would have been my fault.*

She felt a nudge on her arm and looked up. Jalthrax blew a puff of cold air in her face that made the tears on her cheeks cold.

"I'm sorry," she said.

He huffed again, blasting her with more freezing air.

"I know. It was foolish. It won't happen again."

Jalthrax leaned in to nudge her arm again and push her off of his body. Elody rested back on her knees, and the dragon moved his head to lay in her lap. It was how he said he was sorry when they had an argument.

"You have nothing to be sorry for," she said. "I should have listened to Eliath."

He rubbed against her chest, and she laid her arm across his neck. Another gentle nudge reminded her to keep rubbing, so she did. Elody sighed and laid her head down on Jalthrax's long neck. They lay together like that for several minutes while Elody's mind drifted between thanks that they were both alive and thoughts of what could have happened.

Lying there against him, she sighed deeply and hugged him tight. The dragon let out a squawk. Beneath the silver scales that seemed to grow larger and thicker with each day, she could hear the slow, rhythmic beat of his heart. Her whole body rose and fell with each breath.

Her ear pressed against him, she heard a low rumble from within. She suddenly realized her own hunger and lifted her head.

"Can you walk?"

Jalthrax picked his head up and then slowly got to his feet. Elody stood on wobbly legs and held onto the dragon for support.

"I'm really hungry. Let's go get some food."

Jalthrax didn't fly. He walked beside Elody where they could support each other.

***

Rinn leaned over one of many tall stacks of books in his aunt's library and stood to one side of a window peering out. He'd been watching the street outside the house all morning but had so far seen nothing that should alarm him.

Which only made him more nervous.

"You expecting someone?" his aunt said from the kitchen.

Rinn snapped the curtain down and looked back at her.

"No. I just had some trouble with a couple of guys yesterday, and I was worried they might come by here and cause problems."

"Well, no need to worry. No one is getting in here."

She went back to her work with a little whistle on her lips, and Rinn went back to his window. After watching for a little while longer, he finally went to the front door.

"I've got an errand to run," he called out. "I'll be back in a bit."

"Be safe!"

"I hope," Rinn muttered under his breath.

Opening the door just a crack, he peered outside for a second before opening it further and poking his head out. Satisfied that the street was clear, he stepped out and pulled it closed behind him. As quickly as he dared without arousing suspicion, he slipped into an alley and safely among the shadows. Picking his way through the back streets, Rinn kept one eye behind him, but he saw nothing.

When he reached his destination, Rinn stood across the street in the same alley he'd stood in last night and stared. The spires of the temple of Threyl were big through the fog last night, but in clear skies, they towered over the whole city. As though they were built to touch the heavens themselves. Rinn could only gawk.

A slight, almost imperceptible, sound from down the street pulled him out of his reverie. His head snapped in the direction he thought it came from but once again saw no one. He turned back to the temple with a sigh. Taking a deep breath, he stepped out of the alley and walked toward the great, golden doors of the temple. A light push found them opening wide as if by their own will.

Rinn stepped inside and froze.

The foyer of the church was crawling with temple guards, and every one of them turned to glare at him as he entered. With a disarming smile, Rinn put his hands up in a gesture of peace, which seemed to relax them a bit. A few of the guards directly in front of him moved to the side to reveal an even larger and ornate set of doors ahead of him. With a start, Rinn realized they must have thought he was there to pray. Not being one to make them wrong when they were obviously in a foul mood, Rinn put his head down and slipped quietly past them all and into the chapel.

The rows of pews were completely empty. Only a small group of priests knelt near the front where they were crowded in a circle around the altar and praying loudly. He watched them for a moment not knowing whether to stay or run. The hole in the altar stared at him like an empty eye. The feeling of it staring into his soul made him spin around to leave.

"Are you here to pray?"

Rinn started at the voice and nearly bumped into the robed figure in his path. His eyes went wide, and he did his best to hide his surprise when he saw who it was.

"Would you like me to pray for you?" Oryna asked.

Rinn cast his eyes down and shook his head.

"There's no need to be shy. Many people come every day and ask for Threyl's blessing. That is why we are here after all. To help her chosen people."

"Are we her chosen?" Rinn asked without looking up and making sure to keep his voice low.

"Of course. We are her creations. Threyl promised

when we were first created that she would always watch over us. It was her vow to mankind."

Despite his better judgement, Rinn looked up and into her eyes.

"And you believe she still keeps that vow?"

"Threyl does not break a vow."

Rinn took a moment to look at her face. He had seen her last night, but in his rush to get out of the church alive, he hadn't directed much attention to her. Her face was younger than he remembered. She didn't look much older than he was, but there was a worldly sadness behind her eyes. Oryna tilted her head at his staring, and he looked down quickly.

"So you help people because she asks you to?"

"Because she allows us to. She has never asked me to do anything, but neither has she denied me when I ask of her."

"You've never turned anyone away?" he asked after several seconds passed.

"Never. The priests of this church have healed some of the most vile men I have ever met. It is not for us to judge who should be saved. If Threyl deemed one unworthy of help, she would refuse us our gifts to heal them."

"And has she ever refused?"

"I cannot speak for everyone, but she has never refused me. Good or bad, we are all her children."

Rinn nodded and looked back at the ground. Oryna turned her head and nodded to the priests kneeling at the altar.

"Someone broke into our temple last night."

"Oh?"

"Thankfully, no one was hurt."

"No one was hurt?" he asked.

"Some were wounded, but we were able to heal them before any life was lost. One of the thieves who broke in was killed, and another badly wounded, but we were able to save his life."

"You saved someone who tried to rob you?"

"It was not for us to judge his guilt. He was turned over to the city authorities once we had healed him."

"That was very kind of you."

"Sadly, something *was* taken from the temple."

She raised her hand and pointed at the altar.

"An artifact of great power used by members of the church to heal the sick."

Rinn looked to where she was pointing and saw that more priests had gathered around the defiled altar. All of them were kneeling and praying loudly enough for him to hear them even across the great chapel.

"It healed the sick?"

"Not specifically. It allowed us all to have a higher connection to the goddess. With it we were able to channel greater healing magic from her. Without it, I fear some of the sickest who come to us will be beyond our help."

"Why would you leave such a powerful artifact out for anyone to steal?"

"Because it was a gift from Threyl and meant to be seen by her people."

Rinn thought for a second before responding.

"Still a stupid place to put something so precious."

"Well, after last night I might agree with you. But I imagine if it is returned it will go right back to its rightful place on the altar for all to see."

"What makes you think you'll get it back?"

"The goddess has taught me to believe in the goodness of her people."

Rinn looked her in the eye and nodded. Reluctantly, he turned to leave.

"Wait," she said. "What's your name?"

He stopped and looked down again.

"Rinn."

"Do you want me to pray for you, Rinn?"

"Won't do any good."

"If it's all the same to you, I think I will."

Rinn left without looking back. As he left the chapel, he reached into his vest and pulled out the pouch Oryna had given him the night before. He dropped it into the offer box and hurried out.

***

Rinn's thoughts were swirling as he left the temple. He knew now what he had to do, but he knew that it might cost him dearly. He walked up the street back toward home. Lost in reflection, he didn't notice his surroundings until he felt someone in front of him. He moved to step around them, and they moved to the side to block his path. It was then he realized his mistake.

Ariss was smiling like an old friend. An old friend with a couple more friends standing behind him.

"Rinn. I've been looking for you."

"I was running errands for my aunt."

Rinn took in his surroundings as quickly and fully as he could without whipping his head around him in a panic. It wouldn't do him any good to look like he was about to run. He still had a chance of talking his way out of this if he thought fast.

"Something about needing a priest for a birth next week," Rinn said. "She asked me to go to the temple and find one."

Two men behind Ariss. Another down the alley. He could feel someone else behind him, but he couldn't turn and look without appearing nervous.

"Sure thing," Ariss said. "I was kinda surprised to see you going in there after last night. But, I guess they wouldn't really recognize you with your disguise off, so it's probably safe."

Rinn shrugged with a smile.

"No one said anything or tried to run me through, so that's a good sign. Lot of guards in there though. They look pretty pissed. We should probably lay low for a while."

"Why? No one knows who to go after as far as I know. You know any reason they'd come after us?"

Rinn looked around and shrugged again.

"Not that I can think of. Unless Ferix or Balk told 'em something."

Ariss's eyes narrowed.

"I thought you said they were dead."

Damn.

"Maybe not," Rinn said. "I, uh… I heard the guards talking about healing and saving one of them. Don't know which though. They gave him over to the watch."

"Poor son of a bitch, whichever it was. Shoulda just let him die. I don't think the law is gonna be too easy on someone stealing an artifact of the church."

"I wouldn't think so."

"Funny thing about that, Rinn. See, when I woke up this morning, you can imagine my surprise when I found that the ruby wasn't in my belt anymore."

"What? Where'd it go? Maybe you dropped it at the bar. We need to get over there and search the place before they open up!"

"No, no. I'm sure I had it when I left the bar. I touched my hand to my pouch as we walked out the door to make sure. Lotta thieves in the Coop, you know. Can never be too suspicious."

The two behind Ariss, neither of whom Rinn recognized, both chuckled, and he heard another laugh from behind him, confirming his earlier suspicion. Rinn forced a laugh, but his entire body was taut. He could feel the sweat above his hairline just waiting to drip down his face.

He knows. He knows, and he knows I'm just stalling for time.

"Maybe it fell out along the street somewhere," Rinn said. "We were both pretty drunk last night when we left. We should all go back and scour the route from the bar to your house."

"You don't think Delek might've taken it when we were both drunk?"

"Uh… I don't know. I don't think so. Delek seemed a decent enough guy."

"Well, he seemed pretty convincing when I asked him this morning. He was very insistent that he didn't have it. After I sacked his place and cut off a few fingers, I believed he was telling the truth."

Run. Run now.

Rinn's knees went weak. They trembled and threatened to give out and drop him to the street where he would no doubt lose what little breakfast he'd had. His stomach churned, and he felt the bile rise in his throat.

"Thing is," Ariss continued, "after I cut off his second finger, he had a sudden recollection that you didn't actually drink that much last night. Certainly not as much as him or me. He thought maybe you were just playing drunk and maybe *you* took it."

Rinn felt the sweat roll down his forehead and knew he was done. *He's just playing with me. He knew I took it before he ever spoke a word.*

"I gotta hand it to you, Rinn. Not pointing the finger at Delek?"

He stopped and laughed hard.

"Pointing the finger."

The other men laughed too. Rinn didn't even bother faking it.

"Not pointing the finger at Delek, though? You're a good man. A good friend to a man you've only met twice. Me, on the other hand? I'm beginning to doubt our friendship."

"I am your friend, Ariss."

"Then why do you want to kill me, Rinn?"

"I don't want to kill you!"

"You took it. I know you did. While we were drunk, if you even were drunk. You snatched it right out of my pouch."

"I would never hurt you."

"Do you know what those Deathbringers are gonna do to me if I don't show up with that ruby?"

He let the words hang in the air. No one dared move.

"They're going to kill me, Rinn. If I don't show up with my half of the bargain, they're going to kill me. They'd love to do it. One more soul for their ugly god."

Rinn wanted to run, to hide. *Can I let Ariss die? Is that the right thing to do?* His thoughts were going in every direction, and he needed time to make sense of them. If he didn't return the gem, sick people might die in his place. He needed time to think, but Ariss didn't look like he was in a giving mood.

"Let me go and talk to them," Rinn said. "I'll make some other deal."

"Doesn't work that way, friend. You don't renege on Deathbringers."

"I'm sorry," Rinn whispered, his head dropping.

"What was that?"

Rinn looked him in the eyes.

"I'm sorry. I can't let sick people die because you chose to make a deal with some bad people."

"What about Nira?" he shouted. "You'd let her die?"

Rinn locked eyes again and glared hard.

"Ahh, you know," Ariss said with a shrug. "Worth a shot, right? Give me the ruby, Rinn, or I'll cut your fingers off. Maybe the whole damn hand. If I'm feeling generous, I'll do the left one like I did Delek and leave you with your good one."

Rinn folded his arms.

"You won't hurt me," he said.

"We aren't the friends you think we are, Rinn."

"Oh, I know that now. You won't hurt me because of what I can do for you. Don't think I don't know about your rise through the guild. And don't think I don't know why. Because you've been pulling off these big jobs and playing the boss. That's all me, and you know it. You need me and my magic to pull those jobs, otherwise you'd be just another thug collecting down in the bazaar."

Ariss's arms shot out fast, catching Rinn off guard and shoving him backward. He stumbled only a few steps before falling into the arms of the unseen man behind him. The man pushed him back to his feet, and Rinn stumbled forward another step to stop back in front of Ariss.

"You probably think you're smart, eh?" Ariss said. "Well, I don't need you anymore. My position within the guild is secured, so you're not as damned important as you think yourself."

Rinn let his hand drop to his sides and bent his legs a little to be ready to spring.

"On account of what we had, I'll let you live. But I've run out of patience. Give me the gem, and I won't lay a hand on you. Refuse, and I'll take a hand from you. Maybe both if I have to. Either way, I'm gettin' that ruby."

"I've already hidden it someplace safe and told someone in the church where to find it."

Ariss slumped and sighed.

"Rinn. Just tell me where it is, and you can go. Don't make me do this. I promise it won't hurt me as much as it'll hurt you. In fact, it really won't hurt me at all. I promise you that."

"I won't. You'll have to kill me. And don't be a goblin and let one of these guys do the job for you. You were always willing to let someone else do the dirty work, weren't you Ariss? Be a man and do it yourself for once."

"Oh, I'll show you—"

His threat was cut short as Rinn lunged forward and slammed his fist into his chin mid-sentence. Ariss let out a yelp as blood spurted from his mouth, but Rinn didn't see it because he was already moving past him. Slipping around a stunned Ariss, Rinn already had his dagger in hand as the two behind Ariss were still gaping in amazement. Rinn wasn't about to wait on them to recover.

He stabbed his dagger into one, easily slipping

beneath his leather jerkin and into soft flesh. Rinn was pulling his shortsword with his other hand before the man realized he'd been stabbed and cried out. The other beside him recovered enough to grab for his own sword, but Rinn was moving too fast. Slamming him with his shoulder, Rinn pressed his sword arm against him and hit with enough force to throw him back a step.

Free of all obstacles, Rinn took off at a full run.

He heard shouts and screams of pain and anger behind him, but he didn't care. He ran as fast as he could. He heard a loud rattling sound behind him followed by a thundering crack that made him duck instinctively. He tempted a look back and heard a thwack as a crossbow bolt struck the wall next to his head and exploded into shards of wood. He saw the man who was previously behind him reloading while the others were already taking up the chase.

Got to get someplace safe.

Rinn ducked down an alley to at least get out of sight of that crossbow and then pumped his legs harder to put some distance between them all. He came to a smaller cross street and turned up that heading back toward home. He had the brief thought to maybe run back to the temple. No way Ariss could get him in there. But he'd left the ruby hiding in his bed at home, and he knew Ariss would look there.

He didn't relish the thought of putting his aunt in real danger, but he had nowhere else to go. Ariss was his only real friend, and he'd seen how much that meant. The only safe place he could trust was home. And he did feel safe there, though he didn't know why. It was just another old house in a row of old houses, and Ariss knew it well. He knew exactly where Rinn would run.

Up ahead, Rinn saw movement in the periphery of his vision. Up high. A man jumped from the low roof of a building and landed on the street in front of him. Rinn didn't recognize him, but the shortsword in his hand spoke volumes about his intentions.

Rinn started to break left down another alley, but a flash of something in that direction caught his eye and he stopped in his tracks. Another man he hadn't seen earlier was coming down the alley toward him. Ariss must have brought more men with him than Rinn had counted. His power in the guild had grown if he was able to get this much muscle for a job.

Rinn was trapped.

He could run back the way he came, but he had no idea how far behind him the others were. He had to keep moving forward. And these two were in his way.

Rinn tried to find a way he could engage them one at a time, but they wouldn't have it. They advanced steadily from each direction toward him, and all he could do was back up. Tightening his stance and the grip on his weapon, he waited for them.

They came at him shoulder to shoulder, both grinning wide. Rinn wanted to avoid a fight if he could, but they didn't look to be in the mood for a chat. Still, Rinn held his stance and waited. Berym had often told him that two on one usually meant death for the one. But maybe they wouldn't attack.

They both lunged at the same time, each one making a simple thrust straight for his gut. Rinn jumped back a step and out of their reach easily enough. One of them lunged again, the same exact attack Rinn noted, and the other tried an overhand chop. Rinn skipped back, again just out of reach. He thought they would follow on with another attack, but they just stood there watching him.

Now it was Rinn's turn to grin.

Apparently the local thieves guild didn't require their members to practice weaponry and dueling for hours every day. Not like Berym did. In those first moments of combat, Rinn knew instantly that these men were no match for his skill.

"Turn and run," Rinn said. "Now."

They glanced at each other and then back to him.

"This is your last chance," Rinn said. "I know you're only following orders, but I have no fight with you. If you keep this up, I'll kill you both."

One of them chuckled nervously and gestured with his sword.

"There's two of us and one of you. I like our chances."

The other one lunged again. Rinn knew it was coming. It was the same lunge as before. Rinn followed his training and moved to the side while stabbing back with his own blade. Though a stab to the gut would no doubt have ended this man's life, Rinn meant what he said. He had no real fight with these two.

Rinn slashed to the side, biting deep into the man's sword arm. His blade flew from his grasp, and he stole his arm back tightly against his body with a scream. The other shot him a glance and then looked back at Rinn.

"Still like your chances?" he said.

Rinn could see the doubt on his face and in his feet as they shifted nervously. His stance had rapidly changed from one of attack to one of retreat.

"Go," Rinn said. "I don't want to, but I *will* kill you both."

They looked sideways at each other, neither wanting to be the first to flee. Rinn made a half lunge at the unwounded one, and that was all it took. He skipped back a step and then bolted down the alley, leaving the other man staring at Rinn in terror. Rinn waved his sword after the other, and the wounded thief needed no further invitation.

Rinn didn't wait for backup to come. He took off down the street, running as fast as he could. A shout from behind and the familiar rattle and crack of a crossbow made him instinctively dodge and roll, which probably saved his life. Another bolt flew past him as he came up, making him run all the harder.

He dared a glance over his shoulder at the pursuing crossbowman and saw to his relief that he was still a long way down the street. He spun his head back around and came face to face with Ariss as he jumped out of a side alley just ahead of him. The grin on his face told Rinn there would be no discussion and no mercy this time.

He decided in that instant that he would offer none himself.

Another thug, the one Rinn had shoulder blocked, came out beside Ariss, and Rinn silently cursed. Why were there always two or more of them? An uncontrollable groan escaped his lips.

"Aww, don't worry, Rinn. I'm not gonna kill you until you tell me where that pretty little gem is. You're gonna wish I would though."

Rinn shook his head, but his eyes never left Ariss. He brought his weapons up in a ready stance and waited. Ariss was no swordsman. Long ago, he could best Rinn with a few licks from a tree branch. But that was a long time ago. Before Rinn had trained with a knight. Rinn knew he could end this in a single strike, but something stayed his attack.

"So it comes to this," Rinn said. "Don't do this, Ariss."

Ariss chuckled.

"Kill him," he said pointing with his sword.

The other man lunged for Rinn using the same clumsy stab he'd seen from the others. Was the gut lunge the only move they taught in thieves' school? Rinn feigned a stab with his own sword while moving to the left. The man tried to stop the sword aimed for his stomach and missed the dagger sliding through his leather jerkin and into his side. He clutched the wound and fell back against the wall with a scream.

"Always letting someone else do the fighting for you," Rinn said. "Now it's just you and me."

The grin on Ariss's face vanished with the scream of his companion. The blood pouring through his shirt and over his cupped hand turned the man white. Rinn didn't smile or taunt. This was no fun for him.

"This isn't over," Ariss said as he stepped to the side to let Rinn pass.

Rinn paused and then ran past him. Even if it was a ploy, Ariss wasn't fast enough to catch him off guard. He heard another crack from the crossbow behind him and then Ariss yelling something down the street he couldn't make out. Stealing a glance over his shoulder, he saw Ariss standing next to a couple other men watching him run. They made no further move to come after him, so he slowed down a bit. The chase had winded him, and his legs were burning from the exertion.

He jogged the last few streets and turns until he reached the door of his aunt's house. Twisting the knob, he yanked it open and flung himself inside and straight into the big reading chair. Panting loudly, he sat for several minutes until his breathing slowed.

"Did you get what you needed?" Aunt Jelena called out from the kitchen.

"Yes," he shouted back.

Rinn leaned back and closed his eyes.

I got what I needed.

Chapter Fourteen

Razed

Berym stretched his back in the saddle trying to relieve some of the discomfort from the long ride, but it didn't seem to help much. Two days of riding had taken its toll on him, but the pain did little to diminish the smile on his face. It had been almost a year since he'd visited Derne, but he remembered the landmarks, and he knew he was close. Maybe another hour, maybe less.

He clicked his tongue and put his horse in a light trot, which didn't help his backside much, but he was tired and ready to be done. The thought of Narissa kept him going. The thought of her smile. He was so focused on how happy he would be to see her that he almost managed to ignore that she might not feel the same to see him.

It had been a year since he'd seen her, and though she was always glad to see him, he could sense the sadness behind her smile. It was the same sadness he hid behind his. The one that knew the moment was fleeting and that sooner than they both wished, it would end and he would leave again.

The last hour to Derne was lost in thought. When he

felt his horses's hooves clomp over the bridge on the river Southfork, he looked up from his reverie with a smile. He was almost there.

Berym's smile disappeared when he felt the hair on the back of his neck stood up. Something's wrong. His head searched in every direction for what it was he felt. Something was odd about the area, but he couldn't quite place it.

As he crossed the bridge and back onto the road nearing Derne, he paid close attention to the forest around him. That's when he realized. No birds. He didn't hear the sound of a single bird around him. There was a light breeze blowing across the road, but nothing else made a sound.

Berym's hand strayed instinctively to his sword. The wind picked up for just a moment, and he caught a whiff of something. Smoke. It was feint, but there was smoke in the air. He tucked his heels in and galloped hard for the village, drawing his sword along the way. The smell grew stronger the closer he got, and he could see it trailing above the trees before him. He rounded the bend toward the village, and it all became clear.

The village of Derne was gone.

Left in its place was a smoldering wreck. Berym pulled hard on the reins, bringing his horse to an abrupt stop that almost pitched him off. He stared in disbelief.

All around him were the remains of the village. Homes, farms, shops… everything was burned to the ground. Berym sat and listened for a moment for any sign of continued fighting, but he heard nothing. He leapt down from his horse and stumbled slowly down the main road. What happened here? Where was everyone?

Berym stopped at the first house on the edge of town.

In the midst of the burnt remains he could still see the bottom of a bright, red door. Narissa's door. There was nothing else left of the little cottage that he thought might be his home some day. Berym's knees went weak. He felt as though he'd been hit in the gut.

Narissa.

With a deep breath, he pulled himself up and kept going. One by one he passed the houses of people he'd known. People who'd been kind to him. People who'd cared for him when he was in need. Their homes, too, were nothing but smoldering bits of wood and crumbled stone.

"Narissa!"

He clapped his hand to his mouth almost as soon as the word had left his lips. He hadn't meant to shout. It was stupid given that he didn't know what had attacked or whether it was still lurking nearby, but he couldn't hold it in.

"Narissa!"

No answer. Nothing.

Something in a nearby building collapsed in a loud crash. Berym jumped at it and held his sword ready, but nothing emerged. Just more smoking rubble.

"Narissa, please!"

Something moved.

Up ahead, at the old church. Berym ran to it without pausing to see if it was friend or foe. He didn't care. He ran as fast as he could.

The church of Threyl was a fairly large structure for a village so small. It had been built by the people to praise the goddess for all of her gifts. Berym had not been inside it for many years, but there it stood. There was very little left of it, but because it had been built mostly of stone, some of the lower wall was still intact. It was inside that wall that Berym heard a scraping sound.

He peered inside with his sword at the ready and saw the burned remnants of the church pews moving up and down. Someone was buried or trapped beneath them and trying to lift the wreckage off. Berym sheathed his sword and ran for what remained of the door, yanking it free from its remaining hinge and tossing it aside.

Running to the spot, Berym started throwing debris aside trying to dig up and rescue whoever was trapped. The thought briefly crossed his mind that it might be one of whoever did this, but he pushed it aside. Please let it be her. Please. When enough of the smoking wood had been moved, the rest of the pile suddenly burst up in a cloud of smoke and ash.

Rising from the cloud, Berym could hear someone coughing. He saw a hand appear and grabbed it. A man yelled, and Berym yanked him forward.

"Are you all right?" he asked. "Are you hurt?"

The man's eyes were wide in terror until he heard Berym speak. Berym grasped his arm and pulled him to the side.

"Thank the goddess," he said.

"Are there others?"

Berym was frantic. He tried to calm himself down, but finding a survivor, even just one, meant there was a chance. Just a small hope was all he asked for.

"Down there," the man said. "We hid in the basement of the church before they came."

Berym dove forward as another hand appeared through the smoke. A woman screamed, and Berym's heart leapt.

"It's all right," he shouted. "I am a Knight of

Gondril."

The woman appeared from the smoke, and a look of relief washed over her face. Berym heard murmurs coming from the hole in the floor, and more and more people began streaming from it. As the men came out, they turned and started helping him pull others up.

They kept coming.

The whole village it seemed. With each new face, Berym dared to get his hopes even higher. Faces he recognized, friends he'd known, they were all alive. Finally, Berym reached for a woman's hand and pulled her up from the darkness. The look on her face was one of total confusion, but Berym could not hide the tears in his eyes.

He yanked Narissa so hard he feared he might tear her in half. She flew toward him, and he grabbed her up and crushed her body against his. Her body shuddered, and he could hear the quiet sobs that shook her shoulders.

"I'm here," he said. "Oh, Narissa, I'm here."

The rest of the village was pulled from the church basement and slowly spread out into the street. Berym could feel people staring at them, but he didn't care. As long as Narissa held her grip on him, he wouldn't let go of her. Finally, she pulled her head back to give him a long kiss. When the kiss broke, she looked into his eyes.

"I don't know how you're here, but I've never been happier to see you."

"I thought I'd lost you," he said. "I saw your house, all the houses."

"How are you here? How…"

"I came for you."

"Berym?" someone shouted from outside.

Berym felt Narissa let him go. He looked into her eyes just a few seconds longer before turning. Reluctantly, he went outside where the rest of the villagers were all standing in a cluster and looking around them. He knew what they all must be feeling. He'd witnessed this kind of destruction before. Turning a half circle, he found the man who'd called his name.

"Father Meral?"

Both men stepped forward to greet each other and met with an embrace.

"Thank the goddess you're alive, old man," Berym said.

"Not so old," Father Meral said, "but we'll have time for a reunion later. Where are the knights?"

"What knights? There is only me."

"You didn't bring an army of knights with you?"

"I didn't know I needed one. I only arrived just now and alone. I came to see Narissa."

"I'm sorry. When I saw you I thought that you'd come with the knights to stop the goblins."

"Goblins did this?"

Everyone around nodded.

"We didn't see them come through," Father Meral said, "but we heard it from down below."

"When did they attack?" Berym asked.

"With the dawn. We'd been hiding down in the church cellar all night waiting for them."

"How did you know they were coming?"

"*I* told them," someone shouted from behind everyone. As Eryninn stepped around the outside of the crowd, he gave a little smile when he saw Berym.

"Eryninn? Merciful mother, what are you doing here?"

"Following a goblin army. A big one."

"Your friend there came through yesterday warning us that a goblin army was coming and to run," Father Meral said. "We had nowhere to run to, so we hid in the church."

"Good thing," Eryninn said coming close, and Berym swung back to him.

"I just can't believe," Berym said. "Tell me again why you're here."

"I might ask you the same."

"This is my home. Or... it is when I can get here. Why are you here?"

"I told you. I am following the goblin army that just walked through here and destroyed this place."

Berym scanned the looks on the faces around him and stepped forward, keeping his voice low.

"We should speak more privately."

Eryninn glanced around and nodded. The two of them walked up the street a ways before turning back to each other. Father Meral ambled up behind them, and they made room for him to join them.

"Why?" Berym asked.

"It is what goblins do," Eryninn replied.

"No, why are you following them? When last we parted you were going home to leave all this mess behind you."

"The goblins made raids into my forest, and I could not let that stand. I heard them all talking about burning down a village as they marched, and as much as I wanted to ignore it, I could not let that happen. I fear I became even more of my father when I donned his sword and cloak. I will most likely live to regret it as I'm sure he would have had he lived."

"I do not think you will grow to regret saving these people, but it matters little. You have my deepest thanks for it."

"Don't thank me yet," Eryninn said. "The goblin horde is on the march, and they won't be stopped by the likes of you and me."

"What kind of army are we talking about here?" Berym said. "As big as the tribes that attacked Jornath?"

"Thousands," Eryninn said. "Maybe ten thousand. Too many to count."

Father Meral gasped.

"That many? Goddess help us."

"She can't, Father," Eryninn said blithely, earning him a glare from Berym.

"Where did they come from?" Berym asked.

"The same goblin who sent them against Jornath. He's been very busy over the winter, gathering a goblin army the likes of which we've never seen. He calls himself the champion of Ogrosh."

"Ogrosh?" Father Meral said. "What does the blood god want with our little village?"

"Probably nothing," Berym said. "One doesn't set a force of thousands of goblins after one village. Derne was probably just in the way."

"They just needed someone to wet their blades on, but I wasn't going to give it to them." Eryninn said. "After a nasty attack, I managed to get around them and get here in enough time to warn everyone."

"I dare say he was near death when he stumbled in," Father Meral said. "But we got him fixed up."

Eryninn nodded.

"Where are they now?" Berym asked.

"North," Eryninn said with a nod in that direction.

"They've been marching steadily north for days. I don't know where they're going, but *they* certainly seem to. One thing is certain, burning down a few farmhouses is not going to do much to slake their bloodlust."

"Molner," Berym said. "The old road north of Derne leads to Molner. It's a long road through heavy woods. Even cuts through elven borders in some places, so it's not used much anymore. It's a quicker and safer route through Havnor."

"Why would they march on Molner?" Father Meral asked. "Are they looking to start a war?"

"There is another destination to the north," Eryninn said. "And maybe they do mean to start a war. Just not with humans."

"You think they'd march on the elven lands?"

"Ogrosh holds no love for elves. Ogres, his chosen people, in particular, are fond of elven blood. This champion travels with many ogres at his command. What better way to provoke them than to march right through their lands?"

"Then why attack a village in the daylight?" Berym asked. "If you were marching to war, wouldn't you hide your presence until the last moment to strike?"

"Perhaps they figured on no survivors," Father Meral said.

"Perhaps," Eryninn said. "I will follow them to the north and see if I can discover where they are headed. There's not much I can do to a force of that size, but I can still get out ahead of them and warn whoever is their target."

"I must return to Havnor and raise the knights," Berym said. "If the goblins do lay siege to Molner, they will need all the help they can get."

"What of us?" Father Meral asked. "We can muster some men and march to Molner behind them."

Berym and Eryninn both looked around and shook their heads.

"There is much to do here, Father," Berym said. "Your people need you here, and these women need their men. Stay and rebuild your village. Start with the church."

"Yes," the father said with a nod. "Yes, you are right."

The priest looked at Eryninn and laid his hand on his shoulder.

"Take care of that shoulder now, but if you're ever in need, I am forever in your debt."

Berym smiled and laid his hand on Father Meral's shoulder. When he stepped back, Father Meral left them and rejoined the villagers. Berym could see Narissa standing at the edge and watching him.

"Good travels, my friend," Eryninn said, grasping Berym's arm tightly. "I only wish we could have seen each other sooner and without the stink of goblins in the air."

"They do seem to precede us," Berym said. "Be careful out there."

With a final squeeze, Eryninn let go and jogged off down the road. Berym watched him go and then turned back to see Narissa taking slow, steady steps toward him. He gave her a weak smile, and she returned it. But only just.

"You have to go, don't you?" she said.

"Yes."

"But… you just got here."

"I know. I had planned to stay awhile—"

"Stop. Don't tell me you were going to stay awhile this time. I've heard it so many times before. Right now I can't bear to hear it."

Berym looked down and nodded.

"I need you here," she whispered.

"And I want to stay."

"Then stay. Stay with me. We'll scrape away all the burnt rubble that is both of our lives and build a new one together. A better one for us both."

He stared at the ground, unable to look up. Berym knew she was waiting for an answer, but he could not give her the one she wanted.

"Narissa…"

"Stop."

Berym couldn't bring himself to look into her eyes, so he stood silently with his face cast down.

"Just tell me goodbye and then go," Narissa said softly. "Anymore than that and I'll break."

"Goodbye," he whispered.

Berym reached out to take her in his arms, but she was already turning to rejoin the rest. She disappeared into the crowd and was gone. With a deep breath, Berym turned up the road and followed in Eryninn's lonely footsteps.

CHAPTER FIFTEEN

WE MEET AGAIN

GORTOGH WATCHED THE nightly spectacle of the shamans in their dance. It would all look rather silly to an outsider. It did to Gortogh. Right until the moment when it all turned bloody.

Around a great bonfire, the shamans all twisted and turned, shouting the name of Ogrosh to the heavens. When their cries reached a crescendo, each one drew their blade and cut into their arms. The goblins and ogres watching shouted and roared. The shamans flung their arms about, splashing blood on everything and everyone. Drops sizzled as they flew into the fire.

Kurgh stood at the fire closest to Gortogh. He was never far away. Instead of his own blood this night, Kurgh cut the arms of an ogre standing next to him who didn't seem to mind. The blood swirled up out of the wounds to flow into Kurgh's waiting hands. He raised his hands to join the others.

The other goblins watched with looks of awe. Among the goblins, the shamans were second only to Ogrosh himself. They spoke with his voice and called down his vengeance. And Kurgh was one of the most powerful and revered among them. One of the five high shamans.

"Praise Ogrosh!" Kurgh shouted.

"Praise Ogrosh!" everyone repeated.

"Ogrosh gives us life in blood. The Blood God has always cared for us. He makes us strong. He nourishes us. We owe our lives and blood to Ogrosh."

"To Ogrosh!" they chanted.

Kurgh began chanting. As one, the shamans joined and raised Kurgh's chant to Ogrosh. They cut into their arms to let their own blood flow and power their prayers. Droplets began to swirl around, forming a gory, red cloud that enveloped them. Higher and higher the blood swirled until it blasted out from them and into the forest. Despite his feelings toward the shamans and their blood rituals, this part always amazed Gortogh.

The rustle of branches and leaves signaled their coming.

Deer, rabbits, squirrels, boar. All the animals of the forest walked from the trees as though entranced by their bloody chanting. Slow and prodding they came, none noticing the deadly trap of steel that awaited them. As the chanting grew, the goblin warriors drew their blades and slaughtered the beasts.

The noble creatures never even moved as their life left them. The goblins slit their necks from ear to ear, letting the blood flow. Blood was a gift of Ogrosh. The goblins let it wash over them, covering their arms. They painted their faces with it. Drew symbols on their chests with it.

This is the way of the children of Ogrosh.

When at last the chanting and sounds of slaughter died down, only Kurgh kept going. The ogre that stood beside him had fallen from the loss of blood, but the shaman paid no attention. He just took more. When at last he flung his hands out, sending the blood into the forest, he fell to the ground and whispered softly into the earth.

Everyone waited in silence.

A shout went up from beyond the firelight. Then another. The goblins began to move aside quickly as something approached through the darkness. Gortogh could feel the footsteps of the beast as it neared and drew his sword in answer. When the last of the goblins moved aside, a great bear lumbered into the circle around the fire.

It was like no bear Gortogh had ever seen. Walking on four legs, the beast was taller than a goblin standing at full height and wider than an ogre. Kurgh lifted his head, and Gortogh caught the toothy smile on the shaman's face. The bear walked up and stood before him, unmoving.

"Ogrosh has truly blessed us this night!" Kurgh shouted.

He reached out and ran his hand through the bear's black fur. Grabbing the back of its neck with his hand, he jammed his dagger into its throat with the other. The bear never moved. It gave a low huff and breathed heavily as its lifeblood poured out, but it stood perfectly still until it fell. The goblins wasted no time in hacking up the carcass, offering their blades up to Kurgh for blessing. Gortogh could see the looks of adoration in their eyes.

He knew them all too well.

Kurgh turned and bowed to Gortogh who could only nod in approval. Giving a nod around to all of his men, he stepped back into his tent and began pacing in circles. Why was he nervous? Because he could not hold them together much longer. The meat would satisfy them all another night, but he was running out of distractions.

Gortogh walked the perimeter of the great tent his men had erected for him. He stumbled over the assortment of gifts that had been left and silently cursed. A fire pit, mounds of soft furs, a table soon to be covered in fresh meat. It was everything a king of goblins could ever wish for.

Gortogh hated all of it.

The smoke from the fire collected near the roof of the tent and swirled about, making the air hazy and gray. The furs had gotten wet from the rains a few days earlier and now smelled like the carcasses from which they were stripped. All of it sickened him. The meat was good, though. He liked the meat.

Still, Gortogh couldn't bring himself to eat much of it when he knew that at any moment a fight could break out that could be the last. He'd let the beer flow freely since leaving their mountain caves, and it had worked to pacify most of the tribes, but even that was running in short supply. He'd had to allow even more of it after the village of Derne failed to provide them with fresh blood. Thankfully they had stolen enough from the village before burning it to satisfy a bit of their desires.

He stopped pacing and growled when he heard the voice of Kurgh coming from outside. Now that Gortogh was spending more time among his troops, their adoration of him had only grown since leaving the forest. Despite the growing unrest among the tribes, whenever he walked among them, all rivalry ceased, and they bowed to him.

He had quickly learned why.

What began as some fool's tale of glory had spread

through the tribes like a wildfire. When word of it reached Gortogh's ears, he could only shake his head in frustration. The tribes all believed that he was the embodiment of Ogrosh. They looked to him as their almighty god made flesh and walking among them.

The whole thing made him uncomfortable.

Mostly he hated the change that had come over Kurgh as a result of this madness. Being a priest of their terrible god, and being the personal servant to Gortogh, he believed himself to be the right hand of Ogrosh. And, oh, how he reveled in his newfound station. He had been taking the blood of ogres instead of his own to cast stronger and more powerful spells to show his power.

When a great storm blew in, Kurgh had taken blood from himself and the other shamans and sent it away. Like damming the heavens themselves, the rain simply stopped. Though the shaman was always respected, as well as feared, among the goblins, they now saw in Kurgh much more than they had ever before. Gortogh could hear him outside ordering troops around, whipping the backs of his men, even shouting at the ogres in his high-pitched scream.

And they all obeyed without question.

The flaps of his tent fluttered open, and Gortogh heard footsteps. He turned, ready to punch the ugly shaman in the face but instead found himself eye to eye with a golden-skinned elf. Gortogh grabbed for his weapon and almost shouted for his guards when Velanon stepped into the tent beside the elf.

"He's smaller than I thought," the golden elf said. "The whispers I heard walking through the army made him out to be ten feet tall."

"He's just a goblin," Velanon said.

Gortogh stared, his mouth agape, but managed to gather himself enough to speak.

"What in the nine hells are you doing here? We had a deal, wizard. No one is to know of your part in this. You could have been seen!"

"No," Velanon said, "we could not."

"Goblins are such small things," the gold elf said. "It has been many decades since I have seen one. I had forgotten how small they are."

Gortogh narrowed his eyes at the strange elf and tightened the grip on his sword.

"And aggressive," the elf said. "I thought you said this one was smart."

"Smarter than most, but that is still saying very little."

"You haven't answered my question, wizard. What are you doing here, and who by the gods, is he?"

"I am Kalus. Velanon and I are old friends."

Gortogh didn't miss the sneer that briefly crossed Velanon's face, but he hid it quickly and turned back to face him.

"I'm here to see how things are going," Velanon said. "You are making good progress, I see."

"Yes, a *great* journey," Gortogh said. "If there are any of us left alive when we reach Molner, it will be a sight to behold."

Velanon frowned. Kalus chuckled, which only deepened his frown.

"Must I be behind your shoulders at every turn? You have a simple task. March. One foot in front of the other. Are you so incompetent you cannot even do that which you were born to do?"

Gortogh growled, which earned him a glare from Velanon, but he didn't back down.

"These are goblin tribes, wizard! They have fought and killed each other for millennia! They will not just lay down their arms and sing drinking songs together because you *ask* them to. There is only one thing that brings goblins together. Blood. Lots of blood."

"Was the village not enough to satisfy your bloodlust?"

"The damn village was empty!"

Velanon and Kalus both looked sidelong at each other.

"Empty?" Velanon asked with a raised eyebrow.

"Empty," Gortogh said. "Not a soul to be found. My men took all the livestock we could find, but filling their bellies will not slake their thirst for blood."

Kalus looked all around him as if completely bored by this conversation and began wandering around the tent examining any little thing he could find. Gortogh watched for a moment and then turned his attention back to Velanon.

"Empty," Velanon repeated. "Well, there will be more than enough blood for everyone soon enough. At your current march you should arrive in Molner in four days. After that, you won't be able to stop the blood from flowing."

"*Four days*? The only thing keeping them from killing each other right outside that flap is the beer I'd managed to horde before our march, and it's all but gone."

"Then you shall have to find another way to pacify them. A game perhaps? Hold a tournament when next you camp. A few goblins killed in an arena might keep them going a few more days. Have you stayed among them as I ordered?"

"Yes, and that has helped. They seem calmed by my

presence."

"They are enthralled, and the more they see you, the more they will be. You are too nice to them. You need to show them that you will not tolerate the killing of other goblins."

"They have started calling me Ogrosh made flesh."

Kalus laughed and looked back to Velanon so they could laugh together, but Velanon only crossed his arms.

"Because you are," Velanon said. "You are a god. At least in their eyes. You should start acting like one."

Kalus turned from the pile of furs he was poking at to stare at Velanon with confusion. He swiveled his head around to stare at Gortogh, looking him up and down, trying to see whatever it was Velanon was looking at. When at last he saw it, his mouth dropped open.

The golden elf stared at Gortogh's chest.

"Dunatis's amulet?"

Moving faster than Gortogh could register, Kalus leapt across the room and grabbed for his chest. His golden hand closed around the amulet that hung on the simple leather cord around Gortogh's neck, and the the elf yanked hard. Gortogh felt a hum against his skin. A surge of energy blasted forth from the disc. Kalus tried to hold on, but the power was too great. He let out a scream that became a great roar. An entirely inhuman roar that fluttered the walls of the tent.

Kalus let go and fell back, clutching his arm. His breath was rapid and deep, and he stared first at Gortogh and then to Velanon with his eyes and mouth wide.

"You gave the blood amulet to this *toad*?" he screamed.

Velanon rolled his eyes.

"Who else was to wield it? I needed a son of

236

Ogrosh."

"Where in Gondril did you *find* it?"

"My master had it for many centuries, tucked away in his laboratory. In truth, I don't know if he even knew what he possessed. It was only by stumbling upon an old drawing in a book that I began to suspect."

Kalus opened his small, elven mouth and let out another beastly roar. When he finished, Gortogh could hear shouts coming from outside the tent and feet rushing for them.

"Stay out!" he shouted. "On your life, do not enter my tent!"

"Mighty One!" Kurgh called out. "We heard a beast! Are you all right?"

"Yes, now leave."

The shadows of the men slid away down the side of the tent until they were gone completely. Kalus stood staring at Velanon, his breath heaving.

"You gave an artifact of the gods to a sniveling *goblin*?"

"What good had it ever done me? Or my master. I cannot wield its gifts and neither can you. Only a son of Ogrosh can."

Gortogh lifted the little amulet from his chest and stared at it. Aside from the surge of power he just felt, and he could truly feel its might, it had done nothing since he put it on. It had just laid there on his chest as a reminder to him who he owed his good fortune. It was a manacle around his neck, but he dared not take it off. He had felt Velanon's wrath once before, and he dared not anger the elf again.

"What is so special about it?" Gortogh asked. "It's just a bronze disc. I've never even seen it do anything until now."

"You didn't tell him?" Kalus asked.

"It wasn't important," Velanon said.

"Tell me what?"

Kalus shook his head and finally managed to stand up straight.

"That amulet contains the blood of Ogrosh. And not some foolish ritual where you bathe in the blood of a chicken and *call* it his blood. I mean the *actual* blood of a god."

Gortogh's eyes nearly bulged out of his head. He brought the amulet higher to stare into it and suddenly felt queasy. He let it fall from his hand as though it might destroy him at any moment. He stumbled back a step and fell into a pile of furs, just managing to stay sitting and not tumble over the back.

"How is that even possible?" he said out loud but more to himself.

"I suppose they don't teach much history in goblin school," Kalus said with a chuckle. "The dwarven god, Dunatis, cut Ogrosh in a great battle and took his blood to forge an amulet to rule over his brother's creations. He gave it to his most faithful servant and commanded him to use it and lead the goblins and ogres in a great war against each other."

"I thought you said the amulet could only be worn by a goblin," Gortogh said.

"A son of Ogrosh, yes," Kalus said. "The amulet contains the blood of Ogrosh, and as such, the dwarf who wore it became poisoned by it, eventually becoming raving mad. The amulet Dunatis had forged would not serve him or his people."

Gortogh held the amulet in front of him and let it

dance on the end of its leather cord, twirling in the firelight of the tent.

"Then what does it do? Besides contain the blood of a god?"

"That's not enough for you?" Kalus asked.

"No, I just—"

"To the children of Ogrosh, that amulet makes you appear to them as his living avatar," Kalus said. "Those wretched souls out there actually *see* you as Ogrosh made flesh on Gondril. And they will follow you to their own deaths if you order them to."

"Which is what you'll be doing soon," Velanon said. "Continue your march north until you reach Molner. Once there, wait for me to arrive. Trust me, your men will have their fill of blood before this battle is done. Ogrosh will be pleased."

Gortogh let the amulet drop and stared back at them.

"What do I do until then? How can I keep them under control?"

"Become Ogrosh," Kalus said. "The minute you start acting like the Blood God is the minute they will obey you without fail."

Gortogh looked at Velanon who nodded.

"We have to go," Velanon said. "March north. I will meet you in Molner."

Kalus stepped closer to Velanon, and with a swirl of his hand, the two of them disappeared. Gortogh jumped up so fast that his foot kicked out too near to the fire and struck an ember. He leapt back with a yelp and then immediately covered his mouth.

"Mighty One?"

Too late.

"Go away, Kurgh."

Kurgh walked in through the front of the tent as if Gortogh had said nothing at all.

"I heard many voices. The elf and someone else."

Kurgh was doing his best to keep his voice even and calm, but Gortogh saw his eyes. They were locked on the amulet that hung at his chest. Gortogh took a few steps in one direction and then back the other way and watched as the shaman's head swiveled to track his every step. His gaze never left the bronze disc.

Kurgh had heard everything.

"I told you to stop listening to my conversations," Gortogh said with a growl.

Kurgh hit the ground and buried his face, but Gortogh cut him off before he could launch into his usual apology. He drew his sword with a flourish and held it out in front of him.

"Tell me, Kurgh. How powerful is Ogrosh?"

"All powerful," Kurgh said with confusion.

Gortogh brought his sword down to touch Kurgh's shoulder and saw a shiver ripple across the shaman's back. Gortogh slid the sword down just an inch, but the sharp blade cut right through Kurgh's skin. Gortogh pulled the sword back and watched the skin heal itself only a moment later.

"Do you think Ogrosh will grow you a new arm if I were to take yours off?" Gortogh said calmly.

"Ogrosh will heal my arm back to my body," Kurgh said, never looking up, "that is the power he gives his priests who carry his will and his word, but he will not grow me a new one."

"Do you think Ogrosh is forgiving?"

Kurgh looked up confused and then buried his face again.

"No, Mighty One. Ogrosh punishes the weak until they are strong. Ogrosh does not forgive, he demands blood in vengeance."

Gortogh didn't have his boots on, but it didn't matter. He gripped his sword for strength and kicked the shaman hard in the face, sending him sprawling onto his back with a bloody look of horror and betrayal.

"I am Ogrosh made flesh," he said calmly. "If you disobey me again, I will cut both of your arms off and feed them to the ogres where even Ogrosh cannot heal you."

For once the shaman was silent.

"Never forget, Kurgh. I am Ogrosh. And Ogrosh is unforgiving... *I* am unforgiving."

He looked up from the ground, and Gortogh could see that his kick had done quite a bit of damage. The shaman's nose was smashed in, and blood was gushing from it down the sides of his mouth and dripping from his chin. His eyes darted from the amulet to Gortogh's face until he slowly nodded.

"Go."

Gortogh turned his back and stood with his sword raised until he heard the clacking sound of the shaman's finger bones as he scuttled out. He took a deep breath to calm himself.

"I am Ogrosh."

***

Velanon stood beside Kalus on a hill overlooking a large, open field. Behind them was the beginnings of a forest. Beyond the field stood the gates of Molner.

"I must confess, wizard," Kalus said. "I have seen all of your pieces now and all of their movements, but I can't figure out what game it is you play."

In answer, Velanon raised his hand and pointed a finger toward the lone mountain that stood like a sentinel over the city, protecting it in its great shadow.

"Oh, I know what you're after. I just don't see how it is you think you can defeat her."

"She will fall as all the others have fallen before me."

Kalus snorted.

"You think she is like the others you have faced? The Eldest is more than a thousand years old. She is older than me even. Your little magic tricks mean nothing to her."

"If all I had were mere tricks, I would say you were right."

"I was very young during the War of Ways, but not so young I don't remember the great battle. I saw the Eldest of that time do battle from the sky with some of the most powerful elven wizards of the day. And he was not as old as she is now."

"But he did die if I recall my history."

"Oh, yes, he died that day, but not without first destroying *many* of your kind. You are but one. You'll be lucky if your spells can even penetrate her hide. And while you're busy twiddling your fingers at her and singing pretty words, she will roast you like a pig."

A grin spread across Velanon's face, and he couldn't help shaking his head.

"I know," said Kalus. "You think that field protecting you will stop her."

Velanon arched an eyebrow and cocked his head to look at him.

"I can feel the protection around you," Kalus said, "but I promise it is not as strong as you might think. And what are you doing with the goblins? Do you think they can help you somehow? Even an army as large as that cannot help you against the Eldest. They serve no purpose that I can see."

"They will serve their purpose quite well, I think."

"And what of the elves?"

Velanon swiveled his head around and looked at the forest beyond.

"What of them?" Velanon said. "They will not interfere. They will not cross the border."

"Maybe not, but you're certainly testing their resolve bringing an army of goblins this close to their home."

Their heads both jerked back as a screech echoed across the valley from above. A dragon leapt into the air from the wall surrounding the city and flew off toward the distant mountain.

"And now dragonmages," Kalus said. "Did you think they would not protect her? She is the eldest of our kind. They will not let you simply walk in and try to kill her. No, you'll find nothing but defeat here, goblin army or not."

"Tell me again why I'm keeping you around?"

"To talk some sense into you. If you stand any chance at all of defeating the eldest, and I don't think you do, you'll need my help to do it. That's why you haven't tried to get rid of me. I may be the only being on Gondril powerful enough to defeat her, and even with you beside me, it may still not be enough."

Never taking his eyes from the mountain, Velanon brought his hands up to tug at the chain around his neck. Pulling it up, he tugged a pink crystal from beneath his robes and held it up where it sparkled in the moonlight. Kalus turned to look at it and then stopped cold when it caught the light. He stared at it twisting slowly on the end of the chain and brought his hand up to touch it as if in a trance.

"Do you really want to do that?" Velanon said.

"Is it… Is it real?"

"Quite real. You know it to be true, you already said that you can feel it."

Kalus yanked his hand back and stepped away from the wizard. Velanon had to smile watching him try to act calm.

"You seem to have a knack for finding forgotten artifacts. Where did you find it?"

"My master was the most powerful of his kind before he entered twilight. I studied with him for more than a hundred years and cared for him until his death. When he was gone, I inventoried all of his belongings and found it hidden among his personal things."

"Old Lorin was hiding a Dragonbane crystal under his damn *mattress?*" Kalus shouted.

"In his armoire underneath a folded cloak, actually, but yes."

"You cannot keep it! Do you know what that crystal is capable of?"

Velanon swung around to face him.

"It protects me from your kind. As long as I wear it, you cannot harm me. Not your claws, not your bite, not your breath. And neither can the eldest."

"You only think you are invulnerable. You may be immune to her claws and breath, but her magic can still harm you. She draws from the same song that you do for her spells, and the crystal cannot protect you from that."

"Maybe not, but I am no court magician. The crystal protects me from her greatest weapons. I will handle the rest."

"Then why are we just standing here? With the two of us together and a Dragonbane crystal, she stands no chance of winning. Let's march in there now and destroy her!"

"No. Killing her while she hides in her hole in the dark of night would only be one more dead dragon. I want her death to be a message to all those who continue to oppose me. Especially the elves, who are harboring the silver and gold dragons and protecting them from me."

"What message? That you want open war?"

"That war is upon them already… And I will win."

Kalus shook his head and smiled.

"I underestimated you, wizard."

"They all have. No more. Let them see what I am capable of. In five days they will all know. In the meantime, there is still more trouble to make."

Kalus laughed and stepped near Velanon as he began casting. Kalus was cautious not to get too close to Velanon's neck, but the wizard paid no attention. With a swirl of his hands, they were gone.

CHAPTER SIXTEEN

TAKEN

"*I'M SAFELY IN Molner. Send word soon.*"

That was the message Elody awoke to in her head. There was a slight tingle as it arrived, tickling the back of her mind until she woke to hear it. Eliath is safe. For now at least. Thinking of him made her sad all over again, but she forced herself up from her bed. The late morning sun poured through her window, nearly blinding her.

How long was I asleep?

Elody stumbled a bit going down the stairs. The ache in her head made every blink of her eyes hurt, and she found it was easier to just keep them closed on the way down. She remembered coming home and she and Jalthrax eating, but then what? The details were foggy, but she had woken up in her room, so she must have gotten there before the exhaustion overtook her.

The stairs seemed longer than they had ever been, but she finally reached the bottom. Her heel hit with a hard thud when she took a step expecting a stair and found the landing instead.

"Elody?" Aunt Jelena said. "Is that you?"

She groaned something and turned toward the voice, which was coming from the *very* bright kitchen.

"Are you okay?" Aunt Jelena asked.

"Just tired."

"You look like you got drunk last night."

"No. Nothing like that. Just too much practice."

Her aunt set a plate of cold eggs and bread down in front her, and she tore into it without so much as a thank you. Her aunt snorted and shook her head.

"Sorry," Elody said between bites. "I'm so hungry."

"Well, you slept like the dead. I came home in the early afternoon yesterday and found you already in bed, and you didn't stir until just this morning. You're working too hard. Magic takes a lot out of you, you know."

"Believe me, I know."

"Be quiet you two!" she heard Rinn call from the front room.

Elody stopped eating and looked down the hall where she could only see a leg sticking out.

"What are you doing?" Elody asked.

"He's been like that since I came home yesterday," Aunt Jelena said. "Sitting on the floor, watching out the window."

Elody finished her eggs and grabbed the bread as she walked over. Rinn was huddled down beneath the front window, one hand lifting the bottom of the curtain there to peer out through a tiny slit of light.

"I'm watching," Rinn said.

"Get away from the front window, Rinn." Aunt Jelena said. "I don't know what you're so paranoid about, no one is coming in here."

Rinn frowned and picked the curtain up a little more to peer outside. Elody sidled up and peeked out from beneath his hand.

"What are we looking at?" she said.

Rinn brought his hand up slowly and pointed to a man laying in an alley across the street.

"The drunk in the alley?" Elody asked.

"He's not drunk," Rinn said. "He's been there all morning."

Elody squinted and looked again.

"He's sleeping, Rinn."

"He's not sleeping."

"What is going on with you?"

"He's been like that for days!" her aunt shouted.

"You've been like this for days?" Elody asked.

"Just yesterday and today."

"Is this some game you made up to scare me?" she said.

"I wish it were."

Elody got up with a frown and went back to the kitchen for some water.

"What's with him?" she asked in a whisper.

Jelena shrugged.

"I think he got into some trouble, and now he's scared someone is after him."

"What if someone *is* after him?"

"Then he needs to take care of it."

"What if they want to hurt him?"

"Then he *really* needs to take care of it."

"Has he told you anything?"

"He hid out in here all day yesterday and tried to tell me to stay here too. Wasn't too happy when I left to run some errands."

Elody nodded and then walked back to Rinn. He hadn't moved from his post in front of the window.

Behind them, they heard Aunt Jelena tromp up the stairs.

"Rinn?" Elody said.

"Hmm?"

"What did you do?"

Rinn looked down and shook his head.

"What was right," he said.

Elody pursed her lips.

"And that got you into trouble?"

"It usually does."

Elody waited for him to continue, but when he didn't she couldn't stand not knowing.

"You gonna tell me what happened?"

Rinn reached into his breeches and tugged at something. Before Elody could launch a protest, he pulled a small pouch that hung from his belt and opened it up. He gestured to her to put her hand out, and as she did, he turned the bag over and dropped a ruby into it.

A *huge* ruby.

Bigger than any gem she ever thought imaginable. It sparkled red in the sunlight streaming under the crack in the curtain, sending red shafts of light dancing across the scattered books. Elody's breath caught as she turned it over in her hand.

"Oh, Rinn," she said. "What did you do?"

"I stole it."

I knew it. She closed her eyes and shook her head.

"Where did it come from?" she asked after a moment.

Rinn sighed and stared at the floor.

"The temple of Threyl."

"Rinn, no!"

He nodded.

"Mercy of the gods, what were you *thinking*?"

"I thought I was trying to help a friend. But it was all just a lie."

"Well, take it back to the church then. They might arrest you, but if they get it back, they might be lenient. I've heard them say before that Threyl loves all of her children."

"I can't take it back."

"You'd rather hide out in here from them for the rest of your life?"

"I'm not hiding from them."

"Then who are you hiding from?"

"The thieves guild who helped me steal it right before I stole it back from them."

"Rinn!"

"I know."

"What are you doing with a thieves guild?"

"I *know*."

Now Elody was the one checking the window.

"The drunk just moved!" she said.

"He's not drunk. He's one of them. They're all over out there."

"Where?"

"You won't see them. They left the drunk just to let me know that they're watching, but we'll never see them all."

Elody slapped the curtain down, darkening the room a little as the light was cut off.

"Okay, what do we do?" she said.

Rinn shook his head.

"I don't know. Returning it is what's right, but if I return it, they'll kill me. Or worse."

"You need to tell Aunt Jelena."

"No. I won't get her involved in this. She's already in

danger because of what I've done. I won't have her running off to tell the guards or something stupid."

"Then what are you going to do?"

"Hide here. That's the only plan I've come up with so far."

Elody frowned.

"That's a terrible plan."

"I'm ready to hear yours then."

"Well, I don't have one yet. I only just found out about all this ten minutes ago."

They sat silently for another moment when Elody's fist shot out and punched him in the arm.

"Ow!"

***

Elody shifted when she felt her arm start to tingle from a lack of blood. Bolting up, she realized she'd fallen asleep. She rubbed her eyes and looked around. It was dark out. Her aunt had lit a single candle on the table near the window she was sleeping under, but other than its tiny glow, everything was dark.

Rinn groaned beside her and turned away, and she realized she'd been sleeping on him. She tapped him on the arm, lightly at first, and then more insistent until she was slapping him.

"Stop it, El!"

"Some guards we are," she said.

"What?" Rinn mumbled through sleep.

"We fell asleep on our watch."

Rinn bolted up and looked around.

"Is it night already?"

He flipped over and stayed low as he slowly rose to peek over the rim of the windowsill.

"The drunk's gone."

"Probably woke up while we were sleeping. Or maybe they gave up."

"No, they didn't give up. They won't."

Elody leaned close to his face to peer out the crack he'd made in the curtains. They watched in silence for a while, neither daring to move. Elody finally grew bored and shrunk down below the window to put her back against the wall. Rinn scanned the other windows to the side of the house.

"Jalthrax is gone," he said.

"I know, I didn't feel him when I woke up. He's probably hunting. We had a rough day yesterday."

"*You* had a rough day?"

"Maybe not as rough as yours, but rough enough. Have you even thought about what you're going to do? You can't just stay locked up in this house every day."

Rinn sighed and sat down beside her.

"I don't know. The more I think about it, the more I don't see a way out. The only thing I can see is to give Ariss the ruby."

"He's the big one?"

"Yes. Very big. And he has a lot of friends now."

"But you were once friends?"

"Once."

"You think he'll just let it go if you give it to him?"

"I don't know. Maybe. But I don't know if I can."

"Well, you know my vote. You made a big mess of things, but if you give the ruby back to the church, the thieves are going to kill you. I don't want you dead. I say give it to them."

"It's not that simple, El."

"It is for me."

"Well, it's not for me, okay?"

Elody could only nod. They'd already gone over this a few times, and though it kept coming up, neither would give on their position or suggest an alternative. Knowing that, Elody really didn't see a way out for Rinn. They both stood and stretched out their backs with loud groans and cracks.

"Where's Aunt Jelena?" Elody asked.

"She's gone up to bed early the past few nights."

A loud thud hit the door so hard, they both jumped into each other's arms. A loud rapping against the wood followed, jarring them even more. They looked from each other to the door and back again, neither one able to move. Finally, Elody forced one step and then another until she stood in front of the door. She reached her hand, and Rinn shot forward to grab her.

"Don't!" he said.

She laid her hand on the doorknob and felt nothing. She reached for the door and then jerked her hand back when she heard a loud banging noise from above. Spinning around to look at Rinn, she saw his dagger in his hand. They both relaxed when their aunt's feet came into view, tromping loudly down the stairs.

"Who in the nine hells is banging on my door? If this is about you Rinn, you and I are in for a *serious* talk."

She stepped off the final stair toward the door, and before either of them could mouth a warning, yanked it open. Rinn and Elody both jumped back, neither sure what they were expecting, but whatever it was, it wasn't what they saw. A piece of paper fluttered against the door with a short dagger stuck through it into the wood.

Without ceremony, Jelena yanked the dagger with a single pull and then turned the note over in her hand. With a deep scowl on her face and a quick glare at Rinn, she turned it over and read. The note must have been short because her hand dropped away after only a moment. She spun on Rinn, her face like stone.

"What have you done?"

"I—"

She held up her hand and stopped him cold. Her eyes softened as she turned to Elody. Elody faced her, ready to defend Rinn.

"Elody, honey…"

"He knows he made a mess, Aunt Jelena."

"Elody, honey—"

"We're trying to clean it up now. You don't have to worry about—"

"Elody!"

Elody stopped and jerked back in surprise.

"Elody, honey. They've taken Thrax."

The room went deathly silent.

Elody stared at her, once again unable to move or speak. The words hit her like a stone fist, knocking the wind from her. She could feel the panic rising in her, but she didn't know what to do. Thoughts flew through her head like leaves in a storm, and she was barely able to remain standing as her knees went weak. She wanted to run, to find him, but her body would not move.

Jelena was the first to break the tension. She threw the note in Rinn's face and then stomped into the kitchen. Rinn took the note and read it.

"Ariss, no."

He turned to Elody and grabbed her by the shoulders, but she only stared off into space.

"Don't worry, El. I'll get him back. The note says to meet him at dragonmage field. I'll just give him the ruby, and he'll give Jalthrax back."

Elody could only nod. Her knees were wobbly, and she feared she might fall over if she moved at all. She started to say something but was cut off.

"You've done enough already!" Jelena shouted from the other room. "You won't be doing anything else!"

"This is *my* mess, and *I'll* clean it up," Rinn shouted back.

Aunt Jelena appeared from the kitchen, and Elody turned to look at her. Through the haze of fear in her mind, she noticed that her aunt was wearing a belt of rope tied around her waist with many small pouches clinging to it. A small twig was tied by a knot in the rope and hung harmlessly to the side.

"Come," was all she said as she yanked the door open and stepped out.

Rinn took Elody by the hand and dragged her the first few steps toward the door.

"Come on, El. We'll get him back. This won't take long. They only want the ruby, and I'm going to give it to them."

Elody took one step and then another until they were both out the door. Then they had to run to catch up with their aunt who was marching straight up the street toward the open field outside of town.

When they arrived, the stage had already been set for them. Standing across the field, surrounded by men, was Ariss. Or, Elody guessed it was Ariss by his size and the way he stood in front of them all. There was a ring of torches behind him, lighting up all the men. Jelena stopped in front of them and stood calmly with her hands on her hips.

Movement behind Ariss caught Elody's eye, and then she saw him. Jalthrax was lying on the ground in a heap with a large net thrown over him, wrapping him tightly. The men behind Ariss were all standing near the prone dragon, some of them with their feet on the net or even on Jalthrax to keep him from struggling. Elody started to move, but her aunt's arm reached out and pushed her back.

"Rinn!" Ariss shouted across the field. "Glad you could make it. I was hoping we could have another chat. Our last one was… cut short."

The men all laughed. There were at least a dozen of them, and Elody had no doubt there were more she couldn't see. Rinn fidgeted beside her, but they both held their ground just behind and to the side of their aunt. For some reason it felt safest to stay behind her.

"It didn't have to come to this, Rinn. I don't want to hurt the poor lizard. I just want—"

"You give him back to me!" Elody shouted.

Jelena's arm shot up again in just enough time to stop her charging across the field at them, even before she realized her feet were moving. Rinn stepped forward to speak, but a glare from his aunt made him shrink back again.

"Come on, Rinn," Ariss said. "Let's make this easy. You give me the ruby, and I'll let you have the dragon back. Plus, to show we can all still be friendly, I'll let you live."

"*This* will be the deal," Jelena shouted back. "You walk away and leave Jalthrax unharmed, and I will do the same for you."

The men all laughed, and Ariss nearly doubled over as he held his stomach.

"What are you doing?" Rinn whispered.

"Oh, Rinn!" Ariss shouted. "Did you bring your

bodyguard with you?"

More laughter.

"Just let me handle this," Rinn said.

"And what would you do?" Jelena said, spinning on him.

"I'm going to give it to them. They'll let Jalthrax go, and this will all just go away."

"And you think that's what will happen?"

"That's what he said."

"Well, I'm certain you can take him at his word."

Rinn looked down and fondled the small pouch at his belt.

"No, Rinn," Jelena said. "Your friend there will not let you live after what you've done. He cannot. I will clean up your mess for my little sister and for *your* little sister. Now, you and Elody stand back."

The men had finally stopped laughing as Ariss was wiping a tear from his eyes.

"My fight is not with you, old woman. Let Rinn be a man and deal with this himself, not hide behind your sizable skirt like a babe."

"Walk away now," Jelena said calmly. "Or I promise that I will rain the nine hells upon you."

Ariss laughed again, and the men joined him. But with a little less vigor this time. Ariss seemed not to notice.

"You know, you remind me of my mother," Ariss said. "She used to love to order me around and threaten me. And I killed her too."

"Stay behind me," Jelena said over her shoulder, "and whatever you do, don't interfere."

With a clap of her hands, everything went dark. The men across the field began shouting. Elody tensed and started to say something, but then she heard her aunt's voice clear and strong through the blackness and she felt calm. It sounded to her like the melody of a song, but she had never heard the words before. They were foreign, as if another language, yet somehow familiar.

The song finished and the words faded, but Elody could still feel an energy in the air. She heard a ripping sound, and then yelped in surprise as she felt something brush against her. From the sound Rinn made, she guessed something had touched him too.

"Do not be afraid," she heard her aunt say calmly.

Another clap split the night, and Elody nearly stumbled over her own feet as she backpedaled a few steps from the scene in front of her. Her aunt was standing exactly where she had been before the light went out, calm as ever. But standing now to either side of her were two great cats, both with an eerie white glow surrounding them. Their heads reached as high as Jelena's chest where a great mane of thick fur surrounded each of them. They stood deathly still on giant paws as she reached down each hand to stroke their fur. Elody turned to look at Rinn, and the cats gave a great roar that echoed through the darkness and made them both start.

The effect on the thieves was greater.

While they were hidden in darkness, the men had all spread out and moved closer to them. Not knowing what to expect, they had been cautious in their movements, but they were still much closer than before. Whatever they expected to emerge from the darkness, Elody had no doubt it wasn't this.

"This is your last chance for your lives," Jelena called out. "Once I release these creatures, they will not rest until every one of you is dead at their feet."

None of them were laughing now. Ariss stood exactly where he had before, obviously making no effort to close the gap between them. Only now he trembled as he stood.

"Any— Anyone can make illusions, witch!"

Elody could hear the lack of faith in his words even from where she stood. Ariss backed up a step and drew his dagger.

"You let those things go, and I'll slit this dragon's throat."

"No!" Elody screamed.

"I promise you will be dead before you can reach him," Jelena said.

Elody heard unerring conviction in her words. Ariss must have heard it too because he stopped inching back toward Jalthrax.

"Kill that bitch!" Ariss yelled.

No one moved. The rest of the men stood frozen.

"I said kill her!"

Jelena looked around at each of them, her hands gently running down the backs of the big cats.

"I don't think they want to die tonight. It looks like you might have to do your own dirty work if you want the job done."

"If you don't kill that bitch right now, I'll see you all dead by morning!"

The men looked around at each other, and then one by one started to move. Their steps were tentative, but they were coming closer.

Jelena jerked the twig from her belt and pointed it across the field at Ariss. She spoke a single word so softly that Elody couldn't hear it standing just behind her, but she saw the energy crackle down the wood. A single bolt of lightning, one not unlike Elody herself had almost killed Jalthrax with, arced from the end of the stick and flew with blinding speed for Ariss.

As the lightning bolt flew close enough to make his hairs stand on end, Ariss stood trembling in silence. The front of his breeches soaked through, and the dagger he was holding had fallen from his hand to lay in the grass beside him.

No one else moved. The shock on their faces was clear, and no one dared approach the powerful old woman and her cats. She held the twig in front of her and waved it around in an arc.

"Go home now," she said. "I promise you all that next time I will not miss should any of you try to harm my family again. Count yourselves lucky tonight that you get to go home to yours."

With her last words, she turned her back on them and looked at Elody and Rinn.

"Go and untie Jalthrax."

They looked hesitantly at the men who were still surrounding them with their swords drawn.

"They will not harm you," Jelena said. "Go."

Without question, they walked past her toward the writhing mass of netting that was Jalthrax. As they passed their aunt, she whispered a word, and the two cats followed along beside them. The men in front of them parted to the sides without a word. With the standoff broken, the others ran as quickly as they could into the night. As they got closer to Ariss with the great cats beside them, he fell to his knees and whimpered.

"Go, Ariss," Rinn said.

Ariss looked up and started to say something, but a roar from the cat next to Rinn sent him scrambling back instead. He was on his knees and then his feet in an instant and running in a blind panic for the woods.

Once he was gone, Elody ran for Jalthrax. She reached him first, but Rinn was right behind her, his dagger in hand. He cut away at the rope and net, going around in a circle until it was loose enough that Jalthrax could burst free. As the netting fell away, Elody wrapped his neck in a great hug. A tiny screech escaped his lips as she squeezed.

Rinn walked past her and stood quietly staring into the darkness where Ariss had run off. Elody gave one last, crushing squeeze and then stood up and walked over.

"He has a little girl," Rinn said. "Nira is her name. She will probably lose her father now because he made a deal with the wrong people."

"He chose his fate, Rinn. The minute he signed up with the guild or decided to steal that ruby."

"Nira didn't choose anything. What is she going to do now?"

"I don't know."

Rinn looked down at Jalthrax who had moved to stand beside Elody.

"I'm so sorry, El," he said, his voice barely a whisper.

"It's not your fault, Rinn."

"Don't do that. Don't make this easy. I don't deserve it."

"You were only trying to do what was right. It's not always the easy thing to do. Forgiving you? That's easy."

She reached her arms out and wrapped him in a hug. Rinn pulled her tight and crushed her against him. She could feel his body shudder.

"No one got hurt, Rinn. Maybe shaken a little, but

Jalthrax is fine."

Jalthrax squawked beside her, and she laughed in spite of the tears. Over Rinn's shoulder, she saw her aunt approaching, her cats nowhere to be seen.

"Come on," Aunt Jelena said. "We're going home."

Rinn kept his eyes focused on the ground while Elody knelt down and hugged Jalthrax again.

"Aunt Jelena, can Jalthrax sleep in the house tonight?" Elody asked.

Jelena laughed, and Elody was taken aback when she heard it.

"I suppose he can. For tonight only though. He can sleep on the upstairs landing outside your room where he won't destroy my things. That should be big enough for him. Now let's go."

Elody stood and took Rinn's hand as they left the field and headed for home.

CHAPTER SEVENTEEN

A Sit Down

RINN WAS LAST through the door behind his aunt, Elody, and Jalthrax. The dragon knocked things over as he made his way inside, seeming so much bigger in such a small space, and Jelena told Elody to take him straight upstairs. Rinn started up after her when she stopped him.

"No," she said flatly. "You sit."

Rinn looked up the stairs and wanted to bolt to his room and lock the door behind him. But he'd seen what his aunt could do now, and he had no doubt she could find her way through a simple locked door. With his head hung low, he walked past her and sat across from the empty chair at the kitchen table. His aunt promptly took the other seat.

"You are so lucky," she said.

"I know, I—"

"Not because no one was hurt, though you can say your prayers to the goddess tonight for that one too. You have a sister who loves you so much that she can forgive you for almost *killing* her companion. And make no mistake, had Jalthrax died tonight, it would have been *you* who killed him."

"I know," he whispered.

"You know nothing! Your sister may forgive you easily, but you'll not get the same from me, boy. I loved Elara, your mother, but I am not her. If something had happened to your sister or that dragon tonight, I would have *burned* you for it."

"Then why don't you?" he shouted.

"Do not dare raise your voice to me!"

Rinn slumped back down in his chair.

"I knew what you were up to," Jelena said. "I've known for months. Just as your mother always knew you were getting into trouble. But I thought you were out drinking and whoring and maybe stealing a few coins here and there. I had no idea you would steal from the goddess's church!"

"I didn't want to," he said, keeping his voice steady. "I went that night to tell Ariss I was out, but I couldn't. I didn't know he was going to rob the temple. He told me his daughter was going to die if we didn't."

"Well, she might very well die now. I don't understand you. I've tried to guide you as Elara would have, but I just don't know you at all."

"I thought I was helping."

Jelena scoffed.

"Just like Malcom. Always trying to help and getting people killed for it."

"Don't *ever* talk about my father!"

"He coddled you and your sister after Elara died, and look what's become of it. You should be a man grown with a family of your own, yet you run around with whores and thieves. And, what's worse is I've allowed it. I should have put you to work the minute you came through my door. Maybe then you wouldn't have made such a mess!"

"This wasn't my mess. I'm not the one who made a deal with the Deathbringers. I was trying to get out!"

"Now you're dealing with *Deathbringers*?" her voice raised even louder. "*Great goddess*, what in Threyl's name have you gotten into?"

"Ariss never told me what he was up to. He said the Deathbringers wanted the gem in exchange for healing his little girl."

"No doubt they are still looking for it then, though they will have quite a bit of trouble finding it here."

Rinn took the ruby from his pouch and laid it on the table. Jelena picked it up and turned it over in her hand.

"You truly cannot feel how powerful this is, can you? You have no idea what you've stolen from them."

"A priest at the church said they use it to commune with the goddess or something."

Jelena shook her head and set the ruby back on the table.

"You will return that tomorrow. I will walk you to the temple to make sure you are safe."

"What if the Deathbringers are waiting?"

"Then I will see to it they find the glory of Vorrod that awaits them."

Rinn smiled a little, but when his aunt didn't return it, he laid his head down on the table.

"Stupid, stupid boy. I'm glad Elara isn't alive to see what you've become."

Rinn bolted up in his chair.

"And what is that? What have I become?"

"A thief and a liar. So you did what was right in the end? So what. So do a lot of men when they get caught. Running around with thieves and murderers."

"I never killed anyone!"

"Well, let's all thank the goddess for that bit of good news."

"What do you want from me?"

"I want you to grow up. I've let you grieve long enough, it's time to be the man your mother wanted you to be."

Rinn's lip started to quiver, and he could feel the tears at the edges of his eyes.

"I tried," he whispered. "I tried, and I failed."

"I don't mean a dragonmage. Your mother could not have cared less if you had become a dragonmage. She wanted you to be a *good man*."

"I tried to get out."

"You should never have gotten in."

"What was I supposed to do? I'm a dragonmage with no dragon! I'm a farmer with no farm! Tell me, Aunt Jelena, what was I supposed to do?"

"Grow into a man. Stop acting like a child. Make your mother proud."

"You don't know what it's like. You have power. Power I never even knew you had. More than I ever thought possible, I saw it tonight. I was supposed to have power too, but it slipped through my fingers. Everything I thought my life would be was gone in an instant when I looked into those eyes and saw *nothing*."

"You think you're the first to fail?"

"You don't understand. I looked at that dragon, and knew that we would be bonded forever. And then, just like that, it was gone. But it will never be gone for me."

Jelena reached her hand across the table and closed it over his. He looked into her eyes and saw them soften just a bit.

"What can I do now?" he asked. "I thought I would be the protector of my village, but I failed to do that. When I was a boy, I even dreamed that one day I would save all of Gondril, but I can't even save myself. I've failed at everything I ever thought I would be."

His aunt squeezed his hand and then stood and walked away. Rinn sat in stunned silence, staring after her and then laid his head down on the table and closed his eyes. A moment later, a loud thud nearly made him jump out of his boots. When he looked up, his aunt was standing over him, her hand resting on a leather-bound tome that sat on the table.

"I cannot give you a dragon," she said. "But I can give you magic. Old magic. Magic your mother would be proud to see you use to help people."

Rinn was staring at the book in front of him, but at her words, his eyes drifted up to meet hers. She pushed the book across the table to touch his arm, and he pulled it back as though he'd touched fire.

"What is it?" he said.

"Your future. If you want it."

He reached out and laid his hand on the cover, running it over the smooth, worn leather. Taking the pages in his hand, he flipped it open to a random page. It practically burst with tightly written words in a language he had never seen before. Floating in the sea of text were the odd picture or two of a hand with tiny arrows and wisps drawn around them to indicate movement. The pages were yellowed and old, but they had not grown brittle with time, and the margins were filled with hand-written scrawl.

Rinn brushed his hand gently and cautiously over the parchment as though the words themselves might burn him. He flipped a few pages and saw more and more of the same. Flowing language, meticulous images, and more hand-written notes in the margin. It looked similar to the books he had studied in his dragonmage training, but the words were all meaningless and offered no explanation.

"What is it?" he asked.

"A wizard's book of spells."

Rinn's head shot up and looked her in the eyes.

"Where did you get it?"

"It was mine."

"Yours?"

"And your grandfather's before me, and who knows before that, and Elara's after me."

Rinn looked down and touched the pages again, running his hand through the words as though he might be able to understand if he just followed along with his finger.

"This was my mother's?"

"It was. That is a beginner's spellbook. Your mother was the last to learn from it after me."

"My mother was a wizard?"

"Why do you think they called her a witch, Rinn?"

"Because she birthed babies and knew herbal remedies."

"Oh, your mother knew so much more than all that."

"How did I not know that?"

"For the same reason you knew nothing of me. Anyone who speaks the old tongue is looked upon as a charlatan… or worse. Most witches are truly nothing more than old washer women who learned herbs and poultices and then learned a few words in the language of magic. They can cast simple spells or cantrips, nothing more."

"You pretend to be just an old witch?"

"It's easier that way."

Rinn turned another page and stared at it.

"Is this the language of magic?"

"Yes. I can teach it to you if you want."

Rinn looked up with just a hint of a smile and nodded.

"I can't believe my mother was a wizard and I never knew."

"Neither did anyone else, and that was best for us all."

"When can we start?"

"Tomorrow morning if you like. But before we do, you have something you need to return to the church."

Rinn looked down and nodded.

"I'll go with you just to make sure you're safe. Then we can return, and I can teach you. But we must keep this a secret. Elody can know, but it's best if that is all."

"Of course."

"I mean it, Rinn. Promise me."

"I promise."

She pushed back from the table and stood.

"Good. Then I'll see you bright and early."

"Can we make it bright and later?"

Jelena laughed.

"Maybe you're right."

She walked off down the hall and then up the stairs.

"Bright and late!" she yelled out.

"Bright and late!" Rinn called back.

He sat there awhile longer turning the pages of the little book over and over, each one more fascinating than the last. The notes in the margins he could understand, and some of them gave him enough context to know what was on the page. When he couldn't hold his eyes open any longer, he laid it closed, picked it up, and went upstairs with the book clutched tightly to his chest.

***

Eryninn sat in silence as he turned two rabbits on a spit over his fire. He was camped far enough away from the goblins that he had dared to light it, knowing from following them that they never sent out or set a watch. He was growing tired of apples and cheese and wanted some real food. The rabbits sizzled low over the heat, and the wafting smell made his mouth water all the more.

He poked at the meat a bit and decided it was done. Looking away from the fire for a moment, he let his eyes adjust to the darkness and stared into the forest. He scanned in every direction and saw nothing. Taking the spit from the fire, he pulled it close and blew on the meat to cool it down enough to eat.

"You know, I had a bet."

Eryninn leapt up and spun around to face the voice behind him, wielding the spit like a sword. Someone stood just beyond the firelight in the shadows. Eryninn scurried back a few steps to add some distance.

"Who are you?"

Even as he asked, his eyes looked the man over. He was shorter than Eryninn, which was saying a lot since Eryninn wasn't very tall as humans go. Long, blonde hair fell down across the man's shoulders and dripped over the dark cloak he wore around his neck. Almond shaped eyes twinkled in the firelight as his smile stretched from pointed ear to pointed ear.

"I bet the others that I could walk up and tap you on the shoulder and you would never hear me coming."

Eryninn's eyes narrowed, but he said nothing.

"I decided not to frighten you too badly, but I think I would have won that bet."

He looked pointedly down at the spit that Eryninn was still holding between them.

"Are you wanting to fight me or offer me dinner?" the elf said.

Eryninn pulled the spit back and jabbed it into the ground.

"Neither then?" the elf said. "Shame. The rabbits did smell delicious."

"Who are you?"

As he asked, he saw movement as three more elves walked up from behind to stand beside him. They looked bored. Only the one in front doing the talking seemed like chatting. Eryninn's hand wrapped around the hilt of his sword and pulled it free just enough to clear the front of his cloak but stopped short of drawing it completely.

"There is no need for that," the lead elf said. "You are no danger to us."

Eryninn let the blade slide back down but kept his hand on it.

"What do you want?" he asked again.

"So rude. Is this how you always treat guests to your fire? I expected at least *half* of your blood to be civilized."

"Where I'm from you don't sneak up on a man, talk down to him, and then expect civility. What do you want?"

One of the elves behind him leaned forward to whisper in his ear, and the one in front rolled his eyes and nodded.

"Curiosity, that is all. We were sent to keep an eye on the goblins, and we saw you watching them as well. So I ask what it is that *you* are doing."

"There's no need to watch them any further," Eryninn said. "I know where they're going, and I'm hoping to beat them there."

"And where are they going?"

"Molner."

"The human outpost?"

"Something like that."

The one leaned forward and whispered again, and again the lead elf nodded.

"What is your name?"

"Eryninn."

"I am Alranir."

"And them?" Eryninn asked, gesturing to the ones behind him.

"My brothers."

They stared silently at each other for several breaths.

"Be careful out here, Eryninn," Alranir said. "Even a half-blood does not deserve to be slaughtered by stinking goblins."

Eryninn tensed and pulled his sword a little, and two of the elves in back started to draw their own. Alranir raised his hand to stop them.

"You are so easily offended by a simple truth like half-blood? It is what you are, after all."

"It's not the word I mind, it's the feelings behind it."

Alranir shook his head.

"Be careful, half-blood."

He turned to leave, his cloak fluttering up as he spun on his heels. The others followed without another look except for one who stood at the back. He remained where he was, staring at Eryninn.

"Never seen a bastard half-blood before?" Eryninn asked.

The elf quickly shook his head.

"It's not that," he said. "I was admiring your sword."

Eryninn looked down to where he had his sword half out from beneath his cloak.

"I know who you are," the elf said.

"And who am I?"

"You're Tarinthalas's son."

Eryninn couldn't hide his surprise.

"How did you know that?"

"I know that he is dead, and you carry his cloak and sword. It could only be you."

A whistle pierced the darkness from where the elves had retreated, and he turned his head to look after them.

"Be safe, son of Tarin."

"Wait," Eryninn called out softly.

But the elf slunk back away from the firelight and was gone. Eryninn stared after him for several moments before going back to his fire and kicking it out. He stared down at the rabbits still resting on the spit stuck in the ground, but he found that he'd lost his appetite.

Chapter Eighteen

Prepare for War

RINN LOOKED BACK over his shoulder where Jelena was standing in the street watching him. With a resigned sigh, he pushed the great doors of the temple of Threyl open wide and stepped inside. The guards in the church were gathered in groups as he entered, but they paid him no heed when he walked in.

Just another soul looking for salvation.

The doors behind him made the gentlest click as they swung closed, leaving him in near darkness. Torches were lit all around the foyer of the temple, but it took a few seconds for Rinn's eyes to adjust to the change. Rinn's shadow stretched out across the stone floor, dancing in the flickering firelight as it crept up the golden doors in front of him. Taking a deep breath, he strode right up and pushed them open.

The altar room was much more brightly lit than the rest of the church and was exactly as it had been the night he stole the gem. No guards wandered between the pews, no clergy praying at the altar, and no one kneeling in the aisles. Perfectly empty. Rinn wasted no time in taking advantage as he jogged down the long, red carpet toward the altar at the far end of the room. With another glance around, he pulled the ruby from his pocket and nudged it back into the hole in the golden filigree on the front. He had almost gotten it perfect when…

"I knew you would come back."

Rinn spun on his heels and stared up into Oryna's face. She eyed the dagger he'd taken out to work the stone in, and he saw where she looked and quickly tucked it away.

"I was just trying to wedge the ruby back in."

"No attempt to lie? No story about how you were only polishing it? You admit you stole it?"

"You already know I did."

"Yes, but I had hoped for a good story at least. You gave me a story of a young girl dying when I met you that first night. Why not stick with that?"

"You knew that was me?"

"Your magic does not mask your voice, and though you spoke little, I remembered it very clearly. It was kind and caring. A little frightened. Not at all the voice of a thief trying to rob a church. Which is the only reason I didn't scream for the guards."

"I did think I was trying to help a little girl. Only it turned out the little girl didn't need my help. I was deceived by a friend, and now I'm just trying to make things right."

"Is that why you're here now?"

"Yes."

"Then my prayer was answered. Looks like you were worth it after all, Rinn."

"Are you going to call the guards to arrest me?" Rinn asked glancing around nervously.

"I did not call them that first night when I actually

thought I might be in danger, why would I call them now when I *know* I am in none?"

"To arrest me for stealing the ruby?"

"The ruby has not been stolen. See? It's right there on the altar."

Rinn looked down at the ruby that was now set back in its proper place.

"I don't understand," he said. "Why have you helped me?"

"Because you looked like you needed some help."

"And that's all it takes?"

"Threyl guided you to me for a reason. I don't know why, but I've learned not to ask too many questions where her will is concerned. It used to get me into a lot of trouble."

She laughed quietly to herself as Rinn rose from his knees and stood awkwardly.

"Now go," she said. "Before someone *does* see you and decides to arrest you."

Before Rinn could turn, she moved in and held him in an embrace. Not knowing what else to do, Rinn moved his arm around her and hugged back. When she let go, she pushed him back at arms length and squared his shoulders.

"Go," she said.

Rinn didn't have to be told a third time. He skipped around her and jogged back down toward the double doors. Pushing them open, he stepped out into the darker foyer and stopped awkwardly as his eyes adjusted and settled on a familiar face.

"Berym?"

The knight was standing perfectly straight and stiff and talking to what Rinn guessed was a high-ranking priest of the temple. At his name, he turned his head, and a big grin lit up his face.

"Rinn!"

Berym took two huge steps, grabbed his arm and shook it vigorously. The other hand he used to pat Rinn's shoulder until Rinn thought he might clap it right off his body.

"By the goddess, man, what are you doing in here?"

"Uh… the goddess, actually. I was in there checking the place out. But wait, what are you doing here?"

"I was just chatting with the father here about needing some of their help."

"What kind of help?"

"Nothing good, I fear. But I'll tell you all more of that when I come and find you later. Right now I must make arrangements with the father. May I come by later to talk?"

"Elody would have your hide if you didn't," Rinn said with a smile.

"Well, I want her there too. This concerns her as well."

"What does?"

"I have so many things to take care of. I promise I will tell you everything when I see you next."

"Okay," Rinn said with a shrug.

With that, he pushed open the doors and stepped out of the darkness and into the light.

***

Elody, Rinn and Jelena were all at the table when Berym arrived at the house. The smile on his mustached face brightened Elody up instantly, and she leapt to her feet to give him a big hug. She loved the way her toes dangled in the air as he lifted her off the ground.

"Good to see you, little girl."

"You too, old man."

Berym laughed and lowered her to the ground.

"Jelena," Berym said. "It is good to see you."

"Your trip was not well I take it," she said.

"Why do you say that?"

"Rinn told me you had planned to be gone for a while, yet here you are. He also said you were visiting the priests of Threyl this morning. Sounds like you've got a fight on your hands."

Berym shook his head and smiled.

"You are as wise as you are beautiful."

"Why, thank you, good knight. Now, get to it."

Berym sighed and unbuckled his sword belt, setting it to the side of the table before taking the last seat around it. Elody saw the way he winced as he sat down.

"Are you okay?" she said.

"Just tired and sore. I feel like I've been on a horse for a week now."

"Spit it out," Jelena said.

"I'm sure Rinn told you that I had gone to Derne for a few weeks. But when I got there, the entire village was gone. Destroyed by fire."

Elody gasped and covered her mouth, while Rinn wrung his hands white in a tight circle. Jelena sat unmoving and waited for him to continue.

"No one was killed, thankfully, but the village was destroyed. I ran in to try and help anyone still alive and, by her grace, found them all hiding in the church basement. Eryninn had reached them ahead of the army somehow and warned them."

"Eryninn?" Elody said. "How did *he* get there?"

"He'd been tracking the army since they left the

mountains a few days before the attack."

"Tracking what army?" Rinn asked.

"Goblins," Berym said. "A huge army of them. Thousands of them."

"Oh, no," Elody said. "Those poor people."

"They will rebuild," Berym said. "Thanks to Eryninn, they were spared the worst of it. But now the goblin horde marches for Molner."

"Molner?" Elody asked, alarmed.

She felt a flutter of panic. Eliath was in Molner.

"Why Molner?" Jelena asked.

"We don't know. Big city, borders the elven lands. We don't know why they've chosen there, if in fact they have. We don't know for sure, but that seems their most likely target given their path."

"What are we doing about it?" Rinn asked.

"I rode hard from Derne to get here as fast I could without killing my horse. I've already rallied the knights, and they've sent out riders to all in the area between here and Molner, and even some beyond. I spoke with the priests this morning, and they have agreed to send clerics along with us."

"What of the dragonmages?" Elody asked. "We should be there too."

"Molner is already under their protection because of its proximity to the Eldest."

"The Eldest?" Jelena asked.

"The Eldest dragon," Rinn said. "The oldest of the dragons of light who rules over the rest. We learned a little about her in school but not much."

"She is the dragon who decides the laws for all the dragons of light," Elody said. "Her name is Ferinelis'ul'Wayarr, if I remember right, but all the dragonmages just call her Eldest."

"There have been dragonmages guarding her for several months now," Berym said. "Ever since the attacks on dragon mothers started becoming more frequent. Though I doubt she needs their protection, they believe that this monster will eventually have to come for her."

"When do we leave?" Rinn and Elody both said.

"I had hoped you would say that," Berym said. "We leave in the morning. Rinn will ride close to me as my squire in training, and Elody can be my personal mage."

"Oh, no," Jelena said. "They are *not* going with you."

"I would not ask it, but these times are dire, and we need every man and mage who can fight. They are not children, Jelena, it is their choice to make."

Jelena started to speak but held her tongue as she shook her head.

"You are right," she said. "It's their decision."

Berym looked at the two of them, and they both nodded.

"Good," Berym said. "It will be a long, fast ride, but if we're lucky we can beat the goblins and maybe prepare some defenses before they arrive."

Berym stood to leave and grasped first Rinn's shoulder, then Elody's. With a squeeze, he grabbed up his sword belt and walked to the door.

"We leave at sunrise," he said and pulled the door closed behind him.

***

Rinn felt good being back in the saddle. He hadn't gone anywhere since they arrived in Havnor six months ago. Not since they left Jornath and their old lives behind. He took a deep breath of fresh air.

Nothing like being on the road.

Elody rode beside him, both of them in the saddle of a horse the knights had given them. When he looked at her, she smiled.

"What?" Rinn asked with an annoyed glance.

"You just look happy."

"Glad to be out of the city. I forgot how much I missed open air. We spent our whole lives in a little village, and I forgot how nice the quiet could be. I'm just glad to be out of there."

"Even if it's to go off and fight goblins?"

"Especially to go off and fight goblins."

"You're not scared?"

Rinn looked sidelong at her.

"Of course I am. Berym says these goblins are just like the ones that killed Dad, only thousands of them."

Rinn trailed off and took a deep breath.

"I'm terrified," he said quietly.

Elody sighed and looked up to the sky, and Rinn followed her gaze. There had been no sign of Jalthrax since they started. He had flown off ahead of them as they left the gates of Havnor behind. When he turned back, Elody was staring at the ground, her eyes cold.

"You were waiting for Eliath weren't you?" Rinn asked.

Elody nodded.

"Were you just going to run off without saying goodbye?"

"That was the plan, yes," she said.

"I suppose I would have deserved it."

They rode on in silence for a long while, the rhythmic clip clop of the horses lulling them both in the saddle.

"I'm glad you're here," Rinn said at last.

"Are we being fools?" Elody asked. "What can we do

against an army that big?"

"I don't know. All we can do is offer to help."

Elody looked down the line of horses to the knights at the front of their procession. They rode three-across in perfect formation, their shining armor reflecting in the sun. There were maybe fifty knights and squires that Berym had managed to gather in Havnor, including some that had come from nearby villages to join them.

"Does he really think he can help with so few against so many?"

"Berym would be on this road by himself if no one would join him."

"You're right," she said. "He's the bravest man I know."

"Or maybe the dumbest."

"Rinn!"

"Maybe a little of both?"

Elody laughed, and Rinn joined her.

"That's an awful thing to say," she said.

"Well, what would you say of a man who rushed to meet a thousand goblins?"

"I'd say he was a fool, I guess."

"Thank the gods for foolhardy knights."

***

Rinn climbed down off his horse and stretched. Berym had called a halt for the day to let the horses rest and let them all drink from a nearby stream. They would arrive in Molner the next day, but it would be long into the afternoon before they did. The different groups of riders had broken apart into their own little clusters and begun digging fire pits.

Elody led her horse next to his and watched them all scurry about like ants building up the campsite.

"Where do we go?" she asked.

Rinn looked around at the different camps and counted up their options. At the head of the line and closest to the road were the knights. They had immediately set about building a camp for everyone as they came to a halt and looked on with dismay as some of the others began making their own camps. The only ones to join them were the priests of Threyl. They crowded in with the knights and all mingled together.

The mayor of Havnor had called for volunteers from the city guard and militia, and some had responded. They were off to one side building their own camp, but not too far from the knights. Some of them looked like men you'd want at your back in a fight, but most of them were young boys. Probably hoping to make a name killing goblins. The final group was as far from the others as the trees would allow them.

The Deathbringers.

No sooner had word spread that the mayor was looking for volunteers to fight goblins that the church of Vorrod volunteered their services. Their group was small. Rinn counted a dozen priests and maybe as many paladins of their order. Too small to look that menacing, to be sure, but their reputation was enough to ensure their solitude.

Rinn shuddered just looking at them.

"We could eat with the Deathbringers," he said. "They probably make a great stew."

"Just don't ask them what's in it."

Rinn chuckled.

"I don't like the look some of the men from the militia are giving me," Elody said.

"I guess it's the knights then."

"Good, that's where I wanted to go. At least we know someone."

"I saw someone else I know too."

"Really? Who?"

"Come on, I'll introduce you."

The sun had slowly set as the camps were made, and the fires were now burning bright in the darkness. Food and provisions were passed around from the various wagons, and within the hour, everyone had a nice meal cooking over their fire.

Rinn led Elody over to the knights' fire and stopped beside a robed priestess.

"Lady Oryna," Rinn said. "May my sister and I join you?"

Oryna looked up and smiled.

"Please do. I haven't had the pleasure of meeting your sister."

Rinn sat down beside her and motioned Elody to sit on the other side.

"How do you know my brother?"

"He has come to the church a few times," Oryna said.

"Oh," Elody said.

"We met when he came in with a... crisis of conscience."

"I know a little something about that," Elody said.

"We all need guidance now and then," Oryna said. "Some just more than others."

Elody chuckled and nodded.

"Oh, have a laugh at my expense," Rinn said. "Go right ahead."

A knight walked past and handed each of them a bowl filled with soup from the cook pot. Elody stood and gave Rinn a little wink when Oryna bent down to take a bite.

"I think I'll go and find Berym," Elody said.

She walked around the side of the fire without another word and was gone. Oryna watched her go and then looked back at Rinn.

"Your sister is very beautiful."

"She looks so much like my mother," Rinn said. "She has her strength too. And her stubbornness. Could've done without that last one."

"And you take after your father?"

"I hope so. He was just as stubborn though, so I guess we were doomed either way."

"Where are they now?"

Rinn pushed the soup around his bowl.

"They're both dead."

"Oh, I'm sorry."

"My mother died when Elody was only five. My father died last fall when goblins burned our village and destroyed our farm."

Oryna's eyes softened as she let out a sigh.

"And now it's just you and Elody?"

"And our aunt. She took us in."

"You are lucky to have so many in your life who love you. Even if some are gone now."

Rinn kicked a rock at the fire and looked up at her.

"How old are you?" he asked.

"Why?"

"Because you seem so much smarter than me, but you don't look much older."

Oryna chuckled and shook her head.

"I have seen twenty-three years, but they have been long ones. Some in very dark places. You could say that I have lived a lot more than the years I have been alive. So

I am not much older than you, and probably not much smarter. I've just seen more of the world, I guess."

"Berym said something like that before too."

He looked across the fire to where Elody had sat down beside Berym. Even with the din of conversation all around him, the knight's bellowing laugh cut through the night. They couldn't hear the conversation, but they watched him for a while and smiled each time he would laugh.

"Berym was the one who brought us to Havnor after fighting to save our village."

"He is a good man. He brings in the sick and the hungry he finds in the city. They hide all over, but he seems to find them wherever they are and drag them to us for a hot meal and a warm bed."

"He wanted me to be a knight," Rinn said.

"And you don't want that?"

"I'm no knight. Not like Berym."

"You are not as old and wise as he is now, no. I imagine Berym himself was not like Berym when he was your age. Perhaps all you need is some time."

"Maybe."

"Well, you don't need to be a knight to be brave. You're here now, aren't you?"

"Is it bravery if you're running from something else?"

"Which is more terrible? The thing you run from or the thing you run toward?"

"Well, either one is just as likely to get me killed."

"Then why choose this path?"

"Because this is where Berym is going, and he said these people needed help."

Oryna smiled her little smile.

"I think you would make a fine knight some day."

Rinn chuckled and shook his head.

"I tried putting on the armor one time and fell over. It was so heavy I couldn't get back up. I just laid there on my back trying to turn over while Berym laughed until he nearly choked."

Rinn flailed his arms in the air for effect. Oryna started laughing hard, and Rinn couldn't help but join her. He flailed his arms again, and she burst out again, which only made him laugh harder. He got so loud that when he stopped, he saw Elody and Berym watching them across the fire. Calming enough to take a breath, she wiped a tear from the side of her eye.

"You certainly have the laugh down," she said with a smile. "I think the armor is something you grow into."

"Yes, but it's still heavy. It takes a lot of strength to wear it."

"I believe that it does, yes."

***

Elody couldn't stop laughing as Berym threw his head back and nearly fell off the log he was sitting on. This only made him laugh harder, and she was in tears. The other knights nearby were all laughing along too. She had missed Berym. She tried to catch her breath to finish her story.

"So then Rinn tried sneaking up on him. Only Hogwood had been rolling around in the mud quite a bit by now and was completely covered."

Berym managed to calm himself enough to listen.

"He snuck out from behind a tree and jumped on him, I guess trying to knock him to the ground. But that old pig had some stout legs, and instead of falling, he took off running. With Rinn on his back."

Berym started bellowing again, and Elody couldn't

control herself either.

"In his defense, he did manage to hold on for a few seconds before slipping off and landing in the mud himself. Hogwood sort of stopped and looked back at Rinn rolling in the mud and decided to join him in the fun. So, he jumped right in and started rolling around with him!"

"Stop! Stop!" Berym shouted. "I can't... breathe!"

Elody only laughed harder, which was contagious to all of the knights around them. Her story finished, she stopped to take a few deep breaths and fill her lungs back up. The rest of the knights went back to their own stories while Berym finally managed to right himself on the log and catch his own breath.

"My sides are aching," he said.

He rubbed his stomach and took several deep breaths. They sat in silence for a while, just staring into the fire. Elody reached back to touch Jalthrax who was resting behind the log she and Berym were seated on. She brushed her hand along his neck and found that Berym was doing the same on the other side. Jalthrax let out a low growl of pleasure. Berym reached over to tap her on the arm and pointed across the fire.

"Your brother seems to have made a friend over there."

Elody looked up and watched for a second.

"So it seems," she said.

"He could ask for no woman better than Lady Oryna. She is as strong as she is beautiful. And that is saying quite a lot."

"Then why didn't you ever court her?" she asked, poking him in the side.

Berym chuckled and waved a hand.

"Courting is not the business of knights any longer. Once upon a time, perhaps, but that is not the life we lead anymore. Besides, I save my attentions for someone else."

"Someone important?"

"Very important."

"Tell me about her."

Berym chuckled.

"Why do women always want to know what is in a man's heart?"

"Sometimes we just need to be reminded that we're in there somewhere. Even for a knight, brave and strong."

"If any man were to ever tell you the truth of his heart, you would almost certainly find a woman at its core. From the time we first see you clearly, it is why we do most everything we do. Any man who tells you different is lying."

"Everything you do is for this girl?"

Berym sighed and stared into the fire.

"In one way or another," Berym said. "Things are not always so clear. I can say that the things I do are because of the man I want to be for her."

"That's sweet."

"She would not say so, I think."

"Does she love you?"

"I don't know, she has never said."

"You don't know because she hasn't told you? That doesn't sound like the observant Berym I know."

"It's not so easy to see with your heart," he said.

"Then what do you see with your eyes?"

"Not enough of her."

"And she misses you?"

"As much as I do her. Which is more than I can bear

sometimes."

"But you say you do the things you do for her," she said.

"That is what I have to believe, yes. Otherwise I couldn't do what I must do."

"Then why do it?"

Berym thought a moment and then looked around him and nodded his head at the other men around them.

"There are good men in the world," he said. "But it never seems like there are enough."

"So it's your job to save the world then?"

"Well, when you say it like *that* it sounds foolish."

"I didn't mean it like that. I just don't understand."

"You will. You're young yet, but the path you walk will be like mine. Though I pray not exactly so. When you have the power to help those weaker than you, it's not so easy to simply throw down your weapons and say you don't wish to do it anymore."

He pointed around the camp to all of the fires dotting the darkness, and Elody could see the glow of smiling faces and hear the sound of laughter cutting through the night.

"We are all tiny fires burning in the dark. Each one of us good men trying to ward off the cold and the evil in this world. But there will always be more night than fires to light it."

"My father marched off to war before I was even born. My mother was pregnant when he left. I don't remember much, but Rinn still talks about how hard it was not having him there. We needed him home, and he was off fighting for someone else, for good. He left me before I was even born."

"Your father didn't know your mother was pregnant

when left."

"How do you know that?"

"He told me so. Last fall, on our day trips up to the ridge and back. We had many hours to talk, your father and I. He didn't know she was pregnant, but your mother knew before he left."

"She was a witch," Elody said. "She knew everything. I have memories of her, but they're only little flashes in my head. A wave of her hair. A knowing smile on her lips. Rinn tells me about her sometimes so I don't forget."

"Why do you think she didn't tell him she was pregnant if she already knew?"

"I don't know why, but he was gone for years. I was almost four the first time I saw him. My mother died a year later, and he was all I had. He was like a stranger to me. Rinn had to remind me all the time to respect and obey him, that he was my father, but I only wanted Rinn to take care of me."

"Your father was a good man," Berym said.

"I know that. But when we needed him most, he left us."

"On our trips into the forest he told me a little of his time during the war. He fought for King Dornan, a good king by all accounts. He fought against my king, King Hallex. An evil man by my own reckoning. But your father was not called to fight for his king, he told me. He volunteered along with a dozen other men from Jornath and went off to fight for what was right. Your mother didn't tell your father about you because she knew he wouldn't go if he knew."

"My father went to war when he didn't have to?"

"Because he knew what was right and what had to be

done. Your mother knew too."

"But what about me and Rinn? *We* needed him too."

"Without men like your father, it is likely that Hallex would have won the wars and ruled over all the Three Kingdoms. Believe me when I tell you that is not a fate any of us deserved. Do not be angry at your father for leaving you. Without good men like him, we would all live in a much darker place now."

Elody looked down and wiped a tear from her eye.

"But there is still evil in the world. He's gone now and nothing has changed."

Berym put his arm around her and pulled her close.

"Without the light, the darkness would cover everything."

Berym's armor against her face was cold, but it still felt warm being in his arm.

"Is that how you keep going?"

Berym sighed and patted her shoulder.

"It's all I have."

CHAPTER NINETEEN

ARRIVAL

RINN DREAMED OF a grand entrance when their procession arrived at the gates of Molner. The knights, the priests, the common men of which he was a part. All of them come to save the great city in their hour of need. What he didn't expect was the welcome they received.

Which was none at all.

Even back in the line beside Elody, just behind the knights, he could see the gates of the city standing wide open as they approached. People walked in and out of the city with ease. He stood in the stirrups to get a better look and convince himself it wasn't an illusion. Elody gave him a worried look as he sat back down.

"Shouldn't they be preparing for the attack?" she asked.

"Unless they don't know it's coming."

"Oh, gods. What if Eryninn never made it through?"

Rinn shot her a look and then spurred his horse on. He heard Elody coming up behind him just as quickly. They trotted past the knights, who didn't even look in their direction as they passed, and rode up alongside Berym. Their horses fought to move through the traffic of peddlers and farmers coming in and out of the city. It was as if it was just another ordinary day.

"Something is not right," Berym said as he heard them come up beside him.

"What if Eryninn didn't make it through?" Elody asked.

"Then let us pray he is still alive and hiding somewhere."

Rinn looked around at the wide, open field that surrounded the city walls. Small tents and stalls had been setup all around as an open market just outside the city, but it still struck him as odd that it would be so wide open. It was as if the city was floating in a sea of grass.

"Why are there are no trees so far out from the wall?" Rinn asked.

"Molner was built as an outpost to guard against attack from the elven kingdoms to the west," Berym said. "The forest all around the wall was cleared of everything to make a wide open field that gave the elves no place to hide should they risk an attack."

"I have never seen a city look so barren," RInn said. "Other than the wall, it looks defenseless so out in the open. Does it work?"

"Against elves maybe," Berym said. "They prefer to hide among the trees and spare as many lives as possible. Goblins have no such problem charging across an open field to their deaths."

Berym kicked his horse out in front as they neared the gate.

"Ho there!" he shouted up.

A guard along the wall who had been watching their approach stood up straight and put his hand up.

"Ho there, good knight," he yelled back.

"Go and fetch your captain and tell him to meet me at once! Quickly now!"

The man looked at another standing to the side and behind him. They spoke back and forth a few times before standing up straight and turning back to Berym.

"As you wish, sir knight."

He jogged off down the wall and disappeared. Berym wasted no time in waiting and rode his knights unceremoniously through the gates. The villagers on the road moved swiftly out of the way of the coming horses, but the going was slow through the crowd. Once inside, he leapt out of the saddle and barked orders to the others as they began dismounting. He turned to Rinn and Elody standing there with Jalthrax.

"You three stay close to me for now," he said, and they handed their reins to a nearby knight.

Berym marched off, and Rinn and Elody exchanged a glance. With a shrug, they both fell into step behind him as he continued shouting orders, first to the knights, and then the waiting priests. By the time everyone was in motion, they saw a man running down the street toward him. Rinn wasn't sure, but it looked like the same man who was previously up on the wall. When he reached them, he paused and bent over to catch his breath before speaking.

"My… my lord… my lord Koldar will see you now. If you'll… if you'll just follow me."

Berym's face hardened like a stone, and he glared down at the man.

"I asked you to bring me your captain. And you tell me that he is waiting for *me*?"

The man stopped puffing and stood up straight with a look of fear growing in his eyes. He glanced around for some support and found none.

"Those are my orders, my lord."

Berym growled.

"Well, lead on then!"

The man snapped his legs together and then spun on his heels back the way he came. Berym fell into step behind him and waved his hand back for them to follow. The man kept a casual pace on his walk back, apparently in no hurry. As they marched through the city, Rinn was astonished at how normal everything was. People walking home, people selling wares, guards nodding as they passed.

They have no idea what is coming for them.

A shadow passed overhead, and Rinn and Elody looked up to see Jalthrax sailing out in front of them to land. He chose a spot just down the road where they were walking and glided to a stop in front of them. Elody walked up beside him and gave him a quick pat before moving to catch up to Berym.

When at last they reached their destination, the man reached for the door to pull it open, but Berym was quicker and shoved him out of the way. Elody leaned down to Jalthrax.

"Stay out here. I need you by me until we know what's going on."

The little dragon nodded, and she and Rinn followed behind Berym. The knight stormed into the room and marched right up to the desk that sat near the far wall.

"Captain Koldar?"

"Yes."

The man stood as he answered and held his hand out to the knight even as he looked past him to the two of them standing to the back. He looked every bit the soldier Rinn imagined the captain of a town guard to be. Tall, broad shoulders, cropped hair, and a sturdy sword at his belt. The only thing that stood out of place was his face. It was perfect. There were no scars, no marks, no signs of age or battle. Rinn would think him young if he didn't know better.

"And you are Sir Berym, yes?"

Berym pulled his hand away and drew back a step.

"I've been expecting your arrival," the man said.

"I sent no word ahead," Berym said.

"Did you not send the half-elf, Eryninn?"

"You've seen him then?"

"I'm right here."

The three of them spun at the sound of his voice behind them. He stood in the doorway with a wry smile on his face and bowed with a dramatic flourish. Elody ran and wrapped her arms around him, and to Rinn's surprise, he returned the embrace. He even gave her a squeeze and lifted her off the ground, though he was not much taller than she was.

Berym walked over and smiled as he put Elody down.

"Glad you made it. When we arrived and saw no preparations for battle, we thought we'd lost you along the way."

"Oh, no, I arrived night before last. Ample time to prepare a city's defenses. Especially one already so well-guarded as this one. But they refused to listen to me."

Berym marched to stand across the desk from the captain.

"You mean to tell me you have known the goblin army was coming for almost two days and have done *nothing*?"

"No, we have made some small preparations. We—"

"*Small preparations*? An army of ten thousand goblins will be on your doorstep, possibly within hours, and you've made some small preparations?"

"We are fully prepared."

Berym turned to look at them as though he was waiting for someone else to speak. His face turned red as he trembled, his hands clenched in tight fists. When he turned back, he began shouting uncontrollably at the man.

"Where are your soldiers? Where is the militia? Where are your defenses? Your damn gate stood wide open, and we walked right in as though we'd come for a summer picnic!"

"The gates will be closed when the goblins arrive."

"Oh, well thank the gods for that! Did you hear, Eryninn? They'll be fully prepared just as soon as the goblins arrive. They're going to close up the gates! We'll all be just fine!"

"There's no need for—"

"Gather up your men and have them at that wall in one hour! Draft men into the militia and have them join us! And by all Threyl's mercy, *close the damn gate!*"

"With all due respect to your station, sir, you have no authority here."

"Well, with all due respect to your station, you're a damn fool!"

"You cannot come into my city and start ordering people around."

"Well, aren't we all glad for that. Gods forbid we be prepared when a goblin horde comes to destroy us all. Did you tell them, Eryninn?"

"Until my face was blue."

"The half-elf has told us enough," the captain said.

"The goblins are a ragtag group led by a religious zealot who claims to be a god. They have no armor, they have no siege weapons, and they have no dragonmages. Molner was built as the last line of defense between the Three Kingdoms and the elven lands. It was built to fend off elven armies. If these goblins arrive as you say, they will be cut down like so much wheat."

"By you and what army?"

"We need no army, Sir Berym. Molner has never needed an army. We have a dragon. A very old and powerful one. And she has protected our fair city for centuries. We live up against the elven border, sir, we are no strangers to having an enemy right outside our walls."

"You think that a dragon will save you from an army of this size?"

"As I told your friend yesterday and the day before, the goblins have no weapons to harm a dragon. They have no ballista, they have no catapults, they have no magic. It does not matter if they have a hundred *thousand* goblins, there is nothing they can do against a dragon. The Eldest will destroy them all with nothing but a few arrows scratching her scales for the trouble."

"You want to rely on a dragon to do the fighting for you?"

"Why risk the lives of my men or the lives of these people? The eldest will rid us of this scourge, and no one on our side need die at all."

"And what if she fails?"

"You know little of dragons, sir knight. She is the Eldest. There is no creature more powerful on all the continents. The goblins made a huge mistake thinking they could march on *my* city."

Berym sighed and looked to Eryninn pleading, but

the half-elf only shrugged.

"I've been at this for two days," Eryninn said with a dismissive wave. "The answer is always the same. I say we march out the wide open gate we came in through and leave them all to their fate. Whatever the gods and the Eldest deem it to be."

"No," Berym said flatly. "We have marched here to help, and help is what we'll do."

"We are glad that you are here, Sir Berym. You and all of your knights. When the goblins are gone, I know that the mayor would want to honor such brave men. You must have ridden hard to arrive here so quickly, and for that you have our thanks."

"If you will not command your men, can I at least have them ready the walls?"

The captain sighed loudly.

"I will order my men to make ready on the wall if that will put you at ease. But I will not frighten the people and call up the militia. There is no need to cause a panic."

Rinn saw Berym's fists clench tight just below the desk where the captain could not see them. Then, without a word, he spun on his heels and stormed out. They all filed out after him and then ran to catch up where he was already marching quickly toward the gate. Rinn heard a screech as Jalthrax leapt into the air and flew just above them.

"Stupid arse!" Berym shouted. "Stupid, stupid arse!"

"They won't listen," Eryninn said. "There's nothing else you can do. Pack everyone up and let us leave. Unless I missed my guess, there is still time. A few hours at least before the goblins arrive."

"No. I will not abandon these people simply because

those sworn to protect them refuse to do so. That is when we are needed the most."

"They clearly don't want your help," Eryninn said.

"They will have it just the same."

Rinn glanced at his sister, and they both exchanged a questioning look. Berym jogged back to the knights, and the two of them hurried to keep up.

"Gather up!" Berym shouted as he neared.

The knights all stopped whatever they were doing and collected around him. A few of the priests came over to see what was going on while only a single man from the Havnor militia came.

"The city of Molner has decided it does not need to mount a defense against the approaching goblins, but I will not stand by and do nothing. I ask the same of you. I want my knights going through the city gathering as many arrows and supplies for the wall as you can find. If the clerics can spare some of their prayers, we could use wards and spells on the gate and walls of the city. Everyone else, grab a shovel. We have some digging to do."

The knights began moving as soon as Berym finished speaking while the others stood dumbfounded for a moment. Then, the priests went back to the rest of their group and they moved as one to the outer wall. The militia men did not look pleased at the news, and Berym was already walking in their direction before the complaints began. He stopped in front of them and saluted.

"You all have the most important job here. I need a deep ditch dug across the front gate and around the outer wall. As far and as deep as you can make it. If our information is correct, these goblins have no siege weapons to speak of. If we can keep most of them from the walls, we might actually stand a chance of repelling them."

He paused to lock eyes with the men in the crowd.

"Your work could mean the difference between life and death for these people. Can I entrust this task to you all?"

The men began nodding, some of them shouting yes and raising their swords. Berym smiled and clasped the shoulder of the nearest man.

"I knew I could count on the strong men of Havnor. Knights and priests are too delicate for work like this. I need men with strong backs and stronger hearts."

The men nodded, and Rinn was surprised to see their faces turning from scowls to stern nods and even a few smiles and chuckles.

"Find shovels anywhere you can and get started."

With a final salute, Berym rounded on Rinn and Elody and walked a few steps away.

"Find somewhere you can fit in and help," Berym said.

He walked off back toward the center of town leaving them standing there watching him go.

"What do we do now?" Elody asked.

"You were born a farmer just like I was," Rinn said. "Grab a shovel."

***

It started as a slow trickle.

A few dozen goblins ambled out of the forest and stood on the other side of the open field staring up at the wall surrounding Molner. Elody stood next to Rinn and Eryninn and watched them. Slowly but steadily they came, more and more appearing as the minutes passed.

"This is only the beginning," Eryninn said calmly.

"How long until they are all here?" Elody asked.

"A few hours maybe."

"And then they'll attack," Rinn said.

"Maybe not," Eryninn said. "I've been watching them for a while now, and they do not act as normal goblins. It will be dark by the time the tail of the army arrives, and that is when I would most expect them to attack. Goblins are at a great advantage in the darkness because their vision is like that of my people, and they can see as clearly at night as in day."

"But you don't think they will attack tonight?" Rinn asked.

"No," Eryninn said. "When they sacked Derne, they attacked when the sun was high. It makes no sense, but I have never been in a goblin's head. Perhaps they want to show that even at a disadvantage they have the superior force."

"That doesn't sound very smart," Elody said.

"Goblins are not known for brains," the half-elf said.

They watched in silence as more and more goblins poured onto the field. It was as though a dam somewhere upstream had broken and now they came in great waves threatening to wash away all life. A loud clanking of metal boots stirred them from their trance, and Elody looked down the wall to see Berym approaching. His look was stern as he stopped beside them.

"Here we are again, friends. Vastly outnumbered by goblins and trying to help good people."

"At least there's a big wall between us and them this time," Rinn said.

"Won't matter much when they come," Eryninn said. "Listen."

They all stopped and strained their ears to hear.

"I don't hear anything but goblins," Elody said.

"Chopping," Eryninn said. "They're cutting down trees. Mostly likely to make ladders or a battering ram. A force that size, they won't simply stand there and let us kill them."

"Let us hope this dragon is as all powerful as the people of Molner seem to think she is," Berym said.

"She is even more powerful than they think," Elody said. "The goblins are foolish to attack in her presence."

"Then they know something we don't," Eryninn said. "They have shown none of the ignorance and stupidity of common goblins so far. This Gortogh is a leader like no other I have seen. He commands them with a word, and they fall over themselves to obey. There is more to the story than has been revealed."

"We have done all we can," Berym said. "The men did well. The ditch is deep. Wards have been laid along the walls. Even the Deathbringers were helping. I suppose a goblin soul's as good as another to Vorrod, and they aim to send many his way when the fighting starts."

"Archers?" Eryninn asked.

"As many as we could find among the town guard and Havnor militia. Against a force this size, it matters little if they can aim, so long as they loose in the right direction. Can I leave you in charge of the wall?"

Eryninn nodded and bent over the wall to look at the gate.

"And if they break through?" he asked.

"The gate is solid and strong. If they manage to knock it down, they will meet the knights of Gondril on the other side. And they will not find *us* so easy to break."

"What about us?" Rinn asked.

Elody caught the look Berym gave Eryninn but said nothing.

"You will remain up on the wall," the knight said. "You are both trained with a bow, as much as any of the rest of these men. For his own protection, Jalthrax should stay down there behind the wall."

Elody looked down the side of the wall where Jalthrax was looking up at her and smiled feebly at him.

"I want you to stay close to Eryninn," Berym said. "Follow his orders. He will see you through this if we are fated to make it through."

Eryninn nodded. A loud screech broke up their circle, and they all stared up into the sky as a shadow passed overhead. A dragon whose color Elody couldn't see flew a circle around the city.

"The Eldest?" she asked.

"No," Eryninn said. "Too small. She will not come until the fighting begins, I think."

Another shadow, and then another passed over the wall. Four dragons in all circled the city above, and everyone, goblin and man alike, watched them with awe. One by one they dropped from the sky and glided down to land in the center of the city. Elody smiled as the belly of a red dragon flew over.

"I recognize that dragon," she said.

"Tark?" Rinn asked, but she was already running down the wall.

"Who is Tark?" Berym asked.

"The red dragon of a man named Eliath we met back in Havnor. Elody spent a few days training with him if that really is him."

"I don't imagine there are too many red dragonmages fighting for our cause that would just happen to be in the area," Berym said.

"Let us hope not," Eryninn said.

***

Elody leapt the last few steps down the wall and ran as fast as she could toward the city center. The dragons were all out of the sky by the time she hit the ground, and she looked over to see Jalthrax flap into the air above her. She smiled and ran harder, trying to keep up.

It didn't take long to reach the city square, and she could see the bodies of the big dragons standing or walking around from far back on the street. Jalthrax flew out ahead of her, and she saw him fly down into the middle of them.

"Thrax!" she called out, but he had already disappeared.

When at last she reached the square, she was out of breath. But that didn't diminish her smile when a big copper dragon in front of her shifted to the side and she caught sight of Eliath kneeling in front of Jalthrax. She paused to catch her breath and smooth her hair and robes before calling out to him.

"Eliath!" she shouted between huffs.

She collected herself as much as she could and walked over to him, her breath still heaving through her nose as she tried to hide the evidence of her sprint. Eliath's smile brightened her instantly.

"Fancy meeting you here," he said.

"We only just arrived. I thought maybe you had gone already when I didn't see any dragons anywhere."

"I was due to leave for the elven lands, but then we received word of the approaching goblins and were told to stay. The conclave wants us here to protected the Eldest. Can you believe it? Me, protecting the Eldest."

"Where have you been? I looked for you."

"With the Eldest and the others," he said, waving his arm at the other dragons.

As she walked closer, Eliath stood and put his arms around her. With a little hug, he released her and stepped back. Behind him, Tark gave her a little nod. He was sitting quietly, far away from the other dragons who were all together. He laid his head down and closed his eyes, but he was facing the other dragons. Elody could see his eyes open just a slit.

"We've all been stationed near her lair," Eliath said, "though I don't know how much better we could do than her if someone were to attack."

"We have been outside her cave," Tark said without opening his eyes, "guarding her like a dog on her doorstep."

"Quiet, Tark," Eliath said.

"This is the first time we have even been allowed in their precious city," Tark said with a snort. "Good dragons. Dragons of light they call themselves. I have never treated another this way, yet *I* am the dark one."

"Enough," Eliath said before turning back to Elody. "What are you doing here?"

"Berym brought news of the goblin army and said people needed our help. Rinn and I volunteered."

Eliath started to say something but was interrupted by shouting from across the square where a crowd was gathering. A group of fancily dressed men being lead by one even fancier had arrived, and the other dragonmages had gone over to them. More and more citizens were starting to collect around them, but the guards surrounding the officials were shouting and pushing them all back.

"We should go over," Eliath said.

"You go," Elody said. "I'll stay here."

"Come on now. If you're a dragonmage, go and stand with them."

Without looking back, he walked over to join the others. Elody bit her lip and looked down at Jalthrax. Tark shook his head and huffed, startling her.

"I will never understand you humans and your need to be accepted," he said. "Go with him. You may not be as skilled, but you are as strong as any of them. Perhaps even more so."

Elody smiled and reached out to touch the big red, and to her surprise, he leaned into her hand. With a pat on his cheek, she walked over to stand with the other dragonmages who were now talking with the leader of the other men.

"I thank you all for coming," the one man said. "I am the mayor of Molner. Please tell the Eldest we await her arrival and are confident she will deal with this menace swiftly."

One of the dragonmages, the oldest by Elody's reckoning, stepped in front of the others.

"I am Telidor, your lordship," he said.

"I am no lord, Telidor, I am the mayor."

"Forgive me. I did not know what title to use."

The mayor waved his hand, and the dragonmage continued.

"Forgiving your pardon, sir, but the Eldest is already here."

"What?"

He pushed past them to look at all the dragons in the square and went from one to another before stepping back looking confused.

"She did not come with us, sir," Telidor said. "She arrived last night."

"I heard no reports of her arrival!"

"Because she did not wish to make her presence known. But I promise you, she is here, and she will aid the great city of Molner in its hour of need."

Elody saw the men behind the mayor all smile and nod with a few whispers to each other.

"When this is all over," the mayor said, "I hope that the Eldest will come and dine with me and the other chancellors in my home."

"I will pass the message on when I see her," Telidor said.

With a nod, the mayor turned and walked through as the other men parted to let him pass. The dragonmages all stood in silence for a moment and watched him go. Telidor turned to face them all and drew back with surprise when he saw Elody.

"Hello, young lady," he said.

He smiled nicely enough, but Elody caught the question he looked at Eliath and the almost imperceptible nod back.

"I'm Elody, sir. My brother and I traveled here with the knights from Havnor."

"And I take it by your robes that you are a mage?"

"I am. That's my dragon, Jalthrax, over there."

Telidor looked past her to where Jalthrax was talking with Tark.

"A silver. He's beautiful."

"Thank you, sir."

"I hope you'll stay out of danger once the fighting starts."

"That's not why I came here."

"Of course not, but I would hate to see you hurt."

"And will you be out of the fighting?"

Telidor laughed, and the others joined, save for Eliath.

"No, young lady, I am needed up on the wall to defend the city."

"Then that is where I am needed as well."

Telidor blinked, his face emotionless. He nodded curtly and turned back to the other mages. They tightened into a circle, and Elody had to push her way in. The men discussed their plans for the coming battle and where each would be in defense of the wall. The dragons would remain in reserve until most of the goblin force had taken the field in order to maximize their effectiveness. The mages would stay on the wall, flinging destruction down upon the charging horde.

"Where should I be, sir?" Elody asked.

"Somewhere out of the way," Telidor answered without looking at her.

"I did not come here to stay out of the way. I came here to fight."

"She is skilled in combat magic," Eliath cut in.

"Thank you for your opinion, dark mage. You can stand with her and keep her out of trouble."

"Sir, I wasn't—"

But Telidor had already turned and walked back to his dragon, a huge bronze that towered over the the other two copper dragons. Possibly even Tark. The other mages went to their dragons as well, leaving Elody and Eliath in awkward silence.

"Come on," Eliath said. "I'll show you how to fight from a wall."

He walked off toward Tark, but Elody kept watching

Telidor as she followed. He spoke a few words to his bronze, and Elody watched in awe as the dragon began to shift its form. The loud sound of popping bones and stretching skin echoed across the square. Within moments the dragon was gone, leaving behind a man who looked to be as old as Telidor.

Elody's breath caught.

"I have never seen one transform," Elody said as she continued to stare.

"Tark hates it," Eliath said. "Mostly because he wishes he could do it."

"Can any of the dark dragons change form?"

"No. Only gold, silver, and bronze. I sometimes wish he could though. Most people don't like the sight of a red dragon flying over their town. It would be handy to hide his form once in a while."

"I think he's beautiful," she said with a smile.

"So does he. But a lot of people still get nervous when they see a red. Especially down in the south. They have no trust of dark dragons there. The blue dragons in the Seas of Sand are ruthless, and the people there have grown to fear them and attack on sight. There aren't many dragonmages there either, but they have learned that the dragons of light rarely mean them harm. It took a lot of convincing before they stopped shooting at Tark every time we went somewhere new."

"Jalthrax should be able to change his form after another year or so. I don't think I would want him to though."

"He's a silver. He wouldn't have to unless he wanted to."

Elody pointed to where Tark and Jalthrax were still chatting.

"What do you suppose they're talking about?"

"Probably wondering what we're talking about. Tark is a bit of a gossip."

"I'm really glad you're here," Elody said with a laugh.

"I'm glad I'm here too, but I wish *you* weren't."

"I'm getting that a lot."

Eliath smiled and walked over to Tark while Jalthrax passed him and came up to her. Elody knelt down and scratched his neck.

"We shouldn't be here," Tark said softly.

"Are you afraid, little brother?"

Elody crouched down as she kept scratching Jalthrax and listened to them talking. They kept their voices low, but she was close enough to hear them. She knew she shouldn't, but she couldn't help herself.

"I'm not the little one anymore," Tark said.

"You never were, but I will always be older than you."

"Until you die first, which could be very soon if we stick around here."

"This is where we belong, Tark. They need our help."

Elody heard Tark shift his weight and groan.

"This is not our world, brother. You would die for these men who despise us?"

"I hope it doesn't come to that. How else can we make them see that we are just as good as they are if we don't help when we are needed most?"

"So this is all to impress someone? You will never win their approval."

"I do this for me and no one else."

There was a long pause, and Elody was tempted to look over Jalthrax at them, but she didn't want to let on she was listening. She ducked her head low and just kept mindlessly rubbing Jalthrax, who was definitely enjoying the attention.

"What will I do if something happens to you?" Tark said at last.

"Why should something happen to me?"

"You humans are weak and fragile. One stray arrow, and I could lose you forever. Eight hundred years is too long to be alone."

Elody heard the scuff of Eliath's boots as he moved closer to the dragon. She dared a glance over her shoulder and saw him rest his hand on Tark's neck.

"I'm not going anywhere," Eliath said softly as he laid his head down.

Elody felt guilty for listening. She stood and walked a ways away with Jalthrax behind her. When she stopped, she turned back to see Eliath with his body laid against Tark's side as he stroked the great dragon's scales. Kneeling down, she put her arms around Jalthrax and hugged him close.

"He is beautiful," she heard someone say behind her.

Looking up, a woman in shimmering, silver robes was standing behind her, casting a shadow down over the two of them. Elody stood and smiled.

"Thank you," she said.

The woman knelt down, taking Elody's place and rubbing her hands down Jalthrax's neck. Elody was in shock a moment later when the woman began speaking to him in the dragon tongue. Jalthrax was taken aback as well, but he growled out an answer.

"Jalthrax is a good, strong name," the woman said as she continued rubbing his neck.

"How did you learn to speak dragon?"

"I am a priestess of Anarr, first son of Aeos and father of all dragons. We are all taught to speak in the god's tongue."

"I didn't know there was a church of Anarr."

"Oh, there is, child. You yourself are one of his followers."

"I have only been to a church a few times in my life, but never one of Anarr."

"And yet you are one of his chosen," she said, patting Jalthrax on the neck. "One of his children has chosen you. You are as bonded to Anarr as you are to Jalthrax there."

A crowd of people had begun gathering in the square. People poured in from the surrounding streets to get a look at all the shining, metal dragons. They shied away from Tark and Eliath, who both kept their eyes closed and didn't seem to notice.

"But tell me now," the woman said, "why do you stand apart from the rest?"

"They don't want me in the fight."

"And you would listen to them?"

"Of course not. I will stand and fight."

"Good! A chosen of Anarr's place is always in battle. You wield a weapon far mightier than any sword."

"I'm not certain how mighty I can be from a wall. My spells don't reach very far, and Jalthrax doesn't like when I cast fire spells."

"I imagine he does not, no. If your spells do not reach, then you wait for them to come to you. I promise you will not be kept waiting long."

"That's all we do? Just wait?"

"So much of war is waiting, child."

Elody eyed the older woman and wrinkled her brow.

"Who are you?" Elody asked.

The woman smiled and stood.

"A humble servant of Anarr, child. Just as we all are."

She turned before Elody could respond and walked off into the crowd of people. *Am I really a servant of Anarr?* She had never considered herself a servant of anyone. Jalthrax nudged her, and she reached down to rub his neck. The old woman's words stuck in her mind.

We are all his servants.

CHAPTER TWENTY

WAITING

GORTOGH WAS BEGINNING to regret his decision to open the last of the barrels of beer to the men. The revelry outside was getting out of hand if the sounds alone were any indication. He couldn't see what was going on, but he had a pretty good idea. Still, with this being the last night for many of them out there, it seemed only right.

"Ogrosh will keep them safe," Kurgh said, likely sensing Gortogh's unease at the coming battle. "My shamans will be there to protect them with his blessing."

Gortogh scoffed and went back to his own drink. It was bitter. He'd never much cared for the stuff, really. It robbed him of his wits and made him slow. He smiled at the idea that it probably made little difference to the rest of his kin.

"Tonight I will tell the men of the great war between Ogrosh and Anarr," Kurgh said looking out of the tent. "It is the story of how the children of Ogrosh nearly destroyed every dragon on Gondril. It will give them courage for the fight tomorrow. Will you sit at the fire with your people and listen?"

"No," Gortogh said flatly. "Go and drink and leave me."

"Shamans never drink. It clouds the mind, and we cannot hear the voice of Ogrosh."

Gortogh scoffed again, perhaps a little too loudly this time. Kurgh whirled and stared at him. Taking another swig of warm beer, Gortogh held his gaze, emotionless.

"Do you believe in Ogrosh?" Kurgh asked in a low voice.

There it was.

The little shaman had grown quiet of late, ever since Gortogh's last meeting with Velanon in the forest. Gortogh sensed what it was about by the way Kurgh kept staring at the amulet around his neck when they were together, but neither had said anything. Now it was out there.

Gortogh belched long and loud and then laughed.

"Of course I believe in him! Look at everything he has given me!"

Kurgh sneered, and Gortogh arched an eye. No longer the sniveling dog it would seem. Gortogh was drunk. He could feel his senses dulling by the minute, and his patience for the shaman growing thinner even faster.

"You wish to say something to me?"

"No, *Mighty One*," he said, practically spitting the title.

Gortogh hurled his empty mug across the tent, but Kurgh leapt out of the way. He was fast, he had to give him that. Gortogh hooked his thumb under the leather cord holding the amulet and pulled it up before his face. He let it dangle there, spinning and twisting as if in a light breeze.

"You want this, yes?"

Kurgh stared but said nothing.

"You want the blood of Ogrosh around your neck, don't you?"

"You do not deserve it!" Kurgh screamed. "Ogrosh would never give his blood to you! I am one of his mightiest priests, it should be mine!"

Kurgh tensed as if to leap, and Gortogh's other hand flashed to the hilt of his sword. Good sense got the better of the shaman, and he settled back down, but he still stood ready on the balls of his feet.

"I would like nothing more than to take your head, dog," Gortogh said with a slur. "I could take it now and no one out there would come to help you or shed a tear."

Gortogh continued to let the amulet dangle. He loved watching Kurgh's eyes as they drifted back and forth between the amulet and his stare.

"It should be the Blood God on that field tomorrow," Kurgh said. "It should be *his* praises that are sung, but you don't care. You use the blood of Ogrosh for the will of that elven demon!"

"Who do you think gave me the amulet, fool?"

"And he should die for even touching it! The blood of Ogrosh is not for him!"

"No, it's not. Which is why he gave it to me."

"It is not for *you*. *You* are not faithful. *I* am faithful!"

Gortogh let the amulet drop. He was tired of holding it up and tired of taunting the shaman.

"You are a dog, and I am a god," Gortogh said. "The words sound alike, but they are far from each other in life. So, come and take it, dog. I wear around my neck the blood of Ogrosh himself. Take it if you can, and you can be the one to lead this wretched army to their deaths."

Kurgh tensed but didn't move. Gortogh drew his sword and threw it on the ground.

"Does that make it easier for you?"

With surprising speed, Kurgh growled and made a leap for him, leading with his bone dagger that seemed to materialize in his hand. Gortogh was so stunned that he had no time to react except to stumble back with his arms up. A shout cut the air, a single word, and Gortogh was so drunk and so dumbfounded, he thought it came from the shaman. It was only as Kurgh stopped dead in his tracks and fell to the ground in a heap that he saw Velanon and Kalus standing calmly by the tent's opening.

"I cannot afford a change in leadership the night before a big battle, I'm afraid," Velanon said.

Gortogh looked down at the tiny mass of goblin lying motionless in the dirt.

"What did you do to him?" he said.

"He's only stunned," Velanon said. "He'll regain full function in a moment, so if you have plans to kill him, do it now before he can move."

Gortogh looked from the prone shaman to his sword and back to Velanon.

"It's more fun than it sounds, really," Velanon said. "He'll still feel every cut, he will simply be unable to respond. The spell won't stop his blood from running though, I'd move any nice furs you want to keep."

Kalus laughed and strode right up to Kurgh and kicked him over with his foot. As Gortogh stood in stunned, drunk silence, Kalus grabbed the bone dagger from the shaman's limp hand and unceremoniously cut his ear off. There was no scream, no cry of pain. Not even movement as blood began gushing down the side of his face.

"You need to learn to listen," Kalus said into the severed ear and then laughed.

"What are you doing?" Gortogh shouted.

Kalus looked down at the bleeding shaman, then back up and shrugged.

"He's a shaman, right? I'm sure he can heal an ear."

He tossed the ear to the ground and then walked back to stand near Velanon. Gortogh looked to the elf for some response, but as always, his face betrayed no emotion. As the effects of the wizard's spell wore off, Kurgh screamed and clapped his hand over the hole that was once his ear. Scrambling to his feet, he grabbed his ear up with his other hand and shoved Velanon and Kalus aside as he ran from the tent.

"Why did you do that?" Gortogh asked, seething.

"Yes, why did you do that?" Velanon asked. "You should have just killed the thing. Now he can come back and cause us trouble."

"He is a sniveling worm," Kalus said. "If he doesn't leave tonight, he'll be dead on the field tomorrow."

"And what if he rallies the tribes against me for what you've done?" Gortogh asked.

Kalus shook his head and smiled.

"You really have no idea the power that you wear around your neck, do you? They believe you're their *god*, you fool! They would slit their own throats in your presence if you ordered them to!"

"Which means they will fight without fear tomorrow," Velanon said. "You have told your men to be ready at dawn?"

Gortogh looked at the pool of blood on the ground at his feet. Always blood.

"They will be ready," he said.

"Good," Velanon said.

"I have heard reports of dragons in the city," Gortogh said. "It looks as though they have dragonmages to defend with. Why did you not tell me we would face dragons?"

"I do not answer to you," Velanon said.

"We should have brought weapons to fight them," Gortogh said. "We cannot defeat dragons no matter our size. And the dragonmages will lay waste to my army."

Velanon smiled confidently, but Kalus could not contain a bellowing laugh.

"Children playing with pets," Kalus said. "They will not be alive long enough to harm you, I will see to that."

"And what part will you play, wizard?" Gortogh asked.

"Wherever I am most useful, I suppose," Velanon said. "I'm sure a proper target will present itself once the fighting begins. Have your men prepared the ladders and ram as I said?"

"Yes, but I have seen many men up on the wall. How are we supposed to get across that field without dying?"

"You won't," the elf said. "Many will die, but you will still succeed. You will overwhelm them with your superior numbers and courage."

Kalus chuckled.

"Courageous goblins," Kalus said. "In a thousand years, I would not have thought I'd live to see the day."

"Where will you be when the fighting starts?" Gortogh asked.

"Right beside you," Velanon said. "Someone has to protect you, and it seems your shaman won't be up for the job."

"Not after what he did," Gortogh said pointing at

Kalus.

"I wonder if he can still hear the voice of Ogrosh," Kalus said with a laugh.

***

"So many," Eryninn said. "I have followed them so closely that I could not see the true size of them all."

Berym nodded solemnly. They stood beside each other on the wall above the main gate, watching and listening to the goblins having their celebration. Eryninn looked down the wall at the men who were still standing guard. Not many, he noted.

"There are so few on the wall," he said. "You would think that was a fair filled with fire eaters and fortune tellers outside their gates instead of ten thousand goblins."

"They think they are invincible because of the protection of the dragons."

"We should have left when they refused to help."

Berym seemed to snap and turned to look at him.

"Why did you risk your life to reach Derne?"

Eryninn stepped back, surprised.

"Because they all would have died if I had done nothing."

"Yet you are so willing to let all of *these* people die?"

"Derne did not ask for my help, but neither did they refuse when I offered it. If they had, I would have marched on and left them to burn."

Berym shook his head.

"I think that I understand you, but then I don't."

"I am trying to help these people, that is all."

"By refusing to help if they won't do it your way?" Berym asked.

"I offer my help, but I will not offer my life. I have

already given enough for humans in my lifetime."

"You spit the word humans as if half of their blood doesn't course through your veins. I don't see you walking across the field and into the elven lands. Would they welcome you into their borders, I wonder?"

"It is you I do not understand. You seem ready to lay down your life at every turn for people who do not deserve it. You are worth a hundred of these people, but I have no doubt you would die to save just one."

"Who are you to judge the worth of a life?"

"I judge the worth only of my own life, and I deem it worth more than people who won't even raise a sword to defend themselves."

"And what if they were here on the wall now? What if they were beside us, ready to fight? Are they worth more then?"

Eryninn looked down into the city where the knights were all camped behind the gate.

"Maybe."

"And what if you came upon some highwaymen attacking an armed man and a helpless child. Would you fight beside the man and leave the child to die?"

"These are not children who cannot defend themselves."

"No, they are people who are scared and don't want to die. I don't blame them for not wanting to stand on this wall. *I* don't want to stand on this wall, but someone must. Someone has to do defend those who are weaker."

Eryninn shook his head.

"You sound just like my father. Always ready to give up your life for others."

"I am not ready to die, but if it must be."

"Then likely you will meet your fate as he did. That is

the ending of every hero's tale."

"I don't wish to be a hero."

"Don't you? You play the part well enough. And what will Narissa do when you meet your fate as all heroes do?"

Berym looked down at his hands and sighed.

"She will know that I died defending people who needed me."

"And that will give her comfort? They said the same of my father when they came back from that bloody war. He died with honor. He died defending the weak."

"Did it comfort you?"

"No."

Berym nodded.

"Well, I have no plans to die here tomorrow. And when this is done, I will go home to Narissa."

"Let us hope we all go home tomorrow."

Eryninn reached down and unbuckled his belt. Pulling his scabbard off, he held it out to Berym.

"I want you to take this. In a fight against goblin kin, you will find no better blade."

Berym patted the sword at his side.

"I have my own."

"This is an enchanted blade of my people. It will keep you safe."

"My sword has served me well for many years, and my father for many years before that."

Eryninn sighed and pushed the sword toward him again.

"Please take it."

"And what will you do in a fight with no weapon?"

"I have no intention of getting into a sword fight. My talents are better kept to the wall with my bow. You'll not see me down there with the rest of you armor backs."

"I thank you, my friend, but I would never go into battle without my own sword if I could help it. I doubt you would either."

Eryninn nodded and buckled it back around his waist.

"I will be down with my knights when the fighting starts. Will you be my eyes and voice on the wall?"

"You think these humans will listen to me?"

"In the thick of battle, they will listen to anyone shouting with authority. You know the plan?"

"I do."

"Good. Rinn has asked to stand with the knights on the ground, but I've ordered him on the wall with a bow. When things heat up tomorrow, I want you to keep him and Elody close to you."

"This is a battle, my friend, and they are not children."

"No, but neither are they seasoned. Just keep them close if you can."

"I will guard them with my life."

Berym chuckled.

"You may be more like your father than you realize."

"If I had been more like my father from the start, they would not be here at all."

***

Rinn watched from the corner of the wall as the goblins had their fun. In the darkness they looked like nothing more than a few drunks dancing around their campfires. The night and the forest hid their numbers, but he had seen them as they arrived. He knew the truth of it.

A glint of light behind him caught his attention, and he turned to see Oryna coming up the stairs holding a bright, white light of some kind. He had to shield his eyes for a moment until they adjusted to the new beacon in the night. When at last he could, he watched her as she got closer and saw that it was a great mace she held in her hand. The head of it was flanged with sharp corners and edges he noted as she grew nearer, and the light issued forth from the head with a burning intensity.

"Do you know how to use that thing?" Rinn asked.

"Of course," she said. "You hold it high, and you won't trip on things in the dark."

Rinn laughed.

"You know what I mean."

"I am trained to fight, yes."

"Since when does a priestess need to use weapons?"

"It is hard for some to hear the truth. Some get quite angry at hearing it."

"Is it really that dangerous?"

"The priesthood started training acolytes centuries ago as they began to spread the word of the goddess across the continent. The desert nomads in the south were difficult to track, and our clergy often wandered in hostile environments for months with only Threyl's protection. Which was significant, believe me, but sometimes nothing beats a good… well, beating."

"What about the paladins of Threyl?"

"They travel with us, yes, but we cannot be expected to always rely on others to keep us safe. Spreading the goddess's love is sometimes met with resistance. The barbarians in the north tried to feed us to their dragons."

"You've traveled in the Frozenlands?"

"It was part of my wanderings, yes. We are each required to go out into the world and spread her word. Often in unfriendly places."

"That sounds dangerous."

"Hence my holy smiting stick," she said, shaking the mace, and Rinn chuckled.

"Does it always glow like that?"

"Only when I need it. The light is a gift of the goddess to protect and guide me. It shines when I walk the path she needs of me, but it shines brightest when I walk a dark path and need her. In the darkest nights, it has protected me."

"We could use some of that tonight."

They both turned to look out across the field.

"Where will you be tomorrow?" Rinn asked.

"Behind the knights. Some of my order may stand on the wall to help defend, but that is a job better left to the Deathbringers. Their magic is useful in sending souls to Vorrod. Our job is to deny him as many good men as we can."

"What if they break through the gate?"

"We were told to fall back with the wounded if the fighting reaches inside the walls."

Rinn nodded.

"And where will you be?" she asked. "With the knights?"

Rinn tapped the merlon in front of him.

"Right behind this solid chunk of stone. Berym said he needed more archers on the wall."

Oryna leaned forward and let her lips brush lightly against his cheek.

"Be safe, Rinn. If you get hurt, come and find me. Look for the light."

She touched his cheek and hurried down the stairs before he could respond. He watched the white light of her mace bob as she went and stayed with her all the way down the street until it stopped moving. With a final look, he turned back to the goblins with a new fear in his heart.

Would he live to see her again?

***

Elody jumped as another shout went up through the goblin army. Beside her, Eliath stood looking out over the wall, but she remained seated with her back against it. She was afraid to look, but she could still hear everything.

"Here's hoping they'll be too drunk to fight tomorrow," Eliath said as he sat down beside her.

"Why do they have to celebrate? It's unsettling."

"That's why. And because many of them will die tomorrow. It's always like this."

"Have you been in a fight like this before?"

"In the war," Eliath said. "I've been on both sides of the wall."

"You were just a boy, and they let you fight?"

"I was a boy with a big, red dragon. They could always find a use for me somewhere."

Eliath looked down over the wall to where Tark and Jalthrax were sleeping soundly below them in the street.

"Should they be sleeping right in the middle of the street like that?" Elody asked.

"Who's going to ask them to move?"

Elody laughed at the thought and then fell silent. They sat for several minutes as the party outside the wall raged on.

"What will it be like tomorrow?" she asked at last.

"Chaos," Eliath said, then paused. "Bloody. Lots of screaming. It'll start slow at first. They'll stand across the field and beat their chests and their drums at us, try to make us afraid. And they'll probably succeed for many of us, me included. Then one of them will take up a battle cry, and they'll charge. It will be a thunder unlike any you've ever heard."

"And what do we do?"

"Try to stop them. The archers will shoot, the dragons will attack from the skies, and we will blast them from the face of Gondril with everything we have."

"Where will Tark be?"

"Fighting in the air. Most of these men have never seen a true red dragon in battle, and I *know* these goblins never have. He will rain the fires of the nine hells upon them."

"Aren't you worried for him? I would be terrified if Jalthrax were out there."

"Their spears and arrows can't hurt Tark, but Jalthrax has to stay behind the wall. His scales are not thick enough, and you can't cast your magic with him far away and flying. He needs to stay right below you so that you don't waste time drawing the magic."

Elody put her head down between her knees.

"I'm scared," she said.

"I am too," Eliath said.

"You don't act like it."

"I learned to hide it a long time ago. No one wants to hear you whining about how frightened you are when you have a red dragon beside you."

"I suppose not," she said with a chuckle.

"I'm terrified," Eliath said. "I don't know what will happen tomorrow. Something could happen to me or Tark. Something could happen to you."

Elody looked up and met his eyes.

"That scares you?"

"Yes, it does. I don't want anything to happen to you."

"Well, I don't want anything to happen to you either."

He smiled and reached out to touch her cheek. Elody felt her breath quicken.

"You remind me so much of Ardina."

Elody pulled away and looked down.

"I wasn't there to protect her," he said.

She looked down over the wall to avoid looking him in the eye.

"How do you know you could have?" she said.

"I don't," he said. "But I should have been there to try."

"Someone once told me not to think about the ones you didn't save. Otherwise they'll haunt you forever."

Eliath sighed and nodded.

"That they will."

CHAPTER TWENTY-ONE

WAR

THE DRUMS SOUNDED in the distance.

Elody opened her eyes wondering what had woken her, taking a moment to realize she had actually fallen asleep. Eliath stood still beside her watching out over the wall. The drums beat again.

Elody stood up and looked out across the field. The drumbeat echoing through the air was the only indication of any movement at all from the goblins.

"How long was I asleep?"

"A few hours."

She stared across the open field to where the goblins had formed a long line. She couldn't even count how many deep they were, and the lines disappeared into the forest where no one could see. There were tiny movements here and there, but they mostly stood still, facing the city.

"How long have they been standing there?"

"Not long. We heard shouting, and they slowly started to form up."

"They look ready."

"I just hope *we* are."

Elody looked up and down at the faces of the men and women along the wall. Not far to her left, she saw Eryninn standing near the center over the gate. Rinn was beside him, and he caught her eye and gave her a little nod. She looked down and saw Jalthrax look up at her.

The drums beat louder, and she turned back.

"What are they waiting for?" she said.

"Their leaders. Intimidation. Who knows."

"Is it always like this?"

Eliath nodded.

"What are we supposed to do?" she asked.

"Just wait."

"We just wait for them to attack?"

He nodded again.

"Why not attack them first?" she asked.

"I'm not the commander, but we don't know anything about their forces. They haven't revealed anything yet, so we might just be wasting arrows. Or worse."

Elody looked out at the mass of writhing goblins who were all starting to fidget in anticipation. She could feel it too. Her hands were unsteady, and she held onto the wall for support. Just then, the drumbeat changed. It had an immediate effect on the goblins, who all began shouting at the end of each beat. The sound and the cries beat into her head.

Boom! Boom-boom-boom, eee-yah!

Boom! Boom-boom-boom, eee-yah!

"I feel sick," Elody said.

"Me too."

"Why don't they just get it over with?"

"Because they *want* us to feel this way."

"Well, it's working."

She looked down to try and stave off the wave of

dizziness, but a tap on the shoulder from Eliath brought her back up.

"Something's happening," he said.

He pointed out across the field. They watched together as several lines of goblins parted to let another group through. Even at the distance of the field Elody could see the weapons they carried and knew what was coming.

The goblin archers readied for the first attack.

***

Eryninn ran his finger down the string of his bow, making it sing a low note as he did. He shifted a little next to Rinn as the goblin archers took the field. Leaning over the wall, he called down to the inside of the gate below.

"Archers!"

Berym nodded from below where he stood closest to the gate at the front of his knights. Eryninn turned back to the other side of the wall and watched. Looking down to his right, he saw Elody standing with the other dragonmages spread out in a line and nodded. She returned the gesture weakly, and he could see that she was probably going to be sick.

"Mages, ready first defense!" Eryninn yelled out.

He watched the goblin archers move through the ranks of the foot soldiers and shook his head. They were more disciplined than he'd ever seen from goblins. More so than most human armies he'd had the displeasure of witnessing. Given how well they marched and stayed together, he could only imagine their shooting would not be typical either.

"Hold your fingers!" he called.

The goblin archers pulled bundles of arrows from

their backs and pushed them into the ground in front of them. He heard shouts from somewhere behind them but couldn't make out what they were saying. Not that he would understand goblin anyway.

As one, the archers drew their bows back.

"Go!" Eryninn shouted.

He snapped his head to the side and watched as two of the dragonmages began moving their arms in a whirlwind through the air in front of them. Looking back, the goblins were ready to loose. All they waited on was the command. Eryninn silently cursed himself for waiting so long.

He nearly got dizzy, his head whipping back and forth between the two, hoping and praying the mages would finish before the goblins loosed. A sigh of relief passed his lips when they both finished casting and spread their arms in front of them.

Eryninn instantly felt the wind against his face. He could not see the source of it, but he knew where it should be. Right in front of the city wall, about twenty feet up. Even at this distance, the breeze was strong.

The goblins loosed.

A hail of arrows blotted out the sky as they seemed to all fly together in a flock toward the city. Then, just as they neared their target, they began to wobble in the air. The wind caught them and started blowing them off course just slightly. The arrows flew on and struck an invisible wall that tossed them around like sticks in a hurricane. One by one the arrows whipped through the air and fell to the ground.

A cheer went up from the men on the wall. Eryninn and Rinn looked at each other but didn't join in the celebration just yet.

"Think they'll try again?" Rinn asked.

"Any normal goblins, I would say yes. These seem strangely disciplined."

A strong wind blew out from the invisible wall and made it sound as though a storm were approaching.

"I can't hear them shouting anymore," Rinn said.

"They're still shouting orders," Eryninn said.

The archers drew back and let loose another volley of arrows. Just as the last one, those were turned aside by the wall of wind and tossed harmlessly to the ground.

"Powerful mages," Rinn said.

"Let us hope they have none on their side."

Eryninn turned down each side of the wall and shouted.

"Archers, hold! Mages, give them everything!"

None of the men on the wall moved. Eryninn was only reminding them of their orders, but they had all been told they could not fire through the wind wall, so they stood ready for the charge. There was a silence for several moments. The only sound they could hear from the battlements was the wind blowing across their ears.

Then the mages loosed their magic.

Fire rained down on the goblins from the wall in great bursts and columns. Even the wind could not blot out the screams of the dying as they burned where they stood. The lines broke apart in places as some tried to flee, but the ones who ran were quickly cut down by those who stood.

"I have never seen this sort of behavior from goblins," Eryninn said.

"I've never heard of goblins with courage if that's what you mean," Rinn said.

"That is precisely what I mean."

"They do have us greatly outnumbered," Rinn said. "Maybe they think they'll win with sheer numbers."

"Even so, more of them should be running from those spells."

"It does seem odd."

"Aim your spells at the trees behind them!" Eryninn shouted. "Blast their leaders in the back and set the woods on fire!"

The next round of fireballs flew over the heads of the standing army and back into the forest. They exploded against trees and goblins alike, setting everything ablaze.

"Won't that just drive them forward?" Rinn asked.

"Some maybe," Eryninn said, "but more still will be cut off and be forced to go around the fires or be dead from smoke."

"Why haven't they charged then?"

"I do not know."

Eryninn saw more arrows from the back of the goblin lines flying toward them. He saw in an instant that they were not like the others as the arrows flew right through the wind wall.

"Get down!" he shouted as he yanked Rinn down.

A man beside them was too slow as an arrow took him in the chest. He screamed and fell behind the wall, the arrow protruding from his shoulder. Eryninn leapt up and went to him, but the man was wide-eyed and panicked.

"It's just a shoulder wound," Eryninn said, trying to calm the man.

All around he could hear more screams as men on the wall and down behind it were struck with the new arrows. Eryninn reached for the arrow but stopped when he felt something wrong. The arrow looked like nothing he'd ever seen. It was not made of wood, and it had no feathers on it. As he started to reach for it again, the arrow turned to liquid and fell away. Drops of blood fell onto the wounded man as the arrow disintegrated before Eryninn's eyes.

Rinn was there beside him then, and the man screamed and grabbed at Eryninn's cloak. As they watched in horror, the hole the arrow had left behind began to grow.

"What is that?" Rinn shouted.

The man's flesh and clothing were rotting from the inside, consuming his body.

"I don't know," Eryninn said.

Rinn and Eryninn tried to calm the man's flailing, but they both pulled their hands back as the rot spread. More screams filled the air around them, and they knew that more had been struck by the wicked blood arrows. The man stopped thrashing as his life left him.

"Get back to the wall," Eryninn said.

***

Eliath finished his spell and sent another fireball streaking for the forest behind the army. Elody watched as many of the archers moved back and the ranks of the footmen closed in around them.

"I think they're about to charge," she said.

"Looks like it."

"Dragons, ready!" Eryninn shouted from down the wall.

"Dragons, ready!" Telidor shouted down.

Elody looked over the side of the wall to where the huge bronze dragon, two coppers, and Tark were all making ready to launch into the air. Only Jalthrax stood still beside them. Elody met his eyes for only a second.

Long enough for her to shake her head before turning back.

The goblins had formed up their ranks. Slowly at first but gaining speed, they loped toward the city. The drums beat faster, and Elody heard a war cry that was then taken up by the goblins. Even through the wall of wind she could hear their roar.

"Fly!" Telidor cried.

The four dragons leapt into the air, and with a mighty whoosh that dwarfed the wind from the wall, they took to the sky. Tark roared, and the others joined him. They flew down with the tips of their wings nearly touching, creating a long, unbroken line. They swooped down over the top of the goblin army and roared even louder.

Before they passed overhead, Elody could see some of the goblin archers readying for a shot. When the four dragons' roars flowed over them, the effect was nothing short of terrifying. The goblin line broke apart in an instant. All their discipline crumbled in the moment it took them to look to the sky. Eliath pointed a finger out to where the goblin army was starting to turn and run, even madly barreling into the burning forest behind them.

"Look," he said. "They are more scared of the dragons than of the fire."

Elody watched with eyes wide.

"Have we won already?" she said.

"Some will run, but others will turn back and fight. And that is when they will see the true might of the dragons. If they are scared of them now, just wait."

"Where is the Eldest?"

"I don't know, but just look down there. Perhaps we don't need her after all."

***

"What are they doing?" Gortogh shouted.

"Retreating," Velanon said beside him.

"Why are they running?" Gortogh said, astonished. "The dragons have not even done anything."

"Fear," Kalus said. "Should have known goblins would break in the face of true dragons. Even the fear of displeasing their god cannot keep their knees from wobbling and their feet from running."

Gortogh watched so many of his men turn and run from the battle. It was a familiar sight, he was sad to admit. This is how goblins fought. With sheer numbers and intimidation. When that failed, they usually ran. If he was honest with himself, he wasn't that interested in sticking around either after seeing what the mages and their dragons could do.

"Perhaps we should regroup and come up with a new plan," Gortogh said.

"No!" Velanon shouted, suddenly angry, but then he calmed himself. "You cannot back out of the fight now. They will only make their defenses stronger if you give them more time. You have to strike now and strike hard!"

"What do you expect me to do? I can't even command them over the sound of the dragons and this cursed wind!"

"Stand up tall and tell them to charge. Hold the amulet high for all to see."

Gortogh looked skeptical.

"Stop, now!" he shouted. "Turn and charge the wall!"

No one heard him as far as he could see.

"They cannot hear me."

"Try again," Velanon said. "*Make* them hear you."

Gortogh saw him start to twiddle his fingers and

speak softly under his breath. He reached a hand out and touched Gortogh's lips gently with his fingertips.

"Now," Velanon said. "Tell them. Make them believe you *are* Ogrosh. You are their god made flesh."

Gortogh stood tall and drew his sword. He felt stronger just holding it in his hand, even before he gripped it and released its magic to truly make him strong. Closing his hand around the amulet, he could feel the power it hummed with for the first time. Gortogh took a deep breath and spoke.

"Sons of Ogrosh!"

His voice carried over everything. Over the wind, over the roar of the dragons, over the blazing fires that consumed the forest. Even over the screams and shouts of his own men. Everyone on the field and on the wall heard him.

"My sons, hear me! Do not fear the dragon's fire! Do not fear the mages and their magic!"

The goblins stopped running and stared up at him in awe. His eyes went wide in panic as his feet suddenly left the ground. He looked down to see Velanon smile as he flicked his fingers a little, sending him higher. Now he stood above them all, even the ogres.

"I am Ogrosh, and you are loved by me! Do not fear the death that awaits you! For you will dine with me in the mountains of Gorolock when this day is through!"

A cheer went up through the goblin ranks. Gortogh smiled and let it wash over him.

"You are sons of Ogrosh! You fear nothing! No man! No dragon! No fire!"

Another cheer.

"Give them an order," Velanon said quietly from below.

"Destroy this city!" Gortogh shouted. "Ogrosh commands it!"

He could see the fear leave their hearts in an instant. With no further command, they turned as one great being of ten thousand limbs, and with a war cry that made Gortogh's heart swell, threw themselves at the wall.

As soon as Gortogh's feet touched the ground, he started to charge after them.

"Where are you going, you fool?" Velanon shouted.

"To fight beside my men," he said, confused.

"And *die* beside them? You cannot. If you fall, they will fall. They will lose every ounce of courage you have just given them, and they will break like waves against the rocks."

Gortogh let his sword dip into the dirt.

"You never said I was not to fight."

"I never thought you'd be stupid enough to try."

Gortogh lumbered back to stand beside the wizard and turned to watch his men take the city.

***

Rinn heard the speech from the goblin leader. Saw him rise up over the army and call down to them all to destroy the city. Then he watched as they turned back, picked up their ladders and ropes, and charged.

"I don't think they'll stop this time," Eryninn said as he picked up his bow.

Rinn nodded and readied his own bow. More of the blood arrows flew at them, and they both ducked. Most flew over their heads where they hit rooftops in the city.

"Wait until they are beyond the wind and shoot down into them. Their archers cannot shoot us from out there as long as that wall remains, but neither can we shoot them."

Rinn nodded and kept his arrow nocked. The dragons flew another pass over the charging army, but this time their roar contained more than just fear. Fire, lightning, and acid fell from the sky as though the heavens themselves were torn open. Tark's blast of fire was so hot Rinn could feel the heat even from where he stood. The bronze dragon flew low and sent bolts of lighting from his breath into the goblin ranks, while the coppers rained acid down.

Still the goblins came on.

Faster and faster, they ran at the wall. They will not be turned away this time. Even Rinn felt the power in the words of their leader. No fear of death would stop them now. They fought with the strongest weapon imaginable. Faith.

"They're coming!" Eryninn shouted back over his shoulder.

The goblins ran through the ditch in front of the wall, and the archers began firing. Goblins scrambled over each other to get to the wall as fast as they could, some dying from arrows but even more dying as they were trampled. As the bodies piled up, the bulk of their force crossed the ditch and slammed into the city.

Despite the thickness of the wall, Rinn could feel them hit it. Like a thunderclap, the goblin army smashed against the stone. Rinn wondered what could have caused the loud booms, but then he saw. Everywhere a goblin touched the wall, an explosion went off. Everywhere a ladder went up, they caught fire instantly.

"The wards!" Rinn shouted.

"I know, start shooting!" Eryninn yelled.

Eryninn fired down into the army, and Rinn lifted his

bow and did the same.

"Don't aim, just shoot!"

Rinn fired into the crowd. He saw his arrow plunge into a goblin, but he had no time to celebrate as it seemed almost worthless. There were so many, and his little arrows so few. As the wards activated and then were gone, the goblins hit the wall with renewed energy. More ladders went up in an instant, and the goblins started to climb before they were even steady.

"Shoot the ones on the ladders!" Eryninn shouted into the wind.

Rinn drew back and aimed at the goblins raising the ladders. He managed to hit a few and drop some of the ladders, but the dead were replaced just as quickly with more goblins. Always there seemed to be more goblins waiting to take up the cause. He heard screams and looked down the wall to see Elody blasting all the goblins on a ladder with ice and snow.

He heard a shout across the field and looked up to see a battering ram rolling toward the gate. It looked to Rinn like nothing more than two old wagons lashed together with a giant tree trunk, but it was moving fast enough to cause concern. Directly in front of it was a large group of goblins carrying buckets of some kind and running as fast as they could for the gate.

"Mages!" Eryninn shouted. "Hit that ram!"

Even before he said it, Tark swooped down and blasted the battering ram. Every goblin around it burned to ash within that unstoppable flame, and the giant tree trunk caught fire. Only a few seconds passed before more goblin grabbed hold of the burning wagons and started pushing them forward once more.

The goblins out in front had made it to the ditch and

were quickly dumping piles of rocks and mud into it. Arrows from the wall rained down on them, dropping them one after another. As one fell, another moved in behind them to shove their body into the waiting trench. Bodies and rocks soon filled enough of the ditch that the ram would have no trouble reaching the gate.

"Move! Move!"

Rinn looked up to see one of the dragonmages, Elody had called him Telidor, running to them. He stopped short beside Eryninn and immediately fell into a spell. Rinn watched his hands spinning and tried to guess at what he was casting, but he could tell in an instant that it was far beyond anything he had seen. Rinn could actually feel the power the man had collected in his hands as sparks of blue jumped between his fingers.

Swirling his hands in a flourish, he slammed his palms down against the battlements. He held them there, and Rinn could see his face turn red with strain. It was as though he was trying to push the wall into the ground with his bare hands. The sound of grinding rock filled Rinn's ears, and he suddenly wondered if that's what the man was actually doing.

Rinn and Eryninn both peered over the side of the wall and watched in stunned silence as the rock on either side of the gate came to life and began to move. Growing out in a straight line across the banded wood, the stone flowed out like a living wall, each one reaching hungrily for the other. When the two sides met in the center, there was a rumble as they crashed into each other and then knitted together to form a seamless face.

Telidor stumbled back from the wall and fell to his knees. Rinn ran and wrapped his arm around him.

"That was incredible!" he said.

"Is it finished?" Telidor said as he tried to catch his breath

"They've stopped the ram," Eryninn said. "I do not think they will be breaching that gate today."

"Good," Telidor said.

He made a weak effort to stand, and Rinn managed to help him to his feet.

"Do you want me to walk you back to the mages?"

"Slowly, yes."

Rinn put his arm around Telidor and walked him back toward the other mages. He felt a drop of something on his shoulder. Reaching up to touch it with his finger, he pulled it back and saw blood. Rinn looked to the sky to see if a dragon was bleeding above him, but they were all out over the battlefield.

A drop of blood hit his cheek then, seeming to come from nowhere, or from the heavens themselves. He looked down when another nearly hit his eye and then felt them all around him like raindrops. He hurried on with Telidor, slipping a little on the blood. There were men shouting all around him.

Then the shouts turned to screams.

Rinn heard a sizzling sound around him and felt a sting on his shoulders and the top of his head. The blood that fell from the sky burned everything it touched. Men screamed all around him, and Rinn felt his own voice join them as his skin blistered beneath the blood rain. The screams along the wall grew louder as more and more of the men were caught in the burning blood rain.

Then, just as suddenly as it came, the blood stopped.

"These goblins are more than they appear," Telidor said through clenched teeth.

"What could do this?"

"The magic of the blood god and his wretched people," Telidor said. "Get me to the others, quickly."

***

"Where is she?" Velanon asked. "Does she care nothing for these people?"

"Oh, she cares," Kalus said. "I can promise you she is over there right now watching the whole thing."

"Then what in the blazes is she waiting for?"

"Who are you looking for?" Gortogh asked.

"An old friend," Kalus said. "She won't help them unless things are dire. Ferin has a flare for the dramatic. She prefers to make an entrance and save the day when all hope is lost."

"Does she not see what is going on out there?"

"What *is* going on? Some goblins are killing themselves on the wall. The other dragons are destroying more of your little army with each pass, and the men on the wall have barely lifted their bows."

"We have to break down that wall!" Gortogh said with a growl.

Velanon looked to Kalus who only shrugged.

"Did you think it would be that easy?" Kalus asked.

"I thought she would help them."

"She will. You just have to convince her that they *need* help. Right now I'm certainly not convinced."

"Can you do something?" Velanon asked. "I must save my strength for when she appears."

"And reveal myself?" Kalus said. "No, I think not."

"Why not?"

"Because *I* have a flare for the dramatic as well," Kalus said with a flourish of his hand.

Velanon growled and clenched his fists. Shaking his fingers out, he let the magic flow into them as he fell into the song.

***

Elody watched as Eliath hurled another lighting bolt down at one of the ladders on the wall. It flew in an arc down the line of goblins climbing up, and one by one they fell, taking the ladder with them. But she didn't stand still long.

Elody ran up and down the wall, flinging spells of ice and magic as she went. In the street below, Jalthrax paced her to stay close. She could feel his presence every step of the way and waited until he had caught up before beginning to cast again.

Everywhere goblins climbed ladders, Elody threw her spells. The ice and frost of the spell Eliath had taught her would freeze the goblins where they stood, dropping them dead from the wall, their corpses falling to the waiting crowd below. The ladders quickly froze over where her spell touched them, leaving them slippery and impossible to climb.

But she was growing tired.

The magic was taking a lot out of her, but she could not stop now. Not while she still had strength. More and more goblins fell in her wake, and Elody even allowed herself a moment of satisfaction before she glanced out over the field and saw the writhing sea of goblin bodies packed against each other.

"So many," she whispered.

Then she was moving again, running to the next ladder. Along the wall she passed the priestess of Anarr she had met earlier, who was throwing spell after spell down into the waiting goblins. Elody stopped to watch for a moment, and the woman turned with a nod before turning back. Elody returned the nod and then ran back down the wall to where Eliath finished casting. His hand shot out, and balls of fire the size of melons flew from his palm and out into the waiting horde. Each one exploded as they hit, blasting holes in the black mass of pressed bodies.

Out in the air, Tark continued to cut a devastating path through the goblin army, leaving burnt swaths of corpses in his wake. The other dragons, though older than him, were doing far less damage in such large areas. He truly was an awe-inspiring sight. Eliath watched for a moment and smiled.

"My boy," he said.

"He's amazing."

"Wait 'til he gets going!" Eliath said with a laugh.

More and more goblins threw themselves at the wall, fresh soldiers picking up the ladders when others fell, all trying to climb the walls. Elody looked down the line to where the battering ram lay stalled on the open ground.

"Are we really going to do this?" she asked.

Eliath loosed another fireball and looked around.

"It's not over yet, but the odds are tilting slightly in our favor."

Elody saw something out of the corner of her eye followed by a shout and whipped around to see what had caught her attention. A tiny orange light streaked toward the wall surrounding the front gate so fast that she didn't even have time to yell before the explosion went off. A ball of fire, bigger than any she had ever seen, almost as big as Tark's breath, exploded against the stone wall.

She heard gasps from down the battlement that were quickly replaced by the screams of the dying goblins caught in the blast. And there were many. The fireball reached all the way to the top of the wall, and the men there had to fall back from the flames. Then it winked out and was gone. The stone Telidor had shaped into place in front of the gate was gone, nothing but molten rock puddled on the ground.

Elody heard a screech from below and looked down to see Jalthrax flapping his wings.

"No, Thrax! Stay down there!"

"They have a dragonmage!" Eliath shouted.

In another moment, a blast of frost flew from the trees across the field to cover the ground in front of the gate. As the cold wind passed over the battering ram, the fires consuming it blinked out, and just like that, the molten rock around the gate hardened.

"And a powerful one too!" he shouted.

The goblins shouted a cheer and picked up the abandoned ram and rolled it forward.

Elody shook her head. Something stuck in her mind, but she couldn't quite grasp it. They had not seen a dragon from the other side. It would have to be big for a mage so powerful. They couldn't just hide one that big in the trees. She was so lost in thought, she nearly fell off balance when the battering ram hit the gate. Eliath caught her by the arm and hauled her back up.

"Are you hurt?" he said.

She didn't respond. The ram hit the gate again, and the whole wall shuddered beneath her feet.

"Elody!" he shouted. "Are you hurt?"

There was something they weren't seeing.

Boom! The ram hit again, and somewhere in the periphery of her mind she heard the sound of splintering wood. The smell of burning flesh and smoke rose up around her and made her cough.

"Elody!"

Something clicked in her mind. The burning body of the Silver Queen. Her head completely destroyed by magical fire. The kind of power that it must have taken to do that.

"The wizard!" she yelled over the din of the fighting.

"What?"

They were both shouting to be heard.

"It's the wizard!" she said.

"What wizard?"

"The one killing the dragon mothers!"

"What, you saw him?"

"It *has* to be him! Don't you see? That's what this is all about! He's here for the Eldest!"

As if speaking her name alone was enough to awaken her, they heard shouts from down the wall. Elody looked past Eliath to where the priestess of Anarr had stood only a moment ago and saw her shimmering robes rip apart as her body popped and cracked in transformation. Great wings of gold spread out from her body, catching the morning sun and sending shards of sunlight cascading across the field.

When her body finally ceased changing, she stood tall on great, scaly claws, her talons clutching the battlements atop the wall. With a single flap of her wings, she flew out across the top of the goblin horde. Everyone, goblin and man alike, stopped and stared as the Eldest of all dragons on Gondril sailed overhead. Elody's mouth hung open, and she made no move to close it.

The Eldest was the biggest dragon she had ever seen. Her golden scales reflected the sun as she turned her flight, blinding Elody and forcing her to look away. When she looked back, the Eldest swooped down over the goblin army and let loose a roar so powerful that it shook the stone beneath her.

The goblins felt it too and crumbled.

The commands of their god were all but forgotten in that moment. The fear that washed over them was too much for even faith to hold back. The goblin lines broke apart, and they all turned and ran from her shadow. Elody watched them run and looked up to see them breaking through the trees and heading for the safety of the forest.

But as the goblins ran away in fear, Elody saw a small group of odd-looking characters step out of the trees and into the open. Two elves, one as pale as snow, the other as gold as the Eldest herself, stood perfectly at ease in her shadow. The fact that they did not cower in her presence told Elody all she needed to know of them. Her own words echoed in her thoughts.

He's here for the eldest.

***

"Now we can begin," Velanon said.

Goblins all around them screamed and ran in terror from the mighty gold dragon that flew above them, but the two of them just stood and laughed.

"Goblins are such weak creatures," Kalus said.

"They've done their job," Velanon said.

The eldest roared again, and more goblins screamed and scattered.

"She looks old," Kalus said, and Velanon laughed.

"All the easier for us then."

Velanon started casting. He could feel as much as hear Kalus chuckle next to him, and it bothered him, but he pushed it from his thoughts. He flung his hand to the sky, and a pea-sized marble of fire flew toward the eldest. It erupted as it hit her, bathing her entire torso in fire.

When she cleared the blast, she swooped back around toward them. Even from this distance Velanon could see she was unscathed.

"Did you think a few fireballs could destroy the Eldest of our kind? She is practically a god, second only to Anarr himself! Your puny magic can't even penetrate her hide!"

Velanon sneered and started casting again. As he sang through the notes of the spell, the Eldest turned her attention to them. Velanon was too busy casting to see, and Kalus made no move to flee, though he did step a little closer to the wizard. With an inhale of air, the Eldest blew out a cone of fire that instantly vaporized every living thing around them. But the fire did not touch them. It swirled around them and to the side without ever nearing their bodies.

Kalus threw back his head with a laugh and shouted up.

"You're getting old, woman! All those years sleeping with elves has made you soft!"

Velanon finished his spell and pointed a finger at her, loosing a cone of freezing ice. It struck her full in the face, but once again, she flew right through it and out the other side unharmed.

"Dammit!"

"Did I not tell you your plan would fail?"

"Isn't that why you said I needed you? You get up there and do something!"

"Challenge her in open combat? I'm no fool."

"Then we have nothing that can harm her!"

"Not true," Kalus said and paused. "There is one thing I know."

"Stop her!" Gortogh yelled as he approached from

behind.

"I'm trying!" Velanon shouted and then turned back to Kalus. "Tell me."

Kalus pointed up to where the Eldest was coming around for another pass. Velanon looked up and waved his hand behind his head dismissively. Gortogh's eyes went wide, and Velanon sighed as the goblin turned to run. Grabbing the back of Gortogh's leather armor with one hand, Velanon stopped him and pulled him close just as the fire enveloped them all.

"Run, you fools!" Gortogh shouted even as the flames licked at them.

The champion of Ogrosh screamed for his life, and then the fire was gone, leaving all three of them untouched. With a shove, Velanon threw Gortogh away and spun back to Kalus.

"Tell me what you know."

Kalus folded his arms over his chest and smiled.

"I thought you knew everything. What do you need *me* for?"

"I am running out of patience, wyrm. I may not be able to harm her, but I'm willing to try my hand at you."

Kalus laughed and held up his hands in mock surrender. With a single finger, and careful not to get too close, he pointed to the pink crystal that hung around Velanon's neck.

"The Dragonbane crystal," Kalus said. "You can use it to destroy her."

Velanon picked it up on the end of its chain and looked at it.

"It has no such power."

"No? I seem to remember that it did."

"I read every tome I could find, and there weren't

many. Those that even mentioned it spoke of it only as a defense against dragons."

"That is its primary purpose, yes, but it *can* be used as a weapon. I have seen it with my own eyes, though it's been a thousand years, so my mind could be playing tricks."

Velanon held up the crystal and let it dangle in front of him as he looked at it.

"How do I use it?"

"You think I've ever held the thing in my hand? How should I know? Just try."

"If this works, pray that I don't turn and use it on you next."

"If it works, I don't think you'll hurt me."

Velanon closed his fist around the crystal and turned back to where the Eldest was coming around again. As she got nearer, Gortogh suddenly jumped forward and hugged Velanon from behind, but he ignored it. Velanon focused his thoughts into the crystal. Only a part of him was aware as the Eldest flew low overhead and scraped her claws out for them. Those too could not penetrate the protection of the crystal and bounced aside, and he heard her roar with frustration.

Opening his eyes just a slit, he watched her turn in the air and fly back toward the city for another pass over the army. Velanon concentrated on the crystal. He could feel its immense power in his hand, pushing out to form a cocoon around him that he could feel as if it were solid. He pushed deeper into the heart of the crystal, searching its will for its true power. One he did not even know existed until a moment ago.

The world around him went silent.

All he heard was the flap of the dragons above him.

With his mind turned inward, he could feel their presence all around him as though he could reach out and touch each one. Nothing else mattered. He could feel no other soul near him. Only the dragons.

One, two, three, four, five, six... Seven, another small one behind the wall. He was acutely aware of each of them, but he knew instinctively that they could not feel *him*. They could not hear his heartbeat the way he now heard each of theirs. Almost by instinct, he pushed his mind out for the strongest soul.

His mind drifted from Kalus right beside him and out across the sky. He felt the red dragon, so strong and violent. The bronze and copper dragons hardly gave him pause. There above the rest, flying over the trees and toward the city, was the Eldest. He could feel every bit of her power, and it was immense. The crystal seemed to lunge for her when he latched onto her. Not knowing exactly what to do, he made no move to control it and just let the power go, feeling a rush as the energy left him.

Velanon opened his eyes as a beam of gleaming light shot forth from his hand. It ignored Kalus beside him. It flew past the other dragons who were wheeling around and blasting the army. It had a single target and a single purpose. With nothing more than a thought, Velanon focused the beam on the eldest of all dragons on Gondril, and it hit her without so much as a sound.

Then, it was as if her life just suddenly left her and was gone. As if the magic that bound her together was unmade. Her wings stopped flapping the instant the beam struck her, and her massive body plummeted toward the ground. With a boom that shook the world, the Eldest crashed into the wall surrounding Molner and lay still.

Kalus laughed and slapped him on the back.

"Now it's time for some fun!" he shouted.

And with that, his body took its true form as he leapt into the air with a roar.

***

Like everyone else on what was left of the wall, Elody stood in shock. Eliath was beside her, tugging on her arm, but she didn't hear him. Like blowing out a candle, the Eldest was simply gone in the blink of an eye. Her body lay, seemingly unscathed, half in and half out of the ruined walls of Molner.

"Tark, get out of there!" Eliath called out and then turned back. "Elody, we have to go!"

There were screams and shouts of panic. Everyone on the wall was running for the stairs. The goblin army had turned and was coming back for the wall that was now wide open to them.

"Elody, come on!"

Eliath was pulling her arm, but she didn't move. Somewhere over the screams she heard a cheer. She looked up and saw a gold dragon fly out over the goblin army and for a moment thought the eldest had survived. But her body was still where she had crashed. Still, like the others, she felt some hope seeing another gold dragon arrive.

Then it slammed into the bronze dragon, gashing and tearing with its giant claws and teeth. The bronze screamed, a horrible noise that cut the air and made many turn and stare. The bronze dragon managed to get away, but the gold was right behind it. It sucked in its breath, ready to blast the bronze from the sky, when a red streak flew between the two of them. Tark swiveled to face the gold just as it loosed a gout of flame.

Elody screamed.

"Tark, get out of there!" Eliath shouted.

As the flames died out, Tark appeared mostly unscathed. Where the fire had engulfed his body, there was only some black and smoke left. Tark wheeled around and flew away as fast as he could, but the gold gave chase. Elody and Eliath stared in horror as the gold caught up. Tark flipped over, raising his claws in the air, and the gold crashed into him from above.

The dragons became locked in a snarling, roaring battle of fire and wings. Turning over and over in the air, they would plummet toward the ground and then break apart at the last moment to gain air and then clash again. All the while their own fires surrounded them, each one trying desperately to destroy the other in the flames.

"We have to help him!" Eliath said.

"What can we do?"

Eliath wasn't listening. He ran down the stairs and out into the city where the two dragons raged above.

"Thrax!" Elody shouted as she ran down.

Jalthrax was in the air and flying beside her as she tore after Eliath. She could still see the two dragons fighting above, but she turned her head away from it, unwilling to watch the outcome. She could already see the great gashes in Tark's belly as his blood rained down over the city. She knew there was nothing any of them could do.

She heard a roar behind her and looked up to see the other dragons flying fast toward Tark and the gold. Like a pack of wild birds, they dove at the gold and ripped it off of Tark, all of them becoming a great, spinning storm of claws, blood, and roars. Acid splashed and rained down as lightning crackled and boomed across the sky. As the gold's claws let go of Tark to turn on the others, he fell fast. Elody ran on faster and could see Eliath up ahead of her.

Everyone in the city felt the boom as Tark's body slammed into the ground. Ahead of her, Eliath roared and disappeared around a corner. When Elody rounded the corner and saw Tark she stopped short. The great red was on his back and staring at the sky, his head looking up, but his eyes closed. She could see his insides staring back at her from his soft, open belly, his lifeblood running down and pooling beneath him.

"No," she whispered, choking back tears.

Eliath threw his arms around Tark's neck and screamed. The tears fell freely down her cheeks, and she found her steps slower as she tried to approach.

"No, no, no!" Eliath roared. "Elody, help me!"

Elody shuffled the last few steps to stand beside him. Eliath laid his hands on Tark's side and pushed against him.

"Help me! We can heal him. Put your hands against him and send your magic into him."

Elody cried harder now, but she put her hands on Tark. Taking a breath, she pulled all the magic she could from Jalthrax and sent it into the red dragon. Tapping the well deep inside of her, she took all that she had of herself and pushed it along as well.

There was nothing left they could do. The life had left Tark's body. Eliath kept pushing and shouting at her, but she had stumbled back near Jalthrax.

"Help me!" Eliath shouted.

"He's dead, Eliath," she said.

"No, he's not! We can save him!"

"I know you can feel it," she said.

"No, no, no!"

Eliath cried a long, low wail and slid down to his knees, sobbing into Tark's body. Elody wanted to reach for him, but her hands were tight against her chest as she wept. Eliath tried to speak, but his words caught in his throat. All that came out was a roar of agony.

Above her, Elody heard the screams of dragons. In the distance, she heard a cheer from the goblin army. She reached out to put her arms around Eliath, but he shoved her back so hard it knocked her from her feet. She sat there next to Jalthrax and cried.

She cried for Tark.

But mostly she cried for Eliath.

***

Eryninn saw the goblins pour through the gaping hole in the wall left by the Eldest's lifeless body. Berym and his knights stood ready to meet them as they came, one by one at first, and then in a sudden flood.

Eryninn ran down the wall until he was right over the top of the fighting below. Taking careful aim not to shoot close to the knights, he fired down into the crowd of goblins. Berym stood at the front, fighting off a half dozen goblins pouring through the wall as Eryninn tried hard to give him some relief.

Choosing his shots, he picked off goblin after goblin as they got near Berym. When one fell close to him, the knight glanced up for only a second and caught his eye. A brief nod passed between them, and then the fight was back on. With the battle suddenly in their favor, the goblin army had completely turned around now as they all charged back for the wall.

Eryninn ran out of arrows and snatched up a quiver

from a dead man lying next to him. Firing one shot after another as fast as he could, he killed almost as many as Berym.

Despite the sheer number of goblins pouring through the gap, Berym and his knights were holding the wall. A few scratches here and there, but their heavy armor made them almost invincible in the face of the crude goblin weapons. Their greatest enemy was fatigue, but Eryninn knew they would hold the line for as long as needed.

But out over the wall, Eryninn saw the ogres approaching. There were hundreds of them. And they were headed right for the breach. Right for Berym and his knights.

"Ogres!" he shouted to anyone listening, and then he was running.

Eryninn ran halfway down the stairs nearest him and leapt to the street below, hitting with a roll and coming back up. Slinging his bow across his back, he pulled his sword and ran on.

***

Rinn charged down the stairs as fast as he could. They were slick with blood, so he had to step carefully, but he wanted to get to the fighting. He wanted to fight beside Berym where he was needed. He looked down from the wall to the group of knights standing firm at the gaping hole left by the Eldest's fall.

Berym stood at the tip of the wedge like a beacon of light. The goblins poured out of the breach like some dark river of blood and evil that could not be dammed, but Berym stood in the middle of the flow and chopped and hacked at it. And it had no choice but to flow around him or else meet his blade.

Rinn jumped the last few steps and ran to stand

beside his friend. He couldn't reach Berym's side with all the goblins around him, but he took the opportunity to stab any goblin that got near him, killing several in a short span. There were so many coming through that everyone had enough to occupy their hands.

Still the knights held.

Every goblin through the wall was cut down by one line or another of the knights. Even when they charged in a group and tried to overwhelm them, the knights did not break. They would not move or flee in the face of such evil. And Berym stood as the point of their sword, driving a wedge between the goblins and forcing them to either side to be cut down by the next knight.

Then, as if someone dammed the river, the waves of goblins stopped coming. Rinn heard a shout from the other side of the wall and saw the remaining goblins scuttle back and out of the hole. They all stared in amazement for a moment, and Rinn almost cheered at their seeming retreat.

"Ogres!" he heard someone shout and looked up to where the goblins were retreating.

The ogres are coming.

The first one through the breach met Berym head on and without a hint of fear, and more followed behind him. They flowed around Berym, who continued to hold his ground, and crashed into the other knights. They were trained well, and they wore the finest armor, but even they could not stand firm against the might of the ogres.

Swinging clubs the size of small tree trunks, the ogres came on, all muscle and rage. One knight and then another went down in seconds, their heads crushed as their metal helmets collapsed under the awesome strength of those clubs. Still more ogres poured through the breach.

With the goblins out of the way, Rinn could reach Berym. He stayed behind him and out of the way, but if he saw an ogre coming at him from the side, Rinn would step in and stab him. He saw a club swing for his head and only managed to dodge at the last minute, taking the hit on the shoulder. He heard something crack and felt immense pain radiate down his arm.

Rinn fell under the might of the hit and lay stunned on the ground. He looked up to see an ogre raise a club over his head. He had enough wits to raise his arm to cover his face, but he knew it wouldn't matter. The ogre yelled, and Rinn felt blood splash onto him. A sword burst through its chest, and then the ogre was tumbling over him.

Eryninn stood there, a bloody sword in one hand, his other hand down to Rinn. Rinn grabbed it, and Eryninn pulled him up.

"You're hurt, get back!" Eryninn said over the roar.

Eryninn turned and disappeared into the crowd of knights and ogres, but Rinn could still see his sword flash through, usually followed with the bellow of an ogre. With his left arm hanging limp, Rinn still held his sword and stabbed an ogre or two where he could, refusing to leave the fight.

***

Velanon watched with fascination as Kalus killed one dragon after another, each one falling from the sky like so many swatted flies.

"You never said he was a dragon," Gortogh said.

"It was not important. I needed him, and now I'm done with him."

They watched as a copper dragon fell from the sky with a crash of blood and snapping bone.

"He is a gold dragon," Gortogh said. "Why does he fight his own kind?"

"I don't think he has a kind anymore."

Even high in the sky they could hear Kalus's cackles of glee.

"He is insane," Gortogh said.

"Perhaps. But he has served his purpose."

With the last dragon dispatched, Kalus swept down over the goblin army and blasted them with another great breath, sending them screaming in pain and terror once more. Hundreds of goblins were burned away in a moment, leaving nothing but ash behind.

"What is he doing?" Gortogh roared.

"Having fun, I guess."

"He's killing my men!"

"Well, you did say he was insane after all."

"Stop him!"

Velanon cocked his head and looked at Kalus flying over for another pass. He toyed with the crystal that hung at his neck, rolling it around between his fingers. With a laugh, he let it drop back to his chest.

"I think you may be right. He is insane."

Gortogh growled and drew his sword.

"I don't think I would do that."

"If you won't stop him, I will!"

Velanon laughed.

"Very well, I shall like to see this."

Kalus finished his final pass, blasting more goblins as they ran in fear, and then flew down to land in front of them on the field. Taking only a moment to change, he popped and cracked his way back into his elven form.

"My, that was fun! I haven't had that much fun in a hundred damn years!"

Kalus looked to where Gortogh was seething and standing with his sword drawn.

"What's wrong with him?" Kalus asked.

"You killed my men!"

"A few hundred at most. They're only goblins. It's been so long, and I needed more practice. A furnace can't stay low forever. Sometimes it must flare to life, even if only for a moment."

"You lunatic! You killed my men for nothing! You are supposed to be on our side!"

"Side? I'm on *my* side. I came here for one reason only, to watch the Eldest die. Now that she's dead, I can get on with my business."

Kalus turned and chased after Velanon who made no effort to wait for him.

"What about my men?" Gortogh shouted after them.

"I would call a retreat if you want any of them to live," Velanon called back. "Or just leave them be and they'll retreat on their own. Goblins always do."

Velanon heard Gortogh growl and raised his hand. Looking over his shoulder he could see the point of his sword pointing at them, ready to loose its lightning.

"If you do that," Velanon said without turning, "I can promise that not only will it do nothing to me, I will kill every remaining goblin here."

Gortogh roared.

"Why did you do this?" he screamed at them.

"I needed a distraction and an audience, and your men provided just the spectacle that I needed. Keep the amulet, I no longer have need of it. Become the king of your great goblin society if you like. I have bigger plans."

Velanon heard Gortogh scream again, and it brought a smile to his lips. Kalus bellowed with laughter, and the two of them trailed off into the forest. When they had walked far enough away, Velanon spun to face Kalus.

"This is where we part ways, I fear."

"But we work so well together," Kalus said.

"I have no more need of you, and I grow tired of your company."

Kalus laughed.

"Always honest. I like that about you. It's one of the reasons I stay."

Kalus's hand shot out in front of Velanon, and they both stopped short. Pulling his arm back, he pointed off to the forest. Velanon looked to where he was pointing, but all he could see was smoke, fire, and fleeing goblins everywhere.

"What am I looking at?"

"Look closer," Kalus said.

Velanon followed down the line of Kalus's finger to where he was pointing deeper into the forest. He saw them standing there, staring back at them. Two elves. He knew it from their height and lithe shape, but he could see nothing else of them.

"What are they doing?"

"What elves always do. Observe and do nothing."

Kalus's hand went high into the air as he waved excitedly to the elves. The two of them just stared back, stone-faced, unmoving. Velanon shook his head and started walking again.

"Goodbye, Kalus."

"Wait. I have one last thing to offer you."

Velanon rolled his eyes.

"You have nothing else I need or want."

"Would you like to see how a new Eldest is anointed?"

***

With Eryninn standing beside Berym, the knights held against the ogres. Berym continued to fight, though Rinn could see his strength waning. He had sparred enough to know when the knight was getting tired. His swings were getting sloppier and weaker. It was only Eryninn's blade that saved him from several mortal wounds.

Rinn's whole left arm was limp and numb, but he still held his shortsword and lunged anywhere he could to help drive the ogres back. More and more fell, and the knights were forced to back away from the wall just to have room to move with all the bodies piling up. The ogres and a few goblins that still attacked were forced to climb a mountain of their dead just to enter the city.

Rinn heard Berym cry out and turned just in time to see him fall, an ogre standing over him. Eryninn was there in an instant, and a single swipe of his elven blade cut the ogre's belly open. Blood and entrails spilled out over Berym as it toppled to the side to join the pile.

The knights at the back began shouting. Eryninn moved to take Berym's place at the tip of the wedge, and the other knights rallied around him. Rinn moved up beside him, standing over Berym's prone body. He glanced down and saw the knight's helmet crushed on one side and desperately wanted to drop his sword and drag Berym from the fight, but there was nowhere to turn. The press of ogres from the front and the knights behind gave him little choice but to keep fighting.

Rinn jabbed and stabbed at any ogre or goblin who got near him. Eryninn was just in front of him, standing before the flood of ogres through the wall and killing them one by one. His blade danced in every direction, faster than Rinn could even see, always seeming to find the perfect opening. Ogre blood covered the ground and the bodies around them.

An ogre slipped past two that were fighting Eryninn and charged Rinn. It stood nearly double Rinn's height, and he wanted nothing more in that moment than to run. But even if there were a path out of the melee, he would not leave the fight. Not while the rest still stood. The ogre loomed over him.

Rinn didn't wait for it to attack. The ogre started to raise its club, but Rinn was already there, stabbing it in the leg. The ogre howled and stumbled back, but several goblins rushing in from behind kept him close. Rinn jabbed again in the other leg, and it stumbled back, toppling over the goblins. The ogre fell, crushing the goblins under its weight.

Rinn ran up between its flailing legs and stabbed the ogre in its gut. The ogre roared and grabbed at its open belly, trying desperately to hold the blood in. It kicked out, catching Rinn in the chest and flinging him away where he landed hard on his back. His breath suddenly forced from his lungs, Rinn's eyes teared up as he tried to draw air.

A shout went up from the knights behind him. Somewhere above him, Rinn saw a glint of white. When at last he caught his breath, he turned to see the priests and paladins of Threyl charging up behind the knights. They looked bloody and torn, and Rinn wondered where they had been fighting. A renewed energy seemed to flow through the knights. Rinn felt it too. The pain in his shoulder lessened. He scrambled to his feet and took his place beside Eryninn once again.

The priests of Threyl waded into the fight, the paladins leading the charge with their massive swords. The ogres and goblins shrunk back from the onslaught. The knights used the opportunity to strike at them, driving them back up the hill of bodies and out of the city. The remaining ogres were all too happy to oblige as they turned and ran, wounded and screaming goblins nipping at their heels.

And like that, the battle was over.

Many of the knights collapsed where they stood, the last of their energy gone with the fleeing army. Rinn suddenly felt woozy and stumbled back and into someone's arms. He turned, confused, to find Oryna holding him up.

"You're hurt," she said.

He looked at her and smiled and then slipped out of her arms and fell to the street.

"Rinn!"

"I'm... so tired."

"Your arm. Your shoulder's broken. I can mend it, here, lay back."

She laid him flat on the cobblestone and pressed her hands against his shoulder. He grimaced for a moment and then a smile spread across his lips. She stopped with a confused look.

"What?"

"You look pretty," he said.

Then he passed out.

***

"Retreat! Retreat!"

Gortogh shouted as loud as he could, but he knew most of the remaining goblins couldn't hear him. It didn't matter. Most of them were running with or without his command. Seeing him standing there, some stopped to ask if he was hurt, but he just told them to run.

As the field emptied of the living, Gortogh could see all of the dead. Thousands of goblins, dead. Ogres, dead. Dragons, dead. There was so little left, Gortogh thought it would be easier to count the living to find out how many died than to count the dead themselves.

Turning from the field, he sheathed his sword and followed what was left of his army into the woods.

CHAPTER TWENTY-TWO

AFTER THE FIRE

ERYNINN DIDN'T TURN when Berym moved alongside him. Even with a slow, lumbering limp, he had recognized the knight's footsteps coming up the stairs long before he reached the wall. Berym followed his gaze and looked out over the field. The sun had just risen behind them, the shadow of the wall creeping out to gobble up the dead.

The men of Molner were already out there with wagons and spears cleaning up the mess. Most of the dead within the wall had already been removed and taken out of the city, but the mass of bodies lying in the open field was going to take a while. Much of the work had been done by dragon fire during the battle, but there were still many dead goblins to burn. The bodies of the dragons themselves posed an even bigger problem.

Berym put his hand to his head and winced. Eryninn glanced sidelong at him and saw a long, pink scar running up the side of his face from his jaw to his hair.

"Glad to see the priests saved your head."

"Too bad they could do nothing for the face," Berym said.

Eryninn shook his head and smiled.

"The scars will fade in time," Eryninn said.

"Aye. Fade, but never disappear."

Below them, men from the city watch were standing around the body of the eldest and staring up at the massive corpse. Eryninn had watched all morning as the people of Molner had come to pay respects. Some brought flowers or stuck a torch in the ground near her. Braver ones leaned in to touch her dull, golden scales. Some even wept.

"They are still arguing over what to do with her," Berym said.

Eryninn nodded. The city officials had been locked away behind closed doors discussing the preparations for the city ever since the goblins fled.

"She should be burned in dragon fire," Eryninn said. "As should all the dragons."

"I have told them your request, but they do not want to give her body to the elves. They say that she lived among humans and should be buried among them. They may give the others though."

"She belongs to no one but Anarr now, and she should go to meet him as all his dragons would."

"In the meantime," Berym said, "they are going to try and move her back so that repairs can begin on the wall."

"They believe another attack could come?"

"Not from the goblins, no."

"Humans," Eryninn said, shaking his head. "Always afraid of the elves in the night. Do they know anything of the kingdom beyond those trees?"

"They know spooky tales of missing children," Berym said.

"I suppose if it keeps them from crossing the borders,

so much the better."

"What about the goblins?" Berym asked. "Will they go into elven lands?"

"Not if we catch them first."

"I don't know," Berym said, shaking his head. "I'm tired. Perhaps it is time I find some rest from all the fighting."

"We promised to hunt them down after Jornath," Eryninn said, "and look what happened when we didn't."

"Aye."

"The job is not done, my friend."

Berym groaned as he stood up straight.

"One last time then," he said.

"Are you sure you can manage?"

"The priests say they will further my healing once others in greater need are tended to. I shall be fine in just a few days. I will lead the knights to find the rest of the goblins."

"Then I would join you. If you would have me."

"I can think of no one better to have at my back."

"Then you'll be surprised to find me out in front," the elf said with a grin.

***

Elody found Eliath sitting on the wall, staring down into the destroyed part of the city where Tark had fallen. The dragon's body wasn't visible from where they were, but that was where he stared. Taking slow steps, she walked over and sat down next to him.

Eliath didn't move as she scooted toward him. His head was down and his eyes closed, but she knew he couldn't be sleeping. Not after yesterday. She reached out her hand to take his, but he jerked it away.

"Eliath, I... I'm so sorry."

Eliath remained silent.

"I... I don't know what else to say."

Still he didn't move or respond. His eyes just stared out at the broken rooftops. She reached her hand out again, and again he pulled away.

"What can I do?" she pleaded.

"Nothing."

"I won't do that."

"You can't fix this, little girl. Go away and leave me."

"And what would you do if I did?"

"Shove this dagger into my stomach and twist it until I no longer feel pain."

He held up his other hand and showed her the dagger in his grip.

"No," she said, her voice quivering. "Do you hear me? No!"

She felt the tears in her eyes and used the anger to push them back.

"Go away," he said.

"No! Not when you're like this."

"Like *what*? You think this is a phase? That I'll get over it and be better tomorrow? *Nothing* will be better tomorrow. Nothing will be better ever again!"

"You don't know that."

"I don't? What is going to change tomorrow to make this okay? What is going to... bring him back?"

She saw the tears stream down his cheek before he buried his face in his hands. She tried to put her hand on his shoulder, but he jerked it away from her.

"We don't know what tomorrow brings," she said.

"Pain! Loneliness! Suffering! That is all tomorrow will ever bring for me!"

The tears flowed freely from both of them now, and

she couldn't control the sobs in her voice.

"You don't know that. You don't know—"

"Just another neutered mage with no dragon! He was my brother and my only friend!"

"I know that."

"You know nothing! You've had your dragon for, what, six months? For eleven years it has been just the two of us! And nothing will bring that back."

"At least you had eleven—"

"Go away! Leave me alone and go away!"

"I don't want to."

"Well, I want you to! Leave me alone to join Tark in peace!"

"Eliath—"

Eliath stood and turned on her with the dagger in his hand. Elody leapt up and backed away.

"Eliath, don't."

"Just go away," he said, his voice just above a whisper. "Go away and let me go to him."

"Please think about this. I am your friend. You don't have to be alone."

"Please, just go away."

Elody turned and walked away.

**

Gortogh stood among the remnants of the largest goblin army to walk Gondril since the days of Ogrosh himself. Gone was the drink and the laughter. Gone was the bloodlust and revelry. All that remained were the wounded goblins who'd had enough sense to flee.

And they were all looking to him for orders.

There were still at least a few thousand goblins that he could see, and he'd managed to hold them together enough to build a camp. They didn't have much in the way of provisions left. They had eaten everything the night before the battle in preparation for all the spoils and riches they would bring home after.

Gortogh sat staring into the fire, and the goblins around it sat staring at him. He could feel them all watching him, but he couldn't look up to meet their gazes. He heard the sound of clacking bones and closed his eyes with a grimace.

"A mighty army," Kurgh said as he sat across the fire from him.

Gortogh stared through the fire into the shaman's eyes.

"What has happened to this *mighty* army?" Kurgh asked.

"Be quiet, dog."

Kurgh rolled back with laughter. The sound was unsettling. Gortogh leapt up, drawing his blade and pointing it across the fire.

"Silence yourself, or I will kill you here and now!"

Gortogh no longer kept up the pretense of being just another goblin. He was too angry and too distracted to concentrate on dumbing down his speech. Kurgh stopped laughing as he stood and stared at him down the length of steel. He held his arms wide and walked forward to put the point of the blade against his chest.

"Do it," Kurgh said defiantly. "I will go to Ogrosh where so many went yesterday. Will you say the same when you die, Gortogh? Will you go to Ogrosh?"

Gortogh held his blade steady and did not relent.

"Ogrosh will destroy you," Kurgh said and spat at his feet. "You followed the elven demon and look what you have done!"

Gortogh swung his sword, and Kurgh skipped back

to avoid it. He moved faster than Gortogh could have imagined possible. Before he moved to attack again, Kurgh drew his bone knife and slashed both of his arms open. Blood gushed out with every heartbeat, but Kurgh didn't notice through his chant. With only a few words, the blood swirled up and formed a spinning circle of blades around the shaman. Gortogh stumbled back, keeping his blade leveled for a strike.

"Will you fight me now, *Mighty One*?" he shouted.

The other goblins around the camp backed away from the two combatants in a widening circle. No one cheered as the shaman and the champion of Ogrosh stood facing each other. Perhaps they had all lost their taste for blood. Kurgh flicked his finger, and one of the blood blades streaked toward Gortogh. He jumped to the side, landing hard on his stomach, and heard Kurgh laughing.

"Does your elven magic not protect you?"

Gortogh growled and gripped the hilt of his sword. Feeling the magic flow through his muscles, he sprang up and pointed at the ugly shaman. With a thought, he released the energy stored within and watched it race down the blade. Kurgh raised his arms in front of his eyes and leapt to the side, but he wasn't fast enough.

The lightning stuck the swirling blades and seemed to dance across them in blue arcs, some of the magic passing through the barrier to strike Kurgh in the chest. His body shook and fell back from the blast, landing hard on the ground while his shield continued to whirl around him. The goblins nearest where he landed were not quick enough getting out of the way and were cut down by the spinning knives. As blood flowed from their wounds, it was quickly sucked in and formed into more blades, making the barrier even larger and more deadly.

Kurgh pulled himself to his feet.

"Ogrosh protects me" he shouted, though with a little less strength after the blast. "Strike me down with your stolen magic if you can. Even if you succeed in killing me, you cannot win. I will stand before Ogrosh and smile."

Gortogh held his blade up a moment longer and glared at the shaman, his body trembling with rage. With a final twist of his hand, he sheathed his sword and turned his back. Taking long strides, he pushed through the throng of goblins and walked away from the fire and off into the forest.

"You cannot run from Ogrosh!" Kurgh yelled. "He is not done with you! Do you not remember? Ogrosh is unforgiving!"

He heard thunks as blades flew at his back, striking the trees around him. Gortogh ran. He ran as far and as fast as he could, putting as much distance between himself and the other goblins as possible.

Kurgh was right.

It was all his fault.

Thousands of goblins dead because he was offered power that was not his own, and he took it. All so he could rule as a king. Now he truly felt what it was like to be king.

Gortogh stopped running and fell, huffing and puffing, to his knees. He roared at the trees and the sky above.

"How could you let this happen?" he shouted as he tore the amulet from his neck and held it up to the heavens.

"Do you hear me, Ogrosh? Why did you do this to me?"

He fell forward and buried his face in the soft undergrowth of the forest. He lay like that for several minutes, breathing in the smell of the earth and trying to calm himself. When at last he sat up, he leaned back on his legs and stared up at the sky again. He gripped the amulet tight in his hand and felt the power humming through his fingers.

"*You* did this."

He rose from his knees and stood up straight. He tried to crush the amulet in his fist. When that didn't work, he moved to throw it away, but something stayed his hand. Dangling in front of his face, he stared at the amulet for a long while as it danced on the end of its cord. Dropping his arms to his sides, he looked off into the distance. Gortogh turned away from the rising sun and walked into the forest.

To where, he did not know.

CHAPTER TWENTY-THREE

THE COUNCIL

KALUS SAUNTERED UP the sandy path away from the beach with a big grin on his face. He was late, he knew, but that was how he preferred to arrive. Beside him, Velanon twitched nervously.

"Stop fidgeting," Kalus said.

"It was a long flight. My backside is sore. Perhaps you could have gotten a saddle."

"No man, elf, or dwarf, none but dragons, has ever set foot on this island. I would expect a little more awe and majesty from you."

"It's an island. The only reason none have ever been here is that it is so far out over the ocean and with nothing on it. There is nothing to come here for."

"This is where one can come to speak directly to Anarr! You are the first of your kind to be here, and you will witness the crowning of an Eldest. It is an auspicious occasion."

"Why could we not just teleport here instead of flying for days?"

"There is no way to teleport on or off of this island. Anarr himself raised it from the sea and blessed it for his children. It is shielded in his protection."

Velanon scoffed and walked the rest of the way in silence. Up ahead of them, Kalus could see the circle. A great ring of tall, stone slabs standing on the edge of an empty ring of stone. It always made his heart swell a little to see it. Kalus had not seen it in over a century.

The ring was the seat of all dragon power on Gondril. Bigger than any arena made by man, it was the place where the dragons of light met when there was business to be done. If there was a judgement to be made. If there was an edict to pass.

Or when a new Eldest was to be named.

Kalus could hear the others talking as they approached. He knew he would be the last to arrive, which was just how he wanted it. Normally he would have flown right into the circle and landed, but he wanted to make a more reserved entrance this time.

"Stay here and hidden until I call for you," Kalus said. "I would not want you to be killed before it's time."

Velanon chuckled and touched the crystal on his neck.

"I quake at the thought."

Kalus could barely contain his swagger as he strode into the circle.

"At last, Kalus is here," an elf standing near the center of the circle said. "Late as usual."

"It's been so long I had nearly forgotten how to find the place."

There were a few chuckles from the others who were gathered. It was a favorite old joke. Kalus quickly counted all the usual faces. Two other golds besides himself, three silvers, one copper, one bronze, and one brass. Everyone was here. He truly was the last to arrive.

A casual observer, knowing nothing of dragons, might think this a simple gathering of elves to discuss the day's news. Except for the single copper and brass dragon standing on the outside of the circle, everyone present was in elven form, as was common practice. The circle was not big enough to contain the entire council in their true forms, so the ones who could transform did so. Everyone had known each other for centuries, but they all still made the tone of their skin match their true color. It was a measure of pride and power for them.

The circle of elves parted to let Kalus in.

"Olania, Thalaras," Kalus said, acknowledging only the golden-toned elves. "I apologize for my tardiness. I wanted to look my best for my big day."

"Yes," Thalaras said, "we've just been discussing that."

"There is nothing to discuss," Kalus said. "I am ready to take the mantle that is rightfully mine."

"It is not so simple," Olania said. "Ilyaren has given cause."

Kalus rolled his eyes and looked at a silver-skinned elf who stood directly opposite him in the circle.

"Ilyaren always gives cause. But the decree of Anarr is clear. It does not matter that you are older, only a gold can be anointed."

"That is not why he has given cause," Thalaras said.

Ilyaren looked right into Kalus's eyes and smiled.

"I watched you kill Ferin with my own eyes."

"Ha!" Kalus said. "Is *that* your cause? He's lying."

"He does not lie," a silver beside Ilyaren said.

"Alyniryn lies too! Of course another silver would lie for him!"

"We saw you," Ilyaren said. "In the battle of Molner, we saw you attack Ferin and the other dragons."

"You were too busy hiding in the bushes to see anything," Kalus said with a sneer.

"Enough, Kalus!" Thalaras yelled. "A dragon of the council has given cause and another has stood for him."

"Evranon, do you wish to stand for him too? All you silvers stand together."

"I cannot stand for him," Evranon said. "I did not see what they saw. The question is, will anyone stand for you, Kalus?"

Kalus laughed.

"You know that they won't."

"Then we have your word against theirs," Olania said.

Kalus looked around the circle and met their eyes, his gaze growing harder with each one.

"You are all in on this!" Kalus screamed. "You cannot break the decree of Anarr! I am the eldest gold, you must anoint me!"

"Not if you are killed for betraying your kind," Ilyaren said calmly. "One cannot claim the right of Eldest by blood. The decree is clear."

"This is madness!" Kalus said. "Do you think I would violate the decree so close to my turn?"

Kalus looked around the circle to the bronze and then up to the copper and brass dragons.

"Will one of you say something?"

No one moved. Kalus screamed and began shifting. The others in the circle backed up but stayed close together as his body snapped and stretched into his true form.

"One of you speak!" he roared.

"They have already spoken on the matter before your arrival," Thalaras said.

Kalus roared again, like a wounded animal.

"Why do they even get a vote?" he said. "The weaker dragons should have been banned from the council millennia ago!"

Smoke drifted from his mouth, and fire flared around his teeth, enveloping his snout, as he spoke.

"The decree of Anarr is clear on that as well, so all your ranting is meaningless," the bronze elf said, "but your constant reminding us of that has not made you any friends in this circle, Kalus."

"This is revenge," Kalus said. "You knew as soon as word reached you that Ferin had died that I would be the next Eldest, and you couldn't stand it. You can't bear that I will finally be able to pass the laws you should have all had the courage to pass centuries ago!"

"Enough of this!" Thalaras said. "Evidence has been presented, and the vote has been cast. You have been found guilty of murdering the Eldest in an attempt to take the mantle by blood. Kalustroth'ul'Grallitharr, you are hereby sentenced to die for your crime."

As one, the circle began stepping back, growing wider and wider, leaving Kalus standing alone. The copper and brass dragons spread their wings and sucked in a breath as the others moved far enough away from each other to shift.

"Wait!" Kalus shouted. "Not all of the evidence has been presented!"

They all stopped and looked back and forth to each other.

"Ilyaren has given us his account, and Alyniryn has given the same account," Olania said. "Your words hold no more weight here."

"Yes, but I foresaw this. So I brought my *own* evidence."

Curious glances were exchanged between them.

"Velanon!"

The wizard stepped out from the overgrown trees and into the circle wearing a bigger grin than even the one now on Kalus's face.

"What have you done?" Olania whispered.

"You brought a *man* here?" Ilyaren screamed.

The copper and brass dragons roared and turned their heads on him.

"Stop!" Kalus shouted.

Velanon only smiled and reached into his tunic to produce the small, pink crystal that hung there. He raised it between his fingers and dangled it on the end of its chain.

"Waste your breath if you must," he said. "You cannot harm me."

"A Dragonbane crystal!" Thalaras shouted. "Kalus, what are you *doing*?"

Kalus stood up tall on his great claws and puffed out his chest.

"I knew that you would do this. That you would betray me *and* the decree. You feared this day, when I would be anointed, and you all couldn't wait to stop it."

"So you brought a man here?" Alyniryn said. "To the circle? This is Anarr's home on Gondril!"

"And I feel welcome to be in his home," Velanon said, never losing his grin.

"I *had* to bring him here," Kalus said. "I knew that you would all find a way to deny me. And I knew after the events a week ago that you would try and blame me for Ferin's death."

"You *are* to blame," Ilyaren said. "*You* killed her."

"Actually, I killed her," Velanon said.

They all stared at him, mouths open in disbelief.

"It's true," Kalus said. "He did."

"And you brought Ferin's murderer into Anarr's home?" Olania screamed.

"I had to so that you would believe me," Kalus said. "Would I really bring a man here otherwise?"

"He speaks the truth," Velanon said. "I killed the Eldest, Ferin. I destroyed her with a thought, and I will do the same to any of you if I must. You cannot harm me, but I can surely hurt you. But I have no quarrel with dragons."

"You are the one who has been killing the mothers," Ilyaren said.

"That is true too," Velanon said, "but Kalus has shown me that we can work together."

"You have killed countless of our kind, including the Eldest, and now you wish to be friends?" Thalaras said.

A couple of them moved forward, but Velanon held up the crystal and smiled. They quickly backed away.

"We can work together," Velanon said. "I believe that many of you share my goal if not my methods."

"We will never work with a murderer," Olania said calmly.

"I would kill you first," Alyniryn said.

"It matters not," Velanon said. "When Kalus is Eldest, you will have to follow his orders. You will help me whether you wish to or not."

"Kalus, what have you done?" Thalaras said.

"It is *you* who have done this," Kalus said. "I knew you would plot against me, so I brought some assurances."

"And you bring this murderer into our circle carrying a weapon against our kind?" Thalaras said.

"Only so that he could present his evidence and then

pay for his crimes," Kalus said plainly.

"What?" Velanon said.

But before Velanon could turn his head to look at him, Kalus raised one of his razor-sharp talons, and with a single swipe, took his head from his shoulders. It flew from his body and across the circle like some great cat had simply batted a toy. Velanon's body fell forward and hit the ground with a thud, his blood splashing from his open neck to fleck and sputter over the stone. Having no neck to hold it in place, the Dragonbane crystal flew from his corpse and clinked across the stone to lie a few inches away.

Everyone stood in stunned silence and watched as Velanon's blood gurgled out in a pool. It spread out and puddled around the Dragonbane crystal in front of him.

"Now that that matter is resolved," Kalus said.

They all turned to stare at him.

"What have you done?" Thalaras said.

"Why, I have slain the madman who has been murdering our precious dragon mothers. And at the same time, brought our beloved Ferin's killer to justice right before your very eyes. *That* is what I have done."

The bronze elf, who was closest to Velanon's body, took a step toward it and the crystal.

"I wouldn't touch that," Kalus said. "Its power is completely drained from killing Ferin, but it will still disintegrate any of our kind who lays hands on it."

He backed away quickly, and Kalus spun back to face the council who were all glancing nervously at each other.

"Ilyaren, your cause is a lie," Kalus said. "I did not kill Ferin, I killed her murderer."

They all looked around at each other and then back to

Kalus.

"I am the eldest gold," he said, his eyes narrowing. *"Anoint* me."

"He cannot!" Ilyaran shouted. "We all know what he wants. We cannot allow this. The laws were made a thousand years ago, and he would seek to change them with a single breath. He will destroy all that we have worked a millennium to preserve!"

"It matters not," Kalus said. "I am the Eldest, and I shall choose the laws. It is decreed. I do not care what you think of my choices."

"We cannot let this happen," Olania said to Thalaras.

"I give cause," Thalaras said.

Kalus arched an eyebrow and folded his arms.

"Kalus would seek to break the peace between the dragons and humans that has existed for more than a thousand years," Thalaras said. "Are all of you so young that you forget how many died in the War of Ways? So many of our kind, murdered. Kalus would have us bring back those old ways."

"That is no cause," Kalus said.

"The death of thousands of our kind, our possible extinction, is not cause?" Thalaras said. "What madness is this?"

"Giving cause that *may* happen because of something I *might* do is not cause. You cannot deny me because you dislike my beliefs. Would you go against the decree and risk open war between us?"

The elves all began to back up, widening the circle and space between them. But before they could shift to their true forms, the copper and brass dragons moved forward.

"You cannot break the decree," the copper said calmly

as she moved beside Kalus.

"Why are you defending him?" Ilyaren said. "You are nothing to him! He would have you thrown from this council if he could!"

"But he cannot," the brass said. "He cannot break the decree anymore than you can. If you would make war, know that I will stand with Anarr."

"As will I," the copper said.

"And I," the bronze-skinned elf added.

Everyone in the circle twitched in nervous silence, each one looking to the others, waiting for someone else to move or speak, to end this madness. But there was no further argument to be made.

"I am the eldest gold," Kalus said evenly. "No other evidence matters. *Anoint me.*"

Thalaras and Olania both looked to Ilyaren and the other silvers. One by one, they hung their heads and nodded. Looking to the others, the bronze-skinned elf and both the copper and brass dragons nodded as well. Thalaras turned to Kalus and took a deep breath before he spoke.

"Kalustroth'ul'Grallitharr. You are the chosen of Anarr and the eldest and wisest of our kind. We bow to your wisdom and judgement."

As one, the elves all knelt on one knee, and the two dragons bent their necks low to the ground.

"Excellent," Kalus said, a thin smile on his lips. "A new world begins for us today, my friends. And as my first law... the practice of bonding our children to dragonmages will cease *immediately*. Anyone found giving away eggs will be hunted and put to death. Rejoice, my friends. No more will our children be given as slaves to mankind."

Their eyes narrowed as they raised their heads, and their mouths formed into thin lines. Each one around the circle glared at Kalus, but he stared them all down.

"This is my decree. And it is law."

Note from the Author

This was a hard book for me to write. And not just because it's twice the size of the first book. I think, in part, because of some of the unexpected things that happened in Book 1, I was forced to take a really hard look at where things were going. Gortogh was never meant to play such a big role in the events of things, but I found as I wrote him that I wanted to explore the goblin culture in a deeper way. That led to a lot of nights thinking about where all of these characters were headed and whether my original designs for the trilogy would still work. Turns out a lot of them wouldn't.

I'm glad to be done with this book and put it out into the world. The first one felt like I was really just trying to get it out there. Just to see if I could do it. Once I had that out of the way, then it was time to really get to work and see this thing through. The Burden of Faith is the result and the next step, and I really hope you liked it. Just one more to go…

If you liked the book, drop me an email and let me know. I love to hear from fans, if I can call you that. It makes me happy to know that people enjoy my little stories.

Damon J Courtney
http://damonjcourtney.com/
damon@damonjcourtney.com

Now, a preview of the final chapter…

The Fate of Champions
Dragon Bond Book 3

Prelude

"These are some of the finest dragonmage trainees on Gondril today," Cythyil said, waving his arm at the group in front of him.

The man beside him folded his arms and nodded as they watched the boys go through their spell practice. Cythyil looked on with approval as each cast their spell perfectly. He waited a few moments longer so that the man could see how good they all really were.

He was not disappointed.

The man watched with approval. He looked to his servant beside him who nodded his approval as well.

"Of course, these are the third years and very near to hatching their eggs," Cythyil said. "Your son would begin at age twelve like those boys and girls over there, but I can promise he will be casting his first spell within weeks."

That pleased the merchant well enough. He walked past the older boys to observe the younger ones practicing their motions on the other side of the yard. With a few flicks of her wrist, one girl finished her spell and created a small ball of light in her hand. She held it for the three men watching to see, looking into her master's eyes most of all.

"Very good, Denara," Cythyil said. "Denara is my

new prize pupil. She only started here two weeks ago, and already she has surpassed the other boys in her class."

"Impressive," the merchant said, and he did look impressed. "How is it they can cast such spells with no magic to call from? I thought they needed dragons to draw magical power."

"Most trainees have some magic of their own," Cythyil said. "That is why they are chosen by their village or parent to train. They have already shown some aptitude or some well of magic within themselves."

"And if my son has no such well?"

"I doubt that your son has *no* magic," Cythyil said, "else you would not have chosen this path for him. It matters little either way."

Cythyil reached out a finger and lifted the amulet Denara wore around her neck. He held it up to dangle on its chain before the two men. Then he held up his own, a golden sun encircling a blue gemstone.

"These amulets give the children enough of a magical well to cast from until their own can mature and their dragon is hatched. Once their dragon is bonded, the amulet is no longer needed."

"Because the dragons give them limitless power?"

"Not limitless, but immense, yes."

The men nodded, and the merchant waved his arm to continue the tour. Cythyil gave Denara a pat on the shoulder and turned toward the large manor house, not looking back to see if the men were following. They passed the older students again, and he gave them a stern look when he saw them beginning to flick simple, annoying spells at each other.

"This way," he said, "I'll show you the library."

Cythyil touched the sun amulet at his chest and drew the magic held within into his waiting hand. He gave a wave, and the door in front of him swung open at their approach. It was a simple parlor trick any first year could perform, but it never hurt to give a little show for the parents. This merchant had come looking for a school for his third son, and Cythyil was not above a little theatrics to ease his mind that *his* was the right choice.

"Where is your dragon?" the man asked coming up behind him.

Cythyil involuntarily winced but hoped the man had not seen it beneath his robes.

"I lost my dragon many, many years ago."

"Oh. I assumed that since you trained dragonmages you must be one yourself."

"I was once," Cythyil said. "The best masters are the ones who no longer have a dragon."

The man snorted, and his servant chuckled beside him.

"Of course you would say that."

"No, it's true," Cythyil said evenly. "Without a dragon I have no further place in the world of mages. Though I live above Baglund, I no longer have means to protect it. That is no longer my job. Instead, it falls to me to train the best dragonmages I can to send out into Gondril to protect her."

The man shook his head and motioned for Cythyil

to move on, which he did, though with his shoulders and head a little higher. The double doors to the library stood open wide. He stepped aside to allow the two men to stand fully in its grandeur. Cythyil's library was one of his biggest achievements and greatest pleasures, and it was impressive even by a rich merchant's standards.

The men were sufficiently impressed, he noted with pride. The stacks of books stretched from the floor to the second-story ceiling high above. Each one lined with tomes and manuals he'd collected throughout his life. Aside from training new mages, collecting rare and wonderful works had been his life's work since losing his dragon so many years ago.

"Impressive," the man said, admiring the books. "What are they doing?"

He pointed to the students sitting at the long table that extended the length of the room.

"Studying," Cythyil said.

"How can they learn magic sitting in chairs?"

"The casting of spells is very precise," Cythyil said with a bristle. "The students must first learn the proper motions before weaving the magic. If the movements are not correct, the spell could have unintended effects."

"And my son will spend his time reading *books*?"

"A good deal of his time, yes," Cythyil said, spinning to face the man.

"My son already has a tutor," the man said. "I pay a fair coin to teach him to read and write, I want *you* to teach him to cast spells and find him a dragon."

"That all comes in time," Cythyil said, pulling

himself up to try and match the man's height, but it was no use. "I have trained many young mages, sir, and I can assure you that this is the best method. Your son will have to work just as hard as everyone else, but I can promise you that he will leave my school a *proper* mage."

The merchant looked to his servant who only shrugged.

"Carry on," the man said. "I want to see the dragons."

"Oh, there are no dragons here today," Cythyil said.

"No dragons at a dragonmage school?"

"Why would there be? Once a mage bonds his or her dragon, they go off into the world. They definitely do not want to stay here with *me*."

Cythyil laughed, and the men chuckled politely.

"Then show me the dragon eggs," the man said.

"Of course," Cythyil said.

He led them through the library. He walked slowly to admire his own books and give the men time to do the same, but they no longer seemed interested. Exiting the other door and back into the long hallway running the length of the house, he followed it to the large, wooden door at the far end. Pulling it open, he braced himself for the wave of heat that always followed. It blasted from the doorway like a dragon's fiery breath and made him catch his own. The two men behind him didn't seem bothered by it.

"The incubation chamber is kept quite warm for the eggs," Cythyil explained.

The merchant nodded and waved his arm for Cythyil

to lead on. The stone staircase went down several stories, lit only by dancing, magical flames of light that rested in tiny nooks along the wall. There were no handholds, and Cythyil reminded the men several times to watch their steps. The deeper they went, the hotter it got, until Cythyil felt tiny beads of sweat on his forehead.

When they finally reached the bottom, the stairs ended in a floor of sand. Cythyil slid his light shoes off to enjoy the feeling between his toes. The men behind him did not follow suit, he noted.

"Just around the corner," Cythyil said, leading on.

As they rounded a bend, a cavern opened up in front of them. It wasn't high, just tall enough for a man to walk without stooping. But the cave was not what impressed visitors. Cythyil always liked to save this for the last stop on his tour because of what it contained.

Dragon eggs.

Eight of them at the moment, all in various stages of incubation. Though it was impossible to tell just by looking at them how far along they were. It didn't matter. The men behind him seemed appropriately stunned.

"We have eight right now," Cythyil said. "Three copper, three bronze, one brass, and a silver."

A look passed between the men that Cythyil couldn't interpret, but he only smiled as they both walked past him to get closer. The merchant walked to the first egg, a bronze gleaming like the metal in the magical firelight that illuminated the whole chamber. The man reached out and ran a hand over the outside of the smooth, flawless shell while his servant stood back a few steps and watched.

"A bronze," Cythyil said, in case they couldn't tell. "One of the older boys'. Should be ready to hatch in just a few months. Though sadly, its mother was killed."

"Killed?" the man asked.

"By the dragon-hunting wizard," Cythyil said as though the man should know exactly why.

"Is that what they're calling him these days?"

"He tried to hunt dragon mothers to extinction and killed the eldest gold dragon."

"Yes, that was a terrible thing," the man said. "Good thing someone killed *him*."

Cythyil eyed the man and gave a cautious nod of agreement. Why was this man so callous about the death of the dragon mothers? Cythyil had to remind himself that some people outside of his world did not care about its goings on as much as he did. The man was a merchant and probably cared for nothing more than his coin. He had told Cythyil from the beginning that he wanted to train his son so that he could protect his holdings.

The man ran his hand over the egg once more and then looked around the rest of the cave.

"If I send my son to your school, when will he receive his dragon?"

"Well, assuming we can find him an egg after his first year, he should receive his dragon after his fifteenth birthday."

"What do you mean *assuming* you can find him one? Isn't that what I'm paying for?"

"Dragon eggs are not for sale at any price," Cythyil

said. "You are paying me to *train* your son, nothing more. We will do our best to find a dragon mother willing to give us an egg."

"And what of this ban on dragonmages business?"

"That is… unfortunate," Cythyil said. "The new Eldest has made it law that no eggs shall be given to dragonmages."

"Then how do you plan to get my son an egg?"

"Truthfully, I don't know that I can. The dragonmage council is trying to work with the new Eldest to lift his decree. Until then, I can only train your son and hope that we receive an egg from somewhere."

"I could buy him one," the man said. "I know a man who has promised he can get me a dark dragon egg for a price."

"No!" Cythyil shouted. "I do not train dark mages, sir, and you would do well to avoid such dealings. It will only lead your son down a terrible road."

"But you can't promise my son an egg. What else am I to do?"

"I cannot promise him one, no, but I will do everything I can. There have been some dragon mothers willing to donate eggs anonymously since the ban was put in place. That silver egg there was donated anonymously a month ago."

"Anonymously? Is that how it's done now?"

"I'm afraid it's the only way."

"And what if you're caught by this *Eldest*? What would he do to you and your little school if he found out you were stealing dragon eggs?"

Cythyil opened his mouth to speak but only sputtered.

"We have not stolen anything!" he said. "Except for the silver, these eggs have all been here at least a year or more. Long before the new Eldest came along and made his *foolish* law."

"Foolish?" the man said, his voice rising. "You think it is foolish for a leader to protect the children of his people?"

Both men had spun to face Cythyil now. He backed away from them slowly.

"We have bonded dragonmages for more than a thousand years," he said. "The new Eldest is making a mistake by destroying that bond between man and dragon."

The merchant laughed, followed by his servant.

"I don't think my school is right for your son," Cythyil said, turning back for the stairs.

"Don't run," the man said coolly behind him.

Cythyil stopped in his tracks.

"You must have known I would come," the man said.

Cythyil kept his back to the men, trying hard to formulate a plan of escape. But he already knew it was no use.

"Who gave you the silver egg?" the man asked.

"I told you… it was donated anonymously."

"I do not believe for a moment that you don't know *exactly* where that egg came from."

"It was brought in a wagon and left at my doorstep."

"Oh, how quaint," the man said. "Was it in a little

basket with a blanket as well? Did they pin a note to it
and ask you to care for it?"

Cythyil stood trembling, trying hard to find
something to say.

"Why are you doing this?" he managed.

"Because I am the Eldest," the man said, "I make the
laws for all of Gondril, and it is no one's duty but my
own."

"Your laws are over dragons. You do not speak for
mankind."

"There are none higher than dragons in the eyes of
the gods, so yes, I *do* speak for all of Gondril, little man."

"The conclave is not just going to sit by and let this
happen."

"Your conclave means nothing to me. I am
protecting the children of my kind. Now, tell me who
gave you the egg, and I will take it and go. Or, you can
refuse, and we can do this the *fun* way."

"I don't know where the egg came from."

A hand dropped onto Cythyil's shoulder, and he felt
his knees go weak.

"I don't believe you," the man said, leaning to
whisper in his ear.

Cythyil jerked his shoulder away and spun on the
man.

"Believe what you will, Kalustroth, it makes no
difference to me."

"You *dare* speak the name of the Eldest," the servant
said, suddenly stepping forward.

"It's fine, Vaylin," the man said. "Call me Kalus.

Kalustroth is so formal. Not even my mother calls me that, though she *has* been dead for five-hundred years, so I suppose she doesn't call anyone anything."

Cythyil stared hard at the man he feared he might see. Though he never expected him in human form. Kalustroth'ul'Grallitharr, the Eldest of all dragons on Gondril, had come.

Cythyil knew he shouldn't have accepted the egg. But there were no eggs for his students. With Kalus's law forbidding new dragonmages, there seemed no other way. His students had worked so hard for so many years, they didn't deserve to be turned away now.

"Why not come in your true form?" Cythyil asked. "Why this game of a merchant father?"

"Well, it's more fun, isn't it? Watching you squirm like this makes the whole thing *far* more interesting to me. Also, your children up there can't start running before I get to them."

"Please, no, they had nothing to do with this!"

Kalus shook his head with a smile as he strode over to the silver dragon egg resting comfortably in the little nest Cythyil had built for it. Kalus reached his hand out and brushed it over the shimmering, silver surface of the egg with a gentle touch.

"You steal my children, and you want mercy?"

"They are but children themselves," Cythyil said. "Do not punish them for what I have done."

"You humans are so arrogant," Kalus said.

The world slowed as Kalus shook his head again. Cythyil knew in that moment that nothing he said mattered. Kalus turned to smile at him and then moved to brush some sand from the egg.

Then, in one sharp motion, he slammed his fist into its pristine surface. It hit with a loud crack. Dragon eggs are made of hard stuff. But a dragon's hand, even in human form, was harder.

The egg shattered as Kalus's hand went right through it without pause. A hole gaped in the shell, oozing with the precious life inside. When he pulled his hand back, Kalus grabbed at the edges of the hole and yanked, widening it further. Cythyil tried to move, but he could only stand and watch as the egg's innards spilled out. What would one day have become a beautiful, silver dragon, washed over the sands and was gone.

"You…" Cythyil struggled for words, but he trembled, both in fear and anger. "This is how you treat your children?"

Kalus looked over his shoulder with a casual eye and brought his hand to his mouth. To Cythyil's continued and growing horror, Kalus brought his human fingers to his lips and licked the goo from them.

"Honestly, no," he said. "I usually prefer to poach them first."

Cythyil looked at the other man, Vaylin Kalus had called him, but he stood perfectly at attention watching the whole thing. He betrayed no emotion whatsoever.

"You would stand there and let him do this?" Cythyil asked, daring the man to look at him.

"I am the Eldest," Kalus said. "I make the laws for my people. You humans would do well to remember it."

"You're a monster. And a murderer."

"I did this little dragon a favor. Better to die here, now, than to be born a slave."

"The bond between man and dragon was never slavery. It was brotherhood."

"Oh, I don't really care," Kalus said. "Vaylin, go back upstairs and kill all of the children. Make it painful if you can."

"You can't!" Cythyil shouted.

"And be slow about it. Let them run a bit to give them a sporting chance. But, you know, not *too much* of a sporting chance."

"Yes, Eldest."

The man nodded and headed for the stairs. Cythyil reached a hand out to try and stop him, to do something, *anything*. But the man just shoved past him without a word.

"You cannot do this," Cythyil whispered. "This is murder. Of innocent children."

"Oh, I plan to murder more than just children," Kalus said.

He raised his hands, and Cythyil heard a spell on his lips.